THE WHISPER OF PERSIA

PREVIOUSLY BY PHILIP J. GOULD

Fiction

The Girl in the Mirror

The Sons of Gyges

Non Fiction

The Book of Alternative Records (Metro Publishing Ltd)

PHILIP J GOULD

THE WHISPER OF PERSIA

A GIRL IN THE MIRROR NOVEL

THE WHISPER OF PERSIA

First Published in Great Britain in 2016
Wildboar Publishing, 3 Ashton Close, Ipswich, IP2 9XY

A CIP catalogue record of this book is available from the British Library

ISBN 978 0 9934167 2 9

Cover Illustrations and Interior Formatting by Streetlight Graphics
Author portrait © Hayley Waller

PART ONE

PROLOGUE
DOMINIC

SITUATED ON ONE OF the furthest, north-western points of the United Kingdom – Hirta – the largest of the Outer Hebridean islands that make up St. Kilda.

Dominic Schilling strolled along the pebbled beach, the strong coastal winds buffeting his thick winter coat and ruffling his long black hair, despite it being tied into a tail. He often ran along this stretch of shoreline, a daily routine that had accompanied a gym workout, but at that moment he was taking it more leisurely. Being active in any capacity had helped him recover from the injuries sustained whilst in America and, more significantly, regain his former shape and marine-corps fitness.

The sea was rough, which wasn't unusual around the islands; whatever the month or the weather, the waves crashing sounded like the roar of some long dead prehistoric sea monster, guttural and angry.

Now it was December and bitterly cold. There had been regular flurries of snow, much of which had settled giving the background a Christmas card look, which was apt owing to the fact that festivities had taken place just a week earlier. Today was New Year's Eve.

Dominic had visited mainland Scotland during winter before and thought he knew what to expect, but winter on Hirta was something else entirely. Nothing had prepared him for it, especially not his previous, unbidden, visitation to the island, when he had been mercilessly dumped there with not a stitch of clothing to his name.

Despite his frequent moaning, Elspeth Brown had warned him of the harsh climate though, he couldn't deny that. Over the telephone, thousands of miles away, moments before forcing Alby Goodall to fly him and his ninety young passengers to an unknown destination, Dominic had listened to the Scotswoman passionately attempt to deter him from seeking refuge on St. Kilda. There was a reason the island was uninhabited and only bore visitors during the spring and summer months. Even she, a hardy Scotswoman, wouldn't ordinarily have spent time on the island during the winter. If it hadn't been for Dominic's insistence (and Jennifer Ratcliff's money) she would have quite happily returned to the mainland with Dougal and Clarence, where she would stay until April.

Dominic stopped walking to gaze out across the sea. The roar of the North Atlantic Ocean filled his ears, the bitter wind caused his eyes to continuously water and the sea spray stung his cheeks; tiny pinpricks of ice that seemed to slice through the flesh and chip divots out of bone.

"We were a wonderin' where ye might've gone a dallyin'. Why yous out 'ere in the dreich?" Elspeth had crept up behind him (as she often was want to do) and enclosed thick, ski-jacket padded arms about Dominic's waist. They had grown close over the preceding weeks. She clasped her gloved hands together, drawing Dominic near.

"I needed to get some air," Dominic said, showing no surprise.

"T'ere's plen'y of air in the doors. Let's not tarry..." Elspeth pulled apart from Dominic, expecting him to follow.

Dominic turned to face the woman. Her thick ginger hair was contained within a woolly hat that looked like an old person had knitted it for her; it neither looked warm nor flattering. In her almost oversized ski jacket, padded trousers and fleece-lined *Dunlop* blizzard boots, she was dressed like a tourist at Everest's base camp. He smiled affectionately. In the two months hiding out on the island, against his better judgement, he'd grown to love her.

"Give me a couple of minutes," Dominic said smoothly. "Believe it or not, this inhospitable, cold, icy, biting wind... it helps me think." His teeth were almost chattering.

Elspeth shook her head and tutted. "Caw canny..." she shook her head. "I can-nae believe it. Ye must come from the north, I am guessing, aye. You'll be a girn-ing on the morrow of frost-bite or, or... shing'es!" She spoke in a serious tone which conveyed her meaning even when the Scottish words she used wasn't clearly understood. Often, Dominic wished he'd brought a translator.

"The cold doesn't cause shingles," Dominic laughed.

"Nay? May p'rhaps it should..."

"And you'd like that, I bet," said Dominic, still smiling. "Anything to stop me leaving."

"Ha! Ya leavin' is not the bother; it's what you a plannin' that causes me... fash," *bother*. Dominic had adapted to learn a little of the woman's strange Scottish dialect, though he sometimes wondered if she didn't just make up some of the things she said.

"As I've mentioned before... It's just part of the bigger picture, El'," insisted Dominic. He heard Elspeth move away a few steps, her feet kicking up stones. "The kids need to put their abilities to the test." He turned to look at the woman earnestly. "I have such great ideas and plans for them..."

He was referring to the sons of *GYGES*. The ninety children he'd helped liberate from the research facility deep under Area 51 in Nevada, USA back in October. The fact that he had then abducted them was a moot point, one which he rarely discussed.

"Aye, plans... Alwa's yous an your plans... But where be us in t'em plans of you's? Am I jus' you' wee bidie-in?" *Live-in partner.*

Dominic trudged after the woman. "It's for us that I make such plans."

"Huh..." Elspeth snorted. It was soft and lacked conviction. She was weak to Dominic's assertions. He always spoke of doing the things for 'them' though she knew, deep down, he did them for himself.

Without effort, Dominic had caught up with Elspeth. He eased his hands about her waist, halting her progress and drawing her near. "I want us to have our own little kingdom," he said, "where we want for nothing, have half a dozen *bairns* and live in peace and prosper..."

Elspeth shook her head. "Nae, sounds braw an' all," she whispered. "But ye' won' stop at tha'. No' enou' for t' gallus," *daring* "Dom'nic Schillin'. Ye' won' stop 'til you's takes t' world..."

"I suppose you're right," Dominic conceded. "With them kids... anything's possible. Why have a *Big Mac* when you could just as well have a steak?"

"Eh?" She didn't understand the metaphor.

"Just a saying, love. Come, let's go back in. It's getting a 'wee' bit cold!"

⁂

No stately home, jeweller, bank vault or priceless artefact was exempt from being targeted; Dominic had quite an extensive list to draw from.

The first of a spate of burglaries and thefts was to take place that New Year's Eve night, whilst revellers were out celebrating Hogmanay and preparing to ring out the old year and ring in the new. Nothing was off-limits or deemed too audacious; just a test of sorts for Dominic's ninety kids. Inspired by the film *Gone in 60 Seconds*, Dominic tasked his gang of invisible cadets (so-called as they were still in training) to steal 100 million pounds' worth of cash or valuables in a three-hour period.

After two months, it was clear to see that George Jennings had improved upon his DNA modification formula. The ninety survivors from George's research laboratory deep below Area 51 were no longer five-years of age in appearance, but more than three times that. If Dominic had to guess, he'd figure them to be sixteen, or very close to it. They were now roughly Sophie's age when he'd first encountered her, and being boys, they were bigger and likely stronger, so he had a good idea what they were more than capable of.

Memories of Sophie distracted him for a moment. It seemed like a lifetime ago when Dominic had seen her last. He shook the memory from his head.

"At ease." A thunderclap of boots stomping and the shuffling of bodies instantly followed. "Gentlemen... you have until 9:00 p.m. to prepare for your final challenge," Dominic started, addressing the ninety young men within the large training hall. His voice echoed. Maxi Bacaunawa, drill sergeants, soldiers and other specialist instructors stood at the fringes of the vast room.

Standing to attention in rows of ten, all identical and all wearing the Kaplan Ratcliff military uniform, the sixteen-year-olds listened intently like this was their graduation day. They were unable to hide their excited expressions as Dominic, their *father*, detailed the final test.

"Your tracking devices have been calibrated so I know that you will all start at exactly the same time, so no unfair advantages; you just need to ensure you are fifteen minutes away from your mark and fully *immersed*." Each of them wore a tracker on a chain around their neck, dangling like a dog tag beneath their shirts.

'Immersed' had become a term Dominic had coined to describe their becoming 'invisible'.

"Okay... fall out... and good luck!" Dominic had felt the buzz of excitement from his cadets as they visibly relaxed.

Now, sitting within the command centre – a purpose built mobile communication and surveillance hub in the shape of a new *Mitsubishi Fuso* truck fitted out with state-of-the-art computer and monitoring equipment – was Dominic, together with two Kaplan Ratcliff field agents formerly of Ryan's Area 51 task force.

The three of them scrutinised a number of video feeds transmitted by the ninety cadets from surveillance cameras attached to headgear or affixed to clothing, their visuals beamed live and appearing within a grid of separate images on a large sixty-inch flat-screen television taking up much of the wall in front of them.

Two-way communication devices were also fitted to each cadet, filling the ears of Dominic and his two associates with the babble of over-enthusiastic teens itching to go about their tasks. Momentarily, Dominic had to switch off the speaker volume to save his ears, fearing the incoherent jabbering would make them bleed.

"T-minus two minutes." One of the two assistants had taken it upon himself to verbalise the countdown; a synchronised digital timer appeared on a computer screen in front of him and half a dozen other VDUs dotted about the command centre.

"Isn't this exciting?" exclaimed Dominic in over-the-top maniacal glee, rubbing his hands together. Rolling his finger across a flat touch-sensitive notepad, which looked like just a thin sheet of black glossy plastic the size of a piece of A4 paper, Dominic was able to control the flashing, moveable cursor on the sixty-inch display screen; he was also able to enlarge the visuals of any one of his ninety cadets by simply swiping his index finger and hovering over an image, double-tapping the notepad when wanting a clearer view.

Two minutes were nearly up.

"Ten... nine... eight... seven... six... five... four... three... two... one..." The assistant made a gun with his right hand and followed it with a shooting gesture and sound.

Dominic pressed a button activating his communication device, his earphones crackled and his microphone clicked on. He addressed everyone. "Okay cadets... let's do this. Remember... three hours... no deviating from your propositions; no window shopping – just get in and get out. Your time has started..." he paused, "... now. Acknowledge."

A chorus of affirmations, soon followed by visual confirmation of movement as each of the ninety teenagers started forth with their individual assignments that would, when successfully collected, add up to a lot more than £100 million worth of bounty.

"D'you think this is a good idea, sir? It's likely to draw attention..." the second assistant dared to ask, receiving a reproachful look from his colleague sitting close by. He wore a striking spider's web tattoo on one cheek, which, coupled with his bald head, made him look scarily sinister. Dominic had offered him a position within his *clique* after the man's involvement with emancipating the sons of *GYGES*, commandeering him from Kaplan Ratcliff and taking him under his wing. Knowing the man's military past and his questionable reputation, Dominic valued the alliance.

But not the inquisition.

"One cannot skulk about in the shadows forever, Garret. Even the most secretive of animal comes out from time to time to eat... or to take a crap."

"We're hardly going out for a bite though, are we?" persisted Garret.

But we're certainly taking a big, long crap on the establishment...

"No... You're right," Dominic conceded. "You're absolutely right. It may well be too soon... but, we need to know what they're capable of."

"I guess," Garret quietly acknowledged.

"Plus... I have another thing at stake," Dominic continued,

offering affably: "We need the cash injection. Kaplan Ratcliff can't bankroll our enterprise indefinitely, we're not a charity; megalomania and world domination doesn't come cheap!" Dominic started to laugh.

Garret laughed nervously with him. He couldn't tell whether the senior man was being serious or not.

On the sixty-inch flat screen, the first of the ninety cadets could be seen (well, their visual perspectives) scaling a twelve foot high wall, falling deftly to the ground on the other side, and soon charging across a wide expanse of ornamental greenery.

Dominic double-tapped the pointer over the image.

In the foreground, and the focus of the cadet's interest, stood a modern building that, one could tell just from its opulent facade, contained more than a few treasures. The cadet skirted the building and stopped just short of the rear entrance.

"Here we go," said Dominic exuberantly.

Unceremoniously, the cadet smashed a small pane of glass within the door, triggering an audible alarm. Halogen floodlighting burst on from all around the house, bathing the area in artificial light. Ignoring the security features, he reached in through the hole and unlatched the door.

On the large screen further scenes of breaking and entering played out; stately homes; castles; tall office blocks; banks; car showrooms; hotel rooms; art galleries; jewellery shops; book keepers. Nothing was too sacred.

Dominic scrolled over each surveillance image, tapping them larger for a quick scan before moving on to others.

"It's looking very promising," said the assistant who'd been counting the time.

"Yes. AND they've still got two-and-three-quarter hours to go."

Dominic, Garret and the other assistant, Melvyn, watched in amazement as the spate of robberies took place before them. How easily the ninety cadets made each theft look. Being invisible, none of them met any resistance.

"Their potential has no boundaries," whispered Dominic to himself.

By the end of the night, lorry-load after lorry-load of misappropriated goods was driven into a warehouse Dominic had acquired in a discreet, out-of-the-way location in Oban.

Making headlines internationally, newspapers would report the mystery surrounding the hundreds of burglaries that took place simultaneously around Scotland between the hours of 9:00 p.m. and midnight. It was hardly the happiest of New Year beginnings.

Parliaments in both London and Edinburgh were convened, recalled early from their Christmas breaks, to debate the tragedy affecting the Scottish wealthy, and insurers were holding separate meetings to discuss how best to mitigate losses that actually stretched beyond £200 million.

With no one taking responsibility for plundering so many treasures many conclusions were drawn, with that faceless enemy – the terrorists – ultimately taking the blame.

Another such event would take place within the UK soon after, causing widespread panic and in turn, forcing the Prime Minister to declare a state of emergency. In an act of repugnance, the Tory-led government voted to bulk up the police presence by using the army, a sight not seen on mainland Britain since the Second World War, and one which only added to the confusion gripping the nation.

CHAPTER ONE
POTUS

DEEP IN THOUGHT, THE President of the United States (or *POTUS*), Avery Harrison, sat behind the Resolute desk. The famous item of furniture had been built from the timbers of the British Arctic Exploration ship *Resolute* after it was decommissioned, and given as a gift to President Rutherford B. Hayes in 1880 from Her Majesty Queen Victoria.

The President's glasses hid the anger that simmered behind his flint-like eyes. There was no sadness, just blind, insane fury.

News had just reached him that George Jennings was dead. At first it was thought that the bio-geneticist had died in his sleep but video footage from the hidden ceiling camera, coupled with a statement given by the Navy officer who was on guard duty at the time (and who had been subsequently court marshalled for leaving his post just for a bag of *M&Ms*) indicated that George's death was anything but natural.

Playing out on a laptop for an audience comprising of the President, his Chief of Staff, the Director of the CIA Thawn Montgomery, the Deputy Director Milo Calland and General Bill Eastman, CCTV footage of George's murder, all in graphic high-definition and *Dolby* stereo sound. They watched, crowding around the President's desk within the Oval office like a litter of puppies feeding from its mother's teats; looks of shock, surprise, befuddlement, disappointment and moot incredulity crossing their faces.

"The traitorous-son-bitch!" exclaimed the Chief of Staff. "Goddam-it, sir, why?"

"You were... friends with him, weren't you Mr President?" Thawn Montgomery asked delicately. "I would never have allowed his re-assignment... I only placed him by your insistence. If only I knew."

"Brayden had his reservations," pressed Calland, seeing his opportunity to regain a little favour.

President Harrison knew where the buck stopped and didn't need reminding, especially from Milo Calland. After the CIA had bungled the capture of Sophie Jennings in Washington, he had personally stepped in and suggested Mitch Youngs assist Brayden Scott with heading the capture crew at Guantanamo Bay. They believed Sophie was going to mount an audacious rescue attempt, and the President had wanted to make sure they were best prepared to thwart and seize her in the middle of the act.

How wrong they were. It turned out to be a wasteful and expensive exercise. Not only had it NOT been the place where Sophie had been heading, but it also resulted in the untimely death of their most valued asset. With Area 51 hit, George Jennings' research destroyed and the sons of his Project *GYGES* all believed dead, thoughts of a genetically-enhanced soldier returned.

"Where is he now?" demanded the President tersely, indicating the CIA agent who had gone rogue.

Enthused by the fact that he had at least been right about something, Milo voiced his opinion. "He's gone to ground, Mr President. Chances are he's hiding in Cuba." It was quite daring, for in his last encounter with the Commander in Chief, his resignation had been all but insisted upon, though a lot had changed since then. With the culmination of events over the past twenty-four hours, getting the call demanding his presence at the White House had come as something of a shock. He had already emptied his desk and a box of his personal effects remained in the boot of his car.

THWAPP!! The President slammed his fists against his desk making the three men close by jump. "Damn him! Damn him to hell! What a farrago of cock-ups!" He shook his head in resignation. "We're a laughing stock the world over; I bet the Russians love this. How can we influence world affairs if we can't even keep our own in check?"

"Things are not that bad…" placated Director Montgomery, as though trying to reassure a kid with a broken toy.

"What? Have I completely surrounded myself with bloody idiots? Which part of this whole friggin' mess isn't bad? One…" he raised a finger on his right hand, "we are attacked on our own soil; two…" he raised a second finger, a reverse peace sign, "Project *GYGES* - our super soldiers - and millions of dollars' worth of research is destroyed; three…" he raised his third finger, same hand, "the only person able to replicate that work is dead, and four…" a fourth finger popped up, "Dominic Schilling and Mitch Youngs are lording it up someplace, both likely in cahoots with one another." The President lowered his hand, seemingly running out of negative points.

"What about Sophie Jennings?" asked Milo, daring to speak again.

"Oh Oh OH, YES… thanks for reminding me. Five!" The hand was back up; all five phalanges splayed ahead of him. "How she and her friend fits into all this I can't imagine, but they do. And now she's going to be real pissed at hearing daddy dearest is dead. What a catalogue of f–"

"Sir, if you don't mind," General Eastman interrupted. "Perhaps clear heads might prevail?" He was suggesting, without actually saying it, that the President should calm down. No president was immune to the occasional outburst. Even JFK had turned the air blue with expletives over the Cuban missile crisis. "What we need is a strategy to counter these ramifications. No battle is unwinnable; it's just ensuring the right tactics are employed."

The President sighed. He closed his eyes and massaged his temple. "You're right Bill." A moment later he stood up from his desk and walked to one of the three windows behind him that overlooked the well-tended garden and lush green grasses. "The way I see it," the President spoke calmly, "we need to bring those responsible to justice; leave no stone unturned. Put all law enforcement on standby; alert the media. It's vital that Mitch Youngs and Dominic Schilling are brought to heel. Dead... or alive. Doesn't matter."

"And Sophie?" Once again Milo reminded the President of her suspected involvement.

President Harrison turned back from the window. "We need to find Sophie too. Crucially, in one piece. With her father gone, she is all that remains of his research. She could work with us, if she likes... preferably... or, if not, I'm sure our top scientists would love to dissect her; it wouldn't be too hard to clone her DNA. We could still have our army of super soldiers yet."

CHAPTER TWO
SOPHIE

"**D**OMINIC," RYAN SAID THROUGH the mobile phone's earpiece. "*I think Dominic has hijacked the plane.*"

Barry gave Sophie a severe look, which the young woman made no attempt to decipher; oblivious, she brushed her hair in silence; one or two tangles engaging most of her focus.

"Are you serious?" Barry asked walking slowly across the hotel room. "I mean, are you sure?"

"*There's no doubt,*" Ryan continued. "*But, surprisingly, that's the least of our troubles. Have you turned on the TV yet?*"

"I've barely woken up Ryan," said Barry jokingly. "No."

"*Don't. I'm afraid word has filtered through from Stateside about George.*"

"What about George?"

Sophie stopped brushing her hair and turned her attention to Barry. "What's that about my father?" she whispered moving up to within arm's length of Barry. Barry raised a hand to shush her. She turned away and crossed to the twenty-one-inch television perched on a side table in the room.

Fitting in with the decor and the 1980s' furniture, the television was an old CRT one that, unlike modern, ultra-thin LCD flat screens, needed two people to lift it. Sophie switched it on and started flicking through the channels using a remote control that could easily double as a doorstop. A news channel filled the screen and with it an image of Sophie's father. It was a photograph Sophie was getting used to seeing, the one which Ryan had shared with her when he'd told her that George was a traitor.

"*He's dead, Barry. Someone killed him during the night. It's apparently all over the news over there. It's been substantiated I'm afraid. I feel awful. I dread to think how Sophie will take it.*"

Sound from the television filled the room. "*... top of his field, was found dead today. Video footage identified the geneticist's murderer as Mitch Youngs, a former US Army Ranger within the 75th regiment and an Iraq war veteran who is rumoured to have worked within the intelligence community, though Federal government have been quick to distance themselves...*" An old photograph of Mitch Youngs flashed up on the screen, replacing the one of George.

Sophie recognised the man from the night she and her father had gone to rescue her mother from the warehouse in Norfolk back in July. She'd knocked him unconscious and taken his security pass, using it to access the cell within which her mother had been detained.

"Ryan. I'll call you back." Barry disconnected the call and moved to stand behind Sophie. She was statuesque, staring at the TV screen, like time had frozen, her right hand tightly squeezing the hairbrush in a way that threatened to snap it. He wanted to take hold of the young woman and comfort her. Absently he made to reach out to her but pulled back at the last moment, sensing she didn't need it.

"Is... this... real?" Sophie asked meekly, childlike. For a moment she felt small, perhaps akin to her actual birth age.

Barry sighed. "I'm sorry," were the only words that he could find to say.

Sophie shook her head slightly. "Don't!" she hissed. "This is Ryan's fault. If he hadn't withheld my father's whereabouts from me, I could've rescued him." That didn't seem right. She verbally corrected herself. "I should've rescued him."

⬦

Having taken a shower, concluded his 'returned' call with Ryan and sourced a simple, *American* breakfast of bagels and muffins, Barry was keen to be on the move. Checking out of the hotel an hour later was inordinately simple. A regular locale for illicit meet-ups and nefarious goings on, the Puerto Rican manager made it his business to be discrete and unobtrusive in respect of all his customers and their dealings. He accepted return of the room keys from Barry with just an acknowledging smile. Even without the fake IDs, Barry sensed that their stay would have been undetected. Although paying by credit card, he tipped the old guy $100 cash to keep quiet, just the same.

Sophie stepped out into the Miami sunshine, although the pavements were wet from an earlier downpour and glistened under the rays. October is the last month of Miami's 'wet season' with an average of 235mm of rainfall over sixteen days generally expected. The temperature was hovering above 23°C. When Barry appeared with their luggage, Sophie was sitting in the passenger seat of the silver SUV, looking tense. Popping the 'trunk', Barry dumped his travel suitcase and Sophie's sports holdall in before slipping into the car. Sophie's backpack was already stowed on the backseat. He sat behind the wheel and took a deep breath.

"So..." Before Barry had chance to continue the sentence he noticed the gun resting in Sophie's hands. He raised an eyebrow. One of the pair of *Glocks* she'd carried during the Area 51 mission. The other one was buried somewhere within her backpack.

"I hope you'll forgive me for wanting to find the man who killed my father," she said. She looked up and held Barry's gaze. "I'd understand if you don't want to come with me. Not for this..."

Barry swallowed hard making his Adam's apple do a little dance in his throat. Sleekly he removed the gun from Sophie's lap, pulled open the glove compartment ahead of her, and concealed it within. Tenderly he stroked her knee and gave it the littlest of squeezes.

"I know I should be running to the hills... but... I think you might need a friend... crazy I know! I don't think it's the right thing to do, but," he shrugged, "I believe I can help you."

Sophie visibly relaxed, a slight smile appearing at the edges of her mouth; it looked sad, lacking humour.

"Besides, who else can guarantee me a chance of getting shot at?"

Sophie elbowed him in the ribs. "Much more of that and I'll shoot you myself!"

The MI6 man laughed nervously as he started the car's engine. He rubbed his right side where the young woman, though playfully, had bruised him; she didn't realise her own strength. He put the automatic car into drive and set the SUV forward.

"Any ideas where we start? I'm guessing Guantanamo Bay would be a waste of time." Absently, Sophie started playing with her shoulder-length blonde hair. Normally it was tied in a tail. For the moment, it hung down loose.

"And a bad idea," replied Barry. "Other than seeing your father's body, I don't think Guantanamo Bay will yield much. Plus MI6 sources indicate that a 5,000 strong force is waiting for you there; they've been expecting you. Which is why Mitch Youngs was there in the first place. He was sent, together with another CIA agent, to spring an ambush to capture you."

"It doesn't make sense. Why would a CIA agent sent to catch me, kill my father?"

"Ryan said that the man went rogue; he wasn't following instructions or protocols stipulated by his chain of command. The Americans are equally as clueless to his motives – AND extremely pissed with Mitch's actions I can tell ya!" Barry's voice contained a small hint of amusement within it. "It has all but ended their dreams of persevering with their 'super soldier' programme."

"Shame," muttered Sophie dispassionately.

"The FBI have issued an *APB* on Mitch Youngs with a warrant for his arrest, but..." he paused, "little information is known as to his whereabouts. Ryan says the President himself wants him to stand trial for treason and is pushing for the death penalty. I'm guessing there's not been a manhunt like this since the assassination of Lincoln in 1865."

"All very interesting, but doesn't answer my question." Sophie spoke brusquely. "Where are we going?"

"Miami International Airport. The Americans seem to think that Mitch Youngs somehow left Guantanamo Bay and returned to mainland America. Ryan disagrees. He says your father's murderer has managed to pass through the heavily guarded border fence of Guantanamo Bay and is hiding out in Cuba."

"Cuba? That figures."

"Truly. A US no-go area. Not only that, Ryan knows where the man will be hiding – God knows how! Some place called *San Cristóbal*. How's your Spanish?"

"Bueno!" *Good.*

"I told Ryan you'd be keen to check it out. We are booked on the next flight to Havana." Barry was smiling. "We'll be eating *malanga fritters* and sipping *mojitos* at sunset."

CHAPTER THREE
KATHERINE

WHEN GEORGE HAD HANDED her the envelope in the early hours of that morning – within which a hurriedly written note had been scrawled (two hours before Mitch Youngs had paid his bedside visit and ended the geneticist's life) – she had listened to his verbal instructions with mild amusement.

"When I die, can you see that my daughter – *Sophie* – gets this," he had spoken solemnly, speaking with certainty that his demise was imminent. It was almost like he'd had a vision of the future.

"You've got quite a few months yet; maybe even years. Miracles do happen," she'd replied half-heartedly; she was a nurse and it was her job to make him feel comfortable; body and mind. She took the envelope all the same and gave a considered smile in return, which was the best she could give by way of agreement.

How little had she known.

Entering the ward at 6:15 a.m. to carry out George's vitals, Nurse Katherine didn't immediately notice anything disturbing as she crossed the room towards the window. She twisted the venetian blinds' rod, opening a wide ladder of gaps that allowed the first of that day's sunlight to filter in. Behind her, George didn't complain. He lay quietly dead in his bed.

Twisting open the second set of window blinds, Katherine turned back around. "It's morning George... time to wake u-..." Her eyes fell upon George's ashen-grey face, halting her sentence.

His eyes were closed like he was sleeping but she knew that he wasn't. He was dead, she could easily tell. She'd seen dead people many times before, having served in the military for nine years.

George's lips were blue/purple, and, like his face, the colour had drained from his entire body. The embedded medical computer monitor that had been displaying George's vitals, and usually bleeped and warbled above his head, had been pushed to the side of the bed, deliberately turned off.

After the initial shock, Katherine hurried to the orange emergency button fixed into the wall above the hospital bed and pressed it, sounding the alarm. A moment later and the Navy officer guarding the door hurriedly entered, soon followed by a stream of medical staff including an on-call doctor and – not long after – Brayden Scott. A quick assessment carried out promptly confirmed what Katherine already knew.

George Jennings would now be labelled as: deceased. She would have assumed he'd died naturally during the night, but that hypothesis did not explain the monitor being turned off, or the fact that it was turned away from his side.

Katherine had hastily escaped the madness of the ward unnoticed. Her part in proceedings had played out as far as she was concerned; as had her shift, which ended at 6:30 a.m. Of course, there would be questions undoubtedly; it went without saying. The man had been in her care after all. It turned out that her summons and interrogation came round sooner than she'd expected.

At her locker, she reached in and retrieved her handbag. It was quite small and only big enough for a purse and a mobile phone, but she'd tried stowing other things in it too, some chewing gum; a couple of hair pins; a tampon. Sticking out of the top was the envelope George had given her. She'd tucked it in with no thought and it was barely contained within. With sadness she plucked it out and studied the envelope. She remembered handing it empty, along with a sheet of paper and a pen, to George just a few hours earlier.

Written across the centre in George's handwriting was one word: Sophie.

On the back, top left hand corner, where the flap of the seal began, was a series of numbers:

19461183121.

"Oh George," she whispered. "Where do I start with this errand you'll have me do?" She closed her locker, tucked the envelope deep into her small bag and made for her base lodgings. Before she had stepped foot out of the cloakroom a voice called out behind her.

"Nurse Jenkins?" Brayden Scott looked fresh despite very little sleep and dressed to kill in a grey suit bought from *Brooks Brothers*, he stepped through from the hospital corridor. "What's the hurry?"

Katherine turned back and tried to appear innocent. "No hurry. It's just my shift's ended is all... I'm beat." She added a yawn for effect, which she stifled with the back of a hand.

"I have some questions, nurse–"

"It's Katherine," she interrupted

"– Katherine," Brayden corrected himself. "Please... this way." The Navy officer who had been standing guard outside George's room, followed close behind Brayden with a similarly uniformed colleague. Together they escorted the nurse back towards the wards, to one of the vacant administrative offices.

A little over an hour and the 'questions' that turned into the anticipated 'interrogation' were over, though only ending when Captain Will Hancote had entered the room briefly, whispering in Brayden Scott's left ear before quickly disappearing again. Although the captain had spoken quietly, Nurse Katherine had exceptional hearing. She'd heard a little of what was said:

"*...video surveillance proves George Jennings was murdered... I'm sorry, but it was your partner...*" Brayden had straightened up at that, and the look upon his face hardened.

"Okay, I've no further questions Nurse Jen-, Katherine. You can go now."

Katherine gathered up her handbag and quietly left the room. As she closed the office door safely behind her, the sound of a chair was heard crashing against a wall followed by a few choice expletives, some of which she couldn't say she'd heard before. She quickly escaped down the corridor.

A few hours later and it was all over the news. She'd been asleep and the events leading up to the end of her shift had the clarity of a vivid dream, until, that was, she switched on the television. A pair of news anchors reported over-eagerly that Mitch Youngs had murdered the world-renowned geneticist George Jennings, suffocating him – it was being claimed – with a pillow. The FBI was leading the hunt for the perpetrator with warnings to the general public that the man was very dangerous and likely armed. Under no circumstances should he be approached; instead, any sightings should be reported immediately to local law enforcement.

There had been no mention that George had been locked up in Guantanamo Bay without charge, or that he had indeed died within the notorious detention centre.

Furthermore, details of the incident she had relayed to George regarding the 'military attack' that she'd overheard being discussed between Brayden Scott and the now wanted fugitive Mitch Youngs, didn't get the slightest mention. She started to wonder whether it happened at all, but owing to its nature she suspected that most likely it was being hushed up.

From within her handbag her mobile phone began to chime. Warbling, tuneless music rang out. Katherine crossed to a side-unit upon which she'd tossed the bag when she'd arrived in her small apartment, the base lodgings she lived in whilst serving at the military hospital at Guantanamo Bay. She grabbed up the bag and unzipped it. Before picking out her phone her hand stumbled upon George's letter.

Answering her phone, she carried the envelope with her as she spoke.

"Hi dad…"

Her father called her every other day, a trend that she was ordinarily pleased to accommodate as he reminded her of home and she missed the ordinariness of Arizona, where she had spent most of her formative years. Plus he was lonely since her mother had died six months earlier, and she was his only family, but at that precise moment the desire to talk with him was completely overshadowed by the need to act upon George Jennings' final words. There was something about what he'd said that seemed to carry an undercurrent of urgency.

When I die, can you see that my daughter – Sophie – gets this?

She looked at the number on the back of the envelope whilst her father automatically talked into her ear:

19461183121.

She didn't hear a single word her father was saying.

"Dad… listen," she interrupted his flow of speech, some of which she knew she'd heard before. "Can I call you back a bit later…? I'm just getting in the shower then going to hit the sack; I've had a really long shift… is that okay?"

Her father rung off and Katherine walked over to her gold *MacBook* that was placed on the dinner table. It was closed and plugged into a wall socket and the thin layer of dust coating the lid indicated that it had very little use. She opened up the screen and pressed the power-on button to the top right corner of the keyboard.

The number on the envelope meant nothing to her. The first four digits could've indicated a year... but the rest? That was anyone's guess.

Lightly, she tapped the envelope into the palm of her left hand and wondered whether the note inside would shed any light.

Opening the envelope felt wrong, and guilt crept over her like goosebumps. George had sealed it for a reason. It was personal. He had written it to his daughter, for her eyes only.

"But what use is it if I can't ever find you?" she reasoned with herself, her conscience urging her to do it.

The welcome screen on the *MacBook* appeared and Katherine opened up a web browser, revealing the *Safari* search screen. She'd learnt that sometimes the easiest way to find out something, like a vast majority of people, was to simply search for it on the World Wide Web. Putting the envelope aside on the table (down facing) with the numbers 'sunny-side up', she typed in the eleven digit number with little or no expectation and hit the enter key.

A couple of seconds flashed by and the screen changed to that of a fail screen, advising:

Your search – 19461183121 – did not match any documents.

"God-damn!" She knew that would be too simple. "Stupid George... you should have given me more clues!" She returned to the search screen and typed in the number again, this time with a space between each character. The search engine presented her with a list of Sudoku options.

"Although puzzling, I doubt he intended me to play math games..." she whispered to herself.

The nurse keyed in the number again, this time punctuating each numeral with a decimal point. The *Safari* fail screen reappeared.

"Arrrrrrrghhhh!" Katherine slapped the *MacBook* closed in frustration.

Grabbing a can of cola from the fridge and determined not to be beaten, she returned to the computer, reopened it and started keying in the number again, this time using a combination of decimal points and spaces between each numeral.

After almost an hour of painstaking 'trial and error' she typed in:

194.61.183.121

and hit enter.

Katherine almost fell off her chair when the fail screen did not show up. Instead details alongside a *website informer* appeared. The information indicated the number was an IP address, intriguingly belonging to a website identifying itself as mi6.gov.uk.

"Now we're getting somewhere," she whispered, sweeping the mouse cursor onto the site and hitting enter.

The homepage of the official UK website for SIS (Secret Intelligence Service) flashed up.

"What are you getting me into George?"

Scrolling down the page, she searched for a contact telephone number. A quick flick through the pages and, unsurprisingly, she drew a blank. Although not so 'secret' any more, the British Secret Intelligence Service wasn't in any hurry to make themselves easily accessible. Instead, for terrorist threats, they referred you to law enforcement. If you wanted to contact them directly, you had to send them a request via a website form.

"Okay..." Katherine opened up the form, typed her name, her email address, a contact telephone number (including dialling code for the States), and a brief description of her enquiry, which read:

I have a letter for Sophie Jennings from her father. Who do I post it to?

Leaving it at that she pressed the SEND key and turned off the laptop.

Crossing to the kitchen that annexed the room, Katherine tossed the empty cola can into the bin and went to the fridge for another. Before she'd pulled the door of the cooler open, the telephone in the lounge area began to ring.

Leaving the fridge, she casually returned to the lounge and picked up the phone, half-expecting her father to be at the other end, no doubt wondering what was taking her so long to call him back.

"Hello," she said cheerfully.

"*Katherine Jenkins?*" She didn't recognise the voice at the other end. It was male and British.

"...Yes...?" her voice had shifted into a slightly defensive tone.

"*Katherine Jenkins with the social security number: five-five-five, twelve, one-eight-nine-nine... currently enlisted to the US Navy's Medical Corp, stationed at Guantanamo Bay?*"

"Yes..."

"*Never married. The only daughter of Henley and Carol Jenkins – Carol now deceased.*"

"Yes... and you've probably got my bra size! Now tell me... who the hell is this?" Katherine was now beginning to get angry.

"*Have you been in contact with George Jennings?*"

"YES... now answer MY question. WHO ARE YOU?!"

Instead of answering Katherine's demand, the British voice replied flightily, "*Hold please.*" Elevator music immediately replaced him before she could further demand an introduction; it played for barely ten seconds and then abruptly cut out. A new voice came onto the line, filling her ear, no less British.

"*Hello Miss Jenkins. My name is Ryan Barber. You have a letter for my granddaughter. Tell me, does anyone else know you have it?*"

"No." The telephone call didn't feel possible, the same as all the events occurring since that morning after she'd opened the blinds in George's room; it all felt surreal. Unconsciously she picked the envelope up again and was looking at the name written across it.

"*Can I ask that you keep it that way?*"

"Sure." It came across breezy, non-committal. Ryan didn't notice it.

"*Good. Now, Miss Jenkins. I need for you to complete George Jennings' request and deliver that letter to Sophie.*"

Katherine started to laugh. "Oh boy," she said, shaking her head in mock amusement. "Mr Barber... I don't think that's going to be possible, or easy at any rate. I'm in Guantanamo Bay. It's not like I can just get on a plane and fly over to England... even if I wanted to."

"*That's not going to be necessary, Miss Jenkins,*" it was Ryan's turn to laugh. "*You see, there's no need. She's going to be much closer to home. She's already in Cuba... just a stone's throw from you. Get yourself to Havana, you'll find her there.*"

"That's as it may, but for all intents and purposes, she might as well be on the moon. We're locked in here; it's not a holiday camp. Relations between Cuba and the US maybe improving, but it's still not relaxed here. Marines patrol the borders. No one comes in. No one goes out."

"*Mitch Youngs did,*" said Ryan matter-of-factly. "*He found a way, and it wasn't too difficult, either. Find a Lance Corporal Raul Martinez; he knows all about it. Tell him you know what he did and you want his help. He'll get the score.*"

"And what did he do?" Katherine asked naively.

"*He helped your patient's killer flee into Cuba. I doubt you'll need to make too much of a threat before he helps you too.*"

CHAPTER FOUR
RYAN

WHEN THE PARACHUTE HAD failed, Sir Marty Heywood had asked Ryan to do something for him.

"*There's some correspondence in my drawer back in the office. Can you see that it gets delivered…?*" It was an earnest request, and not extraordinary. Many people – agents and soldiers alike – whose jobs exposed them to danger and life-threatening risks, wrote letters to loved ones in the event of their death or something going wrong.

As a personal favour, and hiding his intentions, Ryan volunteered to empty Marty Heywood's desk. The Chief had raised his eyebrows at first, but said nothing regarding the request; it didn't seem such an onerous task owing to the fact the veteran agent mostly 'hot-desked' within the SIS building, flitting from one office work station to another, when he wasn't working from home. He did have a set of drawers (which were locked) that easily moved about on large caster wheels in the corner of a small office which he shared with three other analysts, and it was these drawers that Marty had referred to whilst plummeting from 13,000 feet to his death.

A thin piece of brass with Marty's name engraved was screwed into the side of the drawers for easy identification. Ryan found it, no problem.

Ryan used a skeleton key and unlocked the small piece of furniture, swiftly pulling open the first of three drawers. Ryan reached within and lifted out Marty's laptop. An *IBM Thinkpad*. Standard issue and a couple of years out-of-date. Everyone in the service had one.

Ryan routed around a bit within the drawer. Apart from a calculator, a stapler, a few pens, an eraser, ruler, paper clips and a letter opener, there was nothing further of interest.

He went to the second, which felt heavy as he pulled it on its metal runner. Notebooks, filing wallets, loose sheets of paper, *Post-it* notes and sundry receipts littered the drawer. There was no order or system, Marty had just piled it in thoughtlessly.

"This is gonna be fun," Ryan muttered. He rifled through the clutter and stopped at a thin pile of white envelopes held together by an elastic band wrapped about its centre, each sealed and addressed in Marty's unmistakeable writing. There were five envelopes in total, and on the corner of each were two first class stamps, their value more than enough to cover the postage. Ryan flicked through the envelopes, quickly scanning the addresses. None of the names meant anything to him, but a couple of the addressees shared Marty's surname. He sighed. There was nothing important there he decided; these were just some letters he'd written to his personal contacts, a final word or a farewell to people who were dear to him. Ryan himself kept a couple in the bottom of his drawer... just in case.

Putting aside the envelopes, Ryan resumed with sorting the drawer, pulling out a journal and a wad of expenses receipts before a hand fell upon a small black notebook. Half-interested, he flicked through the first couple of pages, barely taking notice. In the briefest of moments, Ryan was able to determine that it was a list of names, alongside which, telephone numbers had been jotted. With what little enthusiasm he had running out, he leafed through the notebook quickly. In mid-scan, Ryan was about to toss it back down when he noticed a familiar name.

A name that he'd heard recently.

"What... the... hell?" he whispered.

Mitch Youngs.

"This is Marty's book of contacts." Ryan said to himself, almost like he was surprised. He mentally rebuked himself. Really, what else could it have been?

He reopened the book from its start and began slowly turning, page after page, to read the names appearing on it. He wasn't surprised to see a number of high ranking officers and government officials from the world over, including the odd president or a deposed foreign leader.

Ryan closed the drawer and quickly pulled open the final one. It was larger, box-like. A cursory glance informed him there was little of significance within it. A pair of well-worn shoes, a three-quarters finished bottle of Scotch whisky, a box of staples and a pile of ten cassette tapes now made redundant by the advancement of digital recording. Distractedly, he closed the box drawer and stood up; the black notebook was still in his hand.

"I wonder," he muttered, studying the small book. He knew he hadn't finished the task the Chief had set him. The drawers still needed to be sorted through, the contents recycled or disposed of, but something itched at the forefront of his mind.

Scooping up the laptop with his free hand, Ryan returned to his office within the SIS building and picked up the handset of his phone. Thumbing through Marty's notebook, back to the page he'd seen Mitch Youngs' name, he looked up the contact number. There were half a dozen but most of them had been struck through. The last, and freshest-looking, was a mobile number written in red ink.

Without thinking or sitting down Ryan punched in the number and waited. A moment later the ringing tone filled his ear. It rang for ten, then fifteen seconds before totally surprising Ryan by being replaced by a voice.

"Yea... 'ello... 'ello... Marty, is that you?"

Ryan almost dropped the handset in shock. Quickly, he jabbed the cut-off button. It was like he'd been caught red-handed with his hand in the biscuit tin. Still standing, he pondered over the voice at the other end.

Was that truly Mitch Youngs?

Ryan wanted to call him back, to speak with the man who'd robbed him of the opportunity of killing the person responsible for Clara's death. But he knew that the CIA agent would not readily talk with him, instead most likely hanging-up.

Mitch Youngs had probably thought that it was Marty calling, which led Ryan to believe that only Marty knew his number and that Mitch, now in a difficult and precarious situation, had probably been expecting the man's call.

Okay, so he hasn't heard that Marty is dead, Ryan thought. The veteran agent had died less than twenty-four hours earlier when his parachute had failed to open during the operation to destroy Project *GYGES*.

"What were you up to Marty?" he asked silently. An image of Marty scrabbling with the faulty ring-pull on his parachute came to mind. Ryan could still hear the man's final words:

"I hope you can forgive me for what I have done. I did what I thought was best..."

"What did you do?" It came out as an accusation. So much had happened since the man had died; it seemed almost like a lifetime ago.

"Okay, let's see if we can bring you back from the dead and get us some answers." With half an idea and feeling devious, Ryan left his office and almost skipped down the corridor towards the elevator.

⁍⸺⸺⹀⸺⸺⁌

Good, foolproof voice replicating software wasn't available to the general public, and not believed to exist in reality. With businesses investing heavily in voice biometrics in their battle to overcome fraud, having the means to copy anyone's voice would be seen as detrimental and a security concern.

MI6 didn't have such misgivings, instead investing millions in developing and advancing the technology. In the world of clandestine operations, deception and the tools to aid it, helped bring evildoers to justice and kept the good people of Great Britain safe.

Within the basement level of the SIS building at Vauxhall Cross overlooking the Thames, Ryan sat with Emily Porter and Lee McDermott, the head of the Audio Forensics Department. Lee looked like your stereotypical computer nerd; long black hair, round glasses, thick beard and moustache and wearing faded jeans and a black heavy metal T-shirt. Half an hour earlier Ryan had asked Lee if it was possible to change one's voice to replicate another's during a phone call. "We do it all the time," was Lee's prompt response, as if it were natural. Ryan had explained what he wanted to do and thirty minutes later the small room where voice analysis programming and interpretation took place was ready and waiting to expedite Ryan's request.

"How does it all work?" Emily asked Lee, marvelling at the recording and analysis equipment that filled the wall ahead of her. A sound mixing desk ran the length of the wall with hundreds of switches and buttons arrayed in various positions. She suddenly had the overwhelming feeling of being in a recording studio like *Abbey Road*, 'cutting' a record.

"It's terribly boring to explain," Lee started, "but in a nutshell, we've uploaded thousands of recorded sound bites belonging to the person you want to impersonate. Our computers analyse the vocals, including the pitch, tone and resonance. It then replicates his or her voice box, giving it the ability to reproduce sound matching the originator's voice and speech patterns."

"Is it accurate?" asked Ryan.

"97%... which is above acceptance levels for most voice biometric analysis systems. It's very powerful stuff... and something of a nice toy to play with. It's great fun reimagining pieces of music using your favourite recording artist. Can you imagine Ozzy Osbourne singing a Justin Bieber song? Or Ronnie James Dio doing a cover of Kylie's *Locomotion*? It's brilliant, I can tell ya. I've got tons of John Lennon doing different stuff; and Freddie Mercury. And Elvis... to me, he's very much alive!" Lee was speaking exuberantly.

"All impressive but can we get back to the point?" urged Ryan. He collected stamps but doubted he could speak with half as much enthusiasm about a *Penny Black* or *The Tyrian Plum*, both of which were very rare and expensive.

"Ahem... quite." Lee turned back to the wall of equipment. "Once the voice is 'locked in', all you need do is speak into the microphone and the computer does the rest. Here," he handed Ryan a microphone on a long lead, "give it a go."

Ryan accepted the microphone. Holding it, he felt like a compere at a talent competition in a holiday resort, or someone about to burst into song. He had the sudden urge to swing it around like it was a lasso, mimicking a rock star. Shaking off the silliness, he turned to the Forensic Voice Analyst. "What do I say...?" he said, falling silent when he heard Marty's voice flow out of a set of speakers in front of him, repeating what he had just said.

"*What do I say...?*"

"Woah." He couldn't pretend or fail to be impressed.

"Even *you* could do it," Lee said, passing a second microphone over to Emily.

"I don't know… I feel a bit stupid…" Like before, the computer converted her words into Marty's voice.

"*I don't know… I feel a bit stupid…*" Emily started to giggle.

"With regards to doing this over a phone…?" Ryan didn't need to explain what he wanted to know.

Emily handed the microphone back to Lee.

"You make the call through the computer. You wear one of those headsets," Lee indicated a pair of earphones lying to one side, a big over-the-ear set, "and speak into the microphone as though you were talking on your mobile. Your call-ee will be none the wiser. He won't hear your voice, but instead hear the programmed voice. Marty's, in this case."

"All sounds good, Lee. This had better work."

"Like I said, Ryan. 97% match rate. Even if the guy was still working with CIA and they were using voice analysis software, we've bested everything they've got. Every time."

"Okay. I'll go grab myself a coffee and then we can get started."

⎯⎯⎯⎯⎯●⎯⎯⎯⎯⎯

"*Yea… 'ello. Marty?*"

"Mitch?"

"*Where've you been ol' buddy? I've left you about a thousand messages. Never mind, listen: I took care of it, as you requested. George is dead. It wasn't easy, and I'm in a bit of a fix, but it's done. You owe me big time, pal!*"

"I saw that you'd come through. Tell me, how did he die?"

"*Quietly. It helped that he was weaker than a six-week-old puppy.*" Mitch started to laugh. "*The guy's been undergoing treatment for cancer, can you believe that? If you hadn't been in such a hurry, nature would have taken care of him soon enough. But Marty, listen – I now need your help.*"

"Where are you?"

"*Cuba.*"

"How'd you manage to get over the border? I thought you Americans called Guantanamo Bay 'The Island' owing to its remoteness?"

"*I know someone who knows someone. A schmuck called Raul Martinez. I had some dirt on him. Anyhow, Marty, I need you to get me out of Cuba. Fast. And I need a new ID and money. Lots of it!*"

"Okay, Mitch. I've got someone in the area who can assist. I'll get you papers, a new identity and a life some place safe. Where d'you fancy?"

"*Timbuk-friggin-tu if you like... jus' get me the hell outta here.*"

"All right... Where do I send my person?"

"*I'm in a small place a little west of Havana called San Cristóbal. Have your rep call me on this number when they are close. I'll give my location when they are near. And Marty... after this, let's call it even. I can't see how I'll be any use to you now anyway. My career in the agency is finished.*"

Ryan looked across at Lee and Emily; both wore headphones and had been listening to both sides of the conversation. "Fair enough," said Ryan. "Good luck." He disconnected the call with a flick of a switch. "You're going to need it," he said softly into the room, laying the microphone down on the mixing desk and removing his headphones.

"Tell me that wasn't fun?" said Lee, smiling. He was powering down the audio analysis equipment, twisting knobs and pressing buttons.

"I guess you don't get out much," replied Ryan soberly.

CHAPTER FIVE
SOPHIE

"**W**HAT DO YOU MEAN an excursion into the city?" Sophie wasn't keen on sight-seeing, it was a waste of time. She just wanted to find Mitch Youngs. Find him and kill him, and then get a flight to England without using any more serum than she needed. Checking her supply that morning, she'd counted seven days' worth.

Just seven days of appearing normal, that was all that was left. After that...

She tried not to dwell on it, though thoughts regularly strayed to the concern, never leaving her entirely.

They'd landed at José Martí International Airport in Havana two hours earlier and Barry had hired a white *Hyundai Accent* from a car rental stand within the terminal. They had travelled light with just a backpack and a carry-on case for luggage. The rest, including all their weapons, were left in the SUV back at Miami Airport.

Moments earlier Barry had steered the car into a parking area located outside the airport where he'd instructed Sophie to meet him. Sophie was now in the passenger seat having stowed her backpack in the *Hyundai's* boot and looked comfortable in a turquoise flower-print summer-dress. Barry felt his eyes wander down Sophie's slender body, focusing on her lightly-tanned legs that appeared below the hem of her dress, just below the knee. She paid him no notice as she buckled up. He tore his eyes away from her and regained his senses.

"I just got off the phone with Ryan," Barry started. "He says you'll want to do this. We're to meet up with her at a place called *La Fontana Grill, Bar and Lounge*." Barry turned his gaze and set the vehicle moving.

"Her?" Sophie raised an eyebrow inquisitively.

"Ryan didn't elaborate. All he said was she knew your father, albeit briefly. I checked the address; it's about half an hour's drive across the city. Unless you want to take the scenic route."

Sophie looked to seriously consider the suggestion. Had she been a normal young woman the prospect of touring Cuba would have delighted her. Being able to put all thoughts aside of the events from the past four months – even for just a couple of hours – seemed like too much of a luxury.

"No time for sight-seeing," she said gloomily. "Maybe we can come back... when this is all over." Though the words tumbled from her mouth, Sophie lacked belief; she seriously doubted there would ever be a day when the nightmare that was becoming her life, would truly be over.

Barry snorted. "There are better places than this in the world," he said, thinking of many. "Though... you have to admit, it kind-a has a timeless charm to it. Unspoilt by progress."

Sophie was turned from Barry and peering out towards the dusty, hot roads of Cuba.

Although there were modern influences affecting the country, Cuba was relatively unaffected by the advancements of the West, perpetually living in a time long forgotten. Since the Cuban revolution in 1959 and the missile crisis of 1962, Cuba had virtually stood still. As they drove, classic American cars from the 1940s trundled by often, and they passed many locals wearing outfits from a yester-year decade. No new American cars had been shipped onto the island since before the trade embargo was sanctioned between the States and Cuba, and the only modern vehicles passing on the roads were European or from Asia.

"Not tarnished by commercialism," replied Sophie. "I quite like a place that doesn't have a *Starbucks'* or a *Mcdonalds'* franchise."

A little over forty-five minutes later owing to traffic, Barry parked up the car in a space not far from the seafront. Together with Sophie, he crossed a busy road towards a row of elegant buildings, mostly large and grandiose, light-painted or white-washed – all very clean looking. Palm trees stood sentinel within the grounds of each of the properties, giving it a tropical feel. *Well, this is the Caribbean*, mused Sophie.

Barry stepped up onto the kerb, reaching for Sophie's hand. Accepting it she suddenly felt small, like she were the child her birth certificate stated rather than the woman her genetically altered DNA had speedily transformed her into.

A pang of grief hit her as she recalled her father. It wasn't that long ago when he had led her by the hand from that laboratory building. Sure, she appeared to be twenty-one (and would continue to for a very long time, thanks dad), but her heart would only have been beating for four years come the next April.

Barry smiled. "Come, it's this way."

Amongst the scattering of mansions, hotels, restaurants and shops, *La Fontana Grill, Bar and Lounge* was easily found.

A single-storey brick and timber building with a warm, welcoming facade gave way to a sprawling dining and bar area that stretched deep inside; it branched to a covered area outdoors where a bronze water feature of a semi-naked woman stood prominent in the background. A stage on the left was prepared for a band; drums, keyboard and guitars, but no one played. At the furthest point were the kitchens, a glass wall partitioning the restaurant from the chefs preparing food, though the rich smells of cooking wafted through the air.

Even though it was mid-afternoon the place was busy with diners. Waitresses dressed in combinations of black skirt and blouse, or black skirt and white blouse with black aprons tied about their waists, moved purposely around the tables which were placed canteen-like in rows that could each seat twelve or more.

Sophie followed Barry into the restaurant, immediately taken in by the relaxed atmosphere and the coolness of the air-conditioning. Strong aromas of grilled fish and barbecued chicken assailed their nostrils, reminding them both that they'd not eaten since breakfast.

"Do you know what she looks like?" Sophie was peering around the room. Standing at the entrance she felt conspicuous.

"No. Ryan indicated that she was white, so shouldn't be too hard to find her." The restaurant was filled mostly with Cubans but one or two groups of foreign tourists were dotted about the place. "She's masquerading as Canadian. Americans are not permitted in Cuba. Not formally."

A waitress approached from the centre of the room. "Mesa para dos, si?" She spoke in Spanish. A badge pinned to her blouse indicated her name was Maria.

"Um... we're English..." started Barry. Sophie interjected before he could continue. The waitress had asked whether they wanted a table for two.

"Hemos hecho arreglos para conocer a alguien. Un canadiense. Está ella aquí?" *We have arranged to meet someone. A Canadian. Is she here?*

Barry turned and looked at Sophie, impressed.

"Si," Maria replied. "She's in the bar area." She spoke English with barely an accent. "Come... I'll show you."

"You weren't lying about speaking Spanish."

"Nunca miento... I never lie." Sophie smiled and stepped after Maria, a noticeable skip in her step. Barry followed close behind.

Katherine Jenkins was sitting on a bar stool at a small round cocktail table nursing a margarita glass with half of its contents already consumed. Ice cubes and a slice of lime bobbed up and down on its liquid surface. Two empty glasses were pushed aside, but close by. Matching lipstick marks upon their rims indicated they were relatives of the one Katherine was now drinking, a telling footnote to either how long the woman had been waiting, or how in need of intoxication she was.

Seeing the empty glasses, Barry felt the need to apologise. "I hope we haven't kept you too long," he said. Ryan had set the meeting for 3:00 p.m. It was only a little after.

Katherine smiled. "Not long. I just felt like I needed a drink," she said. "Or three. After the day I've had..." she let the sentence trail off. "Please... my manners. Join me. Have you ever had margaritas? These Cuban ones are... woo!" she made a shooting gesture with a hand and it was clear to Barry that she was a little drunk.

"Sure," said Barry.

Sophie and Barry pulled up a stool each and sat opposite, and to either side of the nurse, around the table.

"Maria... *Maria!* Can we get three more of these? Thanks darlin'." Katherine spoke loudly across the bar drawing a little too much attention towards their table.

"Our contact in London says you knew my father. How so?"

Katherine smiled warmly. "You have beautiful blue eyes," she said calmly to Sophie. "I can see George in them." Noticing impatience creep into Sophie's demeanour, Katherine thought to answer her. "I... tended him. I was his nurse."

"His nurse?" Sophie was puzzled. "My father was... why? What happened?"

"Your father was receiving treatment... for cancer. It had gone undetected for quite some time I believe. A brain tumour. The size of my fist. It was terminal. He didn't have much time." Katherine balled her hand up to illustrate. "I don't know what he'd done to deserve being incarcerated in GITMO, but he didn't deserve the hand God dealt him."

Maria carried a tray of drinks over and placed margaritas in front of them. "Buena salud!" Good health.

"Muchas gracias," replied Sophie. Maria walked away, taking the tray with her.

"It was a terrible shock to find him... dead this morning. But to die... like that," she shook her head slowly from side to side. "I'm used to tending battle-wounds. Not cancer and definitely not murder! It's a terrible thing."

"Do you know exactly what happened?" asked Barry, "to cause George's death?"

"The man who did it... such a coward. CCTV security footage caught the whole thing on camera. That CIA weasel used a pillow to smother George whilst he was asleep. Had he not been weak from the chemo or half-asleep... he might've been able to fight him off, but... he had no chance. His death was quick and relatively painless. At first I thought he was asleep, when I came into his room; he looked so peaceful." Tears leaked out and the American pulled out a napkin from beneath her margarita and used it to dab her eyes.

"Thank you Katherine... for helping my father." Sophie laid a hand on the nurse's and gave it a gentle squeeze.

Katherine braved a smile, grateful for the young woman's comfort. She reached for her margarita and took a deep pull. "It was my job," she said, a hint of sarcasm in her voice. It was aimed towards no one but herself. "Still... it's nice to get off the 'island' and see Cuba properly. It wouldn't have been possible without your friend in London; illegal for us Americans." Katherine tried to smile. "It's like stepping back in time... the place so unsullied by capitalism. Even GITMO has a *KFC*."

"I can understand you wanting to have a day out; pass on your respects even, but meeting with us... Seems terribly bold... or stupid," said Barry. He sipped at his drink. It tasted strong and he winced a little.

"It wasn't my idea, believe me," she said. "No... You can thank your dear father, Sophie. He made me promise that I give you this." Katherine reached for a small neon-pink handbag, unclasped it and reached within. A moment later she gently handed Sophie the envelope she had smuggled out of the hospital.

"What's this?" asked Sophie timidly. She recognised the handwriting across the centre as her father's. The envelope bore her name. On the back of it was a number she didn't recognise.

"A web address," Katherine answered Sophie's puzzled look. "All very cryptic. It was how I found your contact in London.

"During the night your father asked for a piece of paper and an envelope and wrote you something. He said it was important that you get it... after his death. Only AFTER his death, he said. He called it his will."

Using her right index finger, Sophie tore it open.

"It was like George had a premonition... or something. Like he knew he was going to die... well, we're all going to die, but you know what I mean. Soon."

With a pincer grip, Sophie pulled free the slip of paper inside. It was folded in four. She opened it out.

Across the centre in George's familiar scrawl was the word 'FAT' and a series of numbers:

8-8-0-5-1

"What IS this?" Sophie demanded.

Katherine shrugged, sticking her hands up in surrender. "Don't shoot the messenger. I only saw the outside of the envelope," she replied. "Why? What is it?"

"A joke. That's what it is. My father's will? Huh...!" Sophie turned the sheet so that both Barry and Katherine could see it. "He may as well have written it in Chinese."

"What? Don't you speak Chinese?" asked Barry in jest.

"That's not the point."

"Oh." From her tone Barry figured that she could. "It's a code," said Barry knowingly. "I'm guessing your father didn't want, whatever it is, to get into the wrong hands."

"I don't have time for childish games. This... *excursion*... serves only to delay Mitch Youngs' death." Sophie finished her margarita – more than half of the glass – and grimaced from the alcoholic bite. She stood up, eager to go. She offered her hand towards Katherine, intending to shake the nurse's. "Thank you for helping my father."

"What about food? We need to eat." Barry had stood up to block Sophie's exit. The rumble in Sophie's stomach agreed.

Sophie sat back down, regretting that she'd finished off her drink so swiftly. The alcohol had mildly affected her head.

"Besides, that letter is probably significant," said Barry. He handed Sophie a menu that had been propped up on a stand. "Your father is reaching out in his final hour; it must mean something. At least entertain that idea."

"And finding my father's killer isn't important? I'm running out of my serum. I want to find peace... I need solace... before it's all gone; before I'm... gone." She was implying her visibility.

"We've got time," replied Barry. "Time enough to eat at any rate, I'm starving. Besides, you won't be 'gone'; just invisible."

⎯⎯⎯◆⎯⎯⎯

An hour later they had left Katherine at the cocktail table and were driving away from *La Fontana Grill, Bar and Lounge*, Sophie having eaten beef steak, mash potatoes and grilled vegetables and Barry picking half-heartedly at the Caribbean lobster which he thought he'd try but didn't like owing to the fact that it looked like it had just entered the restaurant via the front door and perched itself on his plate; its lifeless eyes seeming to follow him with every bite.

"Ryan said Emily will take a look at that code for us, whilst we check out *San Cristóbal* where Mitch is thought to be hiding out." Barry had spoken to Ryan moments earlier, the time difference between Havana and London meant that it was around 8:00 p.m. in the UK; as usual Ryan was in his office. "He's arranged us a package to pick up along the way." *Package* was Ryan-speak for field agent hardware; mainly weapons and ammo. Possibly a *Kevlar* vest, if they were lucky.

"Do we have an address?" Sophie asked, half-interested.

"I have a mobile number to call when we enter town. Ryan says he's expecting a contact of Marty Heywood's to deliver papers, travel documents, cash, etc. He thinks he's getting a new life."

"He will be disappointed. How far?"

The Sat Nav built into the dash of the rental car indicated a travel time of one hour, ten minutes. "Someone from the embassy will meet us en route in half an hour."

CHAPTER SIX
POTUS

"WHAT?"

Deputy Director of the CIA, Milo Calland was back in the Oval office for the second time that day, standing like a chastened child in front of his headmaster; his hands were interlocked behind his back. The President was sitting behind his famous desk looking every bit the most powerful man in the world, which he was, though he also looked tired, and old. The look on his face was grave, his forehead furrowed.

"Dominic Schilling was definitely involved in the attack on Area 51, sir. Surveillance images from cameras within the research facility confirm it. As well as Sophie Jennings, we think that he was working with the Brit Special Forces; MI6 maybe... but we're not sure. We have no evidence. It could've just been a Kaplan Ratcliff operation, though they're denying it. He'd been promoted to Director of their intelligence section a short time ago, so it stands to reason. Plus the *GYGES* research had first been developed by them."

"Have you spoken with the Brits?" President Harrison was leaning forward.

"Not yet, sir... no."

The President pressed a button on his desktop telephone. His secretary came through the speaker:

"*Mr President?*"

"Hilary, can you connect me with the British Prime Minister. Tell him that I need to speak with him urgently."

"*Right you are, sir.*" The line went dead for a moment.

"Let's see what David has to say about this. Milo, do sit down. You're making me feel twitchy."

The telephone on the Resolute desk began to ring. President Harrison stabbed the flashing white button and Hilary's voice resounded.

"*Mr President, the British Prime Minister's now on line...*"

"Thank you Hilary." A crackle of interference was followed by the transferral of the long-distance call. "Ah, Prime Minister Humphries, glad you could speak with me..."

"*Great Britain is always at your service, Mr President,*" said David Humphries saccharine-sweet. "*What do I owe for this humble pleasure?*" he continued. It made President Harrison and Milo Calland squirm.

"It's not a pleasure call, David. You may – or may *not* – have heard; my country came under attack a little less than forty-eight hours ago. We have reasons to believe that a British National, among others, was involved in the attack. It's been suggested that Special Intelligence Services may have been complicit. I want you to assure me that THAT isn't the case."

The line went silent whilst Prime Minister Humphries digested the President's assertion.

"*Mr President... I am unaware of any attacks made on US soil. Can you elaborate?*"

President Harrison exhaled noisily. "Not at this time, no. It's a delicate matter. What of our intel? Are you Brits up to something?"

"*Emphatically I can assure you that SIS would never engage in a military engagement without my prior consent. You say someone British was involved? What's the proof? How can you be so positive?*"

"We have surveillance imagery of one of our assailants that

has been identified, and verified. A man we've named as Dominic Schilling. We believe he is responsible for the attack on one of our military installations, an attack that resulted in more than a hundred American deaths. I owe it to those Americans' families and the American people. It's my constitutional duty to find him – and any others – responsible, and bring them to justice."

Prime Minister Humphries went quiet again. Unseen by the President over the airwaves, his British counterpart was giving instructions to his assistant to call an urgent COBRA meeting, to include the Chief of SIS.

"Prime Minister Humphries? You still there?"

"*Yes, Mr President,*" he replied sharply.

"So, if your Government gave no instructions, and SIS had no involvement, I gather you'll have no qualms in assisting us in finding Dominic Schilling, and supporting us with his extradition?"

"*You have my word that Britain remains a loyal and trusted ally to the United States of America, and that we will lend our resources to assist you with your endeavours.*"

"I'm glad we're reading from the same psalm sheet, David. Any country who tries to hide a mastermind of such atrocities would be met with severe consequences. Look at Afghanistan and Bin Laden. The Taliban were our friends until nine-eleven..."

"*Threats are not necessary. As I said, whatever you need Mr President...*" Prime Minister Humphries severed the connection and the phone went silent. President Harrison expected the leader of Britain's Government was probably cursing him at those exact moments.

"Thanks David," President Harrison said cheerfully, knowing that the Prime Minister was gone.

"That went well," suggested Milo.

"D'you think? I don't know. I don't trust him. I think he knows something."

"It's possible, I guess…"

"Do me a favour Milo; put together a team bound for Britain. Get Brayden Scott out of Guantanamo Bay to lead. When you're ready I'll inform the Prime Minister that your guys are on their way. He said that I could have whatever I needed; I want his Secret Intelligence Service to link in with the CIA. Whilst searching for Dominic Schilling on the surface, they could see what their MI6 is up to from underneath."

"Okay. What about the search for Sophie Jennings? Is that on hold?"

President Avery Harrison raised an eyebrow. "On hold? I said no such thing! Operation Shakespeare and the search for Sophie Jennings goes hand-in-hand with the hunt for Dominic. It looks like together they attacked our base in Nevada, so it stands to reason that they'll still be intertwined, in some bizarre capacity. I don't know what the story is, but he still killed her mother. She won't forget that. Where we find one, the other won't be far behind."

CHAPTER SEVEN
EMILY

THE ROOM WITHIN WHICH Emily worked was open-plan and half the size of the control room at Kaplan Ratcliff. Her short-lived time as Deputy Intelligence Director at the biochemical giant was a memory that had the texture of a long-forgotten dream. Around her, the office was almost empty of personnel; there were three MI6 analysts still working from the ten deployed into Ryan's unit.

It was getting late. The time was 8:15 p.m.

Emily yawned. It had been a long day and she was feeling the effects of almost zero hours sleep since the motel room she had shared with Sophie a little less than sixty hours earlier. That had been after Washington, but before the attack on the American airbase at Area 51. Since then Dominic had hijacked a plane, taking with him the ninety children that they had liberated, all but disappearing from the face of the earth. Putting that into the shade, Sophie's father had also been killed, murdered during his sleep.

She wondered whether things might've worked out differently had she listened to Sophie in the first place and insisted on rescuing her father, instead of working under Ryan's fixated plan of destroying George's Project *GYGES*?

"We'll never know," she muttered under her breath.

Ryan walked into the room through electronic sliding doors and fast approached her desk. "You should go home," he said. "You look good to drop."

"I will," said Emily, combing a hand through her dyed dark-auburn hair. It was the same colour she had picked up in Washington when she had disguised her appearance to avoid detection from law enforcement and those who were intent on capturing her. "Once I've located Alby Goodall and his plane." Alby was the pilot of the missing *Boeing Globemaster III* that Dominic had hijacked.

"Get someone else to do it," Ryan said, "you need to sleep and freshen up."

Emily removed her glasses and rubbed her tired eyes. "Okay," she replied, caving in. She replaced the spectacles. "You're right. Though, be warned, I'll likely sleep for a week..."

"Good. Before you go... would you mind taking a look at this code?" Ryan handed the young woman a slip of paper upon which he'd scribbled: *FAT 8-8-0-5-1.*

"Always something, huh? What is it?"

Ryan shrugged. "Barry just relayed it to me over the phone... says that George left it for Sophie and insisted on her getting it in the event of his death."

"Oh."

"Might be important... doubt it though. But, seeing we screwed up in Sophie's eyes with regards to her father, think we need to give her something... you know, to keep her on side."

"Okay. I'll see what I can do."

"Of course... if you're too exhausted... go home... get some rest, and tackle it in the morning."

Emily smiled falteringly. "No, that's fine. This should be a piece of cake. I can quickly write an algorithm to assist. You know... you should go home yourself and get some rest too."

It was Ryan's turn to smile. "I appreciate the concern... but there's plenty of time to rest… when I'm dead." He turned away and headed for the room's exit.

Which will be soon if you don't slow down, Emily thought, watching the man who'd been like a father to her disappear through the sliding doors.

———※———

Seven minutes was all it took for Emily's algorithm to produce the report that would help decipher the unintelligible message left by George. Twenty minutes later and she had concluded, out of the list of sixty-eight possible interpretations, it belonged in all likelihood to an airport code.

"FAT is the IATA code for Fresno Yosemite International Airport, California. The number sequence is, I think, a combination for a luggage locker." Emily was speaking to Ryan on an internal phone line.

"*That's all well and good… but there are probably hundreds of lockers. How do we locate it?*"

"George must've left other clues with his letter," asserted Emily.

"*Barry said there was nothing else… except…*" Ryan dithered. He wasn't sure.

"What?" Emily pressed anxiously.

"*There were numbers on the envelope. The nurse used them to contact me. She was quite clever really. George had put our SIS IP address on the back,*" he proceeded to read them out slowly. "*1-9-4, 6-1-1, 8-3, 1-2-1. I'm not sure that it helps any.*"

"I don't know. Leave it with me. There must be something here; most likely it's staring us in the face."

"*Thanks Emily… and Emily?*"

"Yes?"

"*Don't forget; go home!*" Ryan hung-up the phone leaving Emily with her handset pressed against her ear for a moment longer than needed.

"Okay…" she whispered. "Where to start? Coffee…" She stood up and crossed to the drinks machine at the centre and along one side of the room. She pressed a number of buttons, selecting her drink. It really didn't matter what she chose; they all tasted equally disgusting.

The hands on the clock – any clock – always seemed to travel much faster when time was needed, and tremendously slower – or not at all – when it wasn't. Frequently, since ringing off with Ryan, Emily had looked up at the large *Rolex* wall clock positioned on the wall next to the room's exit, placed proudly above a row of smaller clocks, each showing the times and time zones of faraway capitals around the world. Even though it seemed like barely a couple of minutes had passed between each glance she was perturbed to find that big chunks of time had escaped her instead.

At 9:15 p.m. she had the answer. Two international phone calls; one to Fresno Yosemite International Airport; the other, to the manufacturer and supplier of the lockers used at the airport. Both had confirmed and corroborated her hunch. Still holding the handset after speaking to the Americans, she dialled Ryan's internal number.

He picked up on the second ring.

"I know exactly where George's locker is," she said excitedly.

"*Go on.*"

"It's definitely at Fresno Airport."

"*I thought we'd already established that?*" griped Ryan.

"No, we guessed it was there. I now know it IS there, AND the locker number. Three-three-one-one." She started to laugh.

"*How?*" asked Ryan.

"The IP address served two purposes. In addition to the obvious,

George meant it for use as a code breaker. The number thought to be the combination to a lock, also had dual functions. When correlating the numbers against the IP address, a new number is formed. The eighth number of the IP address is three. This gives us the first two numbers. There is no third number so we skip to the fourth. The fourth number is a one. As is the fifth. Three-three-one-one."

"*O-kay...*" Ryan wasn't convinced, and he was tired. It all sounded very confusing, like trying to teach a child algebra.

"There are four locker areas at Fresno Airport," Emily continued. "Each has four hundred small-to-large luggage locker facilities. Being proactive, and knowing your scepticism, I gave the airport a call. They confirmed their lockers are numbered by area and box number. I asked them to check whether 'three-three-one-one' had been booked out. They checked and said it was. They also confirmed the locker had a long lease, and, with a little gentle persuasion, the name of the lessee."

"*George Jennings...?*"

"George Jennings. Indeed."

CHAPTER EIGHT
SOPHIE

THE 'PACKAGE' WAS MORE or less what Barry had expected. Two hand guns (not *Glocks* but *Heckler and Koch USP*s, favoured by US government security and some UK armed police units); four magazines of ammo (each containing fifteen rounds); 'his' and 'hers' matching, very conspicuous, bulletproof vests (black) and two combat knives concealed within a pair of ankle sheaths. The embassy official had worn a shirt and tie and looked like a bank manager. He had handed the plain black nylon holdall he had dragged out from the back seat of his car to Barry with barely a word or acknowledgement. They'd met in a parking area at the back of an abandoned service station along a remote part of highway that led towards *San Cristóbal*, and the embassy man swiftly departed.

"I thought Mitch was on his own. I'm not expecting much opposition," said Sophie, picking up one of the guns and examining the feel of it in her hand. She wrinkled her nose as though being presented with a bad smell. "They feel like a cheap children's toy." Even had it been loaded the weight would not have increased greatly.

"Beggars can't be choosers, I guess," Barry said wearily. He handed Sophie a couple of magazines for the gun before picking up the open holdall by its twin straps and stowing it in the back of the car.

"Anyway... I don't intend wasting a bullet on him. I want it to be more... intimate. I want my face to be the last thing Mitch-bloody-

Youngs sees as he slips into death. It'll be slow... and it will hurt. The very least I can do... for my father." Sophie inserted one of the magazines into the gun and carried it carefully as she climbed back into the *Hyundai*, barrel downwards.

Barry keyed the ignition and set the vehicle in motion again. "Sounds like you've given it some thought."

"Not really," Sophie replied casually. The gun was resting on her lap. "It's the same thing I have in mind for Dominic, I've just adapted it. Now, *his* death I HAVE spent a lot of time imagining."

"I bet. Of course, it's conditional on whether we find him," stated Barry.

"I'll find him," Sophie said with certainty.

The Sat Nav indicated that there was less than ten minutes travel time to their destination of *San Cristóbal*. Barry had brought the car to a standstill along a dusty stretch of road, a right turning off the highway. He dialled the number that Ryan had discovered in Marty's small black notebook. The call connected immediately without ringing. The man had been waiting with his hand nursing the mobile phone.

"*Y'ello!*" Mitch Youngs sounded cheerful, like he had just learnt he'd won the lottery and been given a tax refund all within the same hour.

"Hi... Mitch?" Barry tried disguising his voice with an accent that Sophie next to him did not recognise. He was trying Canadian but sounded a cross between Australian and English-brummy. "I have a... delivery. Marty said for me to call you... when I was near." Ryan had told Barry that he had masqueraded as Marty Heywood, evidently Mitch's MI6 confidant, and the likely instigator of George Jennings' murder.

"*Yeah, yeah, yeah. Good, good. D'you have my papers?*" Mitch spoke impatiently.

"Yes... and plane tickets. Where can we meet?"

"*I'm staying at a place called Jamas Aqui, two blocks away from San Cristóbal Cathedral. I'll give you the postcode.*"

"Jamas Aqui?"

"*Yeah... quite apt. Means 'Never here'.*" Mitch laughed before proceeding with the postcode.

Updating the Sat Nav, Barry noted and confirmed the travel time. "I'll see you in twelve minutes," he said just before ending the conversation. Cruising slightly above the national speed limit, Barry made it in nine.

Parking in Zocalo Square, the cathedral could be seen prominently in the background.

"You ready for this?" Barry asked Sophie, stepping from the car and opening up the rear door. Reaching in, he pulled the black holdall towards him. Behind it was Sophie's backpack. Discretely he secured one of the knives to his ankle, concealing it beneath his jeans' leg. He took the gun and two of the magazines, quickly heeling one into the weapon, securing it in place with a satisfying click; the other, he stowed away in a pocket.

"You know, Barry... you don't need to do this. I don't need your help. I promise you, it won't be pretty."

"Just because I look like I've just left Uni doesn't mean I've not seen action." He looked at the bulletproof vest, thought about wearing it... then thought better of it. Too conspicuous. San Cristóbal Cathedral was a tourist attraction and with the time close to five, there were plenty of people milling about. He didn't want to stand out, or alert the local authorities to their presence.

"I'm just saying... it's my grudge," said Sophie meekly.

"Do you want one of these?" Changing the subject, Barry was

offering Sophie one of the vests. "I assume you're going to vanish shortly... no one would notice."

"I went without one in Nevada... and bullets were flying all over the place there. No thanks. Besides, I don't think Mitch Youngs will be too much of a problem. He wasn't last time." She remembered how quick he'd been knocked out cold within the warehouse the night her mother had died.

"Your funeral..." Barry smirked, tossing the vest back down. "What about the knife?"

"Don't need it," she replied nonchalantly. "I'm only going to need my hands."

"But you're taking the gun?"

"What can I say? I'm a hypocrite. I like to have a backup option." She considered what to do with the weapon, glancing about her body pointlessly. The turquoise flower-print dress gave her no options for concealment.

"Too hot to wear jeans you said, back in Miami. But look–" Barry slipped the *Heckler and Koch* between the waistband of his denims and his hips, "–fits nicely. And hidden beneath the shirt. See... no sweat... well, a bit of sweat, but... you get what I mean."

Sophie scrunched up her eyes and concentrated for the briefest of seconds. Subtly and very swiftly, she disappeared beside him.

"Or you could do that," Barry said, deflated. His argument no longer valid.

"My gun is now out of sight," Sophie asserted, "without it pressing into my flesh. Cold metal against my skin isn't exactly a turn-on."

"No one loves a bragger."

"What? Don't you love me no more?" Sophie teased, retrieving her backpack from the backseat.

Barry coughed. "Well... I wouldn't say that," he said coyly, closing the rear door of the *Hyundai* with a gentle slam. "Come, the Sat Nav indicated it is this way." Not waiting, or able to see whether Sophie was following, Barry crossed Zocalo Square and headed in a north-westerly direction.

The house, 'Jamas Aqui', was old, dilapidated, and a visual carbuncle within the neighbourhood of grand apartments and stately homes that stood around it. Situated at the end of a row, barricaded by undergrowth and the rusted remnants of an old *Chevrolet*, 'Jamas Aqui' looked like it hadn't been called 'home' since Fidel Castro seized power in 1959. Mitch had said it translated as 'Never here'. Barry could see why as he followed a path through some overgrowth coming to a stop at the front door. Although much of the house was in disrepair, the door was strong and fully-functional, solid oak with iron furnishings that included a rusting door knocker and a round handle.

"You knock – and act like I'm not here." Sophie stood to the left of him and spoke quietly, close to Barry's ear. She had walked the two blocks by his side without a word, contemplating what she was going to do when she finally set eyes on her father's killer.

"For a second I forgot you were there," he replied, lifting up the door knocker and forcefully rapping it against the metal plate beneath it.

Thrap-thrap-thrap!

The sound of movement from behind the solid oak door was sudden, expectant, almost like the occupant was waiting on the other side. Three heavy bolts were slipped across – top, middle and bottom – and a key was turned; locking mechanisms noisily retracting as the resident of the house relinquished all security measures.

The door creaked as Mitch Youngs opened it slowly. Casually dressed in three-quarter-length grey trousers, white button-up collared-shirt and dark blue deck shoes, within which he wore white ankle socks, the fugitive CIA agent looked like he was happily on vacation.

"Almost on time," said the American irritably. "You said twelve minutes. It's very nearly fourteen." He poked his head out nervously and surveyed the distance. The road behind Barry was deserted and as far as Mitch Youngs could see, there was no one skulking beyond any shadows.

"There was a bit of traffic and a small gridlock," Barry lied. He had adopted the Australian/English-brummy accent once again which, unseen, Sophie was cringing at.

"Really?" Mitch sounded surprised. "In Cuba?"

"Perhaps a cow strayed onto the road... you know how sacred they are in these parts."

Mitch smiled. "Isn't that the truth?" Barry had read somewhere that cows were so valuable and so scarce in Cuba, that to kill one would result in a custodial sentence far greater than what you would receive for killing a kid. "Come in," Mitch continued, opening the door wide and stepping aside to allow Barry through.

Barry crossed over the threshold and, before stepping in, took hold of the door and pushed it open a little further, feigning interest in the entryway. "What a fascinating door," Barry said, making out that he was genuinely impressed by the texture of the wood, caressing the surface with the flat of one hand as a gap large enough for another to slip into the house was created behind him. "Tell me. Is this solid oak or a hardwood from a South American rainforest?" Barry felt a hand gently tap his upper arm; Sophie confirming that she was in.

Mitch shrugged. "Who gives a rat's ass?" Effortlessly he wrested the door from Barry's grasp and closed it. He twisted the key in the lock and secured two of the bolts, leaving the one in the middle free.

"This way. I've got a pot of Cuban coffee on the boil; d'you want some?"

"Sure." Passing four closed doors, Barry followed Mitch and the rich aroma of coffee along a dingy hallway and disappeared into the kitchen.

Out of view, Sophie opened the first door onto the corridor and slipped into the room. Inside she set aside her gun, tossed down and unzipped the rucksack and pulled free the jet injector. Most of her possessions she'd left back in Miami in the back of the SUV, choosing just essential items for Cuba and this excursion.

"I really shouldn't waste these," she muttered, remembering that she only brought enough serum to Cuba for two days, and had very few remaining in her supply.

Pressing a vial of ochre liquid into the injection gun, she raised it to her upper arm and squeezed the trigger, flinching from the sensation. For the best part of a full day's visibility she needed five vials, though she mostly rationed them, making do with four. For a temporary fix and to counter what she considered her 'disorder', she required just two. This would only last a couple of hours – three hours tops.

Ejecting the empty vial of serum from the jet injector, she replaced it with another. Promptly she injected herself again.

The effects were instantaneous. Sophie saw her shadow increase across the room, even though the descending sun that streamed in through the filthy windows continued to radiate undiminished. Tossing the jet injector back into her backpack, but leaving the empty glass vials on a side table, she zipped up the bag and carried it out of the room, picking up the gun on the way. Holding it in her right hand, she pointed it ahead of her.

In the hallway, carefully, quietly, she placed the backpack on the floor and walked towards the kitchen where sounds of cups were tinkling and a kettle was boiling on an old fashioned stove, steam causing it to flute through the fixed whistle in its spout.

Mitch was talking animatedly about something or some such and Barry was responding with pleasantries and verbal nods. They were like two old buddies getting reacquainted.

Closing in on the open doorway, Sophie flicked the safety catch that was on the side of the gun from 'safe' to 'fire ready' and deftly chambered a round using her left hand. Peering through the doorway, she spied Mitch standing over the stove, his back to her. Barry was sitting at a table and, sensing her presence, turned to look her way. He gave her an acknowledging nod as she stepped into the kitchen.

Sophie crept fully into the room, the gun held at arm's length, pointing seriously towards Mitch Youngs' back.

"I'm guessing you thought you'd got away with killing my father," said Sophie earnestly, walking to within two feet of the American. Her face was stone-hard, her lips turning into a sneer.

Mitch whirled round from the stove, his left hand instinctively reaching for the kettle that was boiling, his intent clear in Sophie's eyes. He wrapped his hand about the kettle's handle.

"I wouldn't," Sophie said coolly. "I'm betting my nine millimetre bullet will travel faster than you can throw that at me."

Mitch relaxed his hand and slowly withdrew from the stainless steel water boiler, gently raising his palms up in surrender. "Sophie...," he smiled. "I guess if anyone was going to find me... I'd rather it be you." Mitch spoke in a dejected, half-sighing tone.

Sophie took a couple of steps forward, closing the gap between them.

"I somewhat doubt you'll still be thinking that in a minute." Sophie was now within striking distance of the man. Observing quietly, Barry sat at the kitchen table just two feet to Sophie's left.

"No?" Mitch turned back to the kettle, a hand once again vying for it. "Can I get you some coffee? It's Cuban."

Sophie pressed the barrel of the *Heckler and Koch* against the American's neck. "I'm not here for coffee," she said, foregoing further preamble. Anger was consuming her, bubbling within the pit of her stomach. Images of her father lying in a bed being smothered by this excuse of a man caused a tsunami of emotions raging inside her chest. Her finger began to apply pressure to the trigger. "Why did you kill my father?"

Mitch turned the stove off and took a quick step away before turning to face Sophie once again; her gun was now levelled towards his head.

Barry could see the dangerous look in his companion's eyes. "Sophie... you said you weren't going to need a gun... remember?" His voice, so calm, snapped her out of her trance.

Sophie blinked a few times, as though waking from an enchantment. She lowered the gun. "Sit." She was in complete control, but the steel in her voice was still there, uncompromising.

Mitch took up his seat at the kitchen table opposite to where Barry was sitting, unsure where the young man fitted into all this, but guessing he'd been part of a set-up by Marty Heywood.

"Why did you kill my father?" Sophie repeated. "Tell me. I'll make it quick... I know places where... pressure points... all I need do is gently lay a finger... you'll slip away as though going to sleep." She was standing next to Barry to the side of the table, the hand holding the gun now hanging down to the floor.

"Please... it wasn't my bidding. It was an MI6 operation."

"MI6?" Barry piped up.

"Yeah. My contact, Sir Marty Heywood... He called me asking if I could assist with a covert operation he was involved... a sort of personal favour to him."

"And you agreed to do that for him. Why?" Barry sounded incredulous, not buying it.

"We have a deal... a sort of... how you English are fond of saying; *you scratch my back and I'll scratch yours* arrangement. A hit like this gives me a lot of leverage... Plus, I'm tired of the agency and wanted a way out. This was my retirement party."

"You say it 'gives you a lot of leverage'. You mean 'gave'," said Sophie. "Past tense..."

"What?" Mitch looked puzzled, almost stupid.

"Haven't you heard?" Barry chipped in. "Marty's dead. His body is no doubt feeding some of Nevada's turkey vulture population as we speak."

Mitch started to laugh heartily. "You're so clever, the two of you. He's not dead. I spoke to him the other hour..."

It was Barry's turn to laugh, shaking his head at how dumb the American was acting.

"Dead... alive... it's beside the point. Why would Marty order my father dead?" Sophie spoke above Barry's laughter.

Mitch looked down towards his hands resting on the dinner table ahead of him. He laced them together. "Naturally, I asked him that same question," he sounded solemn. "After all, my allegiance is to the United States and we'd gone to great lengths in bringing him in. Doing what he suggested would result in me being labelled a traitor. But Marty was insistent. He said that *GYGES* had to be terminated... That it was within all our interests, America's too. I'm guessing the man had his orders."

Barry had stopped laughing and had turned to look at Sophie. The pair of them shared an unspoken question which Sophie allowed to go unanswered. She walked around the table so that she now stood behind the former CIA agent.

"My father is dead because of you. You need to answer for this."

Mitch shrugged. "I guess... but I'm answerable only to God. The way I see it, I was just following his will."

"Then I guess you haven't too long to wait for your judgement." Sophie lifted the *Heckler* and *Koch* up and pointed it to the back of Mitch's head.

"Sophie?" Barry's eyes pleaded for her not to do it.

Without warning, she struck the man forcefully across the back of his skull with the gun, knocking the man hard to one side, his chair slipping from beneath his weight and clattering across the kitchen; the big man slumped to the floor.

"Jeez!" Barry jumped up from the table, moved around Mitch's unconscious body, and crouched down to check a pulse. "Nicely done... but I wish you'd give me the heads-up next time."

"Is he dead?" Sophie asked quietly. "Tell me he's not dead; I've not finished with him yet."

"No," replied Barry, removing his hand away from a place just above Mitch's throat. He'd felt the man's carotid pulse strong beneath his fingertips. "But... I think you've done enough. Mitch was just a puppet in all this. Marty had played him. He doesn't deserve to die... not at our hands at any rate. Come, let's truss him up. We'll deliver him to the Americans. He'll be wishing you HAD killed him by the time they've finished with him."

CHAPTER NINE
JENNIFER

JENNIFER RATCLIFF HAD ISSUED a statement to the press that morning, distancing herself from the frenzied reporting circulating the globe at that moment. Dominic Schilling had not, contrary to reports, been appointed as Director of the Intelligence section of the biochemical conglomerate she was CEO of, she had stated. He had merely worked for them in an 'advisory' role, a role which had ceased days before his disappearance; that's what the press release had said.

Jennifer had been met by an angry mob of blood-thirsty reporters upon arriving at the Kaplan Ratcliff command centre, staving off verbal demands for further clarification and ignoring the questions and calls for her to resign.

She clambered through the doors to the building, security personnel swiftly creating a barricade between her and the throng of tabloid journalists. Richard Cullum was within the thick of it, jostling a cameraman to the floor.

"I'll be in my office," Jennifer had said, slightly flustered by the ordeal of walking the short distance between her chauffeur-driven car and the door. Taking big strides, she hurried away to a waiting elevator and leapt in. Half a minute later and she was standing within her comfortable office, the pandemonium left behind where they would wait to stalk her when she left.

Within the safety of her private space, she poured herself a drink from a crystal decanter. She hated whisky but needed something to still her nerves. A sip of the dark amber liquid caused a burning sensation in her throat; its effects started to be felt immediately.

Taking the glass with her, she sat behind her desk and reached for the small remote control. With a quick jab to the red standby button, she switched on the large-screen plasma TV on the wall. She took a second sip of whisky, grimacing at its harsh taste.

Sky News was on. As she half-expected, the news was focused on the events to which she herself was tied despite her spurious denials and distancing attempts.

The media was hungry for more information, salivating like half-starved pit bulls; though receiving and reporting only what the American and the British governments had leaked, which in contrast, was far shy of the truth; a British airliner had been hijacked and had gone missing somewhere over the North Atlantic Ocean with a number of passengers missing. The entire specifics of the event were fabricated, with Dominic's name the only truth to feature in the press. With tensions heightened between the American and British governments, both sides were conjuring elaborate stories to hide the facts about their involvement with what was, a culminating incident. The attack occurring at Area 51, the multiple deaths in combat, and the complete destruction of George Jennings' underground laboratory never featured within the news at all.

Having agreed to 'work' with the Americans in the call made by the President earlier that day, Prime Minister Humphries had contacted President Avery Harrison with the news that a British aircraft had gone missing, with MI6 intel suggesting that Dominic Schilling was involved, and the likely transgressor. All other details, including MI6's collusion with regards to destroying Project *GYGES*, were withheld, any subsequent accusations refuted. At no point did the President make any further reference to the attack on Area 51.

With President Harrison already heavily featured in news

bulletins across the US regarding the manhunt for former CIA agent Mitch Youngs, a further press conference came as no surprise.

Jennifer listened as the most powerful man took to the podium inside the press briefing room, the White House backdrop emblem prominent on the wall behind him, the Stars and Stripes and presidential flags standing to either side of his prominent frame.

"It is believed that the traitor, Mitch Youngs, was working with the known terrorist, Dominic Schilling, who a day earlier you'll remember killed several police officers at Dulles International Airport here in Washington DC." The President looked down solemnly, pausing for effect. Around the room flash photography splashed light and shadows about the stage until the man looked back up.

"In his attempt to escape American justice, Dominic Schilling boarded a plane that was destined for London, England. During the routine flight, contact between the cabin crew and air control was ceased. Regrettably, it's my duty to inform you that it's believed that Dominic has taken control of the plane and with it, all 256 passengers."

The room erupted into bedlam as reporters and journalists vied to gain the President's attention.

President Harrison gestured for the room to quieten with a gentle lowering of his hands.

"This is all the information I have at this time," he said. *"Rest assured I am working closely with the British Prime Minister,"* he didn't hide the disdain in his voice, *"and together we will look to end this emergency favourably."*

Jennifer switched the television off. The fact that she had issued a press release denying that Dominic had been appointed as the Director of Kaplan Ratcliff Security and Intelligence Division was nothing; not compared to the truth of the matter.

Borne from the same lie cooked up between Ryan Barber at MI6 and herself, the two of them had shared a long conversation the night before. There was a plan, but as could be expected, Dominic had done things his own way.

"What we do for love..." she said softly, swirling the whisky around against the insides of the glass.

The telephone on her desk began to ring, a soft jingle. She picked up the receiver, ending the chiming noise.

"*Jennifer?*"

"Dominic. I thought I told you not to call me. It's not safe... you don't know who might be listening..." Jennifer drained her glass.

"*We both know your line is secure.*"

"That's not the point. I did what you asked. Everything else here on in, you'll need to do for yourself. I can't get involved."

"*You're already involved, darlin',*" Dominic said. "*Besides, I'm doing it for us.*" She could tell he was lying. "*Just hear me out... I need something more.*"

"More? Dominic... you've got a state-of-the-art training facility and a burgeoning army of invisible soldiers... and then there's the equipment, the vehicles, helicopters, a boat. What more do you possibly need?" Jennifer snapped.

"*Sophie's data implant training programs.*"

Jennifer laughed. "You know as well as I do George destroyed them when he sabotaged the research facilities. They were blown up with most of his notes and team."

"*Jenny, Jenny, Jenny... you seem to forget how resourceful George was. The training material... he kept it backed up on an external server. He made it look like it was all destroyed, but someone told me it wasn't.*"

"Who?" Jennifer was curious. As far as she had believed, George had been very thorough with destroying his work.

"*A former friend of George's; Malaxi Bacaunawa. Small Filipino martial arts guy, answers to the name MAXI. Taught Sophie all her tricks and helped facilitate all her other training.*"

"Maxi? Never heard of him."

"*Strangely, he said the same of you. He knew your father though; he said he was a despicable excuse of a man who had little or no morals. I said the traits ran in the family,*" Dominic laughed, slightly amused by his comment aimed at Jennifer. "*Before I jetted off to America with Ryan's army of misfits, I sought Maxi out. I half-expected to find that he'd returned to Zamboanga City or wherever-the-hell he came from; but no. Seems the multi-ethnic culture hub of the world took his fancy and I easily found him holed up in some illegal kick-boxing facility towards the arse-end of Soho. He gave me a free lesson in 'Yaw-Yan' before coming around to my way of thinking. One of the perks of being fat; plenty of cushion for a few kicks and thumps.*" Dominic paused for a moment. "*The good news, he's now assisting me with our recently acquired initiates... but for his work to be effective, he needs George's data implant training programs.*"

"Are they important? Can't we just get some stuff off the internet?"

"*When making a chili en nogada,* would *you just improvise and make it without a recipe?*"

Jennifer didn't reply. She hated analogies almost as much as she disliked Mexican food.

Dominic continued. "*No. The data implant training programs are more than just a few pages of instructions; they are complete training solutions that are subliminally transferred without thoughts or interpretations getting in the way. George's D.I.T.Ps can give over a hundred years' worth of information and experiences, perhaps even a thousand, in just a fraction of the time, all with just the press of a keyboard button.*"

"Okay Dominic, I get it. But, why do you think I'm going to be able to get you these data programs?"

"*George hid them on a server within Kaplan Ratcliff, which he was able to connect to via the net.*"

"Why can't you do the same?"

"*It's encrypted, and I don't have the codes to decipher. The only way to access the information, is to collect it directly from the source.*"

"And where did George keep them?"

"*Well, that's the easy part. Maxi told me he kept them saved on the back-up server...*"

"The back-up server? That's..."

"*In your office, yes. All you need to do is access the server, and using SEARCH, type in 'CHAMELEON', followed by the second command: 'Redivivus'.*"

"Latin?"

"*It hardly matters, but, if it truly interests you, it literally means 'come back to life'. George destroyed everything, including all files relating to Project CHAMELEON. However, he embedded a number of hidden files which he needed to complete Sophie's training. Maxi assured me that they would present themselves by using those over-ride codes.*"

"Ingenious," exclaimed Jennifer.

"*Well... if it works, it will be,*" said Dominic optimistically.

CHAPTER TEN
DOMINIC

DOMINIC WAS BLOWN AWAY by how fast the 'kids' were growing. A couple of days earlier they had appeared no older than five-years; now, stepping into the sleeping quarters, they had all radically changed, seemingly overnight. The loose clothing that they had slipped into on arriving was noticeably small now and splitting at the seams. No one was asleep. It was late-morning, close to lunch time. The boys – all identical-looking – sat on beds or milled around looking bored, gathering in small groups about the enormous room. It was certainly the largest dorm room he'd ever seen, housing over a hundred beds (with just ninety of them filled).

Next to Dominic, Malaxi Bacaunawa had crept into the room, all five feet two inches of him. Dressed in black jogging bottoms and a T-shirt, the martial arts trainer stopped intimately close to the overweight man.

A shrill, warbling sound from a whistle that dangled on a thin blue ribbon from Dominic's neck echoed about the cavernous room, demanding attention. He removed the small silver sports' whistle from his lips and allowed it to fall back to his chest.

Upon hearing the signal, the boys stood from their beds or hurried back to their dorm places, preparing themselves for inspection. With discipline, they stood to attention, forward facing, backs straight, arms by their sides.

"They are well trained," observed Maxi, his voice soft but accent-rich. His eyes scanned the assembly. "And so young... how old?"

Dominic shrugged. "Age as from birth...? Or physically? They've been breathing approximately a month... but my guess is they have the bodies of six-and-a-half-year-olds. Or maybe seven now... I don't know. I'm not good with kids' ages. Yesterday I thought they were around five. I'm struggling to fathom it all."

"Extraordinary," said Maxi. "Even Sophie didn't mature this rapidly. They could be fully-grown within a matter of weeks," he asserted. "George is quite a brilliant man."

"Was... George is dead," said Dominic coldly.

"Dead? No... how?" Maxi had the stature of a twelve-year-old girl, and from behind could easily be mistaken for one. But Maxi's face didn't belong to a child, small or old. It was furrowed and, having seen many days, his skin was dry like paper and heavily wrinkled; the image that appeared to Dominic belonged to a wise man... but evidently not *completely* knowledgeable.

"Don't you watch the news?"

Maxi shook his head. "I don't watch television. It's just soaps, reality shows or doom-and-gloom," he said quietly. "See no evil; hear no evil... speak no evil. Makes for a far happier life." It wasn't the first time Dominic had heard that phrase in recent days. Elspeth had said it too.

"I can see the logic," muttered Dominic disinterested. "Your old pal was killed last night it seems. Whilst he was sleeping."

"How cowardly," Maxi whispered sadly.

"Quite." Dominic turned to the boys patiently standing to attention. Not one moved a muscle or gave the appearance of breathing.

"Initiates..." Dominic addressed the dormitory. "This is Grand Master Malaxi Bacaunawa... you will simply address him as 'Master'."

Maxi bowed slightly in acknowledgement.

"As far as you are concerned, he is your God. You will abide by his rules; you'll talk, eat and sleep when he tells you. Master Bacaunawa will help you develop your... *abilities* and sensibilities, and hone your skills. There is no one in the world like him. I'm not going to lie, the coming weeks are going to be intense, insane and terribly difficult... but the rewards... *oh the rewards...* they will be beyond imagining..."

Dominic allowed silence to descend upon the room. His audience made no sound. It was as though he was addressing a gathering of shop-floor mannequins.

Maxi raised an eyebrow but said nothing.

"Well then... I'll leave you to it. At ease."

The dormitory sprung to life as all ninety boys started talking once again and moving about the room freely.

Dominic patted Maxi on the shoulders twice, before leaving his hand to rest there for a long moment. "I want them ready in two months," he said seriously.

"Ready? Ready for what?" enquired the Filipino.

"Everything and anything; but mostly violence and chaos," replied Dominic cryptically. "Have fun."

"Are yous sure of ya-self Dom'nic Schillin'?" Elspeth was standing in a corridor outside the dorm-room, her arms folded beneath the rise of her breasts. She wore a serious look and her eyes were hard and flint-like.

"What's wrong?" Dominic looked like a kid's football coach with the silver whistle still hanging around his neck.

"Yous! That's what's wrong! Ya take me for a dunderheid!" Elspeth spoke angrily.

Dominic didn't understand. He shook his head. "What's happened? Why the hostility?"

"When wis you gonna tell me aboot the hijacking? Yer fizzog's all over the papers... an' in the news; the Americans has ya on their mos' wan'ed list... What's you bin draggin' us in ta?"

"When did you get the chance to see the news?" Dominic spoke in an amused tone.

"There's a toaty t'ing called a telephone... p'raps you've heard of them? Aye, twas Dougal who tol' me... They're sayin' ya also involved with killin' that scientist guy... George Jennings."

"Ellie... everything I told you before I arrived has not changed. Most of what Dougal's heard is lies; they're saying I hijacked a plane and took 256 hostages. I didn't. Sure, I took a plane... but only the one hostage. And he was the pilot, but that was all part of an elaborate plan. Everyone else on board you'll find here... and they weren't passengers."

"Where's t' pilot noo?"

"Safe... a bit fuzzy headed and a little concussed, but he'll live. As for George Jennings... how was I supposed to kill him? Even the stupidest person should work out that there was no way I could travel to Cuba from Washington, kill the man, and then get to Los Angeles to steal a plane; not in the timeframe being indicated. They'll be claiming I have the ability to fly AND shoot lightning bolts from my backside next!"

"There's nah need to be reekbeek," said Elspeth meekly.

Dominic tenderly placed his hands on Elspeth's shoulders. "Believe me Ellie. You're in no danger here. I would never see any harm come to you."

Elspeth leaned forward so that Dominic's hands could slip beyond her back, and descended into his chest, burying her head in the crook of an arm. She casually snaked her hands to the back of his body. "I b'lieve you, Dom..." she said softly. "But please tell us, why here? Why me?"

Dominic planted a gentle kiss on Elspeth's ginger head. "Because I... *like* you," he said quietly, just loud enough to be heard. "And... I needed someone to trust." he said.

"What aboot Jennifer Ratcliff? Aren't you and her..."

Dominic sighed. It was true. Complicated, but true. He and Jennifer had been intimate. Many times. But the truth was, he was fonder of *her* than she was of him. He was just a plaything to her... something she was happy to use when the mood suited and dispose of thereafter. Jennifer's denial that he had been Director of Security and Intelligence at Kaplan Ratcliff was simple proof of that; although he knew she had her reasons, he wished she could have come to his defence. But that wasn't how Jennifer Ratcliff operated. It was a thing she would call self-preservation.

"Once," replied Dominic after a long pause. "Now... she's just a means to an end."

"An end?" Elspeth was looking up from below Dominic's chin.

"Yes. An amazing, wondrous end," he said in a bewildered tone. "I promise." For the slightest second, thoughts strayed back to July in London, and the *Whisper of Persia* came to mind.

CHAPTER ELEVEN
EMILY

"I'VE MISSED YOU..." EMILY sounded sad and spoke tiredly. "Being back behind a desk in dreary England is soul-destroying. It's mostly been raining since I've been back," she continued. "You and Washington, it feels like a lifetime ago." Emily was in her kitchen, the cordless phone propped up between her left shoulder and ear whilst she spooned out cat food from a tin into a ceramic bowl. Circling her feet was a young tabby cat that meowed every few seconds, despite knowing that she was about to be fed.

After informing Ryan that she had deciphered the code, Emily had insisted that she would pass on the information to Sophie herself, a deed that hadn't proved simple. Within the office her call had gone to voicemail twice. On the second attempt she left a message asking for the younger woman to call her back.

It was whilst she was in the midst of feeding her cat – Sally – that Sophie returned her call.

"*Any joy with the code?*" Sophie skipped the small talk. She sounded weary at the other end; her voice was barely recognisable. Emily guessed that the death of her father had something to with that.

"Yes, it was quite easy. Your father has a safety locker at Fresno Yosemite International Airport. The number 8-8-0-5-1 is the combination code."

"Okay, genius... but I assume there's more than one locker there. Which one is my father's?"

Emily didn't much like Sophie's tone. Ignoring it, she picked up the cat bowl and placed it down next another containing water in front of the kitchen cupboard below the sink. With the cat no longer bothering her, she transferred the phone to her hand and left the kitchen in favour of her living room. She made herself comfortable on a sofa, tucking her legs up beneath her.

"Well... *that* wasn't so simple. I shan't bore you with all the details."

"No?"

Emily further ignored the note of sarcasm in Sophie's voice. *What is wrong with you?* she thought. Sophie was really *off* with her.

"The locker number is 3-3-1-1. Listen... I'm sorry about your father. I mean..." *What could I say?* she thought. "I should've listened to you and insisted on helping to find him... instead of, you know..."

Sophie didn't respond to Emily's platitudes, instead sounded preoccupied. *"Hold on... let me write... that down."* The phone line went quiet for a moment. *"Okay, I'm back. You know... it's an amazing coincidence that my father dies the same night I learn of his whereabouts. Uncanny, really."*

Emily didn't understand what Sophie was suggesting. "What are you saying?"

"I found Mitch Youngs. He told me why he did it; why he killed my father."

"Oh. What did he say? Is... is he dead?"

Sophie sighed. *"No,"* she said sadly. *"A little concussed, but he's going to wish he was. Barry's gifting him to the Americans at Guantanamo Bay as we speak. I hope they're as hospitable to him as they were to my father. But, first he was most forthcoming. I asked him why? Why did he kill him? He just said he was following orders..."*

"Yes... we know that. Marty Heywood gave him the instructions."

"*It wasn't Marty, Emily; it was Ryan,*" she spoke through gritted teeth. "*It was Ryan who ordered the hit! He probably killed Marty too, to try and mask his tracks and cover it up.*"

"What are you saying? That Ryan is to blame?" Emily was shaking her head. "No, uh-uh. You're wrong. I know he blames your father for Clara, but what you're saying doesn't make sense. And ask yourself, why now?"

"*Simple: he didn't want to lose me to George, so he got to him first. For him, I'm someone to replace Clara, someone he can dote on as he grows old; someone to cling to.*" It didn't truly sound plausible, but Sophie didn't stop. "*He says he's my grandfather. That he might be, but you don't go killing members of family, or seeing harm come to them. No matter what...*"

"I know Ryan, he's honourable. I assure you, he didn't do it. If he wanted your father dead – and I know, he does blame him for Clara's death – he wouldn't get someone else to do it. He'd do it himself!"

Sophie considered her response. Seeming not to have listened to Emily's argument, Sophie spoke further: "*The question bugging my mind is: did you know about it too? After all, back in Washington you pretty much sided with Ryan from the get-go; you never gave any consideration to what I needed or wanted to do.*"

"That's not fair! You know it made better sense to put a stop to GYGES first. You aren't being rational."

"*Rational? And look how being rational has ended up. Dominic going AWOL with a third of the children and my father DEAD!*"

"So-phie," there was pleading in Emily's voice. "I swear! I knew nothing about the plot to kill your father. And I know Ryan had nothing to do with it either!" Emily's voice had taken on a vehement pitch.

"*We'll see,*" Sophie replied ominously, and hung up.

CHAPTER TWELVE
SOPHIE

"**A**LL SET?" SOPHIE WAS standing by a row of payphones to the far side of the airport's waiting area having just finished with her call to Emily, her hand luggage at her feet. Barry had returned, looking very hot, but relieved that he was back. She felt uneasy, and a little guilty for the way she had ended the call, and the way she had spoken to her friend. She didn't mean to accuse Emily of conspiring against her. It was the grief of losing her father and the anger bubbling up inside.

It was at José Martí International Airport that Barry had left her three hours earlier, transporting Mitch Youngs (still unconscious) to the American base at the south of the island. He had now returned and on approaching, Sophie could see that he was brandishing a pair of tickets for the return trip to Miami.

"We're booked in Business Class," said Barry, "the only seats available on the next scheduled flight."

Sophie shrugged. She couldn't care less. "Did the Americans like your gift?" She reached down to her backpack and hoisted it up to her shoulder. Together they started walking casually towards the departure lounge for the *Sun Country Airlines* flight to Miami.

"I guess. I didn't stick around long enough for the reward or a thank you card. I'll be glad when this is all over…"

"I doubt it'll ever truly be over," said Sophie glumly, almost with foreknowledge.

"You know what I mean," grumbled Barry. "All this; all what we've done over the past couple of days." He looked downcast and a little glum.

"What's wrong?"

"In the car, on the way back, I couldn't stop thinking about all those kids, the ones on the helicopters." He shook his head miserably. "They didn't have to die."

Sophie looked momentarily distant, as though grappling with an uncomfortable thought. Finally, she voiced it: "Whilst you were away, I couldn't help thinking exactly the opposite, about the kids that got off the helicopter; the ones that Dominic now has."

"Oh?"

"I'm actually wondering whether we made a huge mistake keeping them alive, and that Ryan had been right to order their deaths all along. I have this terrible feeling that whatever Dominic has planned for them, it's not going to be good."

"I guess we will find out soon enough," opined Barry.

They stopped at a sectioned-off corridor that zigzagged towards a security checkpoint having walked the short distance across the airport's terminal building. Beyond the checkpoint was an x-ray scanner and half a dozen armed officers waiting for them to pass through, mean and menacing-looking.

"No doubt," replied Sophie. "But for now, we have an errand to attend."

"Oh?"

Sophie recounted the conversation she'd had with Emily just before he had arrived. "She deciphered my father's code," she said off-hand, retrieving her passport (in the name of her alias, *Sophie Mason*) and holding it ready for inspection. "The number is a combination code for a locker at Fresno Airport."

"Fresno? If I'd known, I could've booked tickets to LA... would've saved time and money."

"Doesn't matter; we'll get connecting flights," asserted Sophie. "Besides, we need the things we left in the SUV," indicating her serum, "anyway; Emily was able to locate the locker number."

They arrived at the security checkpoint and Sophie waved her British passport and travel documents frivolously, like she had no cares in the world.

The Cuban security guard checked Sophie's visa cursorily without a word before stamping the passport and swiftly handing it back. Barry, close behind, had his passport scrutinised more thoroughly, the guard checking and double-checking the photograph on the passport up against the man standing in front of him. After a long moment, the guard stamped the passport and handed it back. He urged him to move on with the wave of the back of his hand.

Passing through the 'step-through' metal detectors, their hand luggage drawing no attention, they were safely clear of security. On the other side, Sophie continued updating Barry on her latest development:

"All we need to retrieve what my father intended for me is to go to Fresno Airport, locate the locker, and key in the code."

"Sounds simple," suggested Barry, slightly scornfully.

"Knowing our luck, it's likely a trap," replied Sophie flippantly. She tried to smile; tried to lighten the mood. "We've got an hour to kill; come... let's treat me to some duty free..."

"All well and good if you like cigars," mumbled Barry, following her into the shopping area of the departure lounge.

Two-and-a-half hours later the *Sun Country Airlines* flight from Havana landed at Miami International Airport. The actual flight only

lasted fifty-seven minutes, but it felt longer owing to the cramped aircraft cabin and the lack of any refreshments. It was close to midnight when they reunited themselves with the silver SUV parked within the airport's long-stay car park.

"Take everything you need or want to keep; everything else – including the guns – we'll need to abandon." The boot door to the SUV was pulled up and Sophie was leaning in for her holdall. Unzipping the large sports bag, she rifled through the clothing, re-discovering her *Glock* handguns. She lifted one up just high enough for Barry to see.

"Shame about these though," she whispered sadly. "I've grown quite fond of them."

"I'll buy you a new pair when we're back in London," said Barry, as though discussing footwear or sunglasses. "Come... let's be quick." The car park was full of cars and empty of people, but Barry couldn't pretend that he didn't feel nervous and exposed. Dotted around were CCTV security cameras. He knew that Sophie was still being sought by the authorities, and couldn't be certain that there wasn't a warrant for his arrest also.

Ruefully, Sophie put aside the guns, zipped up the sports holdall and carried it out. She slammed the door closed. "What time's the flight?"

"Half-six in the morning," said Barry tiredly. "We'll doss down for the night in the airport."

"Doss down?" She had never before heard the expression.

"Yes. Sleep it rough. There may be someplace we can go grab a bite to eat, though unlikely at this hour."

"You really know how to impress a girl," muttered Sophie, walking away with her backpack flung over her right shoulder and her holdall slightly off-balancing her, gripped in her left hand.

"Chivalry has always been one of my stronger points." Barry countered, smiling.

"Clearly."

Unsurprisingly the domestic departure lounge at 12:30 a.m. was practically deserted. A cleaner on a ride-on scrubber drove around the large hall washing the black *Terrazo* floor tiles that decorated the airport, manoeuvring the small vehicle around corners before completing the journey back-and-forth several times over, cleaning and polishing. A quick survey of the room confirmed that there were no shopping or recreational facilities open at such a late hour, which included places to eat or drink.

Disheartening them both, supper consisted of bags of *Cheetos* and *Planters Peanuts*, washed down with cans of coke. Afterwards, Sophie used a washroom to freshen up and change from her turquoise flower dress into denim jeans and a white loose-fitting T-shirt. Barry managed to find sleep stretched across four padded seats.

Morning and the flight to Fresno Yosemite International Airport came about slowly for Sophie. Barry was still asleep when the first call for passengers was announced over the public address system. Despite the number of people arriving in the departure lounge, and the increasing noise level, it took a hard shove to wake Barry.

"Rise and shine."

"Wah..." Barry swung his legs out and sat up. "I wasn't asleep." Bones cracked as he stretched out his arms and arched his back.

Half an hour before the flight was due to take off, the boarding gate was opened and Barry and Sophie sauntered towards the security guard manning the entry point.

"Identification and boarding passes please?" the guard on the desk requested. He was not much older than Barry, but had slightly longer and darker hair. Sophie noted that he had bright bluey-green eyes that sparkled and which she found herself magnetically drawn to. "Ma'am?"

Sophie's cheeks reddened as she realised that she had been staring. "Sure... sorry... I didn't mean to gawp. Here."

"British?" the guard enquired on hearing her voice a moment before receiving Sophie's burgundy passport.

"Yes..." Sophie tried an endearing smile which faltered on seeing the CCTV screen on the security guard's desk. Sophie's image was staring out from it, the frame frozen for biometric analysis.

The guard checked the passport and ticket and smiled. "Where in England are you from?" He was studying the passport.

"London... originally," Sophie heard herself say nervously. For a terrible moment she feared her passport stated her birth place as somewhere else. She couldn't remember. Her heart was thumping hard in her chest and suddenly she felt nauseous.

The guard handed Sophie her passport and tickets back. "Have a safe flight to Fresno Mrs Mason," he said with a warm smile.

CHAPTER THIRTEEN
BRAYDEN

I T WAS A TIRED cliché and originally a hit song for Dinah Washington back in 1959, but 'what a difference a day makes' were the words that came to Brayden as he returned his mobile phone to his trouser pocket. He'd just disconnected the call from Deputy Director Calland at Langley and was pacing the room, unsure as to whether to be angry or elated. Milo Calland had given him the 'great news' that he had been selected to head a joint CIA/FBI detail headed to London on orders from the White House. Moments before calling him, Milo had returned from his meeting with the President and he wanted to brief him as swiftly as he could.

"I don't want to go back to England... it's cold and always raining," he asserted. "I have allergies, and... and... it's full of the *English*! I can't go; I won't go!" He winced at how petulant he had sounded as he feebly protested.

"*I have my orders Agent... as do you.*" Milo stated and terminated the call, ending further argument. Brayden was in an office Captain Will Hancote had temporarily commandeered upon arrival at Guantanamo Bay. His ship, the *USS Princeton,* was docked in the bay with most of his crew on board, though some were on land checking out the recreational facilities *GITMO* offered, such as *McDonalds.* The *Ticonderoga*-class guided missile cruiser was easily seen from the second floor window and a number of naval seamen were busy at work out on deck.

Hancote was sitting behind the desk. "You look a little agitated," he said. Before Milo Calland's call the two of them had been making small talk. It was late in the day and neither had better things to do except wait for further commands and share a bottle of whisky that Hancote had found buried beneath a pile of papers in the bottom drawer.

"Is it that obvious?" Brayden snapped.

Hancote raised his hand in mock-surrender and reached for his glass. He sipped the liquid neat, and winced at the fiery taste. An uneasy silence descended upon the room. Brayden walked to the window behind Hancote's desk and stared out towards the ocean. Although it was nearing 7:00 p.m. it was still light enough to see, although the sun had recently set.

The telephone on the desk began to ring its electronic warble. Subtle and quiet, the previous occupant of the office clearly hated the intrusion of sudden, abrupt noises. The captain scooped up the receiver, answering it by just saying his surname. "Hancote..."

It was switchboard located elsewhere within the compound. *"Captain... I have Lance Corporal Raul Martinez on the line for you... he says it's urgent."*

"He asked for me specifically?" grunted Hancote. In his free hand he roiled the small amount of whisky left in the glass.

"Well no, sir... but he said he had someone in custody I thought you might be interested in. Someone by the name of Mitch Youngs?"

Without any hesitation Hancote asked her to patch him through. A couple of sharp crackles on the line filled his ear before a Hispanic voice sounded.

"Lance Corporal Martinez... tell me, is it true you have that sorry sack of faecal matter in your keeping?"

Brayden peered back round to where the captain was sitting, his interest stirred.

"*It's the damnedest thing. A civilian car pulls up outside the north perimeter fence and this white dude with a strange accent climbs out. 'Tell whoever's in charge I have a gift for you', he says to us. I'm with Pillegi, and we both are wonderin' what's he on about? Then he goes to the back of his car and drags out this sweaty bald guy who's a little banged up – a real sight for sore eyes.*"

"Is this a long story?" asked Hancote seriously.

Ignoring the comment, Martinez continued, "*The dude brings him up to the fence. 'Courtesy of Her Majesty's Secret Service,' he says. It's only the son-bitch who kills that guy here this mornin'. I recognises him from the bulletin my NCO briefed earlier.*" Actually, he recognised him from when he'd let Mitch slip past the border fence, but he wasn't about to admit that.

It was Brayden's belief that for every pound of bad luck there came a pound of good luck, akin to Newton's third law: every action has an equal and opposite reaction. A bit of 'ying' and 'yang' or 'rough' with 'smooth'. Learning that Mitch Youngs had been apprehended and in their custody certainly enhanced his mood, so much so that he had all but forgotten his pending trip to London, adopting a definite skip in his step as he left Hancote to his office and his whisky.

Hitching a lift from a Private in a *Jeep*, Brayden speedily arrived at the building where Mitch was being transported, but had as yet to arrive. Known as Penny Lane, it had recently been prepared for George Jennings' stay before his collapse forced alternative arrangements; it was good and ready for a new inmate.

Now George was dead and the man responsible was going to

spend time imprisoned in his place. A further example of 'ying' and 'yang' thought Brayden.

A short convoy of vehicles kicked up a dust cloud which followed them close behind. It was now almost dark and headlamps from the procession glowed brightly, illuminating their progress as they drew near.

The first vehicle to arrive was a *Humvee*. It stopped a short distance from where Brayden was standing. Four military policemen climbed out as another *Jeep* escorting at the rear and a white van transporting the prisoner travelling in the middle came to a halt.

One of the MPs opened the side-panel door, sliding it aside with a grunt. He climbed up into the van to retrieve its only occupant, slouched in a heap against a corner at the back, his hands cuffed and his feet shackled. He dragged him to his feet and shoved him out into the waiting arms of a second MP. The other two stood close by with their hands resting menacingly on holstered side arms.

Brayden stepped forward from the shadows and approached the prisoner being jostled forward.

"Hello Mitch," said Brayden. "I never thought I'd ever say this... but, I'm actually happy to see you. Really I am." Brayden smiled, seemingly exposing all of his teeth; they glowed in dusk's dimness.

"I bet," muttered Mitch beneath his breath. The chains clasped around his ankles jangled as he shuffled past, an MP guiding him into the building where armed guards stood by the door.

"Check him into his 'hotel'. Make sure he has enough 'pillows'," Brayden chuckled. He retrieved his mobile and was pressing it up to his ear. "I'll let the President know the good news," he said cheerily, loud enough for Mitch to hear as he disappeared into the detention facility.

He pressed a hot-key on his phone and waited.

"*Calland...*"

"Milo... It's Brayden..."

"*You calling to berate me some more on my decision to send you to London?*"

"I'm past that, no sir; we've got him!" Brayden walked towards one of the vehicles that had escorted Mitch's van.

"*What?*"

"We have Mitch Youngs. He's locked up and being tucked up in bed for the night..." Brayden gave a short account of what had happened.

"*Do we know who the Good Samaritan was?*" asked the Deputy Director.

"British Intelligence I'm guessing, from the description given; we didn't get a chance to question him further," said Brayden. "What do you want done with Youngs?"

Calland gave the question a moment's thought. "*I know how much you love the guy; let him experience the delights of Guantanamo for a few days. Have him questioned; don't be soft on him, tell base interrogators. After, we'll have him transferred to Langley. He'll be tried and charged for treason; his sentence will be the death penalty. The President will motion for it to be swift...*"

"Do you want me to oversee all this?"

"*Nice try Brayden... I know you'd love to hold his hand through to the end; no, London still beckons for you I'm afraid. I've expedited your mission... it's imperative we locate and apprehend Dominic Schilling. I've chartered a flight to take you to Utah where you'll meet your detail.*"

Brayden sighed. "Detail? Okay... when?"

"*Tomorrow. Your new partner will be waiting for you at Hill Air Base. She will brief you on the rest.*"

"Partner? She? I thought I was heading this detail on my own." Brayden made no effort to hide the torment or disappointment from his tone.

"Agent Mullins is very accomplished. You'll like her."

"Is she attractive?"

Calland ignored the comment. *"She's also a junior pro-wrestler,"* he said, as though it mattered. *"I'll speak to you again when you are in London in a day or two. Don't forget to take an umbrella!"* The Deputy Director terminated the call. Brayden kept the phone pressed to his ear for a little longer as he deliberated over what had just been said.

Early the following morning, Captain Hancote was shaking him by the hand as the *Sikorsky Seahawk* helicopter landed on an expanse of bare land just behind the main detention building. A side door opened outwards and a Navy officer stepped out.

"I've arranged transport to Puerto Rico. From there, Calland has chartered a plane for Utah. Good luck Agent Scott…"

Brayden took his hand back, nodded and turned away. The rotor blades of the helicopter buffeted him as he jogged towards the aircraft, ruffling his hair and lifting up the flaps of his suit jacket. Climbing into the helicopter, he was handed a set of earphones. No sooner were the doors of the *Seahawk* closed, the helicopter hurriedly took off, jostling Brayden from side to side in his seat.

Everything went pretty much according to plan. The Naval aircraft landed on a helipad within Muñiz Air Force base at San Juan, Puerto Rico shortly before 7:30 a.m. Less than 400 yards away was a runway upon which a *Gulfstream G650* business jet aeroplane waited take-off. The twin-engines of the aircraft were powering-up and preparing for flight even before the *Seahawk* had appeared on the horizon. Brayden's transfer between aircraft was swift in a jog, and within five minutes he was airborne again with a drink (warm diet coke) in one hand and a sandwich (ham and pickle) in the other.

The flight time to Utah was just shy of five hours. It had been a long, exhausting day. An hour into the flight, Brayden reclined his seat and closed his eyes to get some sleep having slept very little over the past forty-eight hours and thinking that when he awoke he would be at his destination.

Sometime later, whilst flying above Mount Elbert in Colorado, the highest summit of the Rocky Mountains, the captain piloting the *Gulfstream* received fresh instructions, together with a new set of co-ordinates by order of the Deputy Director of the CIA. The jet aeroplane continued towards Utah, but instead of descending to land, it carried on further, flying past into Nevada and beyond, towards California.

At 1:15 p.m. the jet aeroplane that Milo Calland had chartered landed smoothly on the secondary runway at Fresno Yosemite International Airport, taxiing its length to come to a halt outside the passenger terminal, a modern building built in 2010 and currently handling close to one-and-a-half million passengers every year.

Brayden stirred within his reclined seat, a bit of dribble escaping the side of his mouth. As the *Gulfstream* started to power down, a flight assistant unbuckled her seatbelt and crossed to where the CIA agent was sleeping. Tall, dark-haired and wearing a lot of make-up, she gently shook his arm to rouse him.

"We've landed Agent Scott," she said softly. Her voice was without accent.

"Hmmm?" Brayden had been enjoying his sleep. Initially he was disorientated and a little groggy, as though hungover. Feeling the moisture on his chin, he back-handed it away. "Where am I?" he asked sleepily just as cognisance began to seep through. "Are we in Utah already?" A glance through the window confirmed it was after noon and a number of aircraft were taking-off or landing around him.

"No sir," said the flight attendant casually. Her name was Carol,

Brayden had asked for it when she'd served him refreshments shortly into their flight; she'd given it freely with a smile.

It wasn't all she would have given, he mused. He knew the type.

"Fresno," Carol said in an off-hand manner, seeing the puzzled look cross the agent's face.

"Fresno?" Brayden sat upright, slightly perturbed. "What the hell?!"

"Calm down Agent Scott... new orders came in from the Deputy Director whilst you were sleeping. He's instructed you call him right away."

Brayden checked his watch, confirming it was after noon. The time was actually 1:20 p.m. "It better be good," he said, disgruntled, although not entirely dissatisfied with the delay in going to London.

"I hope so," replied Carol, a hint of annoyance in her voice that she did nothing to explain. "He's expecting your call." Carol left Brayden fumbling to retrieve his phone from his pocket. He squeezed it out between the folds of the bunched-up material of his trouser leg and speed-dialled his superior.

Milo Calland answered almost immediately. "*Y'ello?*"

"It's Brayden," he said. "I'm in Fresno... what-the-hell's this about?"

"*We had a change of plan... it's a bit of a diversion but it's something that should appeal to your ego.*"

"Go on..."

"*Operation Shakespeare is still ongoing, and we've had some good intel. The FBI believes they've found our girl.*"

Brayden's interest went up a degree. "Sophie? You sure?" He was out of his chair and reaching for his jacket which the flight assistant had stowed in an overhead holdall.

"*Biometric scanning at Miami Airport alerted us; she was clearing security to board a flight to Fresno, California. The image was flagged on the FBI's facial recognition tracker; they've had algorithms searching all security and surveillance cameras through the whole of North America since the Dulles Airport incident. Further analysis here at Langley gave a 97% match. It's her, we're certain of it. She's travelling under the guise of Mrs Sophie Mason and has a travelling companion, Mr Barry Mason. We can assume his is an alias also."*

"What do you want me to do?" Brayden spoke with a tinge of excitement in his voice.

"Her inbound flight from Miami is due to land in approximately one hour. We are co-ordinating a joint operation with the FBI in apprehending her – AND her accomplice – and have been communicating with the pilot of their plane. This should be a slam-dunk operation. Nothing can go wrong..."

"Those famous last words," said Brayden, knowing too well that nothing was ever quite that easy. "Okay, where do I go?" He was standing impatiently at the exit waiting for the flight attendant to allow him to disembark.

Carol twisted a lever on the exit door which dropped out and doubled as a set of steps, and stood aside allowing Brayden to pass. As he walked by he blew a kiss using his free hand. She just smiled brightly.

"Agent Mullins will meet you there and tell you the rest; she got an earlier flight from Utah," Calland said. *"She's your new partner."*

At the bottom of the steps leading out of the *Gulfstream* jet aircraft, a woman in her late twenties stood waiting; long brown hair with caramel streaks, and tied in a tail. She wore a small amount of makeup, but hardly enough to notice. Mirrored sunglasses were perched over the bridge of her nose giving her face a casual-look, but the attire she wore looked very official, businesslike. White blouse, black skirt and matching blazer; she looked like typical FBI or law-enforcement. The bulge to the right of her waist gave the telltale sign that she had a weapon holstered at her hip.

"Thanks... I see her." Brayden disconnected the call and re-pocketed his mobile as he ascended the short staircase.

CHAPTER FOURTEEN
RYAN

Emily Porter burst into Ryan's office shortly after 8:00 a.m. eager to share the latest development. A cursory glance was enough to confirm that the man seated behind the desk had not – as *she* had done – gone home the night before, which she established simply by his unkempt appearance and lack in change of clothing.

Without prompting Emily sat down and provided the reason for her sudden appearance. "It's Alby Goodall... we've found him!"

"Thank God! Where? Is he...?" *Alive.* He was relieved and afraid to ask, both at the same time.

"He was found tied up and gagged at the back of a pub, next to a pharmacy in Brampton, nine miles east of Carlisle. He was unconscious and badly beaten, but other than that his prognosis is good. Emergency services have taken him to Carlisle's A&E. The local constabulary are currently investigating and his wife and family have been informed."

"Good, good. I'm glad he's going to be okay. What of Dominic... any news?"

Emily shook her head. "We've not located the plane, either. Our leads are cold. We're working on the assumption that Dominic had Alby dumped far from his whereabouts, probably in an attempt to thwart our manhunt. We're indirectly working with the local police.... but, so far," she shrugged, "no witnesses, and no surveillance footage. A camera at the rear of the pub had been vandalised and the one within the pharmacy next door didn't capture anything. Dominic's disappearance is too perfect to be opportunistic; it was meticulously planned and orchestrated. He needed to have had help." Emily looked agitated. Something bothered her but she couldn't pinpoint it. "Ryan, I think he played us for a load of old fools."

"Jennifer Ratcliff too, I should imagine," Ryan said, trying to sound aloof. The truth was he'd been speaking with the woman earlier that morning.

"She's distancing herself from Dominic," stated Emily, almost in the CEO's defence. It was an expected move.

"As we are too," surmised Ryan with a knowing smile. After a long pause, he added, almost like it was a confession: "I spoke with her soon after I learnt that Dominic had disappeared with the kids. She denied having any knowledge... but if that was the case, why was only Alby disposed of? Dominic took with him three other men, all of them Kaplan Ratcliff had supplied us in our joint task force. She assured me – *to my face* – she had no idea... a yarn she continues to maintain. But it just seems too... elaborate; too obvious. Kaplan Ratcliff has the resources and the finance to pull off such a vanishing act. But... it's going to be difficult exposing her without making ourselves look complicit."

"We are complicit," Emily replied. A look of fear flashed on Ryan's face which Emily didn't notice, then it was gone as he realised that her comment didn't infer anything. "It certainly is a bit of a pickle," she added. It sounded lame and childlike.

"Hmmm," murmured Ryan, becoming momentarily contemplative. Absently, he turned away to look out through the window behind him. London and the River Thames met his gaze marred by another wet, dismal day.

Emily could tell that something was on the man's mind. Whilst he was distracted she discretely, and quietly, leant forward and almost absently touched the underside of Ryan's desk, running her hand along the edge beneath it – as though probing for something. She withdrew her hand swiftly as Ryan rotated back to facing her.

"I spoke to Sophie," Emily piped up, changing the subject and disguising any anxiety. It was also meant as misdirection in case he had spotted anything unusual in the way she had been acting.

Ryan's demeanour softened. "I did wonder..."

"I gave her the location of her father's locker. She's on her way to Fresno as we speak."

"Fresno... at least she's getting to travel a bit," he said lightly. "Is she... okay? About her father, I mean?"

"As well as can be expected, I guess." *She blames you, Ryan, for killing her father*, Emily thought to herself. "She didn't say much on it," she lied, not wanting to repeat Sophie's accusations.

"Oh, okay." Ryan shook his head in remorse. "I do feel somewhat responsible," he said in pity. "I should've let her rescue her father before the *GYGES* mission. In retrospect, might've worked out for the better had we have gone with her wishes." He went quiet, his mood noticeably downbeat.

And Sophie wouldn't now want to kill you, the voice in her head countered. After a moment of uncomfortable silence she stood up to go. "I'll let you know when I have any news regarding Sophie," she said. "Is there anything else you'd have me do?"

"Ah, no. No, just keep me posted, is all," Ryan murmured, sounding preoccupied.

Emily closed the door behind her leaving Ryan to what she assumed was his wishful thinking.

———◆———

"I told you your pilot would be okay."

Ryan was staring out of the large toughened-glass window behind his desk, looking across towards a river cruise boat drifting along on the Thames, tourists in raincoats or holding umbrellas, sat about the upper deck flashing cameras despite the persistent drizzle of rain marring the tour.

"If unconscious and beaten black-and-blue is 'okay', yeah..." he replied sarcastically. "You said you wouldn't call. Damn it, Jennifer... it's too dangerous... I can't get involved!"

"*YOU ARE INVOLVED. Anyway, your MI6 phone lines are secure,*" she said. "*Just thought I'd let you know; the boys are settling in.*"

"I don't want to know. If anyone finds out..."

"*They won't. Not from me... no one should suspect.*"

"The CIA might."

"*CIA?*"

"The Prime Minister has agreed to welcome our American counterparts to work with us to hunt Dominic. They're a little peeved by the attack on Area 51 and have named him as Enemy Number One... and Sophie as an accomplice. They've probably had a pack of cards printed with their images..."

"*You'd better make sure they do not succeed in finding him... for your and Emily's sake. If we go down, I'm taking you there with me.*"

"Is that a threat? Listen... we're in this together. I gave you what you wanted, and we have an agreement. It's for the best for our futures. Now leave me and my family out of it. Or else!"

"*Family? Huh, and else what, Ryan? Now who's making the threats?*" she started to chuckle. "*Just keep to your word, we're a partnership, and we'll be fine.*"

"And you remember your promise. Just don't call again."

"*No promises. Don't forget who you are dealing with Ryan. Say hi to Emily for me...*"

Before Ryan was able to respond further, the line went dead leaving him with his phone pressed tightly against his ear. Maintaining that position for longer than necessary, he once again started pondering over things, more specifically he questioned his most recent decision making.

He was wondering: *What am I getting myself into?*

CHAPTER FIFTEEN
SOPHIE

"*L*ADIES AND GENTLEMEN... WE *are shortly to arrive at Fresno Yosemite Airport... Please can I ask that you secure your seatbelts ready for our descent...?*" The seatbelt sign above the seats throughout the cabin lit up alongside the permanently illuminated 'no smoking' sign. "*We have been advised that there is a build-up of air traffic waiting clearance to land and that we are in a queue. Do not be alarmed, but we will be hanging in the air for a little bit until our turn arrives... this won't be too long and is quite normal. On behalf of United Airlines, I'd like to thank you for travelling with us today...*" The pilot of the *Boeing 737* continued with a standard platitude but Sophie was no longer listening. Almost of its own volition, her left hand reached for Barry seated next to her, and grasped his knee. She squeezed it hard as she peered out of the window; she was surveying the skies around her and then peering downwards towards the earth below. She couldn't see any other aeroplanes in the sky, and owing to the *Boeing*'s height all she could see of the ground was unassuming; swathes of green, dusty-brown lines that were roads and masses of grey squares and rectangles which she figured were buildings belonging to housing and industrial estates. Dots of traffic could be seen moving about in lines like a flurry of worker ants, their backs glistening under the sun's rays.

Barry turned his head towards Sophie. She was still gazing out through the *Plexiglas* window. "What's wrong?"

Sophie didn't immediately respond, her attention now focusing on something in the distance. She could just make out the airport which was coming into view. "Something doesn't feel right," she said anxiously.

An air hostess stopped next to the empty seat beside Barry and leaned over. "Ma'am... please fasten your seatbelt." She wore a winsome smile that Barry barely noticed beneath the thick glaze of crimson that plastered her lips.

Sophie pulled her attention away from the scene outside and fumbled the belt at her waist into the metal clasp, pulling it tight.

"Thank you," said the air hostess as she walked away, inspecting other passengers as she glided down the aisle towards the front of the plane.

"What do you mean?" asked Barry, slightly troubled.

"This..." she used a hand to indicate everything, quickly sweeping it about her. "What the pilot said. It doesn't make sense. If there was a build-up of aircraft waiting to land, you'd expect to see some planes flying around with us... but..." she was peering out of the window again, "... there's no others up here. None."

"Oh... you sure?" Barry stooped down and leaned over Sophie slightly, trying to take a look. It wasn't easy being strapped in.

"Not only that..." she continued, "I've just looked at the airport below us and nothing is landing... or taking off."

Barry was still trying to see out through the window across Sophie, now stretching his torso as far over as his fastened seatbelt would allow. "I can't see anything." He meant that his view was obstructed, rather than being able to confirm what Sophie was intimating.

"Exactly," replied Sophie, taking his comment as a confirmation of what she had pointed out. She didn't allow him to correct her. "The pilot is stalling..." she trailed off, deep in thought.

"What? You don't know that..."

Sophie wasn't listening to him. Mechanical groans and sounds filled the cabin as the pilot of the craft began the landing procedure. Her head was turning from one side to another in agitation whilst she considered the problem. An instant later and she had made a decision.

"We have to get off this plane... before it lands," she said quietly, but sternly.

"Uh? How?" Barry didn't quite understand.

Unperturbed, Sophie continued. "There's a way... but you're not going to like it. Hell, I don't even like it!" Sophie had a crazy, insane look about her.

"Go on," pressed Barry, knowing to argue with her was pointless. The *737* started to judder from turbulence as the pilot began the plane's descent.

"The luggage-hold... under the cabin."

Barry raised an eyebrow.

"We would have an opportunity when the pilot engages the landing gear; there's a gap where the wheels retract in the fuselage. It's not big, but we could just squeeze through and make our exit before the plane touches down."

"That's mental," scoffed Barry, laughing.

"I've seen it done."

"You're serious?"

"Do you have any better ideas?" Sophie asked gravely.

Barry's eyes twitched as he turned up his nose. "I think you're being paranoid. We should just sit this out and see what happens."

"What? And fall into whatever trap they've set?" she snorted. A couple of passengers in close proximity glanced their way.

"What about our stuff?" Barry glanced upwards towards the closets above their seats.

Sophie shook her head. It pained her to even consider it. "We'll have to leave them," she said regretfully, thinking about her meagre possessions, and specifically what was left of the serum.

Barry sighed, conceding defeat. "Okay... how?"

One or two passengers batted their eyelids, but no one thought anything too untoward as Barry and Sophie unclasped their seatbelts and vacated their seats, hurrying up the aisle towards the front of the plane. By this time the pilot of the *Boeing 737* had given orders for the cabin crew to prepare for landing, all of whom were seated and strapped in at the front and rear of the aircraft.

"Sir... Madam! It's not safe! Please return to your seats at once!" One of the air hostesses admonished. The one with the bright crimson lip gloss had seen them advance from her rear-facing seat and was the first to issue the warning. Another cabin member was sitting facing her, quite plain in appearance with unkempt short black hair and looked equally miffed by Sophie and Barry's actions.

"Gonna be sick!" complained Barry. He reached to open the toilet door, finding it was locked. As expected, one of the cabin crew had used a key to lock all the toilet doors, which was the procedure shortly before landing. Barry clasped a hand to his mouth and puffed out his cheeks as though fighting the urge to vomit.

"Hold on!" The air hostess facing him unclasped her belt and crossed to a corner cupboard. Hastily, she pulled free a door and reached in. Before she had time to pluck out the sick bag, Sophie had crept up behind her; Barry pulled across the curtain that allowed partial privacy from the cabin and the hundred-plus passengers.

"Li-a-!" The warning was cut short. At the cupboard the air hostess with the crimson lip gloss turned her head sharply to see Barry had subdued her black-haired colleague.

"What's...?" *going on...* The question was unfinished as Sophie snaked an arm around the woman's neck and applied adequate pressure to a place just above her carotid. The woman promptly slipped to the floor.

"You sure we can do this?" Barry asked doubtfully.

"No..." Sophie quickly gazed out of the window. "But there's no time to debate it." The aircraft was descending fast and Fresno's parched land could be seen growing in perspective beneath them. Turbulence caused the plane to rock and judder some more, jostling the pair from side to side. "Come on," said Sophie. At their feet was the outline of a hatch. "Help me open this." Two small fold-down handles were tucked into the trapdoor's smooth flat surface.

Mere seconds later and Barry was following Sophie down a short ladder into the undercarriage of the *Boeing*. It was dark except for a little light filtering through from where the landing gear was beginning to engage. Noise from the engines and the internal mechanics of the aircraft were amplified down there.

"Come on!" Sophie shouted. They charged down the plane towards the centre where the main landing gear was situated, swaying every-so-often from one side to another, walls of luggage secured by thick netting helping to keep them from falling. Mechanical whirrs and groans increased as the gear lowered into position and slowly revealed a widening slit of daylight. "Here!" Sophie shouted, arriving at one of the breaches.

Through the gap, Sophie and Barry saw the buildings and grassland scurry by in a blur of movement. It took a lot of concentration to keep motion sickness at bay.

The gap around each set of wheels was just wide enough for one person to slip through. Barry positioned himself beside one, Sophie the other.

"I DON'T THINK I CAN DO THIS!" shouted Barry to be

heard. Even with little light Sophie could see that the colour had drained from his face. He looked like he was about to be sick for real.

"TRUST ME! YOU'LL BE FINE!" Sophie looked down as Fresno Yosemite International Airport began below them. They were still between sixty and seventy feet above ground level. "COM'ON! DO EXACTLY WHAT I DO!" Without hesitation she lowered herself onto a section of metal that was hinged and joined just above the set of wheels. Essentially, the side-strut enabled the landing gear to be retracted into the body of the plane acting like an arm; extending when it was deployed, and shortening when it was no longer needed. It was also ideal for Sophie to stand on as the *Boeing* fast approached the runway for landing.

Wind that felt gale-force tore at her clothes, pulled at her feet and pummelled her face, peeling her lips back to reveal gritted teeth and the dark pinks of her gums; she looked like a whinnying horse. Afraid of slipping, she wrapped her arms around the large shock-strut upon which the wheels were attached and laced her fingers together as tightly as possible.

"Oh God!" she muttered to herself as the ground rapidly reached up to meet them. Suddenly she felt the urge to be sick and no longer brave. She closed her eyes, fearing what might happen were her fingers to lose grip or if her feet were to slip from beneath her. It did little to appease her dread; if anything – aided by the whistling sound of the wind and the thunderous noise of the aircraft – it made things worse.

Nothing however, prepared her for the shock as the wheels of the *Boeing 737* hit the ground at 155 knots (or 178 mph). Forcefully, her feet felt kicked-out beneath her. Had her fingers not been laced so tightly together she would have been dragged from the landing gear and dashed against the *Tarmac*. Instead, Sophie found herself clinging onto the shock-strut for dear life, her body horizontally-suspended like a human flag for what seemed like forever but was merely an eye-blink; one second later the pilot applied the brakes, allowing gravity to immediately yank her legs downwards. Her feet flailed uselessly to the side of the shock-strut, and dangerously above the giant rubber tyres that threatened to pull her under. For a heart-stopping second she found her fingers begin to slip, just as her left foot regained purchase on the side-strut, followed by her right. Swiftly she repositioned her hands for greater stability and once safe, allowed a searching glance for her companion, hoping that he had survived her crazy idea.

Sophie was relieved to find Barry was still with her. Clinging to the second shock-strut with both his hands and his inner thighs, his eyes were closed and the telltale signs of motion sickness marring one shoulder of his T-shirt. She was staring at him as he risked opening his eyes. After acknowledging that they were both more-or-less in one piece, Sophie diverted her attention to getting off the plane.

The *Boeing* was slowing down fast. Ahead, she could make out a convoy of emergency vehicles joining the runway, identifying them by their flashing red and blue beacons, easily seen from her vantage point beneath the aircraft.

Sophie turned back to Barry. "WE JUMP ON THREE!!" Despite shouting, Barry couldn't hear over the roar of the turbofan engines. With one hand gripped to the shock-strut, the other she used to gesture a dropping sign with her index finger and a count of three by displaying a corresponding number of digits.

Barry nodded as though understanding, though from his look it was hard to tell.

Ahead, half a dozen police cars, three black vehicles – two SUVs and a *Ford Sedan* –, a fire truck and an ambulance, all sped towards the still-slowing aeroplane. The scene confirmed Sophie had been right to prompt a hasty escape all along.

Sophie started counting down her fingers, closing each phalange into her fist and mouthing the number to Barry.

One.

Two.

Three.

Sophie jumped, relaxing and hunkering down at the same time, trying to make herself small – mainly to protect her head – and falling quickly like a stone. At speed, she landed on the runway hard and rolled several feet, grazing and bruising her arms and legs in the process.

A little behind Sophie, Barry jumped, though opting to try a running landing. As the speed of the *Boeing* was still vastly superior to anything he could muster from a standstill, his legs crumpled two steps in to his sprint and he landed on his front hard, skidding for fifteen feet.

Picking herself up, Sophie ran towards the prone form of Barry, who, from where she was positioned, looked like he could have been dead.

"Barry!" she was at his side and pushing him onto his back.

"Ahh," he winced. "That's gonna hurt in the mornin'." He tried sitting up and for a second, tried to forget his own injuries to check on Sophie's. "What the hell... are you a *cyborg* or something?" Compared to the friction-burns to his chest and stomach, and the cuts and bruising sustained to his upper legs, she was relatively unscathed; superficial bruising and grazing.

"I worked out how best to fall," she said, simply. "Come on... we need to get out of here before they realise what we've done." She reached down to help her companion to his feet.

"Ahh... ow-wow-wow-wow-wow...!"

"Are you a three-year-old?" Sophie demanded, taking his arm about her shoulder.

"It hurts," Barry replied pitifully. "I think I may've broken it."

"Broken what?"

"My leg!" he cried.

"Come-on, Barry!"

He tried bearing some weight on his right leg and pain immediately lanced up through his body, feeling like it was about to bore a hole straight out through the top of his head. He grimaced and bit his tongue; a thin tendril of blood leaked from the corner of his mouth. "Sophie...." he shook his head miserably, "... it's no use. I can't... I can't walk." Grimacing and groaning, he added pitifully: "You need to leave me."

Sophie didn't want to hear any of it. "Just shut-up Barry. We're in this together..." Despite her small frame she half-dragged Barry across the runway, then onto a grassy verge, and further, towards an aircraft hangar, Barry constantly grunting and moaning, Sophie wheezing and panting. Each step was an altogether different challenge, and the exertion was taking its toll.

"Seriously... I can't go on," Barry gasped. "We'll both be caught. It's just a matter of time."

Around the side of the aircraft hangar, Sophie let Barry slip from her shoulder, and although selfish, felt instantly relieved at shedding the burden. He collapsed in a heap on the floor and looked wretched.

"I'm sorry," Barry moaned through gritted teeth. "Forgive me..."

Sophie crouched down, leaned over and kissed him on the side of the mouth that was free of blood. "I'll come back for you," she said softly.

In the background, sirens began to wail urgently, some getting closer, others hanging back in the distance. A look down the airstrip suggested that the *Boeing* had come to a halt and had already granted access to those she believed were pursuing her. If that was the case, she assumed it wouldn't be long before their absence would be discovered.

Barry smiled. "Don't... forget me," he said quietly.

Sophie closed her eyes and willed herself invisible, reopening them once the transformation had begun. She watched Barry's face as she gradually disappeared, his look of sheer pleasure and wonder at what she could amazingly achieve. He looked bewildered, his pain momentarily forgotten. She waved her hand gently – waving goodbye – before fading entirely to nothing.

Precisely then, she remembered that all that remained of her serum – the means to be seen again – was stowed in a bag, left behind on the plane in the overhead closet above her seat.

"Don't forget me either..." she replied dolefully, before slipping away unnoticed.

CHAPTER SIXTEEN
BRAYDEN

BRAYDEN SCOTT WAS PERCHED on the edge of a desk in the centre of the air traffic control room. The FBI special agent, Christina Mullins, was close by, as were two other agents dressed in black body armour and carrying rifles. Four air traffic controllers sat in a line along one side of the building overlooking the runways, large screens and an array of electronic aviation hardware was sprawled out along the entire stretch in front of them. Another controller was standing up, his workstation now vacant. He was facing Brayden with his hands on his hips. He wore a concerned expression, like he had just learnt that his house had burnt down.

"It's nothing to worry about," Brayden tried to reassure. "The plane, its crew and its passengers are not in any danger." The CIA man had burst into the Traffic Control Tower moments earlier slightly out of breath from climbing two flights of stairs. The tower was a small glass-walled cabin topping a drab grey concrete structure that someone had tried to make attractive by placing a checked-pattern; rows of light-grey and Columbia-blue tiles stretched up each side of the rectangular-shaped construct.

"You say that with confidence, but really... who are you?" The senior air traffic controller – Pat, informed the metal pin on his light-blue shirt – a man in his forties and carrying far too much body weight, was annoyed that government agents had forced their way in and were now trying to dictate and bypass protocols and security procedures. When he spoke, excess fat wobbled about his face, but mostly in his cheeks and around his chin.

"I am working on the direct orders of the President. By all means, feel free to call him if you need any clarification…"

Pat sighed. He was in charge here. Not the FBI or NSA or Homeland Security; and definitely not the frigging CIA.

"Look…" Mullins began to speak soothingly, trying to appease the situation. "We're not taking over your airport. We just want to apprehend two passengers who are due to arrive on the United Airlines flight from Miami. We'll be out of your hair in no time."

"Okay, okay," Pat surrendered. "What do you want me to do?"

Brayden took over speaking duties. "Be cool and tell the pilot that there are two passengers on board who are wanted fugitives, and that law enforcement wants to board the plane on arrival to make an arrest. It's imperative that the passengers are not alarmed, and our targets are not spooked."

"Who are they?" Having made a decision he hoped he didn't regret, Pat was mentally preparing what he was going to say to the pilot of the aircraft. He thought it might be useful to know who he was dealing with.

"On the flight's manifest, they are listed as a married couple, Sophie and Barry Mason. Needless to say, those are aliases. That's all you need to know." Brayden was curt.

"Fine." Pat was equally blunt.

Sensing the hostility, Mullins stepped in. "Tell us… when is the flight due to land?"

Pat consulted a screen that Brayden guessed was radar, and then another screen with a whole list of jargon. After, he quickly checked the watch strapped to his left wrist. "Approximately eight minutes time," he replied hesitantly.

"Good. That's good," asserted Brayden. "After you've informed the pilot, tell them to circle the airport for a bit... my teams need to be in place and ready." Adding, quietly to himself: "We don't want any more surprises."

⸻ ⬩ ⸻

Eight minutes later, standing alongside the black *Ford Sedan*, Brayden watched the *Boeing 737* come into view through a pair of binoculars he had found in the glove compartment, and followed it as it gracefully glided down from the sky towards the runway. Inside the *Sedan*, Mullins sat waiting for Brayden to climb in and give the word to set them forward.

The *United Airlines* flight from Miami touched down smoothly and began travelling the runway, approximately 3,000 metres in length, and its speed lessening with the pilot's application of the brakes. Pat had advised Brayden that the pilot of the *Boeing* had been instructed to bring the plane to a halt some distance from the terminal building, within an area that allowed a good deal of space to surround.

With the aircraft fast-approaching, Brayden turned to an airport police officer and gave him the order to proceed. "Exactly as I said," he instructed. "O-kay! Let's go... let's go... let's go!" Brayden climbed into the passenger seat and Mullins set the *Sedan* in motion. Behind them, two black SUVs transporting a team of field agents, followed by half a dozen black and white police cars, a fire truck and an ambulance, all began moving in tandem. The convoy of vehicles fanned out to speed towards the approaching plane alongside each other in a parallel line. Without warning, sirens began to howl from the emergency vehicles accompanied by flashing blue or red roof beacons, or coruscating blue-and-red light-bars.

Brayden turned angrily about. He scooped up a hand-held radio and barked: "Kill the sirens, damn-it!"

"There goes the element of surprise," assured Mullins, staring ahead.

Brayden shook his head in agitation. "That's California..." he muttered to himself. Mullins said nothing, smirking a little to herself.

A set of air-stairs were being manoeuvred from a hangar on the left side of the airfield as the *Boeing* gradually came to a halt; the fire truck driver positioning them at the rear passenger door.

Brayden and the FBI's cars drew level and pulled up just a short walk from the plane's nose; the police cars sped past and took up positions around the aircraft, hemming it in. The fire truck and ambulance stopped a little out of the way, there on standby just as a precaution.

Looking up, Brayden could see the pilot (or co-pilot) peering out through the cockpit window. Climbing out of the *Sedan*, he gave the aviator a short wave.

With the air-stairs in place, Brayden and Mullins advanced up the flight of steps and stopped at the *Boeing's* passenger door. It felt absurd, but Brayden rapped his knuckles against the aluminium-alloy door as though canvassing door-to-door in a residential suburb. Mullins matched him for pace and was at his side.

For a long moment, Brayden didn't think the door was ever going to be opened, feeling how a Jehovah's Witness or a travelling salesman might often feel; then the sounds of metal grating against metal as levers and handles were pulled down, followed marginally by the groan of the door's internal hydraulics as they assisted the stewardess on the reverse side. Painfully slow, the door retracted to reveal a blotchy-red-faced young woman with tears of mascara streaking down her cheeks.

"You're too late; they're gone!" she said. It was hard to tell whether the air hostess was in shock or just plain upset.

Stepping back out of the *Boeing* aircraft, Brayden felt acid bubble at the back of his throat and the sour taste of bile fill his mouth. "Lock down the airport!" he shouted down to a couple of uniformed policemen standing just to the left of the air-stairs. "They can't be far. Have a cruiser circle the perimeter." He started descending the staircase, his feet clanging noisily against the metal steps.

Mullins appeared behind Brayden and quickly followed him down. "SWAT is on stand-by," she announced. "I'll make the call." Once at the bottom of the temporary stairs, she jogged across to the black car. Without climbing in, she reached down and picked up the radio.

"Sir?" An FBI field agent wearing a navy blue windbreaker, *FBI* printed in large yellow letters across the back and smaller ones on the front and sleeves, stepped towards Brayden. He was African-American and younger than Brayden. His hair had been buzz-cut into short fuzz. "We've just got word from maintenance that someone has been seen trespassing at one of the hangars on the south-side of the airport."

"Sophie?"

"Nah... The other one. Apparently he's still there."

Brayden wrinkled his nose, not hiding his disappointment. "Okay... let's go get 'im..." he returned to the *Sedan* and climbed into the passenger seat. Mullins, still holding the radio, slipped in behind the steering wheel and readied to go.

"SWAT is en route. I've also alerted the airport's Chief of Police that fugitives are at large within the compound... in view of what we are dealing with, I've asked him to report anything untoward, no matter what." Mullins emphasised the *no matter what.*

"Good," mumbled Brayden, distracted. *This is how it always goes,* he thought. Nothing ever went his way.

The cavalcade of FBI and police vehicles screamed away from

the stationary aeroplane; the two SUVs leading the way, followed by Mullin's *Sedan* and then two of the black and white police cruisers.

Less than twenty seconds later, they pulled up alongside the first of three immense structures. Nothing beat the sheer scale of an aircraft hangar, mused Brayden. A large gaping doorway was open to reveal an aircraft in a state of reassembly; wings, engines, fuselage and sundry parts sprawled across the concrete floor.

"Yo yo yo... this way!" The field agent that had alerted Brayden to Sophie's companion started to run in the direction of one of the other hangars. Brayden and Mullins quickly exited the vehicle, absent-mindedly drawing their weapons as they followed the field agent around the side of the second hangar.

A moment later: "Over here!"

Brayden and Mullins charged towards the sound of the voice, following it around to the side of the hangar. They came to a stop next to him. He was stooping, surveying the scene.

"He was here," the agent said, crouching down to squat over a patch of dark moisture alongside the wall of the large building. "Blood." He reached down and dabbed a finger against the crimson patch and held it up for inspection. "Fresh too."

Brayden re-holstered his gun, as did Mullins. He looked about urgently, eyes searching, a pained look on his face. Behind him was the airfield, the *Boeing* just visible to his right. Ahead were some smaller buildings and beyond them was a perimeter fence that enclosed the airport.

"We must've just missed him," proclaimed Brayden. "He's losing blood and in bad shape from the looks of things. He can't be far..."

The field agent stood up. "I found some more blood over there... a trail of sorts heading away towards the back of the hangar."

"Okay Agent... Go get some of your guys to follow the trail;

search all the buildings. Make sure you find him. He's gotta be here somewhere..."

"Yes sir..."

Brayden turned to his FBI partner. "Mullins... let's focus on the girl. She's who we really want."

"Okay. So far, there's been no sight of her around the perimeter," Mullins calmly stated.

"And there's not likely to be either," muttered Brayden. "Tell me, do you do much field work?"

"More than most I guess, why?"

"Then I suspect you'll have what I need in your car's trunk."

"I have plenty of weapons, if that's what you mean," Mullins said acutely. "A *Kevlar* jacket too..."

"What about night-vision optics?"

"Brayden... it's day time," intoning it obviously. The two plainclothes agents were casually walking back to the car.

"I'm thinking the thermal setting. There's no way we'll be seeing Sophie Jennings now... not with the naked eye."

"Seriously, her being invisible... that wasn't a joke?" quizzed Mullins, not totally convinced by all that had been relayed to her in the mission brief. She knew absolutely nothing about Sophie's abilities, and even less regarding Project *GYGES*.

Brayden "Tsked" to himself. "I forget; I've grown so accustomed to my adversary being like a ghost that I've taken it for granted." He started to laugh at an unspoken joke, slowly shaking his head. "And to think, I've never *actually* seen her. I'm just following the Deputy Director's orders. For all I know, we're just chasing our shadows!"

"Who are we to question the chain of command?" she asked sarcastically. Stepping into the *Sedan*, further conversation was halted by the radio crackling into life.

"Agent Mullins? This is Stapleton... Chief of Fresno Airport Police." The wheezy, nasally voice of the senior police officer filled the car.

"Yes, Chief."

"You asked to be advised of anything strange or abnormal," he began, *"I thought you'd like to know, a silent alarm has just been triggered at one of the emergency exits near to boarding gate six in the terminal building. It's the oddest thing; CCTV is picking up nothing... but doors..."* Stapleton started to laugh over the radio, *"...they don't open all by themselves."*

"Thanks Chief... we'll check it out."

"What in hell is going on?"

Mullins ignored the question. She looked uncertainly towards Brayden as the *Sedan* sped forward, steering the vehicle towards the terminal building. It wasn't too far from where the *Boeing* was still parked, and the first of the airliner's passengers started to disembark.

Brayden took the radio from Mullins and disconnected the transmission. "It's nothing personal..." he said, unheard by the Chief of Fresno's Airport Police. "It's just one of those 'needs to know' situations."

CHAPTER SEVENTEEN
SOPHIE

Leaving Barry behind was not the hardest thing she had ever done; stepping away from her mother's dead body, crumpled and bloody by the side of a road was much worse. But, she had to admit, Barry came a close second.

Hardly a day passed without her thinking about her birth mother. She feared the image of her lifeless, blood-stained corpse would haunt her for the whole of her life (which for Sophie *could* be a very long time). Already her sleep was tormented by visions of Harriet, often visiting with accusations of blame, feeding from the guilt that Sophie felt. On the positive side she considered, at least she rarely dreamt of her father 'rescuing' her from the burning laboratory; his posting of the gun into the bin by the bus stop had been blanked from memory until Ryan had revealed her father to be a traitor. Then she'd remembered all the heinous details all too clearly. She blinked back the memories to focus on the task at hand.

As she stepped out from the shadow of the last hangar, separated over a short distance from any other building by a strip of land where planes and vehicles sat parked, the sound of sirens continued to scream from a short distance away. A quick look to her left, she picked out the *Boeing* – now stationary – which she had leapt from, and the retinue of emergency vehicles that had been despatched to deal with the event and more significantly, to greet her. Half a dozen were now speeding up the landing strip towards her; official government-issue black vehicles leading the way. Despite the cover invisibility afforded her, Sophie felt exposed like a nudist at a Bar Mitzvah as she started jogging towards the terminal building five hundred metres ahead of her.

Seconds later and the cavalcade of law-enforcement vehicles sped past, the sirens no longer warbling but their flashing light-bars maintaining their urgency. Taking a swift sideward glance as she ran, she caught sight of the man in the passenger seat in the leading black *Sedan*. He was looking out, scanning the vast range, seemingly as though he believed he possessed the ability to see her. And for a heartbeat, the man's eyes met hers and Sophie was almost convinced he could.

There was no way for her to know that this man had played a significant part in her life, or his involvement in the events that led to the deaths of both her parents; an eye-blink later he was gone. Yet, in all their close dealings, this was the first time Sophie had clocked eyes on him.

From the comparatively short distance, she could see that the agent had tidy, blond hair – slightly darker than hers – styled with a side parting, and blue eyes. Completing his look, he had the firm 'all-American' jaw-line, the type that wouldn't appear out of place on a *Levi* jeans model. Sophie continued to run towards the terminal building, her strides getting bigger as she closed in, thoughts of Barry creeping into mind as it became obvious that the *Sedan*, the two SUVs and the black and white police cars, were heading his way.

There was no time. She would dwell on him later.

Sophie skirted the control tower building and sprinted past the airport's fire station, acknowledging an empty space from where one of the fire trucks had driven out to the *Boeing 737* as a precaution, though the fire-fighters remained seated within the vehicle. Seconds later and she was a handful of yards from the exterior of the passenger terminal, its long glass-panelled wall stretching between two buildings; the first structure to Sophie's right, was where ticketing, security and baggage claim were stationed; the other to Sophie's left, was where boarding gates nine through to fifteen were located.

Within the length of the corridor joining the two were boarding gates one through to eight, though only gates six and eight were accessible via Sophie's side; she easily identified them by the large numerals printed in black on a white background above the doors.

Sophie turned to run towards gate number six. An aircraft was parked nearby and airport personnel were busy loading and refuelling or doing safety checks, none the wiser to her presence.

Half-heartedly she tried opening the door. As expected it was locked from the inside. Quickly, she assessed the perimeter for possible ways to access the building, eyes darting to-and-fro, looking for any opportunity of ingress.

"I know," she said, an idea forming. She ran off towards an engineer dressed in a dark-blue, grease-stained coverall. He was leaning into the back of a white van, stretching in to retrieve or replace a toolbox. "Excuse me," she said.

Hearing her voice the engineer turned sharply, only to find nobody there.

Must be hearing things, he thought, and was about to return to what he was doing when, from nowhere, Sophie struck him. Taking him totally unaware, he felt the hard blow connect to the side of his neck.

Sophie deftly caught him as he collapsed unconscious, and hurriedly dragged him into the back of his van.

"Sorry," she whispered, checking his carotid pulse as she gently laid him down.

From the toolbox she removed a large retractable spanner. It was black with grease and rusty with age and felt heavy in her grip. She tested it with an arcing swing. "This'll do."

Stepping out of the van, she pushed the door and secured it closed after her.

Quickly assessing the best way into the terminal, Sophie found herself wandering towards the main building where baggage claim was situated, and the disquieting knowledge that it was also where border security could be found.

As she had expected – and came prepared for – the emergency exit doors had no physical way of opening from the outside. Built within the glass facade of the long corridor-stretch of the terminal, joining the main departure terminal building, the double-doors were steel-framed with glass panels at the top and bottom, and secured firmly from the inside. Sophie could see the easy-to-operate opening bar from where she was standing, tantalising and teasingly close, and could read the basic 'push here' instruction printed on the bar, even though it was upside-down.

Furtively, as though expecting someone might be watching her, Sophie swung the spanner forcefully against the top pane of the nearest door, smashing the glass noisily, sending large shards to rain down on the other side. Without stopping, she struck the jagged, barbed spikes of glass that remained in the door with the spanner, using a circular, anti-clockwise motion. In a moment, the frame was clear from any sharp protuberances.

Still holding the spanner, Sophie reached through the gap to the push-down bar, and applied some pressure. The door swung open outwards and she stepped aside to allow a gap, before walking through, glass crunching underfoot.

Within the terminal corridor, puzzled onlookers stood about

gazing at the smashed window and the open emergency door; others continued walking showing no interest, though mindful of the broken glass. No one was alarmed as nobody could see Sophie.

Leaving the spanner, she walked deeper into the building, heading away towards a door marked *Authorised Personnel Only*, secured by an electronic key card reader. Almost dismissing it out of hand, she made to progress towards the terminal's security clearance section, ignoring the airport's 'No Entry' signs. Just as she stepped forward, the door marked *Authorised Personnel Only* opened out and two airport staff entered the corridor.

Hastily, she charged across to the slowly closing door, stretching herself to keep it open so that she could slip through the shortening gap.

The corridor beyond was short and narrow and allowed permitted staff to bypass security. The door at the other end exited into the 'Welcome Hall' of the terminal building, the glass roof allowing shimmering natural light to fill the room. A large public reception with shops, fast-food outlets, ticket-booths, waiting areas and baggage check-in desks awaited her.

The airport was busy with passengers milling about; men, women, children – old and young – bustled from one place to another, anxious or excited, pulling suitcases on wheels or pushing trolleys laden with piles of luggage and handbags. Armed policemen walked around in pairs nursing automatic weapons on shoulder straps. She counted eight of them around the big, brightly-lit foyer. She couldn't be sure, but she expected that there were likely plainly clothed officers on patrol, discretely operating amongst the swarms of travellers.

Sophie crossed to a signboard upon which an internal map of the airport was displayed. Expeditiously, she scanned the map for the locker areas. A key indicated there were four of them... all situated on the second floor, a mezzanine area that could be seen from where she stood, overlooking the hall from the back and both sides, like a spectator stand in a concert hall.

Hurriedly, she charged through the crowd of people to an escalator, bumping one or two and knocking someone clear off their feet.

"Hey!" a large woman yelled from the floor, not seeing who, or where, the person who'd barged her was.

"Watch-it!" another exclaimed in surprise.

At the top of the escalator, a restaurant area met Sophie. Not being seen, a number of patrons jostled and knocked into her back, grunting and cursing from the hidden obstacle. Oblivious and barely moved, she read the directional signs hanging from the ceiling. None pointed to the locker areas.

"They won't be hard to find..." she muttered, moving away from the escalator and the multitude of franchise-based eateries.

The first locker area she came to was identified as: 'Two (1-400)', placed in the corner of the raised level. Sophie guessed, if she followed the floor round, the locker's area numbered 'one' would likely be found.

Instead, she turned back and entered the dining area full of Americans eating and drinking fast-food purchases. At the end of the concourse was a less-densely populated area that led to locker area advertised as: 'Three (1-400)'.

"Bingo," said Sophie quietly in triumph to herself. However, the elation was short-lived as the whoop and jangle of the airport's emergency alarm began to sound through the ceiling speakers, accompanied by an announcement over the PA by a member of Fresno Yosemite's security team:

"For reasons of security and passenger safety, a state of emergency has been invoked. The airport is in complete lockdown, and we ask that you all remain calm and stay where you are until further notice. On behalf of

Fresno Yosemite International Airport, we thank you for your assistance at this time..."

Sophie sighed, exclaiming "Great!" under her breath. "What is it with alarms?!" With a little more urgency, she ran to the locker area and began searching for her father's depository, numbered three-three-one-one (or simply 311, as the first digit related to the area and not the locker itself).

Metallic-grey in colour with electronic combination keypads, the lockers came in two sizes; small – just large enough for a backpack; and big – allowing enough space for a suitcase (upright) or a golf trolley. They appeared in rows from left to right, in numbered order.

There were four aisles with one hundred lockers to an aisle (fifty on one side, fifty on the other). Sophie quickly ascertained that her father's deposit box was situated within the fourth and last aisle in the locker section, and it didn't take her too long to locate it. Situated at shoulder height, George had hired one of the smaller of the two types of storage closets.

"Three-one-one..." she said, running a finger over the number that was engraved and highlighted in white within a blue background that surrounded the combination lock. Her father's final communication with her had been scrawled on a piece of paper which the nurse, Katherine, had given to her the day before. At first, totally meaningless, but Emily had done her thing and concluded that it was a combination code.

A code for this, her father's locker.

"Here goes nothing..." She jabbed an invisible index-finger at the keypad, punching in digits. Corresponding numbers flashed up on the small LCD screen above the combination keypad, like digits on a calculator: *8-8-0-5-1*.

A slight, muffled 'click' came from behind the metal door, releasing it to glide smoothly open an inch. Anxiously, Sophie took the edge of the square door and opened it out fully. Peering in she could see the item her father had left her.

An aluminium attaché briefcase, secured by two latches either side of a small black handle fitted into its side, had been placed towards the back of the locker. Sophie reached in and slipped it out far enough to be able to inspect it, noticing the latches were locked with a further combination mechanism, these ones mechanical and comprising of four numbered dials.

"Okay dad… I'm guessing you want me to open this thing… so this should be simple." Sophie eased the four dials on each latch to read one-six-zero-four. The day and month of her birth date, the same sequence of numbers she remembered George had used to secure the floor safe back at their old apartment in Chelsea. Guessing correctly, when she pressed the small release buttons the latches popped up. Silently, nervously, she lifted it open, unsure of what to expect.

There were just two objects inside the briefcase.

The first item was a gun, which – she checked – was fully loaded; she slipped it into the waistband of her jeans.

The second item was an A4 manila envelope that contained something that appeared bulky. The package bulged at the centre. Sophie lifted it out and upended it, pouring the contents gently out into the palm of her hands.

A thumb drive lightly slipped out first, about two-and-a-half-inches in length and approximately a centimetre thick. She quickly concealed it within a pocket. Tilting the envelope further, the item causing the package to distend most fell out more heavily and she carefully caught it; a glass vial of blue liquid, slightly larger than the ones she was accustomed to (and which she had left behind on the aeroplane) disappeared within her grasp. On closer inspection she would think the liquid looked a lot like mouthwash. A folded piece of paper had been wrapped around the small bottle, held in place with a red elastic band.

Sophie pulled free the piece of paper and unfolded it, laying it on the shelf of the small closet so as to see it. There were only a few words scrawled across it, but she recognised the handwriting.

Her father's: *A remedy to your predicament... drink me!*

It brought to mind *Alice in Wonderland* and the small potion bottle which Alice drank to make her shrink to fit through the small door.

She scrunched up the paper and slipped it, together with the glass bottle, into the other pocket of her denim leggings. Just before discarding what felt like an empty envelope, she noticed something else within it. Poking her fingers into the manila pouch she teased the glossy piece of paper out. It was upside down but she couldn't fail to recognise one of the faces in the photograph.

The man that was George Jennings. Her father.

Sophie turned the picture the right way up and studied the faces captured within it.

George Jennings was smiling and looked happy. He had his arm around the shoulders of someone else, a woman who appeared familiar. She was pretty and younger than her father, and looked very comfortable within his enclosed arm. It wasn't her mother, and the photo didn't look too old. On the reverse was scribbled what appeared to be an address:

Norská 561/10, 101 00 Praha, Czech Republic.

Although curious, Sophie had no time to give it further heed, the intensifying wail of the alarms accentuating her plight. "Later," she whispered, folding the photo into quarters and placing it into the pocket where the thumb drive was stored. From the corner of an eye she saw purposeful movement; she couldn't see who it was, but dark figures shuffled about across the other side of the mezzanine floor.

Dextrously, she swept up the gun (a *Glock 19*, which pleased her) and retraced her steps back towards the dining hall.

Almost taking her invisibility for granted, Sophie stopped herself at the end of the locker area as she spied a man dressed completely in black and brandishing a machine gun. Purposefully, he walked around a corner. With him facing away from her she could read his unit's identifier printed across his back in large white capital letters: S W A T.

Special Weapons And Tactics.

"Shit," she uttered in frustration. She doubted he was going to be alone. Peering around the final locker, Sophie took a longer look at the specialist law enforcement officer, groaning inwardly on seeing the ocular apparatus strapped to his face just below his armoured helmet.

Infrared/thermal goggles.

I guess that confirms they're not here looking for somebody else... she mused. Taking comfort from the gun in her right hand, she assessed the situation, her eyes darting from one place to another, devising an escape route and a proposed course of action. From where she was standing she could see from the over-hang down into the airport's reception hall, more than a dozen SWAT officers had joined the armed policemen patrolling; together they fanned out and were shepherding people away from the doors.

Through the glass entrance windows, splashes of red and blue from black and white police cruisers oscillated across the threshold; Sophie could see that the doors were closed - likely locked - and guarded by police officers on the outside.

No one else was getting in and it would appear, no one was going to be getting out.

"Shit, shit, shit!" As though nursing a headache, she pressed her left hand against her temple and closed her eyes. She was trying to think but the noise from the continuous braying of the alarm was hindering her. *Com'on damn-it! Think!*

At the top of the escalator another SWAT officer appeared, he began to walk towards her locker area. The situation was getting less stable by the second and she knew time was running out for her. If she was to survive this, she was going to have to take a risk and move, and move very soon.

As the SWAT officer turned the corner, almost parallel with her hidden form, she launched herself at him. Despite the surprise and the force of being propelled off his feet, the black-clothed officer managed to squeeze off a couple of rounds from his rifle, bullets peppering the ceiling. Chunks of plaster and dust fell around them as they tussled. Sophie elbow-punched the man twice against the nose, displacing his goggles and knocking him to the floor, gaining an immediate advantage over her pursuer. Releasing his grip from the gun, he scrambled to reposition his thermal goggles. Not giving him the chance, she side-swiped his head hard with the underside of the *Glock*, knocking him forcefully against the toughened, steel-framed, glass safety barrier that encompassed the floor but which allowed an unobstructed view of the foyer below.

Gun shots were fired from somewhere, pinging and ringing out as they ricocheted off metal and brickwork close by. Instinctively, Sophie ducked down behind the toughened-glass barrier – to the right of the fallen SWAT officer – but knew it afforded her minimal protection. Emphasising her thoughts, the two metre high wall shattered beside her, a puff of air from a bullet caressing her ear (the same one which was still healing from being grazed in Washington the day she first met Barry). Most of the glass wall fell to the floor below, people ducking or throwing themselves aside to avoid the lethal shower, but a few crystals of glass bounced around and over her, one or two nicking her face. She buried her head into her chest, trying to shield herself from the prickly rainfall.

"MISS JENNINGS! YOU ARE COMPLETELY SURROUNDED. GIVE YOURSELF UP; THERE'S NOWHERE FOR YOU TO GO; NOWHERE TO RUN... WE DON'T WANT TO HURT YOU..."

Sophie peered out from her cocoon, and looked down to the man addressing her. He was holding a battery-operated megaphone and was standing in the centre of the airport's welcoming hall. She remembered him from a bit earlier, within the passing *Sedan*, although half his face was now concealed by a pair of thermal-vision goggles he'd acquired from the back of his partner's car. As well as his face, she could now see his body too, noticing that he was quite tall, over six-feet at least.

"WE HAVE YOUR FRIEND IN CUSTODY," he lied. "HE'S OKAY... *AT THE MOMENT*. IT'S UP TO YOU IF HE STAYS THAT WAY!"

If anything happens to Barry, she thought, *I'll kill you.*

The SWAT officer, who had passed whilst she was hidden within the locker area, was approaching from her left. Raising her *Glock* she fired a warning shot, dusting the man with plaster. He ducked around a corner out of the line of fire, his rifle poking out threateningly.

"THERE'S NOWHERE LEFT FOR YOU TO RUN SOPHIE... YOU'RE COMPLETELY SURROUNDED. COME QUIETLY AND YOU'LL COME TO NO HARM..." The CIA man lowered the megaphone to confer with a female agent standing close by.

Lowering so that she was almost flat against the floor, Sophie shuffled backwards, away from the shattered balustrade, manoeuvring herself around the unconscious SWAT officer. She reached out and plucked the wired earpiece she'd spied when brawling with him, out from his right ear and clawed free the radio receiver that was clipped to his belt. Inserting the audio device into her own ear, she listened to the linked-in conversation from the SWAT officers manoeuvring to enclose her.

"*... the perimeter is locked down... and we have a strike team on the roof awaiting orders... over.*"

Sophie glanced up towards the glass ceiling. There were no obvious signs of movement above her head; it could be all a bluff, she thought, but then again they weren't aware she was listening in.

"*... all exits are secure... we are locked tighter than a fish's butt-hole... over.*"

Another voice added: "*... everyone is in place... over.*"

"*Copy. Okay... on five...*" Sophie recognised the voice from the megaphone. "*Five... four... three...*"

Not waiting for the countdown to finish, Sophie bounced up onto her feet and started sprinting towards a now-deserted dining area; when gunshots were fired, patrons had panicked and had hurried down to the lower level, literally kicking and screaming.

Machine gun fire exploded from the floor below as her movement was tracked just a two second count away from Brayden giving the order to advance; more of the glass-panelled balustrade shattered beside and just slightly behind her as bullets tore into it, coming dangerously close to hitting their mark. Skidding to a halt behind a solid beam a short distance from the separate 'up' and 'down' elevators (still operating) and parallel with a fast-food burger bar, Sophie was about to reassess the situation when the glass roof above the place, under which she had moments earlier been cowering, disintegrated beneath four small explosive charges timed to detonate just before a SWAT strike team came falling and swinging in from the sky, attached to *Fast Ropes*, skilfully holding their weapons battle-ready as they descended.

There were five of them in total and Sophie knew she had no time or any advantage, seeing them attired in body armour and thermal vision eyewear. They looked well-trained and keen for action.

The hum of the escalators stopped abruptly, replaced by the sound of boots clattering noisily against the now-stationary metal stairs as a flow of armed officers ascended each separate escalator single file. With eyes darting about the mezzanine floor, Sophie quickly weighed-up the situation.

There was no dressing it up. It was dire and almost hopeless. Time was nearly running out.

She glanced towards a fire escape which was signposted and situated close to the back of locker area numbered 'Two', but was forced to dismiss it as an option. A black-clothed SWAT officer appeared through the door, obstructing the escape route and looked prepared to engage her should she make any attempt at approaching him.

"No... no... no!" In moments she would be completely surrounded, a situation, she decided, that could not happen.

Without thinking, she ran out from her point of cover, her *Glock* gripped in her hand and pointing ahead. She was fast and determined and seemingly, with timed precision, she propelled herself forward in an upward, climbing motion just as the first SWAT officer arrived at the top of the escalator. Her right foot landed hard against the man's chest, knocking him backwards to fall into the flailing arms of a comrade who was close behind. Like a line of dominoes, the officers on that moving stairs crumpled down the flight of steps whilst their colleagues on the adjacent escalator watched on helplessly. Sophie descended, using their padded, crumpled bodies as stepping stones, dropping down to the metal stairs for the final few steps, her gun aimed ahead ready to engage if needed.

The large reception hall was full of both alarmed and curious spectators as she invisibly entered and 'disappeared' within the throng of people. Whereas the upper level had cleared of people immediately after the first bullets were fired, the airport's patrons had nowhere to disperse other than to congregate in the welcoming hall of the main terminal building, hemmed in like cattle at a rodeo.

On the face of it, implementing a lockdown on the airport had been wise and made perfect sense. However, actions – no matter how good the intention – often came at a cost; this being no exception.

Chiefly, it now enabled Sophie a way to move about without being shot at; it also meant she could move even *less-visibly*, using groups of people to mask her movements from those with the equipment that enabled them to see her. She intended to use the camouflage effectively for her exit.

"*Where is she?*" The voice belonging to Brayden returned in her ear. From her vantage point she could see the CIA agent through the crowd. In agitation he had tossed the megaphone to the woman agent standing with him and looked very annoyed.

"*... it seems she's disappeared...*"

The fallen SWAT officers on the escalator had picked themselves up and were now recomposing themselves, returning to the first level floor.

"*Find her! She's in here someplace!*"

Casually, Sophie began to put space between herself and the man who was clearly in charge, startling bystanders by grabbing them roughly with invisible hands, manipulating them into positions that offered greater cover, using them as a shield towards anyone who might have the ability to see her. Stealthily, she carried this on until she was close to a single push/pull set of exit doors that were designated for staff and deliveries only, discretely placed beyond a quiet waiting area. It was a good distance from the terminal's main entrance point, and seemed to have been overlooked by the police placing barricades about the building.

Through the glass door she could see the many dozens of black and white police cruisers parked at various angles, blue and red light-bars upon their roofs coalescing in dazzling merriment. Policemen in their all-black uniforms, collars open at the neck, walked about in pairs or clustered together in groups. Their orders were to barricade the perimeter – no one gets in, and, more importantly, no one gets out. Who they were apprehending they had no idea. That information was classified.

Unseen, Sophie wandered to the door and tried pushing it.

Surprisingly, airport security had taken the 'lockdown' instruction seriously. Even though 'unmanned', Sophie found the staff door was secured shut like, she imagined, the main entrance doors and all other ways in (or out).

She cursed. A sideward look into the terminal hall behind her alerted her to the fact that SWAT officers had further composed themselves after being knocked down the escalator and were now advancing upon her position. It was just a matter of moments, she thought, before she was discovered. *I need to get out now....*

Confirming her fears of discovery, one of the SWAT team started hollering and pointing, "I see her! She's there!"

Sophie swore even more and raised the *Glock*, her finger about to squeeze the trigger; not at the advancing law enforcement officers, but at the staff entrance/exit door, thinking to blast a way out.

Sophie hesitated as screams of alarm and agitation came from outside the airport building. Guns were fired by policemen cowering behind their black and white vehicles, the spectacle from outside puzzling the young woman. *Surely the danger is in here... with me?*

Equally distracted were the SWAT officers – now seven of them – and Brayden, who had halted their progress to stare out at the drama outside. Without warning, the main glass entrance doors imploded as an old red and white *Chevrolet Silverado* crashed into the airport, sending Brayden and the SWAT officers to dive for cover (one, without success, ending up being knocked up and over the windshield).

Gunshots continued to sound from outside as police officers fired ceaselessly at the vehicle that had now breached the airport's lockdown.

Winding down the side window of the *Chevrolet*, a familiar face appeared. Barry, looking like hell, was sat behind the wheel. "I can't see you, but hope you are here somewhere Sophie... come, get in!"

Already running, she was at the driver's side door – her near side – and opening it up to climb in. "Am I glad to see you!"

CHAPTER EIGHTEEN
BARRY

"How?" She wanted to know how Barry had managed to get away. When she'd last seen him he was acting like she needed to find a priest to administer his last rites.

"Long story! Get in!"

"Scoot over... I'm driving!" she dictated, ditching the radio and plucking free the earpiece. Despite the man's brave face, she could see that he was in intense pain. The way his leg had been, she doubted he had been able to 'walk it off'.

Barry didn't argue. Quickly, he unbuckled the seatbelt and pushed himself, with a struggle, over to the passenger seat.

Closing the door behind her, Sophie reversed the *Chevrolet* back out of the airport's smashed-in foyer; tyres' crunching over glass fragments an inch deep, and through the mangled remains of the double-doors.

Staring through the front windshield, Barry watched the first of Sophie's pursuers, climb to his feet. Dressed in dusty plain clothes, the CIA agent, Brayden Scott, leapt into action waving a handgun and readying it to discharge.

"Look out!" yelled Barry as the blond-haired agent fired a shot towards the reversing pick-up.

Unobserved, Sophie instinctively ducked her head at the moment Brayden took the shot. A bullet smashed a ragged hole into the safety-glass parallel to where her head had been positioned moments earlier.

The slug thumped into one of the rear seats, spitting out a puff of foam.

"Here!" Sophie tossed her *Glock* to Barry, dropping it into his lap. "Give him something else to think about besides trying to kill me!"

Before Barry could fire the gun the back windscreen shattered beneath a hail of bullets fired by Fresno police officers manning a blockade behind them.

"Do something Barry!"

"I AM!" Barry squeezed off two shots in Brayden Scott's direction. One of the bullets hit marble at his feet; the other sailed past him harmlessly. Brayden returned fire, this time hitting a wing mirror and smashing a headlight.

Sophie continued to reverse the *Chevrolet* away from the terminal building, manoeuvring it over paving and tearing up a flowerbed, zigzagging towards the road that was crammed with police cruisers. Hastily, she did a handbrake turn, barely stopping as the vehicle straightened up from a spin, before accelerating forward onto the road, the truck ploughing into two parked police cars and scraping the sides of two others. Police officers standing close by were forced to dive for safety in spectacular fashion.

"That's more like it!" Barry whooped, laughing. "Where did you learn to drive like that?"

"I wouldn't celebrate just yet... look!" Sophie indicated a roadblock half a mile ahead of them, fashioned from five police vehicles parked transversely across both lanes and a row of A-Frame barricades. Adding to their woes, police cruisers had started to give chase behind them. It was like a classic car-chase scene from a movie.

"Take the next left," said Barry, seeing a white signpost ahead with the words 'ROAD CLOSED' emblazoned across it at the junction's entrance.

"Are you sure?" Sophie sounded hesitant.

"Just trust me, Sophie."

Sophie took the corner hard; tyres squealed in protest and a hub-cap came free and bounced across the street. Sophie advanced up the side road. It was narrow and hard not to collide with the odd dustbin, sending bags of rubbish and metal bins to bash and fall in the vehicle's wake. She drove for two-hundred metres before an alarm screamed inside her head.

"Uh-oh..."

"What?" asked Barry. His neck was craned behind him as he monitored the convoy of police vehicles closing in on them.

"The road... it's closed," said Sophie, sounding surprised.

"What? Didn't you see the signpost?" Barry started to laugh.

"Glad you find our imminent imprisonment amusing..." griped Sophie, adding slightly panicked: "... but seriously Barry..."

Turning serious, Barry raised his right hand and pointed. "Pull over just up ahead."

"What the hell Barry!" Sophie couldn't see what it was he was getting her to do. There was no throughway and nowhere left to turn.

"Just pull-over!" ordered the MI6 agent.

Sophie slammed the breaks, bringing the pick-up to a skidding-stop. She turned, looking perplexed. Her eyes implored Barry for clarification, but he was oblivious to any of her expressions. Without faltering, he shared his thoughts with her. "This is where you get out," he said matter-of-factly.

"What?" Sophie didn't trust what her ears had heard.

"You've got a much better chance of getting out of here on your own." Highlighting his plight, he winced noisily as he tried lifting his broken leg. Shaking his head he added regretfully: "My job here is done."

"Barry..." she said, fearfully.

Barry reached up to the rear-view mirror and adjusted it so that he could see Sophie's reflection. Her eyes were welling-up, as though she was about to cry, but her features were almost as he remembered them, though a little bloody from some nicks and cuts. He reached out for her with his right hand and found her chin. Pulling her gently towards him, he gave her a kiss full on the lips.

"Oh Barry," she whispered, sounding totally miserable. She kissed him again.

Behind the pick-up, a tide of police cars were piling single file into the narrow road, closing the gap.

Reluctantly, he prised himself away from Sophie. "Go. Go now, get out. Before it's too late. I'll buy you some time." Without further discourse, Barry opened his side door and jumped down onto his good leg, Sophie's *Glock* in his hand. Using the door for balance and as a shield, he crouched down, his broken leg stretched behind him awkwardly. Peering back into the truck he noticed the driver's door had not budged. "Sophie! Go...! GET THE HELL OUTTA HERE! DON'T LET ME DIE ALL FOR NOTHING!"

Sadly, but reassuringly, Barry heard the 'clunk' of the door as it opened, and the heavy thud that followed as it was slammed closed behind her. Despite looking, there was no way to see which way Sophie was heading without thermal-goggles, or to tell whether in fact, she had left at all.

He hoped – and prayed to dear God – that she had.

The leading black and white police car that had been tailing them stopped at a safe distance from where the red and white *Chevrolet* was parked, the driver navigating it into an angle that blocked the road completely, barring any suggestion or thought of escape that way. A pair of uniformed officers climbed out – a man in his mid-forties and a much younger woman – and crouched in the car's shadow, mirroring Barry's stance by unholstering their weapons in readiness for use.

The convoy of chasing police cars piled up behind the lead vehicle and came to a grinding halt, spewing forth an impressive number of officers. Taking up positions of safety, the policemen withdrew handguns and rifles and steadied their hands, preparing to use them.

"*PUT DOWN YOUR WEAPON AND COME OUT WITH YOUR HANDS RAISED!*" The policeman used the car's radio and amplified his voice through a speaker built into the radiator-grill of his car. He spoke with more authority than he actually had.

Barry sighed. He didn't have much of an option.

As though endorsing the sentiment, the policeman began to speak once again: "*YOU ARE COMPLETELY SURROUNDED! GIVE YOURSELF UP AND YOU'LL BE UNHARMED!*"

Uniformed officers cowering behind police cars made a show of steadying their weapons in Barry's direction, bracing themselves for action, contradicting the policeman's amplified assurances.

"Good luck, Sophie," he whispered to himself, standing up and pointing the gun downwards, just ahead of him.

"NOOOOOOOOO!!!!!" Sophie caterwauled.

Barry sighed, turning his head slightly in the direction of her voice. Sophie was close. Too close. He had hoped she would have run and put some distance between them.

The fact she hadn't changed things. *Oh Sophie*, he pondered.

He lifted the gun up and took careful aim at the nearest police officer.

"STOP! DON'T DO IT!"

There was only one ending to this scenario. Before the neurons in Barry's brain had connected to give the command, and the order had filtered through his nervous system to the muscles in charge of the hand gripping the gun, a barrage of bullets rained down upon him, stippling the exposed part of his body and blasting chinks and holes into the truck, obliterating the glass in the door, popping one of the tyres with a 'bang!' and peppering the red body-work with a dozen jagged holes the size of half-dollar coins. Translucent liquid leaked out beneath the vehicle in a fast flow.

Realising the gas tank had been punctured, the lead uniformed officer shouted into the radio: "CEASE FIRE!"

Barry collapsed to the floor, gasping for air, a hand clutching his chest where a bullet had penetrated and was lodged within his ribcage. He couldn't comprehend the sensation... it was almost ethereal, like an 'out-of-body' experience. Around him there was a lot of movement. People charging about him, busy like soldiers in the thick of combat, doing what, he didn't care. He could hear their voices, urgent, harried, though could barely understand what they were saying.

"Ah, jeez! Seriously? Wasn't one bullet enough?" Despite the news reports about how 'trigger-happy' American policemen were, very few of them present had fired a weapon during active duty. This, Brayden surmised, was why, when the occasion required it, they felt the need to let rip.

Barry found his eyes focus on the newcomer running into his field of vision. Having dusted himself down, he was smart and tall, dressed in an official-looking suit. Barry recognised him from the brief encounter at the airport; the man was clearly in overall command.

"Get a medic here!" Brayden shouted urgently. "I need him alive!" The CIA agent removed his jacket, crouched down beside Barry and tenderly placed it under his head. "You just hold on buddy, d'you hear me? I'm not letting you off this lightly..."

Barry tried to speak. Instead of words, blood bubbled from his lips. He choked a couple of times. Inhaling was like fire burning inside his chest, and exhaling felt like he was trying to blow up a lead balloon with a straw.

"Hush... save your energy," placated Brayden mildly, as though not addressing a wanted fugitive but a dying friend.

Barry closed his eyes, taking small comfort from the man's words, and much more from the darkness that gradually drew him near and lovingly embraced him.

"I'M LOSING HIM!" were the last words Barry heard before consciousness deserted him.

CHAPTER NINETEEN
EMILY

IT WASN'T OUT OF the ordinary for MI6 to use 'phone tapping' under intelligence-gathering protocols, protected under law for the benefits of the country and the commonwealth; it was a fact that most people expected it.

However, it was rarely endorsed for use upon fellow members of the same intelligence service. Spying on spies wasn't the 'done' thing, and not an action easily achieved. Most offices were regularly checked for listening devices.

With a dual headset enclosing her ears, Emily sat behind her desk and selected the file on display within the surveillance interface software – a live feed was available, but hardly relevant; all conversations within a five metre radius of the 'bugging device' were recorded for analysis, which made it easier. That way, one could skip through all the unnecessary waffle and blather.

Pressing the play icon, Emily listened as she recognised the two voices playing out a conversation within her ears:

"*I spoke to Sophie,*" she recognised herself say.

"*I did wonder...*" It was Ryan.

Emily had planted the listening device a moment before the recording had begun transmitting – whilst Ryan had his back turned for just a moment. Although she trusted the man, Sophie had earlier planted a small grain of doubt within her mind, which continued to gnaw at her, even now. It was this doubt which prompted her to spy on her boss.

"*I gave her the location of her father's locker. She's on her way to Fresno as we speak.*" She pressed the fast-forward icon, whizzing through the conversation and watching the audio progress bar, green spikes denoting talking on a black background. They flurried by until flat-lining, which Emily interpreted – correctly – as silence. The timer counted through the minutes in mere seconds.

Emily pressed the play button whenever a spike of green reappeared. A new voice filled her ears:

"*I told you your pilot would be okay.*" Although faint, she could just make out the female voice spoken over a phone line. She adjusted the volume setting to a point where the voices could be heard clearly, but with the added annoyance of an electronic drone.

"*If unconscious and beaten black-and-blue is 'okay', yeah...*" Ryan replied. "*You said you wouldn't call. Damn it, Jennifer... it's too dangerous... I can't get involved!*"

"Jennifer Ratcliff?" Emily whispered to herself. She quickly surveyed the room to see if anyone had heard her. Nobody had. There were only two analysts working at that moment. Mac and Rafe. And they were preoccupied with their own tasks.

"*YOU ARE INVOLVED. Anyway, your MI6 phone lines are secure,*" Jennifer continued.

"Not secure enough," muttered Emily presciently, listening carefully.

"*Just thought I'd let you know, the boys are settling in.*" Jennifer again.

"*I don't want to know. If anyone finds out...*" Ryan sounded nervous.

"*They won't. Not from me... no one should suspect.*"

"*The CIA might.*"

"*CIA?*"

"The Prime Minister has agreed to welcome our American counterparts to work with us to hunt Dominic. They're a little peeved by the attack on Area 51 and have named him as Enemy Number One, and Sophie as an accomplice. They've probably had a pack of cards printed with their images..."

"You'd better make sure they do not succeed in finding him... for yours and Emily's sakes. If we go down, I'm taking you there with me."

"Is that a threat? Listen... we're in this together. I gave you what you wanted, and we have an agreement. It's for the best, for our futures. Now leave me and my family out of it. Or else!"

"Family? Huh, and else what, Ryan? Now who's making the threats?" Jennifer was chuckling; it sounded like the scrunching-up of a paper bag. *"Just keep to your word; we're a partnership, and we'll be fine."*

"And you remember your promise. Just don't call again."

"No promises. Don't forget who you are dealing with, Ryan. Say hi to Emily for me..."

"Straight back at ya, Jennifer..." Emily murmured. The green oscillating spike soon vanished, replaced by a red flat-line that hovered at the base of the audio progress bar. Emily fast-forwarded again, speeding through more than an hour's silence before more conversation occurred. She proceeded to listen before dismissing it. A chat between Ryan and his secretary revealed nothing of interest, nor did the next call (Ryan phoning for a lunch order – whatever strain he was under clearly hadn't affected his appetite). She pulled the headphones free, ran a hand through her deep-auburn dyed hair and scratched the nape of her neck nervously. *What should I do with this?* She pondered.

Before she could give it any further thought she received an interruption.

"Emily... I think you ought to see this." Mac, a geeky-looking analyst with long black hair and designer glasses, stood up from his workstation and was speaking across an island of desks that partitioned the room. Emily turned around to see Mac changing the channel on the large flat-screen TV hanging from the wall.

ABC30 News came onto the screen, a 'breaking news' banner scrolling beneath a split transmission showing live footage from an event occurring at Fresno International Airport, together with a broadcast by a female news anchor reporting from behind a desk within a Californian studio.

Mac was pointing a remote control, increasing the volume. The newscaster's voice played over the live broadcast of police officers and FBI agents milling about, some looking serious, whilst others were perplexed, some scratching their heads absently, oblivious to the viewing world watching on.

"*...more strange goings on in the business district of Fresno today after the events affecting Washington's Dulles Airport earlier in the week. Conflicting reports are reaching us about an attack on a Boeing flight from Miami, followed by a good old American stand-off within the Fresno Yosemite International Airport between an unseen assailant and a joint operation conducted by Fresno PD and the FBI, which saw guns fired and the deployment of FBI SWAT teams. Things appeared to turn ugly as the action spilled out into the streets of Central Valley, concluding in law enforcement's favourite pastime of 'police chase' which was soon brought to a bloody end. No law enforcement officers are purported to have been injured, but one of the 'attackers' was shot multiple times and is reported to have died at the scene.*" A male newscaster appeared on the screen, replacing both the woman and the live pictures from Fresno Airport. "*We'll have more from that story as it progresses. Now, let's get the rest of the news...*"

Mac turned the volume down. "You said to let you know if we hear anything 'big' happening in Fresno. You can't get much bigger than this..."

"What about the person shot dead at the scene? Do we know who it is? Is it ours?"

"Male. Caucasian. Mid-twenties. Riddled with bullets," replied Mac, attempting humour. "That's all I've managed to glean from our contacts. However, contrary to what is being reported, I don't think he's dead. Critically injured, yes, but he's hanging in there. It's been suggested that he may be one of ours..." Mac left it hanging.

Emily didn't progress the colloquy, smiling appreciatively. "Thank you. Keep me posted." She sat and reached down for the phone. Plucking up the receiver, she punched in Sophie's mobile number and waited for the long-distance call to connect.

Unsurprisingly, after just one ring the call was connected to Sophie's mobile answer service. Impersonally, it was the pre-set factory answer message rather than a recording of Sophie's voice:

"*The person you are calling is unavailable at the moment. Please leave a message after the tone...*"

"Sophie... I'm sorry how our last call went. Please call me when you get this. I'm worried. It's urgent."

Nervously, Emily sat at her workstation biting her nails, gnawing at them almost to the point of bleeding. Over an hour had moved on since Mac had shared the ABC30 news report, and despite 'tapping' into Ryan's comings and goings, nothing of further importance had arisen, giving little to distract her from the anxiety bubbling in the pit of her stomach regarding Sophie.

The telephone on her workstation began to ring and she snatched it up too quickly, failing to grip it. Instead, she knocked the receiver, which bungeed from its coiled wire to clatter noisily off the desk to the floor.

"Sophie?" Emily hadn't checked the caller ID, failing to notice the small LCD screen indicated the incoming call was internal.

"*No, it's Ryan.*" Inwardly, Emily groaned. "*Can you step by my office? We need to talk...*" Ryan's tone sounded solemn and hard-edged. Emily assumed he'd heard about Fresno.

"I can't Ryan; I'm expecting a call from Sophie..."

"*Forward your phone to your mobile,*" Ryan was insistent, then went quiet for a moment, as though struggling to come to terms with something. "*It's important, Emily,*" he said.

"Okay... sure." She sighed. "Give me five minutes." Emily replaced the handset slowly and leaned back into her chair. Something felt wrong. She'd been listening to almost all his conversations over the past couple of hours (up to the last fifteen minutes); there had been very few visitors to his room, and most of the conversations overheard took place across the phone. Nothing of much import had been gleaned after the Jennifer Ratcliff revelation, and nothing in his tone or inflection had given any clues as to the sudden change of mood. It had to be an outside factor.

"What's going on Ryan?" She whispered the question to herself, picking up the headset and slipping it atop of her head. With the mouse, she pressed the play icon on the audio file still displaying in front of her and fast-forwarded the minutes up to a few jagged spikes of verbal activity that occurred just prior to Ryan's call to her a moment ago.

"*...what the... ?? someone's bugged my room...*" crackling and rustling sounds followed, along with a few harsh bangs. Emily could tell, just by the background noise, that the listening device had been discovered and that Ryan was removing it. She visualised Ryan holding the small microphone between his fingers.

A loud 'pop' later and the transmitted sound ceased, the audio file came to an abrupt end.

"I guess that's what's going on," she answered herself, nervously removing the headset from her head and placing it down next to the VDU and keyboard. Checking over her shoulder to ensure she wasn't being observed, Emily speedily tapped a few buttons on the computer keyboard and deleted the audio file in an attempt to cover her tracks. "Okay... let's get this over with." She locked her computer terminal by selecting 'Ctrl', 'Alt' and 'Delete' and stepped away, heading for the sliding exit door.

Two nervous minutes later and Emily felt like a schoolgirl facing expulsion outside the Headmaster's office. Anxiously, she rapped her knuckles hard against the polished wooden surface of Ryan's solid office door and waited a moment to compose herself before entering.

Thinking the visitor needed an invitation, Ryan called "Come," impatiently from the other side.

"What's this about, Ryan?" Finding strength, Emily walked in assertively, hiding any signs of the uneasiness she felt or the foreknowledge for her brusque summoning.

"Sit down, Emily," he said snippily. Before she had managed to take one of the seats ahead of the desk, Ryan had presented the small black bugging device. It looked like a strange pill.

No bigger than the size of a five-pence piece and only thick enough to contain a watch battery, the item looked tiny in the man's hand. He made to give it to Emily. "I think this belongs to you," he said quietly. He half-turned his hand so that the small item fell to the desk. It bounced a couple of times before coming to a stop just short of reaching the desk's edge and a few inches before Emily.

"Ryan..." she started to talk, shaking her head apologetically. A surge of guilt overcame her.

"You're not going to deny it then?" There was pity in Ryan's voice.

Emily closed her eyes. Involuntarily they started to moisten up. She slowly shook her head, accepting her fate. "No," she added quietly.

"How could you?" Not waiting for a response Ryan pressed on. "I trusted you. You're like a daughter to me..."

Emily looked down sheepishly. For the first time she noticed how short her fingernails were from biting and started studying them. *When did I chew them?* She hadn't realised that she'd been doing it.

"Are you listening to me?"

Ryan had talked some more but Emily had momentarily blocked out his voice. A strange feeling seeped into her and before she knew it, she was speaking. "Why did you have Sophie's father killed?" It surprised even herself. By side-stepping Ryan's questioning, she'd thrown him off-balance with one of her own.

"What?" Shock and confusion flushed Ryan's face. "What d'you mean?"

"Come on Ryan..." feeling suddenly emboldened, she went on: "Cut the crap. Mitch Youngs killed George Jennings on the instructions of Marty Heywood. You and I know Marty was following your orders..."

"Where's this coming from?" Ryan spoke meekly; he looked distant as he tried to comprehend what was being implied.

"I didn't want to believe it Ryan... but then... I heard it for myself. You and... *Jennifer Ratcliff!*"

Ryan clasped his head in his hands, forlornly accepting defeat. "It's not what you think," he said after a long moment, his voice steadily growing as he pulled himself away from his placating fingers, finding resolve. "I can explain Jennifer... but *George*? I didn't have him killed, that wasn't for Marty to sanction. Oh sure, I wanted him dead, it's no secret... but not like that! Not at another person's hand." Ryan banged fisted hands defiantly onto his desk. "He was mine to kill!"

Emily's mobile began to ring from within her handbag. Ignoring Ryan further, she half-twisted away and pulled free the *Samsung Galaxy.* Seeing that the incoming call was from Sophie she stood up and turned away from her SIS superior. "This will have to wait Ryan. I need to take this," she said cold and abruptly.

• • •

"Hi, Sophie?" Stepping outside of Ryan's office, Emily accepted the call as she forcefully closed the door behind her. For the moment, the awkwardness between Ryan and herself was forgotten.

"*He's dead, Emily... he's dead... they shot him!*" She was out of breath and sounded hysterical.

"Calm down Sophie, you need to relax. Where are you?"

The line went quiet for a moment as Sophie tried to think. "*I... I don't know. I've been running, putting a bit of distance between myself and the cops. But Emily... Barry's dead!*"

"Listen to me Sophie, I've had intel. I don't think he's dead. In a bad way, yes... but not dead," adding as a macabre afterthought, "not yet at any rate."

"*Not... dead?*" There was a note of disbelief in her hushed voice along with a discernible tremble. "*But I saw... I watched as they shot him relentlessly... he had no chance.*" There was shaking in the young woman's voice. "*I saw the look on that agent's face. He shook his head!*"

"We need to forget Barry – for now at least – and focus on yourself and getting you to safety. Did you find your father's locker?"

She went quiet for a moment, before perking up "*Yes,*" she said. "*The code you had cracked was correct. Inside the locker I found a case; dad had left some things within it; not much, you could hardly call it an 'inheritance'. I'm not sure what to make of them though to be honest, I'm gonna need your help.*"

"Whatever you need." It seemed the earlier rift had been forgotten. "Can you elaborate?" Emily was pacing the corridor outside Ryan's office. Not really thinking about it, she could feel the thick pile of the carpet beneath her shoes.

"Well, there's a small bottle of liquid with a note on which my dad has written an instruction for me to drink; there's a photograph of my dad with a younger woman... I recognise her from my days locked within Kaplan Ratcliff, and it recently occurred to me; I think it is Clara."

"Clara? Ryan's daughter?" *My friend...*

"Yes. How many Claras do you know?"

But Clara is dead, Emily reflected sadly.

"On the back of the photo," Sophie continued, *"my father has written an address, somewhere in the Czech Republic."*

"Okay... I can help look into that."

"Thanks, but that's not all. There's also a thumb drive, very small, very discrete, the sort used in a camera. I'm guessing it holds a key to something. Knowing my father, it's likely important."

Emily sensed a degree of excitement in Sophie's tone, or maybe it was her own enthusiasm interpreting the upbeat slant. "Well, your father went to a lot of trouble hiding it, so you're likely right. You'd best keep it safe." A moment after saying it, Emily felt stupid.

"Yes, mum! Don't worry... It's safe."

"You need to get it back to me ASAP," she said. "Do you have a get-out plan?"

Sophie laughed sarcastically. *"Barry WAS my get-out plan,"* she replied. *"I guess travelling as Sophie Mason is now out of the question."*

"Leave it with me; I'll see what we can come up with."

"Don't worry yourself. Let's not over-complicate things. I arrived in America on my own, I'm sure I'll be able to depart from it... one way or another. I'll be in touch." With no further thought Sophie disconnected the call.

"Just be careful," Emily said to a dead end.

CHAPTER TWENTY
SOPHIE

STOPPING A SHORT DISTANCE from where she had left the *Chevrolet* and abandoned Barry, Sophie turned her head about and watched from between the gaps of a dilapidated wooden fence that was held up by some frayed rope tied to a ponderosa pine tree and thickly coated green paint. The house behind her was in a similar state of disrepair; faded and flaking creamy-yellow – once white – paintwork, boarded-up windows, moss-covered roof tiles – some missing – and part of the chimney had collapsed.

"NOOOOOOOOO!!!!!" Sophie had screamed.

Heeding Barry's demands she had slipped out the driver's side of the *Chevrolet* and had made to escape, but found after a few hurried steps that she couldn't. She liked Barry... felt something weird burn inside her when she thought of him.

The thought of the sacrifice he was about to make for her was unbearable to contemplate. She didn't want to leave him; couldn't leave him.

Barry turned his head towards her, a look of sadness and regret flashing across his face. She could tell within that look that he was about to do something stupid. She hadn't realised that she gave him little choice.

Sophie watched him lift the *Glock* her father had left for her, raising it purposefully, his intent all too clear.

"STOP! DON'T DO IT!" she screamed.

Calmly, almost reassuringly, he looked again towards where Sophie was standing, making her feel visible and exposed. He then turned away to face the still-gathering police officers and before he was able to squeeze the trigger of the gun a volley of bullets slammed into the *Chevrolet* with metallic clunks and peppered the unprotected parts of his body. The tyres blew out beneath the truck with four quick successive bangs and the glass in the door imploded.

Translucent liquid leaked out beneath the vehicle in a fast flow from the gas tank, punctured from a stray bullet.

The policeman who had taken charge shouted into the radio, his voice amplified by a speaker built into his car: "*CEASE FIRE!*"

A lonely gun fired a further bullet before the order was completely adhered to, taking Barry in the torso. He slumped to the ground, clutching his chest. He was breathing hard and gulping for air like an asthmatic desperate for oxygen.

"Barry..." Sophie whispered, feeling tears at the corner of her eyes. She watched Barry collapse in a heap, entirely defeated, the gun clattering heavily to fall a couple of feet away from him.

Almost in slow-motion, police officers charged around the scene, securing and making safe the area.

"Ah, jeez! Seriously? Wasn't one bullet enough?" The man who she had first laid eyes upon at the airport spoke indignantly and looked around the scene perplexed. She could just hear him over the hubbub caused by the officers milling around. "Get a medic here!" he shouted urgently. "I need him alive!" The CIA agent crouched down beside Barry and, removing his jacket tenderly placed it beneath his head.

The agent said a few more things but Sophie couldn't hear anything further, not until he looked up frantically:

"I'M LOSING HIM!"

"Hold on Barry... *please*... don't you die on me as well," she spoke quietly to herself, almost in prayer.

A pair of EMTs ran from an ambulance parked at the furthest point, to the rear of the motorcade of haphazardly parked police vehicles, a stretcher board carried between them. One had a red medical life support bag flung over his shoulder.

"...search the area.... she can't have gone far..." A new voice penetrated the babble of frenzied police noise... female. She was directing her speech to half a dozen FBI agents as she walked up to where Barry was lying, the FBI agents trotting close behind in what looked like a bizarre follow-the-leader charade, their bodies concealed within black body armour, their hands clasping rifles menacingly.

The newcomer, in her late twenties, bustled onto centre stage; quietly attractive and wearing little makeup, she had long brown hair streaked with caramel highlights and tied neatly in a tail. She looked official in her white collared blouse, black skirt and matching blazer and carried an air of authority that Sophie guessed meant she was partnered with the man still stooped at Barry's side. Her eyes were hidden behind mirrored sunglasses. The woman stopped next to her partner and placed a hand on his shoulder.

The blond-haired guy looked up and shook his head slowly. Sophie could read the body language and felt a gut-wrenching feeling tear at her insides.

Unaffected, the woman turned to face the FBI agents. "Remember... she's camouflaged," she said, not elaborating. "You won't see her without thermal eyewear!"

"Sorry Barry." Taking her cue, Sophie backed into the garden beyond the dilapidated fencing and charged through overgrown grass and knee-deep weeds and nettles, circumventing the house and scaling a boundary wall that bordered another, slightly better maintained property.

With finesse, she leapt over to the other side, landing smoothly and carrying on easily at a run. Despite being unseen, an angry Rottweiler sensed her presence and started barking threateningly. Chained to a post, he posed no physical danger, except for potentially exposing her whereabouts. She ignored the dog's continued snarling and ascended a boundary fence across the other end of the garden. On the opposite side was another garden, and beyond that was another, then another, and so on and so forth. For ten minutes she hurdled walls, fences and hedges, some low and easy, some high and arduous, until she vaulted a mesh-wire fence into an alleyway that followed a short distance between a row of properties. Slightly out of breath, she quickly considered her options. To her left the alley led to a road. On her right, a wall blocked progress and, unknown to Sophie, her FBI pursuers were not far beyond it.

Sophie chose the road side and started running towards it. Not only would it allow her a vantage point for a few blocks, gaining her vital foresight of her enemies, it was – she reasoned – in a populated area. Unwittingly, the pedestrians and drivers passing by would give her plenty of cover and, should her pursuers discover her, provide her with necessary protection. She believed no one in law enforcement would risk killing or injuring civilians in a densely inhabited district.

Sirens in the distance caused her ears to prick up. Spilling forth from the alleyway, Sophie stopped long enough to consider the ambulance speeding off into the distance. It was hard to accept, but she knew Barry was dead. She remembered the agent kneeling next to him, the look of resignation as he shook his head towards his partner. It could mean only one thing. She swiftly dismissed those thoughts.

The ambulance disappeared around a corner, the siren sounding less insistent and gradually fading.

She ran across the road, dodging traffic, and sprinted along a busy boulevard, putting greater distance between herself and her pursuers. A couple of police cars sped past, their sirens screaming, light-bars splashing blue and red. Oblivious to her close proximity, they were heading in the direction from where, a short time before, she had come.

Taking no chances, Sophie kept on moving. In her jeans' pocket she felt her mobile phone vibrate. It had gone a couple of times before but she hadn't noticed until then, the buzzing sending a small pulsation to butterfly against her leg. She could guess who it was but didn't yet feel safe enough to pause for the distraction. Instead, she allowed the call to go to voicemail as yet another police car blazed past.

———————

"He's dead, Emily... he's dead... they shot him!" Sophie had only moments earlier thought it safe to stop running, stepping into a phone booth along a quiet stretch of road that offered seclusion and a blockade to the outdoor sounds. The fact that it was out of order – a sign plastered across the door – was a bonus, affording her unlimited privacy free from intrusion.

She was out of breath and found her emotions brimming to the surface and with them total understanding that her travelling companion was now dead.

"*Calm down Sophie, you need to relax. Where are you?*"

Sophie had explained that she didn't know. Fresno wasn't a place she'd ever frequented, and not likely someplace she'd ever dream visiting again. Her thoughts dwelled on Barry.

"*Listen to me Sophie, I've had intel. I don't think he's dead. In a bad way, yes... but not dead,*" Emily felt compelled to add, "*not yet at any rate.*"

"Not... dead?" she couldn't believe it. "But I saw... I watched as they shot him relentlessly... he had no chance." There was a slight tremor in Sophie's voice. "I saw the look on that agent's face. He shook his head!"

"We need to forget Barry – for now at least – and focus on yourself and getting you to safety. Did you find your father's locker?"

Sophie went on to confirm that she had and proceeded to explain what she found inside. The small bottle of liquid, the photograph of her father with another, younger woman (a strange address scrawled on the back), and a thumb drive.

"You need to get it back to me ASAP," stated Emily. *"Do you have a get-out plan?"*

Sophie started to laugh, almost hysterically. "Barry WAS my get-out plan," she replied between whoops. "I guess travelling as Sophie Mason is now out of the question."

"Leave it with me; I'll see what we can come up with."

"Don't worry yourself," now composed, she spoke with regained confidence. "Let's not over-complicate things. I arrived in America on my own, I'm sure I'll be able to depart from it... one way or other. I'll be in touch." Without further thought Sophie pressed the red icon on her phone and disconnected from Emily. Holding the mobile for a little longer, she stood for a minute mulling over things. This was the first opportunity to really pause and take a break since sitting on the flight from Miami, before the absurdity of jumping from the moving aeroplane, having to fight her way out from being held under siege at the airport, and facing the likelihood that her recently acquired friend was dead.

Oh Barry... She pushed the thought of him from her mind. There would be time to grieve later. She needed to focus.

Her heart was still racing from all the running, and despite all that she had been through, she still felt brimming with energy, still itching to get moving again.

That's the adrenaline, she thought. When it subsided she would be in for a real treat of muscular soreness and fatigue. And then there was the added worry of having no serum – her supply and other belongings had been left in the cabinet above her seat on the *Boeing 737*. She couldn't speculate what the result of using the small vial of blue liquid would be, but her father had left it for her in the safety box for the obvious reason of using it. Its presence dug reassuringly into her upper leg, beneath her right jeans' pocket.

For now, she ignored it, using instead the adrenaline pumping throughout her body to motivate her further into action.

Seemingly, the problem wasn't moving and running, it was knowing where to move to.

She pushed out of the phone booth, the door having the appearance of swinging open of its own accord to an elderly couple out for an afternoon stroll, arm-in-arm, and just a few feet away. Sophie bypassed them as they looked on in shock, muttering words of befuddlement, the utterances of the everyday senior generation.

Sophie walked further up the road, convinced that if she kept moving, it increased the distance between herself and her pursuers, providing greater security. For the time being, this was all that mattered; it helped buy her some time. Along the way, she concentrated on coming up with an idea for how she was actually going to be able to leave America.

At the end of the sidewalk, a pedestrian crossing started to sound its alarm, alerting a group of people waiting to cross into mobility. An old Chinese man wearing dark sunglasses and holding a white stick started forward warily, his right hand swaying the stick ahead of him, from one side to another, seeking out obstructions.

Sophie walked up beside him and gently took the man's arm.

"Here, let me help you," she said, not waiting for protest.

"Thank you... so kind." He had the slightest Chinese accent.

Sophie saw him to the other side of the road in silence. Upon reaching the pavement she released her hand, letting the man go.

The Chinese man smiled gratefully. "'tis very rare for young-uns to help these days... thank you kind lady..."

"You're welcome," Sophie replied, faking cheerfulness. "Tell me, do you know this city very well?"

The Chinese man laughed. "Jus' cos I blind, don' make me stupid! I've lived in Fresno mos' me life... You're English, yes?"

"Err, yes..."

"There's somethin'... strange... about you," he figured. "Other than being English! You're..." he trailed off, not able to pinpoint or choose the right word; he made a face like he tasted cat faeces, his tongue turning over an invisible nut.

"Different?" volunteered Sophie.

"Yes..." he started smiling again. "That could be it..."

"You have no idea," she muttered.

CHAPTER TWENTY-ONE
RYAN

MILY HAD STEPPED OUT of his office, divesting him of any chance to explain his actions or give reasons for why he was secretly in commune with Jennifer Ratcliff. Ryan recalled his earlier conversation with Jennifer which, no doubt, Emily had overheard. It hadn't been until shortly after that, and only by sheer chance, that he'd discovered the small listening device. Before Jennifer's call, he'd been eating the club sandwich he'd ordered from *Rumbles*, a small sandwich shop situated just across the river. As soon as the call was over and after absently taking a bite from his half-eaten toasted sandwich, he realised he was no longer hungry. He had tossed the sandwich to the bin placed to the side of his desk, his aim useless. It had rebounded off the rim of the bin, falling apart upon impacting the carpet, spilling lettuce, turkey, bacon, tomato and a splodge of mayonnaise onto the thick pile. It was whilst cleaning up the mess that his eyes happened upon the small circular disk stuck to the underside of his desk.

"What the..." It hadn't taken him long to realise who had planted it and for a while he had just sat, bewildered and feeling utterly miserable and betrayed. Although he was aware of the events unfolding across the pond in Fresno, his thoughts were momentarily elsewhere, and after an hour of deliberation he'd summoned Emily.

That meeting hadn't gone at all well and had been left unfinished, interrupted by a call which Emily had deemed too important to ignore.

Ryan reached across his desk to the small listening device that he had tossed down in front of Emily, a physical accusation against her treachery. He studied it for a moment between his thumb and index finger before dropping it into a long-abandoned mug of coffee, a small ripple left upon the dark liquid's surface.

Sweeping up the handset of his phone, he punched in a phone number and waited for his call to be answered.

"*Yes...*"

"Jennifer... it's Ryan."

"*Well, well.... I thought we were done talking... you changed your tune.*"

"We've been compromised; it turns out my office was bugged. I told you it was too dangerous to call me."

"*What happened?*"

"My assistant, Emily. She suspected something..."

"*Emily Porter?*" Jennifer recalled demoting the woman from Assistant Intelligence Officer when she'd taken over as CEO at Kaplan Ratcliff after Tom Kaplan had died. She remembered the bespectacled woman had taken it spectacularly badly.

"She's found out... about us... about everything. Damn it! I knew I wouldn't be able to keep it from her. It's just a matter of time before Sophie learns of it." Ryan suddenly burst into laughter that quickly subsided. "Then, we will have a problem! As it is, she believes I was responsible for her father's death." Ryan exhaled a long breath, emptying his lungs.

"*And weren't you?*" She had heard the same thing. Dominic had suggested it.

"Of course not!" he sounded exasperated and slightly aggrieved.

Moving on, not interested the slightest in his protestations. *"Does anybody else know?"*

"No," he hesitated, "I don't think so."

Jennifer went silent for a brief moment. *"Listen Ryan, this changes nothing. You of all people knew that you wouldn't be able to keep this totally under wraps. But you did say, when you agreed to us setting things in motion, that you could control it. As long as the Americans continue to believe their sons of GYGES are dead... things will be okay.*

"You admitted you couldn't take responsibility for them, not with all the heat, which is why you agreed for us to take them in the first place. It made sense. How d'you think MI6 would look if word got out that you were involved with their liberation? It would likely turn into an ugly, diplomatic mess!"

"Which is WHY I didn't want you calling me in the first place! Jeez!" Ryan wasn't happy with how things were freefalling. He was starting to feel how Marty Heywood must've felt just before he'd hit the ground. "I told you, my involvement, until the time is right, ended with my agreement with Dominic's plan. Don't forget, it's in both our interests that MI6 remain in the dark regarding all this. For the long-term future."

"And MI6 will. Relax. Is Emily going to be a problem? Because, if she is, I don't care how close or who she is to you... we CAN do something about her." There was a hint of menace in Jennifer's voice. It was the same hint of intimidation she'd concluded their earlier telephone conversation with. That time she hadn't allowed him the opportunity to retort. This time was different.

"You'll do nothing regarding Emily, d'you hear? I'll take care of her, she isn't a problem," stressed Ryan. "She isn't a problem," he insisted.

"That's good then, I'll leave her in your capable hands... but what about Sophie?"

"She's still in America; I will speak with her... when I can."

"You do that. In the meantime, you should know that we have some leverage... in case things get a little challenging. We really can do without her getting in the way."

"Leverage? What d'you mean? What leverage?!" Slightly perturbed, Ryan needed to know what she meant.

"Oh, you know... the usual. Threats and blackmail."

"None of that stuff would work on her... she's lost both her parents, she's programmed to withstand that sort of thing. Besides, there's nothing left she cares about..." said Ryan emphatically and a little smug.

"No? What about Meredith and her brothers? Have you forgotten about them? Call yourself an Intelligence Analyst... you sometimes don't come across as very bright."

Ryan couldn't help balk at Jennifer's condescending manner. His back stiffened as he leant forward in his chair, almost as though he was speaking to her directly across the desk.

"Meredith and her brothers? She barely knows them," said Ryan tersely.

"Sophie was with them the day her mother died in July." Jennifer replied, challengingly. *"She saved them at Willoughby Rising when Cooper disregarded Tom Kaplan's orders and stormed the house after her. She was also with them the day she decided to head to America, leaving them with you to see them safely into their grandfather's care. Yes, I know a lot about Sophie Jennings, so don't tell me she doesn't care for them!"*

Accepting defeat, Ryan slumped back into his chair. "What are you going to do?" he meekly asked.

"Oh nothing... for now. But if need be, if our hand is forced, her mother's fate awaits her siblings. Goodbye Ryan."

Ryan found Emily in the small meeting room at the rear of the operations centre. The vertical blinds were drawn all along the glass partition wall, shielding her from distractions or outside intrusion. Her back was to Ryan as he stepped in. He closed the door behind him.

"Emily?" Ryan spoke softly, coaxingly. It was how he once spoke to Clara when she too was upset.

"Go away Ryan." Emily was crying. Immediately after her call with Sophie, full understanding of Ryan's deceit flooded her senses and engulfed her emotions. "I don't want to talk to you. Not at the moment."

"Emily... *please*... it's not what you think."

Emily turned to face her mentor, her father-figure, looking forlorn and crushed. He looked tired and withered, like an old man. She shook her head from side to side. "Not right now," she implored. She had removed her glasses and her eyes were red. Moisture glistened on her cheeks. She daubed at one with a crumpled handkerchief.

"Dominic provided us with options, and Jennifer Ratcliff helped implement them," Ryan started, oblivious to Emily's refusal to hear him out. "MI6 couldn't be seen to be complicit with the attack on American soil, or the destruction of George's work," he continued, "and taking those kids, that put us in a difficult spot. We couldn't take them; we SHOULDN'T have taken them! I said as much, but Sophie wouldn't listen. Dominic came up with the ideal solution, and Jennifer Ratcliff came on-board with the idea at his behest.

"He would take custody of them and be the scapegoat, the figurehead for blame, thus shielding us from involvement. It was perfect as Dominic was already a figure of interest to the US authorities, and it was the only way to get them out of America without causing a diplomatic crap-fest."

She didn't want to, but Emily listened. Gradually, her whole demeanour softened, like a weight or burden had been lifted. "Why... didn't you tell me?" she asked in a tiny, deflated voice. "Don't we have trust between us?"

Ryan sat down in a chair opposite the young woman. "Emily, it wasn't that. Of course we have trust, please believe me. I didn't tell you because I didn't want you to get hurt; I was protecting you. This knowledge is dangerous. I just didn't want you, or anyone else to be involved."

Emily blew her nose noisily, straightening herself up. She ran a hand through her dyed hair; the hair band that had kept it neat had fallen loose and was in her hand. "Okay, Ryan. If what you say is true, where are the kids now? Where's Dominic?"

Ryan made to speak, and stopped. He made a face that Emily could tell meant that he didn't know. The man's eyes glazed over as he considered his answer.

"You haven't the slightest clue, have you?" She started to laugh humourlessly.

"Jennifer and I have an understanding, an agreement. They will look after and finish the boys' training, and when the time is right, they'll be made exclusively available to us for clandestine operations. Where she is keeping them never came up, and I didn't want to know to be honest."

"You genuinely believe your agreement – her word – is worth something?"

"I've known Jennifer Ratcliff a long time," Ryan answered timidly, hoping it was justification enough.

"And you believe everything you are told in the spy business? I thought you knew better!" Emily spoke harshly.

Her words and tone stung him. "What other choice did I have?" he pleaded. "Sophie refused to carry out my orders. The sons of *GYGES* were to be eliminated, you know that; along with George's work. Her conscience failed the mission, and as a result forced us to improvise. I did what was best for all concerned."

"Right. And having George Jennings killed, was that what was best for 'all concerned'?" Seizing the moment, Emily decided it was time to bring Sophie's shared suspicion out into the open.

"Now you listen! I had absolutely nothing to do with George's death. NOTHING! You can believe me, or not. But I'm telling you, Marty was working independently, for whatever his reasons. I told him, under no uncertain terms, that Sophie's father wasn't to be harmed. I don't know what he was playing at, contraire to what he may have said, or implied." Ryan was shaking with anger, his cheeks were flushed and a vein stood out on his forehead.

Emily knew Ryan like no other and saw that he was telling the truth. Lightly, she stepped over to the man and laid a hand on his arm, smoothly caressing it. "Okay, Ryan," she whispered. "I believe you. But it's not me you're going to need to convince."

CHAPTER TWENTY-TWO
SOPHIE

THE CHINESE MAN HAD been the most helpful person she had encountered in all her time in the States; the *Alpha Omicron Pi* sorority girls who had given her a lift into Washington came a close second.

Imparting a little bit about himself, Sophie had learnt that he had lost his eyesight one evening eleven years ago when he had worked in a small convenience store. He had been all that stood in the way of a masked robber and the cash register. Despite making no protest and giving the thief what he had demanded – a till full of dollar bills – the thug had clobbered him hard on the back of his head, fracturing his skull and causing a bleed in the occipital lobe part of his brain. When he awoke from a coma three months later he discovered he could no longer see.

"The wors' par' is, I lose job... and dignity as well. No one wants a blind Chinaman serving in shop. No way to feed family... family now gone," he spoke sadly, which made Sophie feel pity for him.

"I'm sorry," Sophie said. She felt the need to say something.

"Why?" he asked. "I'm fine... you, much worse! Police hunt you and you lost. Plus you English. Terrible shame. I'm just blind." He started to laugh. "You much worse," he repeated.

"How can you know all that?"

"I hear," he said. "And smell. Plus your accent..."

Sophie didn't pursue the matter, accepting his explanation. "Can you help me?" she asked. "I need to get out of Fresno, and back to England."

"Sure," he said exuberantly, it came out as *sshhurrre*, slow and elaborate.

Half an hour later and she was winding her way through the Santa Fe Passenger Depot on Tulare Street, just across from Fresno City Hall. Invisibly she hurdled a barrier of turnstiles that ordinarily required a ticket to navigate through, and hurried towards the platform area where the train she needed was expected to depart from. The *Amtrak* station had two train lines, but only one was used for passenger services; the side platform, south of the station where the train was due, was packed with passengers.

The San Joaquin train rolled into the station almost immediately as Sophie jostled through the waiting travellers, startling and eliciting yelps and agitated comments, all oblivious to her actual physical presence.

To get to Las Vegas, the Chinese man had explained she would need to get off the train at Bakersfield and use a throughway connection bus that would then take her to Las Vegas Municipal Airport, but only after a good number of stoppages beforehand. Sophie had thanked him with an embrace, leaving him outside the station's entrance to make his own way back to wherever he had been going. She started to feel bad that she hadn't asked for his name.

The journey time – with transfers, waiting around and travelling – amounted to a little less than ten hours, and included an overnight commute.

It was still dark when she stepped from the bus the following morning. To avoid alerting anyone to her presence she allowed the other travellers to leave first. It wasn't enough; somebody did notice her.

The driver, studying his reflection in the rear-view mirror, noticed the young blonde-haired woman walk towards him through the aisle between the two columns of seats. She was pretty, he thought, and it dawned on him as she approached; he couldn't remember her boarding his coach, and with so few passengers and her cute appearance, there was no way he would've forgotten her.

He decided to ask to see her ticket.

"Ah, Miss...." he started to turn around. "Can I see your..." his question evaporated as he saw that the girl was no longer there. "Damn, I must be going mad..." he muttered to himself. He put it down to it having been a long night and the fact that he was tired. "I need to get m'self some coffee," he said, closing the doors of the bus and setting the vehicle back in motion.

Sophie was relieved to leave America three hours later, slipping unseen and unchallenged through security, helping herself to an assortment of food stuff from a breakfast bar (she was literally starving having not eaten since the flight from Miami) and passing through the boarding gate onto the 7:30 a.m. *Virgin Atlantic* flight destined for London Gatwick. All seats in economy and premium economy class were full, but Sophie took one of the nine empty seats in upper class, a seat towards the front of the cabin, closest to the cockpit, and least obtrusive. Not reclining the seat to avoid drawing attention to her presence, she curled up in the spacious chair and went to sleep for much of the eleven hour transatlantic flight. It felt like the best sleep she'd ever had.

The window of the ground floor apartment in Grampian House was boarded up and graffiti had been sprayed across it without any artistic talent, a series of crude images and harsh lettering in blacks, blues and luminous pinks and yellows. Sophie mentally sighed at the ghastly sight. It looked entirely how she felt; neglected and miserable.

In contrast to California, London was dreary, wet and depressing and Sophie was sodden through, still wearing the jeans and T-shirt she'd donned before her flight from Miami to Fresno, her hair matted dark and hanging shaggily to the sides of her face. Had she not been invisible, her image would have brought about comments and gained her unwanted consideration.

The last time Sophie had walked the path that led to the dark-blue entrance door allowing access to her former home, the world had been an entirely different place. It was hard to believe it had been only three months since she was last here. So much had changed in her life, including her. Mentally and, more especially, physically. No longer sixteen in appearance she was fully developed and had the stature and world-weariness of a more mature person.

A discrete piece of mortar between a brick and the windowsill gained Sophie's attention. Despite being unseen and the earliness of the day (it was still dark), she checked all around her before she stepped through the small shrub just below the window and reached down carefully, fingers probing purposefully for the mortar she knew concealed the keys to the entrance and apartment doors, hidden there by her father. Plucking the keys out, she replaced the mortar and walked back to the short path leading up to the doorway. She climbed the two small steps.

Inserting the key she half-expected to find that the lock had been changed. But no, luck for once was on her side, and the door swung open easily and invitingly. Across the threshold, a little further past her father's apartment door, were some stairs that led to the neighbours' apartments above. There were three in total, but she knew none of them. They, like her father, had kept to themselves.

Sophie took a deep breath and walked blindly into the hallway, relieved to get out of the rain. She closed the door behind her and approached the once familiar front door.

A memory leapt to mind from when she was last here in the apartment. She could almost hear the sounds that went with it, close like the fabric of her wet clothing.

They had been standing right here where I am, when my world took a downward turn...

Sophie could hear the sound of the lock being picked by the intruders who had entered the building, who had been intent on killing or capturing her. She had been within the living room of the apartment when they had come, having let herself out of the panic room shortly after her father had left.

She blinked away the memory and inserted the second key into the lock, twisting it with a flick of her wrist. The door creaked open noisily; dampness and the lack of recent use made the hinges remonstrate against the sudden incursion.

Sophie entered promptly, closing the door behind her. For a moment she felt lost. Standing in the hallway, she felt like she was making a colossal mistake, and that she was trespassing in her own home.

With the windows boarded up and daylight a couple of hours' away, the entire apartment was subdued in impenetrable darkness. One or two windows to the back of the building permitted light, but the barest minimum. Just inside the hallway, a little above Sophie's shoulder height, a light switch operated the two overheads at either end of the hallway. She pressed it on, not expecting anything to happen.

Incredibly, the electricity had not been cut off. Power surged immediately into the light bulbs, but the one at the other end of the hallway, closest to what had been Sophie's bedroom door, popped suddenly in a cascade of sparks and glass fragments. The other over Sophie's head burned brightly.

At first glance, the apartment looked exactly how she remembered it, apricot-white walls, photo-frames with family portraits lovingly placed in various positions along one side, a black *Dynasty* runner sprawling the length of the hallway floor, but she hadn't moved deeper in yet, nor ventured towards the living room just a few feet ahead of her.

The door to the living room was closed and bore some signs of her skirmish with the armed intruders; a few bullet holes splintered the wood, but nothing a bit of *Polyfilla* couldn't fix.

Sophie considered the living room door for a moment. "I'm not ready for this yet," she whispered to herself. Instead, she walked the length of the hallway towards her bedroom, passing the panic room which her father had intended for her to stay in whenever he was away (and which she habitually didn't), and tread carefully over eggshell-thin glass to get to her room, small splintering sounds from the shattered light bulb cracking underfoot.

She opened the door and stepped into her bedroom, clicking on the light that dangled within a pink lightshade from the ceiling, illuminating her familiar surroundings.

Her room was exactly how she remembered it; the duvet was strewn aside on her bed, just how she had left it; her wardrobe door was open to reveal her clothing (now mostly too small), and a deep bookcase filled with children's books and a few toys, warmly reminded her of a fleeting childhood that her father's genetic tinkering had barely allowed her to experience.

"The only thing missing is *Flopsy*," she said sadly, recalling that the stuffed toy had been left in America, having travelled across with her in her backpack. Devastatingly, she'd been forced to leave it behind, stowed in the overhead cabinet of the *Boeing* at Fresno Airport, along with all her other possessions, including the last of her serum.

Crossing to a chest of drawers, Sophie pulled open the topmost receptacle and hastily frisked through it. There was underwear for all ages, her father proactively purchasing knickers, vests and bras in preparation for his daughter's fast growth. She rifled through the drawer and found suitable undergarments for her slender adult frame.

The second, third, fourth and fifth drawers contained other clothing items, socks, tops, T-shirts, trousers, and jeans, again in an array of sizes to cater for sudden overnight development. There was very little choice, but Sophie didn't much care. Functionality was her main concern.

Selecting pyjamas and clean undergarments, Sophie bounded over to her bed and emptied her jeans' pockets of all that she carried. In one was the thumb drive, safely contained within a carefully folded piece of paper – she had packaged it whilst on the *Virgin Atlantic* flight from Las Vegas.

Opening the paper out revealed it to be the photograph of her father with the younger woman. She had discovered it last within the envelope that had been left for her at Fresno Airport. Her other pocket revealed the small vial of blue liquid; the piece of paper with her father's written instruction was still attached to it with the red elastic band.

It was hard to believe, but from the possessions she'd travelled to America with, these small meagre items, along with the clothes she was wearing, was all that she had left.

The only other thing she carried was her father's mobile phone, still functioning if not a bit battered-looking. She tossed it down to land alongside the other items.

She thought about calling Emily upon arriving at Gatwick Airport, and the woman would have expected it, but Sophie found that she couldn't.

She wasn't ready for the reunion, instead feeling the need for comfort only solitude could provide. Plus she was extremely fatigued.

Despite several hours' sleep on the plane she was utterly exhausted; compounded by getting completely soaked through from the great British weather, she now felt chilled to the bone. All she wanted to do was to lay in a hot bath and try and cleanse her body.

Across the hall from her bedroom was the bathroom, and on the way she wrestled free from her sodden clothing, careful to side-step the broken glass and making a mental note to clear it up. Dumping her jeans and T-shirt in a corner and wearing just a bra and panties, she stood and studied her reflection in the mirror above the sink.

"You're a sight for sore eyes," she muttered. Owing to her invisibility and, until now, the lack of mirrors, this was the first time she'd checked her appearance since the hotel room in Miami, where Barry and herself had masqueraded as husband and wife, or Mr and Mrs Mason. In truth, even then she hadn't really looked herself over.

Now, she saw for the first time the adult Sophie Jennings, a fully-grown twenty-one-year old. Her eyes roamed down her body, following the contours of her breasts and further as she drank in her reflected image.

Despite the hair band, her hair was a clump of wild, tousled tangles which she did not look forward to putting a brush through. Cuts and bruises marred her entire body head to toe, and smudges of dirt uglified her face, but she was still faintly attractive. Where the bullet had grazed her ear in Washington, just a couple of inches away from ending her life, there remained just a scab. Fast healing was another side-effect she'd recently became aware of. *Thanks dad.*

Like with the lights, Sophie was again taken aback by the discovery that hot water ran readily from the tap on the bath. She turned it on full and poured a good measure of *Radox* into the flowing stream, instantly creating a waterfall of foamy-suds.

Five minutes later she submerged her naked body into the water, the only evidence of this occurrence being the splash and ripples as her weight dropped down like an oversized stone. Warmth instantly soothed her body, the small pain receptors in her brain that registered the aches and sores blighting her nerve-endings, suddenly evaporated.

"Oohing," and "Ahhing," the cosy feeling transported Sophie back to a time when her mother and her father were alive.

How easy a bath could make things appear almost normal; that nothing of the past four months had truly happened. Sophie could almost hear her father in the living room through the open doorway, him busy behind his laptop tapping the keys furiously. She imagined her birth mother whom she saw only at Christmas or on birthdays. Then images of Meredith leapt to mind, the carefree nine-year-old who, in the beginning, believed she lived in a mirror.

Sophie allowed her head to slip under the surface, her ears filling up with water that gradually subdued her hearing. Holding her breath she continued deeper until she was completely immersed.

For what could have been five minutes, she held herself beneath the water's surface. Closing her eyes, she imagined how it must have felt to be inside her mother's womb. Imperceptibly, she thought she could hear her mother's slow heartbeat thumping as an echo around her, the rhythm calming her. Focusing on the 'thump-thump, thump-thump, thump-thump' of her mother's imagined heartbeat, she felt safe, secure and comforted. So comforted, her body over-relaxed. It felt good, the best she'd felt in a long time. Too good. Suddenly she felt darkness creep in as sleep's fingers caressed the edges of her consciousness, beckoning her to follow.

WAKE UP!! An inner voice screamed at her.

Sophie burst up from the water like a breaching whale, out of breath and inextricably panicked. Gasping and choking for air, the fantasies that she was inside her mother's womb, or that her father was still in the living room, and all other aspects conjured up by her mind dissipated like smoke from a joss stick.

No longer in any mood for a bath, she removed the plug, sat back and brought her knees up to her chest. She watched as the water slowly drained away around her, the plughole gurgling it down noisily. When it was all gone and she started to feel a little cold, she stood up and finished cleansing herself using the shower.

The living room resembled a picture from a war story. The leather sofas were shredded, their springs jutting out like barbed wire, lethal and sharp. What was once a coffee table was a pile of broken wood pieces, demolished under the weight of one of the intruders who'd tried to hurt Sophie and who'd felt the brunt of what she was capable of. Surveying the room, it was hard for the young woman to imagine having spent time happily living here with her father. Bullet holes peppered the walls and ceiling and brass casings littered the floor. Surprisingly after four months, the smell of cordite remained thick in the air.

Sophie shook her head in dismay. She hadn't wanted to go into the living room but felt compelled to. That and the simple need for food and water had motivated her forward; not before holding herself under siege for more than twenty-four hours behind a locked bedroom door. Stepping into the kitchen adjoining the living room, it looked practically undamaged and habitable, compared to the room behind her.

After taking a long pull of water directly from the tap of the kitchen sink, water sloshing over her face and skin, she half-heartedly crossed the small room to the fridge-freezer, hoping to find a few stray vials of ochre serum that may have slipped free during her rush to flee after thwarting the initial attack. Pulling open the door she soon discovered that she had been thorough with her collecting up of the small bottles. As expected, there were none there. Dismayed, she searched the fridge for any other delights it might yield. It was a fruitless exercise, practically bare with just a half-empty bottle of curdled milk, a slab of mouldy cheese, a jar of jam, and leftovers from an unidentifiable meal that was now host to a decomposed mass swimming in a puddle of ghastly brown and green soup.

"Ergh," Sophie exclaimed, closing the disgusting sight – and pungent smell – with a fast shove of the door. In desperation she turned to the waste bin, pressing the foot pedal to open it. Inside were a dozen or more empty vials, but none containing any dregs.

"Bugger it!" she cursed. *Now what?* The only serum in the world had been left in her backpack. It could be found with *Flopsy* stowed in the overhead cabinet of the aeroplane her and Barry had leapt from.

Time to forget about it. That was all gone... and the only person who could have produced more – *her father* – was dead.

Then it suddenly dawned on her, a sound seemed to audibly click inside her head.

"My father!" Running from the kitchen, Sophie rushed to her bedroom and went straight to the items she had carried back from America. Before sleeping, she had moved them from the bed onto the dressing table. They were still there now.

Reaching for the vial of blue liquid, she plucked free the folded piece of paper from beneath the red elastic band. Excitedly, she unfolded it and placed it down so that she could read it. Her father's scrawl appeared to her:

A remedy to your predicament... drink me!

"He knew that I was running out of serum, so made me this..." Sophie picked up the small bottle of liquid and watched it disappear in her hand – a frustrating by-product of her genetic alteration which made it impossible to look at anything she held.

But my father lied to us, she thought to herself. *Who's to say this ISN'T just a serum to counter the effects of my condition, but a cure?* Although she had often wished she had been normal, frequently voicing it, since the events began back in July, she didn't doubt that her abilities had been of crucial benefit and very much a blessing.

She didn't know if she was quite ready to be rid of them, not just yet.

A remedy to your predicament... drink me!

"The predicament I most have is not having any serum and being stuck like this... *invisible...* forever!"

Still, she couldn't be sure. Next to the slip of paper were the other items her father had left her. The photograph and the thumb drive.

Maybe the answers are on here, she pondered as she picked up the thumb drive. It didn't matter that she could no longer see it, she could feel it and almost sense the answers contained digitally within.

Almost as though telepathically responding to a mental summoning, Sophie's mobile began to ring. It was Emily, and it wasn't the first time she had tried calling her over the past twenty-four hours.

Sophie had ignored all nineteen previous calls, the last one only twelve minutes earlier.

The Show Must Go On... played, her father's familiar ringtone. Sophie snatched up the handset and answered.

"*Where have you been? I've been sick with worry...*" Emily spoke like an upset parent, her voice shrill and tinged with annoyance.

"No time to explain. I need your help."

She went quiet for a moment, probably to clear her head.

"*Okay... how?*" The tone Emily used indicated that she would return to the former question.

"I need you to come to me. My father's thumb drive; I need to see what's on it."

"*Sophie, I'm not coming to America... I've only been back here a few days...*"

"No, I don't want you to," she said. "I'm in London."

Emily took a moment to digest this information. "*Where?*"

"Home," Sophie replied softly and sadly.

CHAPTER TWENTY-THREE
DOMINIC

Shortly after **6:00 A.M.**, Dominic watched from the water's edge as Elspeth disappeared across the sea in the *Bell 206* helicopter, the twin-bladed, single engine aircraft floating a couple of metres above the choppy waters of the North Atlantic Ocean, at a height believed to be below radar detection. Sea mist sprayed Dominic's face as he lowered his hand from waving off the ginger-haired woman, her face having turned away even before the black helicopter had taken off. When all he could see of the chopper was a small dot in the distant sky, and the sound of its beating rotors were no longer heard over the roar of the sea, Dominic turned around and began his morning jog along the shingle beach. From within one deep pocket of his hooded sweatshirt, he pulled free his *iPod* and inner-earphones, plugging them into both of his ears.

The album *Black Holes & Revelations* by Muse played, blotting out the noise from the ocean and the occasional howl of the wind. In addition to taking his mind off running, absorbing himself in music helped him think. Shutting out any distractions, the early morning run had become more than just an exercise regime; it was fast becoming a ritual.

Whilst the ninety sons of *GYGES* enjoyed another hour in bed, Dominic would be out running until sweat drenched his clothing and matted his long dark hair, no matter how cold it was outside. The weight which he'd piled on during the three months he'd 'laid low' would drop off fast, his body returning to the shape and fitness he once took meticulous pride in. He anticipated that by Christmas he would be back to peak condition, just in time for when his plans would truly begin.

When he jogged into the hastily erected compound building, some of the identical boys were wandering the corridors and heading towards the mess hall for breakfast. Dominic barely acknowledged them as he advanced towards the private rooms where he spent most of his time.

After a shower and a bowl of mixed fruit, he sat down to read the newspaper. Delivered by the *Bell 206* helicopter with fresh supplies daily, it was Dominic's only way of keeping abreast of what was going on in the world outside – although, a day out of date. It reminded him of when he holidayed in Greece. The papers on the newsstands were always a day behind.

The front page of *The Daily Mail* was reporting a story about a scandal involving a prominent Tory MP and a night spent with three prostitutes in a drugs den. Dominic flipped over the page to more articles of impropriety or impending doom and gloom. He riffled through a couple more pages until a headline caught his eye.

"Interesting," he said to himself.

CALIFORNIA UNDER SIEGE

The news story detailed the events occurring in Fresno, California, where it claimed a gunman was shot and critically injured by cops after a high speed car chase. The journalist glossed over some details about the situation, but indicated the incident started at Fresno Yosemite International Airport when a flight from Miami landed. It was claimed that the gunman had an accomplice – possibly female – and that she had escaped, despite the airport being locked down and completely surrounded by police. No description of the gunman's accomplice had been released; however Dominic read that a joint operation between the FBI and Intelligence Agents was in full swing, and that the events were being linked with the death of George Jennings. Although not confirmed, an inside source had suggested that the gunman and his accomplice had a few hours earlier travelled on a flight from Cuba, possibly using the aliases of 'Mr and Mrs Mason'.

Dominic would have continued to mull over the bulletin, but another caption gained his attention.

"He-llo beautiful," he said quietly, sitting up straight, as though it helped with his attention.

His assiduity could easily have been credited to the photograph of the actress Jennifer Lawrence, looking stunning in a white dress with its plunging neck line and who was out walking a red carpet promoting her latest movie. But in actuality, it was the headline to the left of that image; the mere mention of a certain diamond that got him salivating.

"Why do you keep on teasing me like this," he whispered, sighing. "The one that got away..."

A photograph of the *Whisper of Persia* placed upon a velvet cushion involuntarily excited the former marine. Quickly he scanned the accompanying report, gleaning as much information as he could, his mood darkening as he read of its recent history, a turbulent past that had indirectly involved him. His heart quickened a pace as he learnt of the plans for its future.

"*A gem such as this cannot be kept under lock and key,*" said the diamond's current owner, an eccentric Viscount of Great Britain, eighteenth richest man in the land. "*It would be folly to deprive the nation because of the act of one villainous person,*" continued the Viscount who also happened to be a celebrated horticulturist, often appearing in the media, brushing shoulders with the rich and famous.

"Yes, it so would," agreed Dominic. *And depriving me the chance of getting my hands on you too...* He further scanned the article, learning that the reason for the *Whisper of Persia's* mention was owed completely to the Viscount's decision to put the diamond on display at Holyrood Palace in Edinburgh, the Queen's official Scottish residence.

"*Besides, they had a heart and returned it. No harm no foul,*" the rich fool had gone on, adding clarity: "*So, with that spirit I thought: what better place is there to exhibit one of the finest stones in the world, than at one of the finest palaces ever built. Besides, there's no better security to be had in the country...*" The article further mentioned that the Viscount was loaning the diamond for exhibition for the next twelve months, after which it would be placed in a bank vault for its future protection.

"That almost sounds like a challenge," said Dominic fervently, his heart beginning to race in tandem with his growing excitement. He looked across the room in the direction of the compound where he knew the sons of *GYGES* were gathered, and started to wonder. He dismissed the thought from his head. "Not yet. Soon..." he placated himself. "Very soon."

⊶━⬤━⊷

As the training of the ninety boys was being overseen by Malaxi Bacaunawa, Dominic had very little to do with them, except to gather progress updates on a regular basis, and start plotting on how best to use them. Most of his time was spent drinking cups of coffee or putting himself through vigorous exercise programmes involving stints in the gym, on the squash court and in the swimming pool, all in addition to the early morning jogs along the coast. Some people obsessed over fitness, the endorphins released from exercise akin to an intoxicating drug almost bordering an addiction.

But not to Dom.

The only reason for spending three hours in the gym every day and undertaking all other sporting exertions was to see the waistline of his trousers return to size thirty-four-inches.

Whilst on the *Life Fitness* elliptical trainer – a smooth cardiovascular machine designed to emulate cross-country skiing and which promised an 'all-body workout' – Dominic heard the trill of his mobile phone, the ringtone identified within the settings list as 'Leisure Time'. He stopped pumping the handles on the training machine and ceased moving his legs in the simulated step and glide motions.

Below and to either side of the LCD interface panel were two cup holders. In one was a sports drinks' bottle, an orange liquid sloshing back and forth from Dominic's frenetic arm and leg movements; the other held his ringing phone.

"He-llo..." he was out of breath.

"*Dom?*"

"Jennifer." Dominic uttered it breathily. He stepped off the cross-trainer and reached for a hand towel, quickly wiping sweat away from his face with it. After, he draped it around the back of his neck. It felt warm and damp, but he hardly noticed it. "Hadn't you agreed not to be in touch until the media had died down?" he didn't wait for a response. "Glad you've called though... where are my data implant training programs?" It had been a couple of days since he'd requested the encrypted programmes from the CEO of Kaplan Ratcliff. So far he was yet to receive them.

Jennifer Ratcliff disregarded Dominic's comment. "*I thought you ought to know that Emily Porter knows of our tête-à-tête and Ryan's complicity.*"

"What?" Dominic walked across the gym to a machine well-stocked with health food bars and energy drinks. He pressed a button selecting a *Fuelmax* fruit and cereal carbohydrate bar. Containing 141mg of caffeine and 30.8g of carbohydrate, the energy bar fell with a heavy clatter to the dispensing tray, a reassuring sound that indicated his hunger would soon be abated. He scooped it up, propped his phone between the side of his face and his shoulder and tore open the packaging.

"*The wannabe-spy bugged Ryan's office and overheard a conversation between us. Now she knows...*"

"But not where we are?" Sounding unconcerned Dominic took a large bite from the cereal bar and started chewing it noisily.

"*No... not where we are; not even Ryan knows that,*" she confirmed, "*but, it's just a matter of time before our other friend finds out what they do know.*"

"You mean Sophie?" It came out garbled, surrounded by food.

"*Yes, you know who I mean.*"

"But why should we care? She's no longer necessary to our plans... we have ninety kids like her." *Or WILL be like her if I ever get my data implant training programs*, he thought.

"*You're forgetting how bloody righteous she is. Do you think she will be best pleased to know that you've taken those boys to use for your own purpose? You're also forgetting that there's unfinished business between the two of you.*" Jennifer was referring once again to the fact that Dominic had killed Sophie's mother.

"Old news... she had many an opportunity to kill me whilst in America," he dismissed the woman's concern. "What about Ryan? Isn't he able to keep this contained? After all, he was all in favour of us taking the kids."

"*For his own reasons, yes. But Ryan isn't Sophie's favourite person right now. She thinks he ordered the hit on her father...*"

Dominic started to laugh. "She must be finding it hard knowing who she can and *can't* trust," he continued smiling to himself.

"*Which makes her even more dangerous in my opinion,*" replied Jennifer humourlessly.

Dominic took another bite from the *Fuelmax* bar. "Wha' d'you wan' me ta-do abou' it?"

Jennifer's disgust could be heard down the phone by way of an audible 'tut'. "*I want you and the agents seconded to you on standby. You're going to have to be ready to get your hands dirty, I'm afraid.*"

Dominic was no longer smiling. "How dirty?"

Jennifer took a long pause. "*Oh, you know... Harriet Jennings dirty,*" she said gravely.

He grunted. "You want me to kill her?"

"*Dear boy, I don't think you are capable,*" she scoffed. "*No. But there are other ways to tame a wild animal. Sometimes you just need to know how to push all the right buttons. What do you perceive to be her greatest weakness?*"

"Her family," guessed Dominic without hesitation, seeing exactly where Jennifer was angling at.

"*But, hopefully it won't come to that,*" she said optimistically.

"Okay, I hear you. First, be quicker getting me what I want and maybe then I'll consider whatever it is you require of me."

"*Sounds only fair,*" replied Jennifer incisively. "*You'll have your data files by the end of today.*"

CHAPTER TWENTY-FOUR
EMILY

"**Y**OU SHOULDN'T BE HERE. It's not..."

"Safe?" ventured Sophie, stepping well to the side to allow Emily into the apartment so as to avoid colliding, despite the fact Emily had come prepared and was wearing thermal glasses, enabling her to see through the young woman's invisibility. "I know."

"I was going to say *pleasant*." Emily carried a folded umbrella which was dripping rain water – which she stowed in a bucket near to the entrance door (where one other was standing to attention) – and a shoulder bag large enough to carry a laptop. She surveyed Sophie's former home, her attention focusing on the destruction and disarray of the living room ahead of her, the door held open by a book wedged beneath it, *Dan Brown's Da Vinci Code* she noticed. She wrinkled her nose at the havoc surrounding her, slightly repugnant. Initially her judgement had been formed outside, viewing the boarded up facade and the graffiti gracing it with disdain, but the sight of bullet holes marring the walls and ceiling, and the shredded, devastated furniture added weight to her aversion. "How long have you been back?"

Sophie closed the front door and led the MI6 analyst into the living room. Despite the destruction, she had tidied an area of the room so that it was habitable. The dining table and chairs were relatively unscathed, and the carpeted floor around it had been swept and vacuumed clean.

"I got back almost two days ago, but was so tired... I've been sleeping." Sophie replied, her tone defensive. "Come in. Please forgive the mess..."

Mess was an understatement. "You should've called, I could've helped." Emily followed Sophie through to the living room and sat down at a place set aside for her at the table. She removed the thermal glasses, laying them nearby. In their place she slipped her spectacles on to see better.

The table had a few small items placed upon it, but the surface was mostly sparse and tidy.

"Can I get you something?" asked Sophie, acting the host.

"Tea would be nice," suggested Emily in the direction she'd heard Sophie's voice.

"Um... totally out of tea."

"Coffee?" ventured Emily hopefully. She stood by the dining table waiting for permission to sit.

"There's water... I've not had chance to go shopping since being back." Sophie entered the kitchen, ran the cold tap and filled two glasses with water. A moment later the two glasses of water, as if by magic, appeared on the table.

Emily gasped. She had forgotten that everything Sophie wore or carried became absorbed by the same component of camouflage that she was genetically enhanced with, and without the thermal glasses on, she hadn't seen Sophie come in carrying the two drinks.

"What about food, have you eaten?" *Listen to you. When did you turn into your own mother?* Emily mentally rebuked herself.

"Yes... once," Sophie laughed.

"Okay, let me order in..."

As quickly as it had started, Sophie's laughter stopped. "After." She spoke firmly. Although ravenous, she needed to do something important first. "I need to know what this all means." Though unseen,

Sophie gestured with her hands towards the items on the table. The small bottle of blue liquid stood out foremost. To either side of it were the thumb drive and the photograph of George, his arm around the younger woman. These were all the items her father (excepting the gun which she had left with Barry) had left for her.

"Are these...?"

"Yes," replied Sophie, not needing to hear the full question. "My father's last will was for me to find that locker in Fresno Airport where he had placed these items... for me."

Emily picked up the photograph. She recognised the young woman that George's arm was draped around. Seeing her brought a lump to the throat and a tear to her eye. Her spectacles misted up slightly, requiring her to remove them to wipe clear.

"You knew her?"

"Of course... that's Clara. Your biological mother." Emily replaced her spectacles and studied the photograph some more. "She looks so happy... and weirdly close to your father." Turning the picture over, Emily noticed the address scrawled across the back.

Norská 561/10, 101 00 Praha, Czech Republic.

"Do you know what this is?" Emily asked curiously.

Unseen, Sophie shook her head. "I don't think it's important, not at the moment," being dismissive. "What I do want to know is what's on the thumb drive... And, whether it's safe for me to drink the thing that looks like smurf pee."

Emily returned the photo of George and Clara back to the table and swept up the small vial of blue liquid. The slip of paper George had attached with a red rubber band was still in place. She pulled it free and carefully opened it out, seeing the words in the same writing as used to scrawl out the address on the photograph.

A remedy to your predicament... drink me!

Emily looked up to where she knew Sophie was sitting. "What's stopping you from drinking it?" she asked earnestly.

"I don't know whether I should. What predicament is he implying? Is it the fact that I have run out of serum? Or could it be referring to the whole invisibility thing? What will be the outcome to me drinking it?"

"I couldn't know," answered Emily solemnly. "I guess there's only one way to find out…"

The laptop was powered up and Emily had inserted the thumb drive into the slot in the side of the *Lenovo* machine. Five seconds later and she was presented with a list of options, specifically on what next to do. She selected 'folder open' and almost immediately was presented with a list of files. The topmost one was an AVI file, which Emily knew just by the initialism was a video file (audio video interleave).

"Here… maybe this will help." Emily twisted the laptop around so that Sophie could see, and selected the file, pressing the enter key.

The LCD monitor flickered a few times before presenting a video playback screen which filled the entire area, corner to corner. A play/pause bar appeared at the bottom indicating the file's length was four minutes and twenty seconds, and the video started to run.

George Jennings stepped into view from the right side of the picture, likely having just switched the camera on. He was wearing a white lab-coat and mad, dishevelled hair. He sat down on a swivel chair and looked towards them, his eyes piercing blue, just like his daughter's.

"*Hello Sophie,*" he started cheerily. "*I guess, if you're watching this, things have gone bad and are beyond my control. Most likely I am dead… or will be soon.*" He looked down gravely towards his hands clasped together, as though coming to terms with the situation for the first time. A moment later he returned eye contact. "*I'm sorry about all this Sophie, none of this is what I wanted. By now I guess, you've learnt that I'm not who I said I was; that I was working covertly for the American government, and that my job was not only to genetically engineer a super soldier – you –, but it was to take the research and give it to my employers, sadly destroying the evidence and all avenues that could lead to replicating my work, behind me. Regretfully, I complied with most of this which makes me a terrible man, but I couldn't give you up, Sophie. And it was a condition, for me to continue with my work on the project that you, Meredith, your brothers and your mother, all remain safe. To this end, I've only had assurances that this is the case. I hope to God that it is so.*

"*But I digress. You will notice that in the envelope you found this thumb drive,*" George held up the digital device which, paradoxically, felt impossible to be playing back the same message. "*You also found a photograph and my gift, a small bottle of liquid with a note attached urging you to 'drink it'. Knowing you Sophie, you haven't yet drunk it,*" he started to grin, "*but rest assured it's perfectly safe and completely innocuous. By my reckoning, you would have run out of 'B-twenty-one-L-eight', or what you and I simply called your 'meds'. I bet you are now roaming the earth like a ghost and invisible to all, except for thermal glasses... and of course in reflective surfaces – I never could work that out. Anyway, this is not the existence I ever wanted for you my love... so, covertly, I've designed an antidote especially, and only for you.*" From a table behind him, George reached for a small item hidden from view. When he turned back round his hand was wrapped around the centre of a vial of blue liquid. The same vial which was now placed in the centre of the dining table.

"*I wish I could've tested it more thoroughly,*" George began saying, "*but I simply ran out of time. Don't worry, it's fine... and no animals died making it! You will, however, need to get used to the modification as you won't be requiring the injections any more. I'm sure that'll please you! Plus, the changes it will make to your DNA, they're irreversible, which means nothing can ever be done to change it... so, if you were ever hoping for a cure... I'm sorry... it's not going to happen. Nothing can ever take your gift away."* Sophie's father leaned forward, very serious-looking. *"Remember that,"* he said, adding emphasis to those two words.

"Skipping on, time is of the essence and all. I'm guessing that you will know that I have been coerced into creating an army of genetically enhanced soldiers for the Americans. They are just like you, Sophie, but without a conscience... or are GOING to be without a conscience. I built in a slight inhibitor. As they age, emotional feelings gradually dissipate until the host is fully matured. They will know no boundaries and feel no limitations once that happens, which simply means they will be fearless and all but unstoppable.

"On the thumb drive you will also find a number of files. One is the location and schematics of the American base under which my laboratory is based, where you will find the soldiers of GYGES... the project which I had no choice but to orchestrate. I need you to go there and destroy all my work; it's not going to be easy, but it needs to be done."

"Been there... done that," interrupted Sophie nonchalantly.

"On another file, you'll find a formula. Get it to a bio-geneticist, pronto. The ingredients are to be strictly adhered to and the method of distribution is subcutaneous." Which Sophie understood meant: it needed to be injected below the skin. *"How you administer it to potentially thousands of children could be a concern, but it's imperative for the safety of mankind that it is done; no world power should have an army of such capability... What I am giving you is a permanent antidote to the DNA enhancements I've made to their genetic makeup. It will strip out all the modification and by and large, they will then just be normal, weirdly similar looking kids.*

"I just wish... I'd had the strength... to refuse my superiors... never

creating them in the first place..." He slumped his shoulders and, for a moment, George looked forlorn and traumatised, looking down towards the floor, finding it hard to grapple with something more. He looked like he was about to cry. "*That's the problem with having a conscience... and being emotionally attached to something or someone. It makes you weak.*" He looked back up. "*No matter what has happened to me, whether I am alive or now dead... know this: I've always loved you, Meredith, Stanley and Charlie. And your mother. And I always will. I only did what I did to keep you safe...*

"*Before I go, you'll see that I've written an address on an old photograph. Keep it safe. If you ever need a friend, someone you can trust, or someplace to go and just properly 'disappear'... that's the place. Now, be a good girl. Drink the serum.*" George smiled lovingly. "*Say hello to your mother, sister and brothers for me...*" Now he was crying. "*Goodbye Sophie.*"

"Goodbye dad," Sophie whispered.

On the screen, George stood up from the seat and walked towards the camera and then stepping to the right of it, out of shot. A second later and the image on the laptop went black and the video ended.

"He doesn't know..." reacted Sophie, sounding stunned.

"Your poor, poor father... all that time they had led him to believe that you were all okay, even though your mother was dead." Emily shook her head in sorrow.

"Maybe it was a blessing," said Sophie unhappily. There was no way to know that George had been given the news that his wife had died, although that didn't happen until several weeks after the video was made (the AVI file had a date towards the beginning of September). "Who wouldn't want to leave the world of the living knowing that everyone they held dear was going to be just okay without them..."

"I guess," murmured Emily, not so certain. She exhaled dishearteningly, asking: "So, what now?"

"I drink this I guess." Sophie snatched up the vial of blue liquid from the centre of the table, the glass bottle disappearing in her grasp. Emily heard the seal on the cap snap as Sophie twisted the lid anti-clockwise, followed by the sound of liquid sluicing around in the young woman's mouth like it were *Listerine*, then an audible swallow.

What happened next didn't seem very out of the ordinary to Emily having witnessed Sophie's transformation a few times, but it felt extraordinary to the person holding her father's biochemical concoction.

"Oh God..." exclaimed Sophie, physically beginning to appear. "Oh my..."

"What is it?" A look of concern flashed across Emily's face.

"So... *warm*..." said Sophie, starting to laugh. Although her body was taking on form, Emily could still see through her. "Tingly!" Sophie was standing up as a feeling of intense pleasure engulfed her.

"Should this be happening?" Emily was embarrassed and slightly concerned. *Maybe the antidote was a euphoriant*, she considered, *and Sophie was now in the midst of a 'trip'.*

"Oddly peculiar... in places!" her eyes were closed, but the lids flickered rapidly.

"I should call for help," said Emily abruptly, moving away from the table and setting forth for the room's exit.

As Sophie's metamorphosis concluded, she thumped the dinner table in triumph, anger or relief. The laptop and the few items placed about it jumped up a couple of millimetres and clattered back down. The empty glass vial toppled over noisily and rolled a little, stopping just short of the table's edge.

"Wait..." Sophie was smiling and still clearly elated, but the feeling was lessening. "Emily. It's over..." *How could she explain it?* "I've never had a feeling of such *pleasure*... not like that before."

Emily stopped and turned back towards the younger woman. Sophie was now fully visible, fresh-faced, flawless and looking almost how she remembered her back in the hotel room in Washington, before they had evaded capture at the airport and the battle to destroy *GYGES* in Nevada.

Except she now looked a little older, wiser and world-weary.

The cuts and bruising picked up during the battles, skirmishes and run-ins with her pursuers had all swiftly healed.

"You look..." Emily couldn't grasp the word.

"Amazing? I know!" Sophie ran a hand through her shoulder-length blonde hair. It looked silky and framed her head impeccably. "Another gift from my dad," she replied breezily. "Like my aging; turns out my cells regenerate at an elevated rate too. I first noticed it back in California... a bullet grazed my ear... but didn't think much on it."

"Fascinating." Emily had moved back towards the table and stood facing the younger woman. Studying her unblemished face she immediately became aware of another change. "You've grown too." Before, Emily had stood an inch taller. But now these aspects had switched over. Sophie's shoulders were also slightly broader.

"Stop!" lamented Sophie. "You're imagining things. Besides, I can't have grown. I've not eaten in days... which reminds me," changing the subject, "I'll let you order that food now."

CHAPTER TWENTY-FIVE
BARRY

T HE WHITER-THAN-WHITE WALLS AND the strong smell associated with medical facilities helped Barry pinpoint his whereabouts, even without the sounds associated with ECG and other equipment monitoring his vitals.

Lying on a narrow bed with metal bars to either side of him, he slowly became aware of all the drips and wires stuck to or pinned into his body. An oxygen mask was secured over his face. He figured that he was recovering in some hospital somewhere after some accident, momentarily forgetting the actual fate that had befallen him. That soon changed when he discovered the handcuffs fastened about his wrist, restraining his right hand to the bed railing.

Oh, I remember some of it.

He was surprised to find that he was actually still alive.

Numbly, he tested the cuffs by lifting his arm and giving it a quick, hard tug. The little slack between the railing and his wrist allowed minimal movement and the metal clasp locking him in place jangled noisily as he jerked about.

A nurse walked into the private ward busying over something – Barry assumed it was a nurse, based on how she was dressed and moved. She walked purposefully and hurried about her duties, oblivious to him being awake behind her. He guessed the nurse was in her mid-thirties, although he had only seen her face fleetingly. Her short black hair was neatly tied back and she wore dark blue scrubs that hung loosely from her tall, gangly frame.

"A-hem!" Barry cleared his throat in an attempt to draw attention.

"I know you're awake... *Mister Abney*." The nurse turned from the side of the room and stepped towards him. Barry looked her over, noticing the scar running the length of the left side of her face; it ran from her cheek down to her chin, though faint it was quite prominent. He couldn't help staring. For a second he hadn't realised she'd used his surname. "Mister *Barrington Abney*," she repeated, "of British descent..."

The woman saying his full name felt like a face slap, snapping his attention away from her disfigurement. "How do you know...?" The question sounded muffled, a little sinister. To Barry, he sounded a little like a villain from a famous space opera.

"What? Your name?" The nurse stooped down, her face level with his. Even with the mask on, Barry caught a whiff of a slight scent, a subtle fragrance that reminded him of a gentle spring day back in England. "The Feds told me," she said softly.

"I don't see how...*AHH*... that...*OOO*...is... Poss...*Ah*!" Barry was trying to shuffle up the bed into a sitting position, stabs of pain piercing his body in various places all at the same time, the effect dizzying, bringing tears to his eyes.

"Whooa, hold your horses. No sudden movements, okay. We've only just finished stitching you up!"

Barry closed his eyes, trying to block out the pain, and relaxed, settling back down on the bed. Almost immediately the throbbing, stinging sensations seemed to subside, along with the dizziness.

"What happened?" he wheezed, no longer bothered about how his identity had been discovered. He had some memory of what had transpired before the 'lights' went out, but things were a little fuzzy around the edges.

"Can't remember, no? That's probably the effects of the morphine." The nurse didn't know either, though she had seen some of the news footage. She had also been in the operating theatre for sixteen hours whilst surgeons worked to fix his liver, remove his spleen and extract the nineteen bullets from his body, most puncturing his body from the waist down; but some had taken him high in the chest or about his shoulder, perforating a lung and just narrowly missing his heart. "By all accounts, you've been a very lucky man," she added. "From the looks of you, the PD used you for target practice."

"Feels like it too," Barry tried to smile.

After the operation, the nurse had carried the metal dish used to deposit each bullet, away from the theatre and passed them to the agent who appeared to be in charge. Without smiling, Brayden Scott had made it clear that Barry was under federal arrest, and shortly after that was applying the cuffs to ensure, with absolute finality, no risk of escape.

The nurse mentioning the police department returned him back to the setting where he'd sacrificed himself to provide Sophie cover to aid her escape.

He recalled raising the gun – a *Glock*, Sophie's gun of choice which she'd given to him during their escape – and firing off a couple of rounds. Pain had exploded in various points about his body simultaneously, a long second before the accompanying sounds of gunshots deafened his ears. Like a sledgehammer to the chest, he was knocked to the ground, and still bullets rained down around him. No one was taking chances.

Immediately after, whilst lying there on the dusty road, he remembered seeing feet running towards him, then a face leaning in.

"You just hold on, d'you hear me? I'm not letting you off this lightly..."

He had tried speaking, to tell the man something... *Let me die...* was what he had wanted to say, but only blood slipped from his lips.

"*Hush… save your energy,*" the man said just as Barry closed his eyes. The last thing he heard before darkness relieved him of pain and all his senses was:

"*I'M LOSING HIM!*"

Coming back to the present, Barry sighed in dismay, turning his head slightly away from the nurse. It wasn't due to him lying in a hospital chained to a bed, his body pierced like a hock of meat straight from the oven, or even the fact that he had grown tired of seeing the woman's scar. He knew that, even in the face of all that he had gone through, it was likely to pale against what would befall him soon, once his body had adequately recovered to allow the FBI or the CIA to interrogate him. He worked for MI6, he knew how it worked.

A knock at the door – a quick 'one two' with bony knuckles – shortly followed by the sudden appearance of a tall man in a suit who Barry had first observed at Fresno Airport, walked in confidently. An agent or someone in command, the same one he had seen at the shootout, kneeling next to him, placing his jacket carefully under his head. It was the same jacket which the man was now wearing.

"Barrington Abney… back in the living." Brayden Scott strode to the hospital bed and stood towering over Barry, a knowing smile appearing across his face. A slight shift of his arm revealed a gun beneath his jacket. It looked like a *Smith and Wesson* to the injured man. "We've learnt a lot about you these past couple of days… Mr Abney. Or should I address you *Agent* Abney of Her Majesty's Secret Intelligence Service?"

Barry didn't react or show any emotion.

Brayden turned to face the nurse and communicated for her to leave just by a slight turn of the head, a raised eyebrow and a facial expression.

"Two minutes. I'll be at the nurse's station if you need me," she said haughtily, leaving the ward, though lingering just outside.

"I'm Agent Scott," Brayden said once the nurse had closed the door behind her. "I'm sort-of your equivalent here in the States..." he said, adding, "...only... a few pay grades higher," he chuckled. "Britain and America are allies... MI6... CIA... We regularly collaborate, share intel. There's a lot of give and *take*." He emphasised the word 'take'. "We have common goals... and *common enemies*. You and I, we are cut from the same cloth. Two legs to a pair of trousers. Hell, we're practically brothers..."

"Okay, okay. I get it. We're one big happy bloody family. Thanks for the stirring speech." The oxygen mask weakened the sarcasm in his voice.

Brayden walked around the bed and crossed to the window, pushing open a couple of slats in the venetian blind to peer out. The view offered was dull compared to the hospital room he had been standing in just a few days earlier. Owing to its setting, the Community Regional Medical Centre in Fresno, though offering exemplary health care which ultimately saved Barry's life, wasn't as pleasing to visit as the hospital facilities at Guantanamo Bay had been.

A concrete car park, beyond which North Clark Street could be seen, looked mediocre compared to the crystal blue waters and the white sand south of the island of Cuba.

Thoughts of George came to mind. Brayden could still see his lifeless body lying there in his bed, suffocated with his own pillow by the man who had once been his partner. He allowed the slats of the blind to fall back into place and returned his attention to Barry.

"I have you to thank for delivering George Jennings' killer to us, an act which has earned you a little gratitude from me. That's a perfect example of inter-agency-collaboration." **B**rayden smiled. He manoeuvred a chair so that it was facing Barry, the legs scraping the floor noisily, and sat down, his expression hardening. "It is my job to help protect the United States from external threats – great and small – at all costs." Brayden went quiet, as though considering his words carefully.

"What do you want?"

Brayden's eyes sparkled like quartz under ultraviolet light. "The girl for starters," he said, "and... Dominic Schilling."

"What makes you think I –" Barry was shaking his head apathetically.

"Cut the crap Abney!" Brayden interrupted, jumping up from the chair and placing a hand upon Barry's shoulder, across an area that was bandaged and obviously sore. He lightly applied pressure knowing that directly beneath the dressing was an angry bullet wound. A small dot of blood appeared on the bandage.

Barry tried not to cry out in pain, to brave the torment through gritted teeth. He grunted involuntarily as Brayden dug his fingers in a little deeper, his teeth gritted. The look on the CIA agent's face seemed to be one of pleasure.

"Don't think I won't carry on," declared Brayden, pushing down harder. The dressing was now dark red with crimson beneath his hand, the spot now the size of a five-pence-piece. "Reminds me... I need to stick a bottle of Cabernet Sauvignon in the fridge..."

Barry squeezed his eyes shut, white stars dancing behind them; once again consciousness teetered, threatening to desert him and the acidic taste of bile bubbled at the back of his throat.

"Okay! Okay! Stop... stop... STOP!"

Brayden removed his hand and started to laugh. "I haven't even gotten started yet! Call yourself MI6! You're a disgrace to your profession and your country." He 'tsked' loudly as he laid his hand back on Barry's shoulder, squeezing again. He didn't care that the man was weak and about to answer some questions.

"Ahhhh, no... no... Nurse! Nurse!"

Before the nurse came in to admonish Brayden, the CIA agent

lessened his pressure and removed his hand. "Okay, Abney. I'll stop... seeing as you're now wishing to be compliant."

Barry was whimpering a little from the pain continuing to burn above his chest. "Before I talk..." he grunted, "go get me a coffee. I need a caffeine fix."

"I've already told you once, cut the crap." Brayden moved menacingly forward, a hand half-reaching for the man's shoulder again.

"Wait! I'll tell you EVERYTHING... just get me a bloody coffee. I need a coffee. I want a coffee!"

"All right! ... don't have a coronary." Brayden withdrew reluctantly and stepped out of the room, passing the nurse's station as he sought a coffee machine. He didn't notice the nurse he'd ordered out walk from a neighbouring room and enter the corridor behind him as he headed to where he knew a drinks' machine was stationed.

Using a stethoscope pressed up against a wall, the nurse had listened into Brayden's questioning, hearing everything. She wanted to step in, to end the man's torment, but couldn't; there was something she needed to know first. Now that the agent had momentarily left her patient, she swiftly reappeared at Barry's bedside.

"Are you okay Mr Abney? Your dressing...!" The nurse noticed the growing dot of blood on the bandaging secured over the man's shoulder.

"It's nothing," Barry replied, closing his eyes, making the most of Agent Brayden Scott's absence.

"I'll change it in a minute. First, I need to administer some meds. Something for the pain." She walked around to Barry's right side and removed a syringe from deep within a pocket. She removed the needle guard and tapped air bubbles free from the liquid in the small glass tube.

"I doubt it'll help rid me from all my pain." The oxygen mask still suppressed his voice, but what Barry implied was still clear.

"Oh, I don't know. You might be surprised." The nurse jabbed the needle of the syringe into a vein in Barry's arm. "Just a little scratch," she said, a reassuring smile spreading across her lips. She squeezed the piston plunger, gently administering the drug.

Instantly, a warm feeling spread from the needle site in his arm, coursing through his veins. At first, it felt pleasant, soothing, but without warning Barry suddenly felt like he was drowning, his lungs feeling bereft of oxygen and his chest feeling heavy, like a compression was steadily building against it. He made a long, desperate gasp as he fought for a deep intake of air. Involuntarily, his free hand shot up to his neck, clawing at an invisible barrier that seemed to be obstructing his airway from the inside.

"Shh, Mr Abney... it'll soon be over."

An alarm started to blurt from the monitor displaying Barry's vitals. His heart rate and blood pressure readings were flashing in red, the oscillating lines spiking and falling, spiking and falling, then dropping off altogether into a flat, continuous line.

Barry, his struggles declining, appeared to relax, his eyes staring skyward, transfixed on a spot on the ceiling.

"What's happening?!" Brayden Scott ran into the private room carrying two coffees, black steaming liquid sloshing over the lips of the cups, burning his fingers. Involuntarily, he recoiled.

"Code blue!" shouted the nurse dramatically, at the same time discretely concealing the syringe back into her pocket. She hurried purposefully around Barry's bed to the man's side. "I need a doctor!" she demanded, making pretence of reaching for a crash cart to the side of the room behind her.

Brayden looked around for somewhere to discard the two cups. A corner wash basin was closest. He dropped them down and ran out into the corridor, coffee draining down the plughole. "SOMEONE GET A DOCTOR IN HERE!!!" he yelled desperately.

Barely a second had ticked by when a couple of doctors, one dressed in blue scrubs, the other wearing a striped shirt and a regal-looking tie, appeared in the doorway.

"Step aside!" one of the doctors ordered. Brayden obliged, allowing the doctors to pass unobstructed. They closed the door behind them and started working on the unconscious man lying on the bed.

Through the narrow window set within the panel of the door, Brayden peered in. Muffled conversation – frantic, but purposeful – could be heard and the doctor in scrubs, seemingly taking charge, told the medical staff to "CLEAR" just as he pressed a pair of defibrillator paddles against Barry's now-bare chest.

Thwump!

The doctor turned to the nurse and gave an instruction to change the setting for another charge of the defibrillator. Receiving acknowledgement, he shouted "CLEAR" for a second time as he administered another dose of electricity directly into the man's chest.

Brayden watched the team confer, syringe-inject a couple of drugs, and repeat with the use of defibrillators another three times before the man in charge decided it was no use. He shook his head and glanced at his watch, as though making a deliberate assessment of the time. Wasting little effort, the two doctors who had responded to Brayden's demand for help, exited the room with barely an acknowledgement.

The nurse that had been tending Barry when the CIA agent had arrived was still in the room, disconnecting cables and turning off equipment. Seeing Brayden reappear she looked downcast. "I'm sorry... we did all that we could."

"Oh Jeez," exclaimed Brayden, throwing a hand automatically to his head, dismayed and pained at seeing that Barrington Abney, formerly an agent with MI6, was dead. "I told him NOT to have a coronary!" He shook his head dejectedly. "How do I explain this?" he asked himself quietly.

The nurse stepped up to the agent and laid a hand gently on his arm. "We did our best," she said.

Brayden lowered his hands pensively, looking away from Barry's still staring face, the man's eyes, though no longer focused, were fixated on a point within the ceiling. He walked away from the nurse and reached into a pocket for his phone, pressing a button intuitively to dial a preset number and raised it to his ear.

His call was answered with barely enough time to take a breath. He didn't allow the recipient any time to speak:

"Mullins... Agent Abney is a dead end," Brayden announced sardonically. He trudged out of the room, leaving the nurse to continue with her necessary duties. "I guess Milo now gets his wish," he said with a sigh. "Prepare the field team. We make for London before nightfall."

With Brayden Scott gone, the nurse stopped what she was doing for a moment and retrieved her own mobile phone. Nervously, she advanced to the door and peered out. Brayden was a little way along the corridor still speaking to his partner. Satisfied that no one would witness her, the nurse quickly tapped out a text message:

IT'S DONE.

And followed up by pressing 'send'. Five long seconds later and a delivery confirmation flashed up on her phone with a double bleep. The nurse deposited the small handset back into her pocket and left the private room.

The CIA agent finished his call as the nurse was about to pass, and he stepped towards her, blocking her progress. Initially, she thought the CIA agent suspected something, in the manner with which he was looking at her, almost challenging. His gaze then marginally softened.

"Makes all those hours spent patching him up seem like a waste now, doesn't it," moaned Brayden without sympathy.

PART TWO

CHAPTER TWENTY-SIX
RYAN

Two months had slipped by since news of Barry's death had been reported. He couldn't now recall what had come first, details of the young SIS agent's cardiac arrest, or the arrival of the American agents, all but hijacking his and Emily's command centre as part of a joint operation granted by Prime Minister Humphries by request (or *coercion*) of President Harrison, in their pursuit of both Dominic Schilling and Sophie Jennings, wanted for their roles in the terrorist activities on mainland USA back in October.

Despite the man's failed attempts at catching Sophie, Brayden was still deemed the CIA's top agent and selected choice to head the American contingent taking up temporary residence within the Secret Intelligence Agency building alongside the Thames.

Thoughts of Barrington Abney surfaced, and Ryan couldn't help but feel sad at how his part in the whole saga had to come to an end. "I'll raise you a glass," he said. "Wherever you are."

His thoughts dissipated when his mobile began to vibrate on the table within the small hotel room. He snatched it up, seeing that it was Emily calling.

"Yes... yes... yes. I know, I know. I shan't be late." Ryan was referring to the New Year's Eve dinner date that Emily had badgered him into accepting. It was rare to spend an evening in the company of others not related to work or duty, and rarer still to receive an invitation to a private function. What was most surprising was getting the invite from Sophie in the first place, asking him and Emily to spend New Year's Eve with her and her family in Norfolk. Until then, neither of them had spoken, Sophie still holding him responsible for her father's death, even after hearing the evidence vindicating him, and seeing Marty Heywood's little black book, indicating that the man had worked alone, with his own ambitions. "I'll be in reception in a tick." He didn't wait for Emily to acknowledge him before disconnecting, placing the phone down.

Crossing the room, he checked his appearance in the mirrored door of the large fitted wardrobe that ran to the right, along the length of the short walkway into the room, and straightened his tie. Returning to the small table where his mobile phone was, he gathered it up, along with his wallet and wristwatch, placing them on and around his body as he made to exit the hotel room. Before leaving, he collected a gold-coloured gift bag that could only contain a bottle of wine of some sort, left in a corner near to where he'd stowed his small travel case.

Ryan believed you should never arrive at a dinner party without a gift offering, it was etiquette. He'd picked up the bottle of *Château Musar*, a red wine produced in Lebanon, from *Waitrose* earlier that day.

Stepping out of the hotel room, Ryan waited a moment in the corridor for the door to slowly close behind him before proceeding, taking the elevator to the reception where Emily had been waiting patiently for over half an hour.

⸻ ◆ ⸻

Ryan had never met Theodore Crossley who was, technically, Sophie's maternal grandfather, although it turned out, Harriet only carried her surrogately. After Harriet's death, the old man had happily taken

Meredith, Stanley and Charlie into his care, and would have accepted Sophie too had she not grown into womanhood so rapidly.

Driving the *Jaguar XJ* onto the driveway of the semi-detached house and parking it alongside the black *BMW* in front of the mahogany garage door, Ryan stopped the car and keyed off the ignition. He turned to Emily, looking apprehensive.

"I don't do social get-togethers," he said nervously. He was half-hoping that his phone would ring, a caller providing an elaborate excuse to make his apologies and forcing him to drive away. The mobile was in his jacket pocket and made no sounds at all. He was disappointed.

"Come on," said Emily cheerfully. "It'll be fine. Sophie's offered an olive branch; the least you can do is grab it. We'll enjoy a nice meal and make some pleasant conversations. Try to be happy. It's the end of the year; maybe a new year will see things better. The sooner you two are friends again, the sooner we can work out a way to get those kids back."

The kids... Ninety children who he'd aided Dominic into hightailing with.

"Thanks," groaned Ryan. "I was hoping you wouldn't remind me about the *GYGES* kids... not here, not tonight." She seemed to mention it at least once every day.

"Sorry," Emily muttered, embarrassed.

Since Emily had discovered his involvement with Dominic and Jennifer, and his complicity to their acquisition of the ninety children – plus the arrival of Brayden Scott and his American cohorts in the SIS building alongside the Thames – very little had been heard about them, including their whereabouts. Not wishing his association with Jennifer Ratcliff to be exposed, or to encourage further threat to Emily or Sophie's family, he'd kept a safe distance from the CEO of Kaplan Ratcliff.

"Let's get this over with," sighed Ryan in resignation, releasing the seatbelt and hooking open the car door. He climbed out, reached into the back seat for the bottle of wine, and then ambled across the garden towards the front door, his stride kicking up loose white stones and leaving deep muddy divots in the decorative driveway covering and crunching underfoot. He rang the doorbell just beneath the house number 'seventy-three'. A subtle chime 'dingdonged' from inside, just heard through the white PVC double-glazed door.

A figure shuffled into view, their identity obscured by the frosted glass panel in the door, but soon revealed to be the homeowner and host for the evening, Theodore Crossley. Behind Ryan, Emily was removing a bag of gifts she had purchased for Sophie's family.

"Evening, Ryan..."

"Theodore."

"Jus' Theo, me ol' son... only my dear departed mum and a school headmistress ever called me that..." he laughed, each word dripped cockney.

"Here," Ryan offered the wine to Theo.

"Lovely... Manners maketh the man," Theo beamed, accepting the wine. "Come... make yourself at home." Seeing Emily trot up the driveway made the old man's smile even wider. "My dear Emily... the children have been so looking forward to seeing you. Please, let's get in from the cold." Although winter in Britain, the temperature was more autumnal for December and barely below 11°C that New Year's Eve.

Emily returned Theo's smile and accepted a peck to the cheek as she drew closer, Theo momentarily barring the way in, a kiss the price to gain admittance.

In the corner of the sparsely furnished living room was a six-foot Nordic fir, bejewelled with baubles, fairy lights, tinsel and other festive tree ornaments, including a star at the top; about its base, a sprinkling of needles had been shed around the carpet despite Camilla having vacuumed only an hour earlier.

A few Christmas decorations hung around the room and upon the mantelpiece were a pair of jolly Santa lights, their fat stomachs gently changing colour from the LED lamps contained within. Between them, a nativity scene, and a couple of red pillar candles that, when lit, released the smell of cinnamon into the air.

Beneath the mantelpiece, an ornate gas open fire heated the room, flames dancing lazily across coals designed for visual effect rather than necessity. Ryan immediately felt its warmth as he stepped into the room. The absence of noise disconcerted him.

Above the fire and mantelpiece was the television, turned to standby.

Interpreting Ryan's puzzled look, Theo felt the urge to explain. "The children will be with us momentarily. They've been banished to their rooms for the duration it took to prepare. Sounds harsh, but believe me... five children underfoot, doesn't bode well." He laughed. "Please, take a seat... I'll summon them shortly."

Emily padded in behind Ryan and sat on a cream-coloured leather two-seater. Ryan took a matching armchair placed beside the Christmas tree, opposite to Emily.

"Can I get you two anything to wet your whistle?"

Before either Ryan or Emily could answer, Sophie casually stepped into the room and stopped a short way in front of the doorway.

"Sophie!" Emily squealed in delight, springing to her feet and embracing her friend in a sisterly fashion.

When Sophie had prised herself from Emily's grasp, Ryan quietly appraised the young woman. She looked different to how Ryan remembered her, which wasn't surprising. Wracking his brain, he couldn't remember the last time he had actually seen Sophie in the 'flesh'. Their last encounter had been in Los Angeles, twenty-five miles east of Palmdale, within the small hut where they'd shared a late breakfast and watched the *Boeing* take-off with Dominic and the ninety sons of *GYGES*. But she had been invisible then, and he realised that in actuality, the last time he 'saw' her was before she had left London and headed for America in search of her father.

It wasn't surprising she looked different. Sophie had aged by three physical years since their last meeting; she had been a gangly teen, with straggly blonde hair and dressed for comfort in jeans and a plain T-shirt. Now she was a beautiful woman wearing makeup and a *Savannah Miller* silver sequinned dress. Her golden hair, hanging loose and wavy, was longer than he remembered it, but then he was accustomed to seeing it tied back.

"Ryan." There was a slight edge to her voice. She may have offered an olive branch but she certainly hadn't forgiven Ryan with regards to her father. Even though he hadn't ordered George's death, he had withheld the man's whereabouts to pursue destroying Project *GYGES* instead, which made him tantamount for blame.

"Sophie..." Ryan spoke tenderly, his eyes looking doleful. He locked eyes with her and without thought used the flat of his left hand to rub his knee in a comforting motion. He couldn't help feeling guilty and looked pitiful.

"EMILY!!" Meredith, Stanley and Charlie charged into the room, exuberant and excited.

Theo had to step aside to avoid being clattered by his grandchildren. "Careful there," he grumbled.

The children crowded around the bespectacled woman, Meredith taking the seat next to her and Charlie awkwardly climbing onto her lap.

"Cor blimey, you kids! Give the lass some air to breathe!" admonished Theo half-heartedly.

Ryan turned his head away from Sophie who had been holding a stare, turning to Theo. "I think I'll have that drink now," he said. "Do you have any Scotch?"

The dining room was bigger than Ryan expected and surprisingly larger than the lounge, containing the largest table he had ever seen in a private dwelling. With enough seats to host a party of sixteen guests, the adults were placed at one end of the table whilst the children were at the other. Separating the two groups, there were three seats either side of the long table, though the gap wasn't big enough to set apart the noise levels, with the children talking loudest.

Theo was at the head of the table with Camilla to his right and Emily on his left. Sophie sat alongside Camilla opposite Ryan, but neither had engaged in any small talk and the mood between the two was palpably strained.

A woman in a maid's outfit wheeled in a trolley laden with plates full to the brim of food followed by a young man dressed in a tuxedo carrying a bottle of champagne, a plain white serving cloth draped over an arm.

Spotting the look of bewilderment shared between Ryan and Emily upon noticing the waiting staff, Theo felt the urge to speak. "I could quite get used to this... *opulence*," he said, indicating the man and woman serving food and drinks around the table. "Doesn't come cheap, mind; that I can tell ya. Alas, just for the occasion of bringing one set of friends together with our blessed family this New Year's Eve. Plus Camilla is the most atrocious cook... struggles even to cook beans on toast!" His laugh quickly subsided after receiving an unfavourable look from his wife.

After a starter of warm pigeon breast with a woodland salad of crispy bacon, wild mushrooms and blackberries there followed a choice of roast beef, pork or turkey and a selection of vegetables, with many different types of potato. Before dessert was served, Theo stood up with his champagne glass, a moment earlier refilled by the waiter.

"Okay, okay... listen up – kids at the end, hush please!" Theo waited a moment for silence to descend. "Before I get totally sozzled, allow me to make a quick toast. This year has been a terribly difficult year for us all. With Harriet... and then George," he shook his head mournfully, "My biggest regret is not being able to bury the hatchet with my Harry." His voice was close to cracking. He sighed, his eyes welling up; two dams close to bursting. "But light always follows darkness, no matter how black it is. The children are the light, and taking in Meredith, Stanley and Charlie has allowed me – us..." Theo reached for Camilla's hand, "... to get to know our grandchildren, and to meet our newest grandchild, the wondrous enigma that is Sophie. It hurts to say it... but I wouldn't change this for the world." A tear rolled down his cheek. "Hand on heart." There was a lump in his throat as he pulled his hand away from Camilla and rested it across his chest, "I wish you all good health and a happy, uneventful New Year. Let's bury the past and enjoy the rest of our lives... bottoms up! Cheers!" Theo raised his glass before taking a long sip.

A chorus of "Cheers," emanated from around the table. Champagne glasses being raised by the adults; fizzy drinks or squash in plastic cups by the children. One or two cups and glasses were clinked or tapped together.

"Enough said. Let us now eat cake!" Theo sat back down as servings of black forest gateau were distributed by the waitress and champagne glasses were refilled by the waiter. Unseen by any, the waiter gave the waitress a slight nod, as though confirming something. She acknowledged it with a thin smile.

From within Ryan's jacket pocket his mobile phone began to vibrate. Earlier he'd turned off the ringtone, thinking it would be rude to sound during dinner. Reaching into his pocket he pulled the handset free. "Excuse me," he said apologetically. He glanced at the caller ID; he recognised the number. "I need to take this." He stood up as his dessert was set at his place.

Emily turned and looked at Ryan briefly but gave the matter little attention.

Standing up, he strode out into the living room and pressed the green acceptance icon, raising the phone to his ear. "Hello?"

"*Have you seen the news?*" It was the Chief of SIS, and he sounded grave.

"No, what's happened?"

"*Turn it on.*" The Chief didn't elaborate.

Ryan found the TV remote and pointed it towards the LCD screen above the fireplace. He pressed the red button to activate it. A few moments later he was flicking through the channels until he came to one of the twenty-four hour news channels. A red 'breaking news' banner flashed across the bottom of the screen highlighting details of a string of robberies taking place simultaneously across Scotland.

"*... so far there's been reports of at least a dozen burglaries across Scotland tonight, the first of which occurred around nine o'clock...*" The outside reporter was replaced on the screen by a studio news presenter. "*And what makes these burglaries significant?*" he asked, slightly disinterested. The picture changed back to that of the outside reporter. "*Well, the nature of the burglaries, and the properties being targeted; mostly stately homes, the occupants all owning valuable assets – including jewellery and works of art. The thefts all appear to have been synchronised to take place at the same time... and indeed, we're getting further reports of ongoing incidents, including a break-in at a home that belongs to Hollywood actor Ewan McGregor.*"

"Okay, Chief. You've got my attention... a number of high profile burglaries, hardly a threat to national security. What's that got to do with us?"

"On the face, nothing. But, it's what's not being broadcast that is interesting. Something about 'invisible burglars'. I only know of one person capable of that feat. A friend of yours, I believe."

"It's not her," said Ryan firmly.

"Are you sure?"

"I know for a fact. Unless she has developed the ability to be in two places at the same time," he said stuffily. "I'm with her now..." Using the remote, Ryan switched off the television.

"I've just got off the phone with the Prime Minister. He wants all our best people on this. I want you to head the team."

"What about the search for Dominic Schilling?"

"The trail has gone cold... let the Americans worry about him. I'm to attend an emergency COBRA meeting in the morning; see if you can learn anything by then."

"But sir, it's New Year's Eve..."

"Yes...? But only for a couple more hours..." The Chief of the British Secret Intelligence Service ended the call leaving Ryan holding the mobile to his ear for a little longer than necessary.

"Happy New Year," Ryan whispered solemnly into empty air. He turned to go back to the dining room.

Smash!

The sound of a plate shattering as though from impact halted Ryan's progress. Half-expecting a babble of excited or dismayed voices, the fact no noise followed seemed strange.

"What's go–" *ing on?* He stopped midsentence as he entered the dining room. Around the table bodies lay slumped back, to the side or, in Theo's case, crashed forward, all within their chairs. The force of Theo's head colliding with the dessert plate was what had caused the commotion.

Ryan walked to Emily who was closest to the door. "Emily?" With his right hand he felt her neck for a pulse. It was there, and reassuringly strong. He tried shaking her but she was non-responsive. Out cold. Like everyone else around the table, Emily had been drugged. Swiftly, he scanned the area. Sophie was slouching against Camilla who was sitting propped up with her head drooping forward. The children at the other end of the table lay across each other or rested against the table, heads in plates, drinks knocked over.

"... let him know that we're ahead of schedule." The waiter was talking to the woman when he stepped into the room and stopped, surprised to see Ryan standing and not unconscious, looking accusingly at him. "You should be..." Before he could finish, Ryan had charged bull-like into him, knocking the waiter into an oak buffet and hutch cabinet. Glassware and display crockery toppled and crashed inside from the impact.

"Hey!" Hearing the tumult, the woman came to the door holding a gun pointing ahead of her. "Get off him, man!"

The waiter, restrained under Ryan's full weight, grunted as Ryan punched him hard in the face. "Shoot him!" he half-shouted, half-slurred, his mouth swollen and bubbling blood.

"He said no one was to get hurt!" Torment was in the woman's voice, the gun twitching in her shaking grasp.

"Just do it!" he screamed frantically.

Ryan punched the man again to silence him, oblivious to the weapon pointed at his back. Before he could do the waiter any more harm, the woman pressed the trigger. The silencer softened the sound of the gunshot, but it was loud enough to echo around the house.

The bullet tore into the back of Ryan's right shoulder, hurling him forward. He spun around, lifting a hand either in useless defence or surrender. "No!" he rasped, seeing the danger and the intense look on the woman's face.

"Too bad old man," she said, squeezing the trigger, releasing the gun's deadly load.

CHAPTER TWENTY-SEVEN
DOMINIC

THE WAREHOUSE HAD BEEN purchased through an off-shore investment company that was indirectly linked, though untraceable, to Kaplan Ratcliff. Hidden within an industrial district to the south-east of Oban (a couple of road turnings off Gallanach Road) the huge warehouse was where Dominic stood outside waiting at the large up-and-over roll-up door which was open like a hungry mouth.

A little deeper in, the *Mitsubishi Fuso* truck had been parked, equipped throughout with enough state-of-the-art technology to successfully mount a major surveillance operation, or oversee the launch of a space rocket. Inside, Garret and Melvyn continued to monitor the cadets as they finished carrying out their individual missions and began to make their way home. This place served that purpose, the agreed upon drop-off centre.

The mobile phone in Dominic's hand began to ring, a pre-set jingle that came with the cheap communication device, bought for the occasion and which he intended to dispose of soon after.

"Hello." He heard a note of Scottish in his voice. *Probably from being around Elspeth so much*, he mused. It was funny how easy one could adopt a regional accent if you spent long enough exposed to it.

"Dom, um... things haven't gone all to plan." Dominic recognised the voice, though the hint of nervousness made the man at the other end sound slightly higher pitched. *"Natasha killed one of the guests."*

"Go on..."

The caller began to explain the events leading up to when the man, Ryan Barber, had attacked him. "*She had no choice,*" he offered for reasoning. "*It was him... or me.*"

"It was unavoidable then. Apart from that, did you get the job done?" Dominic eagerly asked.

"*Sure, what do you take us for? Muppets?*"

Do I need to answer that, Dominic thought. "And everyone else... they all right?"

"*Exactly as you instructed.*"

"Good. Killing Ryan is a bit of an inconvenience I'll have you know; we had a bit of a *thing* going on. Aside from that, it's going to be okay. Carry on as we planned within the set timeframes. Make sure the children are comfortable before you set off. They are important and integral to what we're doing here. The roads should be quiet, so I expect to see you around lunchtime tomorrow..."

"*What about the others?*" A note of concern was in the caller's voice.

"What about them?" Dominic volleyed back irritably.

"*They've seen our faces!*"

Dominic sighed. "So?"

"*They'll be able to I.D us...*" He spoke condescendingly.

"Hector, just leave them be. It's imperative no harm comes to them," said Dominic. "Especially the women." *Especially one in particular...*

"*Whatever man.*"

Dominic hastily disconnected so as to make a call. There was someone he thought might be interested to learn of the latest developments. He keyed in a number and pressed connect. Almost immediately he heard the ringing tone.

"Hi, this is Jennifer Ratcliff. I'm not available at the moment. You can leave a message or contact my secretary on..."

"It's Dominic... Why do you never answer your phone, damn it! Call me back as soon as you hear this." Angrily, he ended the connection and placed the phone deep in his pocket and started pacing back and forth alongside the truck, frequently checking his watch.

The kids will start arriving soon, he thought as time ticked closer to midnight. Every so often whoops of glee could be heard from within the *Mitsubishi Fuso* as Garret and Melvyn communicated with the cadets as they concluded their missions.

As the first of many nondescript vans rolled into the warehouse, the first of the night's fireworks began to fizzle and pop in the background, splashing bursts of light and colour in and around Oban's clear night sky, with the most vibrant taking place in George Street accompanied by explosive booms that could be felt underfoot.

The annual Hogmanay celebrations were in full swing.

Although a couple of miles due south, Dominic could hear and see the pyrotechnics clearly from outside the warehouse. Dominic hurried in after the white transit van, directing the driver to pull in just ahead of the mobile command centre.

A cadet climbed out from the passenger seat and ambled cockily towards Dominic. He wore a badge pinned to his chest, like the type presented on an age specific birthday card; the number '15' was printed upon it. Although somewhat impersonal, the cadets weren't given names, but instead allocated a number.

"Was it a success, Fifteen?" asked Dominic. Despite growing accustomed to the cold on St. Kilda, he felt a bit chilled inside the warehouse from keeping the roll-up doors open all night. He planted his hands deep into his jacket pocket, fingers of one wrapping around his phone.

"Moderately, yes," he replied positively. "Two banks, a bookmaker and a small jeweller in Kilmartin. About a quarter-of-a-million quid I reckon," he said cheerfully.

"Excellent. A great start." Dominic removed his hands and rubbed them together either gleefully or for warmth. Five minutes later cadet number '45' turned up in a local hire truck (which he'd stolen). When asked what he had managed to collect, the lad reeled off a list with an accumulative value similar to the first arrival's.

All through the night and early into the following morning, cars, vans, trucks and lorries, pulled into the warehouse loaded with cash, gold, diamonds, jewellery, paintings, designer clothing, bearer bonds, and sundry other items, the combined amount eclipsing £200 million.

By lunchtime New Year's Day, the plunder had been separated and sorted and all the cadets, now exhausted, were accounted for and seated within a ferry cruising across choppy waters destined for St. Kilda.

Dominic had watched them leave the warehouse in a coach, like they were heading on a daytrip or going on holiday. Seeing them off, he felt immense pride swell within him at what they had all achieved in such a little space of time.

Jennifer Ratcliff finally called him back just as a grey *Ford Tourneo* pulled into the parking area of the warehouse. Guards wearing concealed weapons advanced on the vehicle whilst Dominic spoke into his phone. Three men in total, taking up positions either side of the van as it came to a standstill.

"Finally," grunted Dominic.

"*I got your message Dom. Sorry, I was at a party until late... and this morning, well, you know how it is with drinking too much gin.*"

"Sure." His alcoholic nemesis was whisky. In the background the driver of the *Tourneo* opened his door and stepped out, his hands spread out high enough not to alarm the guards. He took a couple of steps towards the rear passenger door and opened it. One of the guards peered inside.

"*I gather last night went well. It's all over the news. The media is having a field day!*"

"It mostly went to plan," agreed Dominic. "It's just the other part of what we discussed we've had a slight hiccup."

Jennifer went quiet for a moment. "*The children?*" she asked fearfully.

"No... Ryan," replied Dominic. "He's dead."

Humourlessly, Jennifer started to laugh at the other end of the phone.

CHAPTER TWENTY-EIGHT
SOPHIE

"HE'S NOT DEAD..." SOPHIE was kneeling next to the MI6 unit leader and could feel his pulse, although weak and the man had lost a considerable amount of blood.

Emily was close by, weeping, completely useless.

Theo and Camilla were still sitting at the dining table, both in a state of disorientation and befuddlement. The twins: Josephine and Henry were both out cold, still in their places along one side of the table; half-eaten desserts just ahead of them beside toppled cups of juice. The seats next to - and opposite - them, were all empty.

Meredith, Stanley and Charlie were missing.

A sideward glance to a clock on the wall informed Sophie that the time was long after midnight. Hands pointed to the three and the six.

3:30 a.m.

Owing to being drugged, they'd missed the ringing in of the New Year, a minor point in the grand scheme of events.

"Where am I?" asked Theo in a daze, slurring slightly. He had lifted his head up from the broken plate in front of him; black forest gateau cream and chocolate sponge had congealed thickly to his left cheek.

"He needs urgent medical treatment," said Sophie, stating the obvious.

"I'm on it." Emily forced herself into action. With her mobile in her hand, she keyed in: '999'.

"Where are the kids?" Theo was gaining cognisance by the second, alarm compelling him to stand. Unsteadily, he fell back into his seat where he looked defeated.

"What?" Sophie looked up from Ryan. She hadn't noticed her brothers and sister were gone. When she had come to, the first sight she encountered was Ryan, sprawled awkwardly behind her with his life fluid soaking into the carpet about her feet. Although she and Ryan were not on the best of terms at that moment, she hadn't wanted him dead. Not yet at any rate.

"Oh God, no..." Emily lowered the mobile whilst she deliberated over the situation. Helplessness bounded towards her, saddled with that other deleterious emotion, fear.

"*Which emergency service do you require?*" a very alert voice sounded loud through Emily's mobile earpiece, galvanising her. Emily returned her attention to the call.

"Ambulance," she said, followed with the nature of the incident and her address.

"Meredith!" Sophie charged past Emily, bounding up the stairs two at a time, beginning what quickly turned into a fruitless search for all that remained of her father's family.

***

Sophie had not experienced many New Year's Days, but this was proving to be the absolute worst start to a year thus far.

Sitting in a waiting area in the Norwich and Norfolk University hospital, Sophie and Emily passed the time by flicking through year-old-magazines and staring at a variety of *NHS* posters adorning the walls surrounding the room with advice and information on a diverse range of illnesses and ailments; cancer, HIV, pregnancy, herpes, impotence... amongst others; there was a notice for pretty much everything, offering plenty of scope to mull and worry over.

After five hours of waiting, a male doctor wearing a blue tunic and matching trousers, stepped in; a stethoscope was draped around his shoulder and his *NHS* ID card was pinned to a pocket. He wore a serious expression on his ageless face, and his virtually-bald head gave him the appearance of a very tall baby. Beneath the bright fluorescents, his scalp shone greasily from the glare.

"Miss Porter?"

"Yes," replied Emily, shuffling expectantly forward on her seat.

"Would you like to come this way...?"

Before Emily had risen, Sophie was on her feet. The doctor gave her a look of disapproval and was about to speak.

"It's okay... Ryan Barber is her grandfather," Emily approved.

The doctor's demeanour softened. "Very well, please follow me." The doctor led the two young women down a short corridor, up a double flight of stairs and into a corridor, off which doors to a number of private wards idly watched as they passed. After stepping past the sixth, the doctor opened the seventh and entered without hesitation. "Close the door behind you," he said as Emily and Sophie followed him in. A light-blue curtain screened most the room from sight but did nothing to hide the telltale sounds of an occupant on life-support or the surgical smells that assailed their nostrils.

"Is Ryan going to be okay?" asked Emily timidly, momentarily returned to childhood where she was a shy and very nervous girl.

"Your father sustained two gunshot wounds and had lost a lot of blood," Ryan *wasn't* her father, but Emily didn't correct him. The doctor continued: "One bullet hit him in the back – just to the centre, beneath his neck – the other was to the chest, where a small amount of damage was sustained to his heart. We managed to remove both bullets and carried out an emergency surgery, and I'm pleased to say that his condition is stable. He will, however, require more operations to repair the damage to his heart, which we've scheduled for later today."

"Oh." Emily felt weak in the knees and desperately wanted to sit down.

"We have kept him on life-support and heavily sedated," the doctor went on, "but come on in, you may briefly see him..." The doctor pulled open the curtain like a magician unveiling a magic trick, to reveal Ryan lying propped up in a bed, a tube protruding from his mouth, hooked up to a ventilator machine that made sucking and wheezing sounds, placed next to him beneath an electronic monitor that displayed the man's vitals.

Ryan's skin was sallow and his face looked gaunt and old, like he had aged more than a hundred years since Emily had last seen him. Where his hair was always tidy and glossy black, it was now unkempt, thinning slightly and showing signs of silvery-grey.

Sophie followed Emily, walking round behind the doctor to stand over on the opposite side of the bed. Seeing the breathing device attached to Ryan's face, and the man's change of appearance made Emily gasp aloud. She threw a hand to her mouth, afraid of what noise or words might next escape through her lips.

Finding courage, Emily twisted her neck to face the doctor. "When will he be... better?" asked Emily, deeply disturbed by the sight of her mentor.

"We can only hope. In time, if the operation goes well, he should make a full recovery. It might not look it, but your father was lucky. Had the bullet entered his chest a fraction to the left, we wouldn't be here now having this conversation."

"Can you give us a date for when we can take him out of here?" asked Sophie unaffected by Ryan's incapacity and affliction. "Assuming the operation later today goes okay."

"Who can say... Miss?"

"Jennings," replied Sophie.

"Miss *Jennings*... Everyone recovers at different rates. Healing from the incision made to his sternum alone is going to take six-to-eight weeks. Also, there will be an element of rehabilitation. And it's not just the physical wounds to overcome, there's the psychological ones too. Your grandfather isn't going to be back to full strength for several months... or years even."

What the doctor said didn't sink in. "And what about his work?" Sophie pressed. "He has an important job."

The doctor held back his feelings of frustration and impatience. Calmly, he replied: "In time, he'll be able to go back to work. But for now, we really need to concentrate on him pulling through the operation this afternoon... and for him to get better first." The doctor smiled revealing a full set of gleaming white teeth, which annoyed Sophie immensely. "Now, if you will forgive me. I have other patients to visit... you can have five minutes with him, then you must leave." He waited a little longer than necessary before turning to leave.

"I hate admitting it, but we need you Ryan," whispered Sophie, leaning over to within an inch of the man's inert face.

Emily thought for a second that the younger woman was going to gently kiss him.

As if in response his closed eyelids flickered. Encouraged, Sophie added: "I need you to help me find my family. They're only children, and they're likely very scared."

"Come on. We're wasting time here. We'll come back later... maybe, after his next operation, he'll be awake by then."

Sophie straightened up slowly. "You're right," she said. "But what now? What do we do? I'm not going to abandon Meredith, Stanley and Charlie... like we abandoned my father."

Emily looked down guiltily. Not a day had gone by where she

hadn't wished she could have gone back to the motel room, last October. She could easily have ignored Ryan and insisted on pursuing the search for George Jennings instead of going after Project *GYGES*. She couldn't help thinking that had they rejected his mission, Sophie's father would likely have still been alive.

"We're not making the same mistake twice," asserted Emily. "But we can't do this alone; and we can't rely on Ryan." Leaving Ryan's room and the noise of the ventilator machine, wheezing and clattering with every forced lungful of air, and the bleeps of the ECG machine, they walked purposefully down surgically-clean corridors and brightly-lit aisles, until they came to the hospital's exit.

"Where are we going?" asked Sophie hurrying behind Emily to keep up. Emily appeared determined.

"Back to London," said Emily breathily. "85 Albert Embankment to be precise."

"Your work?"

"Our help," Emily corrected. "But you're not going to like it."

CHAPTER TWENTY-NINE
BRAYDEN

LESS KEEN THAN A vegetarian at an all you can eat sausage contest, Brayden Scott arrived in London. It was on a cold, wet November morning after a seven hour flight from Washington that had been twice delayed, that the CIA agent stepped foot into Heathrow's arrival terminal in a foul mood. The first problem had been due to a mechanical fault, which was then followed a little later by a 'terrorist threat' within Dulles International Airport, an occurrence that seemed to happen at least once a week.

Now, after two soggy months in England and with very little to show for missing Thanks Giving, Christmas and New Year's Eve with his wife Jordana, his personal morale and motivation had ebbed to an all-time low.

Joining him for breakfast at the London Marriott Hotel County Hall, Christina Mullins, who was dressed casually in black jogging bottoms and a hooded sweatshirt that bore the FBI insignia across the back, had served herself breakfast from the buffet tables, and was holding a glass of grapefruit juice in one hand and her plate in the other as she arrived.

"Mornin'" Christina greeted cheerfully. She sat down opposite the six-foot-two-inch man, placed her breakfast ahead of her and helped herself to the pot of coffee. "Happy New Year," she said as an afterthought.

"Is it?" Brayden asked miserably. He was feeling especially homesick that morning, tired also. To 'see in' the New Year with his wife, he'd had to stay awake until 5:00 a.m. due to the time difference, speaking to her via the hotel room phone and wishing her all the platitudes as the countdown had concluded back in Washington. Unable to sleep, an hour later he'd visited the fitness centre where he was the sole occupant, and did forty minutes' worth of cardio before doing a few laps in the swimming pool.

Around the spacious dining area were a lot of guests eating or picking at food, some looking worse for wear after a long night celebrating the New Year, whilst others appeared surprisingly spritely.

"Did you see the fireworks?" Christina asked, attempting light conversation.

"Couldn't avoid them from my room, really," moaned Brayden. Most people would have been impressed with his accommodation overlooking the Thames, especially with the spectacular views of Big Ben and the Houses of Parliament just over the other side of the river. He had been perfectly placed to watch the annual fireworks display, foregoing the need to purchase a ticket; but instead of watching them avidly like most hotel guests had, he'd closed the curtains tight and watched cable television instead.

"Mmm, mm. We moan about British food, but I honestly haven't tasted bacon anywhere better than here," Christina trumpeted, cramming a forkful of meat into her mouth.

Brayden shrugged, not bothered.

"Lighten up, Brayden. People back home would give a kidney to be doing this. And we're here for free! We should make the most of it. Take some downtime and do some of the sights. Maybe get in a show."

Not hearing anything Christina had said, Brayden leaned forward and looked the FBI agent in the eyes. "You know, I think us being here is a complete waste of time. We're never going to find Dominic... or that *girl*. Let's face it; we're no nearer now than we were back in Washington."

"There have been a few leads," said Christina between mouthfuls.

"Mostly dead-ends," replied Brayden coldly. "I wouldn't be surprised if MI6 are giving us a run-around. DAMN!" he slammed his hands hard against the table startling some breakfast-goers close by. Christina's breakfast jumped up a couple of millimetres from the impact. "We were so close to nabbing her," he complained. Christina had heard it before. "I wish I'd put a bullet into her head when I'd had the chance."

You never had the chance, mused Christina as she continued to enjoy her breakfast.

Brayden stood up. "I'll catch you sometime later; I need to get some fresh air," he said, adding as he left: "I think it's time we see sense and prepare ourselves to go home."

⎯⎯⎯⎯◆⎯⎯⎯⎯

The London Eye was just a bit further along from the hotel. To get to it you passed a number of other tourist 'attractions', including a Sea Life centre and The London Dungeon, and some street performers who, Brayden reflected, seemed to 'entertain' in spots every dozen yards from a visitor attraction. Already by 12:00 p.m. a large throng of tourists were gathered about the Eye's entrance base, many queuing to access it or to collect tickets from the nearby ticket kiosk.

Brayden couldn't be bothered with the big wheel; they had them back home, some a lot bigger. Instead he hurried past with his hand buried deep in his jacket pocket, his shoulders hunched, and headed away along The Queen's Walk towards Jubilee Gardens, a public park created in 1977 to mark the Silver Jubilee of Queen Elizabeth II.

Within the park Brayden found a bench and sat down to ponder the situation. Despite the masses of people passing through the park, he found it peaceful there, almost cathartic, and barely noticed anyone.

Putting an end to the tranquillity, Brayden's mobile phone began to vibrate in his pocket. Sighing, he pulled it free and answered.

"Yea, Brayden..."

"*Are you sitting comfortably?*" Although Christina Mullins was calling from the nearby hotel, the phone reception was awful and Brayden could barely hear her.

"What's up Agent Mullins? It's only been ten minutes, are you missing your babysitter? Or couldn't you get tickets to a show?" He didn't hide his agitation and spoke loudly, startling a young couple holding hands as they passed by.

Ignoring the comment, Mullins continued. "*I think we may have a break in our hunt for Dominic Schilling.*"

Brayden had heard this line before. "If you think you can change my mind about us going home by using that ruse, you can forget it."

"*Have you been watching the news? Those burglaries? Up in Scotland?*"

Brayden recalled seeing something whilst willing away the time, flicking through the channels late last night; this had been a little before seeing in the American New Year over the phone with his wife. "What about them?" He did nothing to mask the lack of interest in his voice.

"*It's not common knowledge, but I'm hearing some peculiarities about those burglaries from our sources,*" said Mullins cryptically. Her sources usually meant a contact within the joint CIA/FBI operation unit. Possibly Mac, the computer-geek-looking guy they'd grown close to these past two months.

"Go on."

"*Some eyewitness accounts make little or no sense...*"

"Mullins YOU'RE currently making little or no sense. Get to the point."

"They're saying that all the items just disappeared or vanished in thin air. As though taken by a—"

"Ghost," finished Brayden. "Our girl?"

"I don't know. Possibly... but I doubt she could be responsible for all of the thefts; there were more than a couple of hundred incidents last night, right across Scotland. Same M.O. She's talented, but I don't even think she could pull off something that audacious."

"Quite. Have you spoken to Emily yet?"

"I've tried, but she had no comment. She's busy dealing with a major incident involving Ryan. Apparently he was shot last night..."

"Jeez. Happy New Year Ryan," Brayden muttered sarcastically. "I think we need to head over to centre command and see what the hell is going on."

"Am I to take it your plans to go home are now moot?" asked Mullins playfully.

"No... Just on hold," he said. "I'll meet you in the hotel's foyer in ten minutes. That should give you enough time to make yourself presentable."

"Sod off, Brayden! A girl needs at least an hour to do that!"

CHAPTER THIRTY
EMILY

THREE HOURS WAS ALL it took for Emily and Sophie to arrive within the small operations room – or what Brayden Scott referred to as *centre command* – which Ryan ordinarily managed.

Despite working there, entering the MI6 building overlooking London's River Thames wasn't a casual affair. Security in one of the world's foremost intelligence agencies was intense, as one might expect. Passing through a variety of checkpoints, including a basic swipe-card operated door, its activation box affixed to the wall just to one side of the entrance; this was then followed by fingerprint analysis, a retinal scan and a body check from a butch woman in an official uniform (black trousers, white shirt and a gold badge like a sheriff's star pinned to her breast), a detection wand in her hand which she ran up and down each of their bodies, clearly savouring the task. Clearing security, the guard looked immensely disappointed, waving them on with a grunt.

"That was easy," stated Sophie, having never been to the SIS building before. "I thought it would be like Fort Knox."

"Ryan had your details uploaded into the system before you disappeared to America months ago."

"Including my retinal images?" she asked doubtfully.

"There are ways," said Emily cryptically, making no attempt

to enlighten her. "Here, I almost forgot." Emily reached into her handbag. "Your ID. You should wear it at all times."

Sophie accepted the plastic card. It was contained within a cardholder on a lanyard. She studied it for a moment, holding it by the cord. "Cool! Sophie C. Jennings, Intelligence Officer," she said. "*Intelligence Officer!*" she repeated, giggling. "Does that come with a salary?" Not waiting for a response, another question immediately leapt to mind: "What's the 'C' stand for?"

"Clara," replied Emily. "Ryan found it on your original birth certificate in George's locker at Kaplan Ratcliff... after the 'accident'." She made inverted commas with both of her index fingers. "It was at the same time he found the photograph and learned the truth about your father's CIA background. It's when he discovered Clara to be your biological mother."

"Huh... how about that," Sophie said softly. "I didn't know I had a middle name," she said whimsically.

Entering Ryan's command room for the first time came as a bit of a shock to Sophie; it was not what she had expected, and looked more like a call centre than a hub for secret intelligence operations.

The room was stuffy, the overhead heaters pumping out hot air unnecessarily. Mac was the only analyst on duty, practically living on site twenty-four-seven. Dressed in Bermuda shorts and a T-shirt, he couldn't have looked less like a SIS officer had he tried.

"Emily!" gasped Mac. "I wasn't expecting anyone else in..." his cheeks flushed red under the two women's appraising looks. "It's New Year's Day..." as though asserting this explained his presence.

"I guess that's why it's so hot in here," said Sophie with disdain.

"Have you not heard about Ryan?" asked Emily, crossing the room to a small electronic panel built into the wall. She punched a button a few times, adjusting the setting of the air conditioning. "Go put some clothes on... this isn't Miami."

Thoughts of Miami sprung into Sophie's mind, and with them, Barry. The man had stayed with her after the *GYGES* operation, offering to help Sophie find and rescue her father. They'd shared a hotel room in Miami, and he'd comforted her after learning of her father's death. Then they'd flown to Cuba together. Two days later he was dead, killed in the line of duty, sacrificing himself to facilitate Sophie's escape.

As Mac was about to protest, the doors to the office smoothly slid open and in stepped Brayden Scott, followed close behind by Christina Mullins.

Alarm flashed up onto Sophie's face before the Americans had a proper chance to clock her. Instantly, she vanished, but not without notice.

"Soph–" Emily started, noticing the younger woman's disappearance. For a moment she'd forgotten Sophie could do that. The last time she had been present when the younger woman had used her ability, it had been back in George Jennings' apartment in Chelsea just after she had returned from America.

"What... just... happened?" asked Mac somewhat baffled.

"She's here." Initially Brayden had thought he'd imagined the blonde haired woman, so swift was her vanishing act, but Emily – beginning to speak her name – all but confirmed it. Effortlessly a handgun appeared in the CIA agent's hand.

"Wait! STOP!" Emily demanded.

"I thought I recognised you. It's been bugging me for ages... you were with *her* in Washington. You had different colour hair then... lighter."

"What's going on Brayden?" Christina who had walked in behind the CIA man hadn't seen anything. "Who's here?" Proactively she unholstered her own weapon sensing the other man's anxiety.

"Our girl... Sophie," replied Brayden triumphantly, sweeping his weapon from one side of the office to the other. "And this... *Emily Porter* is her accomplice."

"Agent Scott, we can explain," started Emily, walking so that she was standing directly in front of the man, between – she believed – him and where Sophie was now likely standing.

"I think you'd better!"

"Lower your gun first," requested Emily, "and then we will."

Brayden held his weapon fast making no signs of re-holstering it. After a long moment he sighed and slipped the gun back in its place beneath his jacket. "Okay. I'll hear you out. And it better be good, your agency is going to be in a whole heap of trouble after this." He moved in closer and sat on the edge of a desk. "After you've finished, you will assist me by letting us take Sophie Jennings into custody." To emphasise the point, a pair of standard FBI-issue metal cuffs appeared in Christina's hand. She twirled one of the rings around her middle finger playfully. "Now, show yourself, Sophie. I like to be seeing who it is I'm speaking with."

As effortlessly as she had vanished, Sophie reappeared. To blink, you would miss the transformation.

After drinking the contents of the glass vial back at her old apartment in October, Sophie's DNA had been irrevocably altered. Initially she had faded back into existence, a warm, euphoric feeling spreading through her body. At first, she was so pleased to have a physical appearance, she hadn't noticed that the effect did not wear off, unlike the serum she'd had to inject herself with three or four times a day. After three days of being 'visible', Sophie wondered whether her *normal* look was permanent, she tried to make herself disappear again. Concentrating hard, she had discovered that the ability, for so long considered a curse, was still available to her – only now under her full control. She vanished as suddenly as light would disappear from a bulb after clicking a switch. A couple of minutes later she concentrated hard again, this time thinking herself 'real'. Instantly she had watched herself casually reappear. It had been exhilarating, and, for the first time, Sophie actually appreciated the gift she had been born with.

"Does it hurt?" Brayden watched as Sophie's physical appearance was restored. She was standing next to Emily, exactly where she had been before the FBI and CIA agents had entered the room. Seeing the lanyard draped around the young woman's neck and the ID card hanging from it, he added with a nod: "Agent Jennings."

"Not if I don't hit you," replied Sophie, seriously.

Brayden smiled. *The broad is funny*, he mused.

"So, you were going to explain to us. What's going on?" Mullins directed the question to Emily. She had re-holstered her gun just after Brayden.

Emily pulled up an office chair on castors and sat down. Firmly, she said: "First, you tell us what really happened to Barry."

A look of sadness and, something else, flashed across Sophie's face. The muscles in her cheekbones tensed and her eyes hardened.

"You've read the report no doubt," replied Brayden dismissively.

"A little too contrived," Emily criticised. "What REALLY happened?"

Brayden sighed, dropping his guard. "Really, there's not much else to add. I went to get him a coffee, when I got back, he was having a heart attack and a nurse was sounding the alarm. I called for help, and then watched as the doctors worked to save his life. I watched him die from the corridor," adding, sardonically, "front row seat."

Sophie shied away. Coupled with her earlier thoughts of the man, it took a lot of effort to fight back the tears that threatened to leak from her eyes. It felt silly. She had hardly known the young agent, but in the few days they'd travelled together after meeting for the first time on the jet at Dulles International Airport, strange emotions and feelings had engulfed her, sensations that she'd never known existed and could never have learned from a computer programme. Two months had passed since Barry had died and those feelings, interlaced with grief, continued to spit and flame beneath the surface.

Accepting Brayden's response, Emily's steadfastness softened. "Okay, what do you want to know?"

Mirroring his boss, Mac also sat down, though on the other side of a desk partition behind two work areas and Emily's office space.

Relieved the tension in the young woman's voice had lessened, the CIA agent relaxed. "Your involvement with Dominic Schilling?" asked Brayden, propping himself up against a desk.

"Nothing like cutting to the chase," replied Emily stiffly.

"He murdered my mother," interjected Sophie, pain still evident in her tone. "After you kidnapped her... and did whatever..." She couldn't finish. Breaking the seal to her emotions allowed heartache to flow flagrantly. The loss of her mother, her father, and then Barry... it was overwhelming.

"Yes, I know that... and I'm deeply sorry. Truly... Sincerely..." They just sounded like words being reeled off an autocue, there was no candour in his voice. "It wasn't part of the plan, I get it. It seems Dominic had his own ulterior motives, of which you surprisingly became allied to, a couple of months later."

"It's a long story," said Emily.

"Oh? I've got plenty of time... it's New Year's Day. There's little on the TV. What about you Mullins?"

"Ditto," she muttered. "It's not like we've any place better to be, stuck over here... away from our families, at *Christmas*, an' all."

Ignoring the sarcasm in the FBI agent's comment, Emily took a moment to compose herself, to clear her thoughts and to get her story straight. Clearly she couldn't divulge everything; to do so would be an admission of guilt and draw attention to their recent operations in Washington, California and Nevada. The fallout would cause a political disaster for Great Britain, tarnish the reputation of MI6 and likely start hostilities between the USA and the British nation. But Emily knew the Americans were not stupid and that they already suspected MI6 were involved somehow. Sophie's presence in the room all but confirmed it.

"Dominic had been made Director of Intelligence at Kaplan Ratcliff," started Emily confidently. "Our organisations had a joint interest and it was felt that we could work together with him to achieve a mutually beneficial outcome."

"And you were happy with that?" Brayden asked Sophie incredulously.

"I would hardly say 'happy'," replied Sophie haughtily. "Far from it. I wanted to kill him. STILL want to kill him..."

"We persuaded Sophie to put aside her differences... for the greater good," offered Emily by way of explanation.

"Greater good? You mean destroying George Jennings' work? Killing countless American soldiers? Killing George, Sophie's father?"

"No, nothing like that," she lied. Quickly she relayed a concocted story which she hoped would exonerate them and bring the CIA on side. "We had received intelligence that Kaplan Ratcliff wanted to steal back their research from America, and at the same time put the American project back in the dark ages."

"Were they equipped to do that?" asked Mullins who had been quietly digesting Emily's explanation.

"Yes," replied Emily. "As their former Assistant Intelligence Officer, I know what they are capable of. Militarily, they have enough resources to take on a small country and beat them in a war; weapons, personnel, you name it, they have it."

"But they're a biochemical company?" Brayden didn't sound convinced.

"On the face of it, sure. Genetics and biochemistry is their main bread and butter, but behind the scenes they undertake a number of other activities. Security and intelligence gathering; fighting private wars is a lucrative business." Emily paused, allowing Brayden an opportunity to challenge her further. He didn't, so she continued. "Our intel indicated that Kaplan Ratcliff were going to use George Jennings' research to better themselves, and enrich their own army for nefarious means."

"Okay," seeming to accept what she said. "How does that tie-in with your involvement?" asked Brayden, folding his arms across his chest and listening intently. His expression indicated that he was finding it difficult to believe the tale.

"We read the danger signs early. As a result, we felt the best cause of action would be to neutralise the threat from within. We set up a unit headed by Sir Marty Heywood, who feigned allegiance with Dominic Schilling - so we thought - to infiltrate Kaplan Ratcliff and sabotage their plans. We've since discovered that Marty had gone rogue and had sided with them instead. Sophie and myself were sent to America to assist with intercepting Dominic, to putting a stop to what they intended to do."

"Sir Marty Heywood?" Brayden wore a puzzled expression.

"Knighted for his charity work, amongst things," replied Emily a little sheepishly.

"It appears he was too charitable," grunted Brayden.

"Quite," Emily replied disappointedly. "We had contact with Dominic in Washington, and went along with the charade, helping him evade capture at Dulles Airport as we had no idea where the planned attack was going to happen. It was shortly after that he discovered our true intentions, presumably from Marty Heywood, and ditched us in California.

"The next we heard there'd been an attack on US soil at an airbase in Nevada. Area 51. We then heard reports that George had been killed by the former CIA agent Mitch Youngs. It didn't take too much to work out that both incidents were linked. It turned out Youngs had been collaborating with Marty Heywood, and had been for some years. It appears he was enlisted to carry out the deed. The fact that he was in the ideal place at the right time was amazing luck."

Brayden's jaw line tensed at the mention of his former partner's name, and Emily observed the man clench both his fists in anger.

"But we got to him, and handed him over to you. Of course, not before we'd done with him first."

"So it was YOU guys who gifted him to me at Guantanamo?"

"It was our pleasure. Sophie and..." Emily couldn't bring herself to say his name, "... another agent apprehended him; Sophie had been driven by revenge for the death of her father."

"It took a lot of restraint *not* to put a bullet in his head," interrupted Sophie, saying it as though she had done the world a favour.

"We found him in Cuba," Emily continued. "It was under interrogation that Mitch Youngs admitted getting his orders from Marty, and the rest 'as they say' is history."

Brayden saw that Emily was finished with her account of events and started a slow clap. "A good story," he said, smiling. "Really, it is." He stopped with the clapping. "What I don't understand is: why didn't you inform us beforehand? We could've been prepared; we could've been ready and protected ourselves!"

Emily shrugged. "It was Marty's call. He wanted to keep it low-key, under the radar." It was easy to pin full blame on the man now that he was dead. "He said he thought Kaplan Ratcliff could be stopped before you would ever know. Of course, it turns out he was a traitorous arse-hole; hindsight is an amazing thing."

"Hmph," grunted Brayden, unconvinced. "Sounds too..." he struggled with the word, "... contrived. I'm not buying it."

"It's the truth!" insisted Emily, gazing into Brayden's eyes, holding his glare. "And now, Dominic Schilling is back in the UK, seemingly with a force of invisible burglars..."

"A force?" Brayden appeared puzzled. He turned towards Sophie. "We believed you were somehow responsible."

"What? All of them?" Sophie's tone carried a note of ridicule. "Hardly... haven't you listened to *anything* Emily said? I'm not involved, how could I be? I'm one of the good guys."

"Our belief... after Dominic – *and* Marty – had orchestrated the attack against Area 51, Dominic escaped back here to Britain, bringing with him some of your specimens." Emily couldn't fight the urge to add further clarification, fearing Brayden was never going to accept their version of events.

"Specimens?" queried Mullins, not understanding what the MI6 agent meant.

"Invisible children," replied Emily gloomily. "We think he took some; now," she looked reluctant, "they are working for him."

The spate of burglaries across Scotland had been featured heavily in the news broadcasts that day. Although details of invisible thieves had not made the hourly bulletins, Emily had learned of the full facts whilst en route to London during a phone call with the Chief.

"And it doesn't stop there," said Sophie ominously.

"I guess you've heard about Ryan?" asked Emily.

"Getting shot? Yes," confirmed Brayden breezily. Thanks to Christina it was old news.

"We believe it is somehow linked to what's happening in Scotland."

"Why?" asked Mullins. The link was tenuous she thought.

"Because whoever shot Ryan has kidnapped my brothers and sister too," answered Sophie gravely.

"And," Emily joined in, "Ryan told me he'd received a veiled threat over the phone a couple of months ago. If he – or *anyone* in the agency – did anything to scupper Dominic's plans, or seek out the sons of *GYGES*, something was going to happen to me," added Emily, recalling Ryan's confession when she had discovered and confronted him about his involvement. "So you see, it sort of makes it difficult to tell anyone anything of what we knew... including the CIA."

"Okay. Is that it?" asked Brayden stiffly.

"Yes, I believe so," answered Emily without emotion.

"Good... okay then." Brayden stood up and smiled. "I'll take everything you have said under advisement. Now that you've finished, I believe we had come up with an agreement. Time to hold up your end of the bargain."

"What?"

"What I said at the beginning. I've heard you out, now I'm taking Sophie into custody under the authority afforded me under special licence granted by the British government..." answered Brayden self-righteously. He turned to his partner. "Mullins..." He indicated for the FBI agent to make use of the handcuffs she was still holding.

"You can't do this," Emily protested. "Not after what I've just said."

"You admitted she aided Dominic Schilling at Dulles International Airport. There's also the incident in Fresno, California to discuss. There's more than enough to warrant an arrest. I'm sorry, this changes nothing." He looked directly towards the blonde woman. "Sophie Jennings. Place your hands behind your back please."

Mullins stepped forward brandishing the metal cuffs, one loop opened ready to receive Sophie's wrist. She proceeded to read the woman her Miranda rights. "You have the right to remain silent. Anything you say or do can and will be used against you…"

Sophie didn't listen to anything more. She instantly vanished and immediately used the surprise it evoked to her advantage.

Moving swiftly to the side of Special Agent Mullins, she tugged out the woman's handgun and in one fluid movement, used the butt of the weapon against the back of her head, knocking her down hard.

Mullins crumpled to the floor like a Premiership footballer hard-tackled, momentarily unconscious and likely concussed.

Seeing his partner felled to the ground, Brayden eased his own handgun free, released the safety and aimed it ahead of him.

"Sophie, halt! I don't want to hurt you!" he shouted, unable to see his target.

BANG!

Brayden dropped his gun and threw his hands to the side of his face, inextricable pain lancing into his brain. Sophie had discharged Mullins' weapon next to the left side of his head, the bullet smashing harmlessly into the ceiling above him. The detonation was so loud, it deafened him to external sounds. All he could hear was a shrill ringing from within his skull, so intense it blurred his vision.

Sophie dropped the gun to the floor where it clattered and bounced harmlessly to the side.

"Sophie! Please wait," implored Emily, standing up and making to go after the invisible woman, not knowing exactly which direction to turn.

"I… I can't," Sophie replied dejectedly. "If I go with them, they'll stick me in a cage and dissect me like a lab-rat; I'll be dead within a matter of weeks. This is the only way," she said pragmatically, adding, "the only way to be of any use in getting Meredith and my brothers back."

Emily turned her head in the direction of Sophie's voice. She was now close to the door. A double-bleep as Sophie used her ID card on the security pad confirmed it. The door glided open.

"You don't have to go with them!" spouted Emily desperately. "They can't arrest you... Ryan and the Chief sorted it. You have *Absolute Immunity*, as prescribed by the Home Secretary. You have been completely exonerated of any wrong doing, and as such cannot be held accountable in any court of law. I did try to say... before you went all schizoid."

At first, Sophie said nothing. Emily believed the young woman had not listened and instead had vacated the room. The door slipped quietly closed.

"A'you sure?" Sophie quizzed close by, uncertain. However, she had never known Emily to lie to her. She reappeared by the woman's side.

Emily exhaled in relief. "I have the signed affidavit here." Emily turned away, stepped around Mullins who was still lying on the floor out cold, and walked to her desk. Brayden was now standing up and shaking his head. "You see, we had expected this day would come... sooner or later," she said with conviction.

CHAPTER THIRTY-ONE
MEREDITH

HER SURROUNDINGS WERE UNFAMILIAR. Lying on a strange bed in an almost empty, windowless room, it took Meredith a long moment to gain her wits and start to fathom what had become of her.

An overhead fluorescent tube burned brightly, illuminating the space around her, allowing the ten-year-old to see that her two brothers were also with her. Both appeared to be asleep on separate beds.

"Stanley?" Meredith spoke in a hushed tone and sat up, a wave of dizziness forcing her to immediately fall back, her head hitting the pillow hard, but cushioned.

"Erghhh." Stanley groaned but didn't move. There were three single beds in the room, placed alongside each other with a couple of feet gap between them. Stanley was in the middle with Meredith to his right and Charlie to the left.

Without speaking, Charlie rolled over and fell out of the bed, quickly picking himself up. Seeing his sister attempting to sit, he ran around the beds, seeking comfort.

"Where are we, Mer?" asked the five-year-old. He hadn't felt this confused since awaking for the first time at Grandpa Theo's house, the day after his parents had gone away; that had been what Theo had told him, temporarily shielding him from the harsh truth.

Meredith swung her legs off the bed and made to stand. Before her feet could take her weight, giddiness off-balanced her and she allowed herself to drop back down, the springs giving her rump a little bounce and creaking in protest. "I don't know," she muttered. Blinking hard, trying to clear her head, Meredith tried to make sense of what was going on. She clawed at her memories, seeking answers to their current situation.

The last thing she could recall was being seated around a dinner table with her family on New Year's Eve. Sophie had been there, as were Ryan and Emily. They'd eaten their dinner and had started the dessert...

Outstretching his arms, Charlie reached up to Meredith, an action that meant he was seeking a cuddle. Frequently since their mother had died, he gravitated to his sister for comfort, unofficially making her an unwitting guardian. Obligingly, as always, Meredith swept her youngest brother up in an embrace.

"Where ARE we?" Stanley was now awake and sitting in his bed. A puzzled look was stretched across his face.

Ignoring the question, Meredith put Charlie to one side, stood up and crossed the room to the door. Twisting the silver doorknob, she was unsurprised to find it locked, the round door furnishing allowed no give or movement.

"Where's grandpa?" Charlie was at Meredith's side, watching his sister desperately seeking a way out of the room.

"I don't know," Meredith replied distractedly to both questions, her attention shifting from the door to a small CCTV camera in the corner on the opposite side of the room, affixed to the ceiling on a ball-and-socket bracket.

Sluggishly, she walked away from Charlie to stand beneath the camera, her frame in clear view of the lens. Studying the security equipment, Meredith could see that it had a built-in microphone and that it was in operation. A small dot of red light to the side of the camera's housing glowed subtly.

"Hello!" Meredith double-waved at the eye-in-the-ceiling. "Where are we?! What do you want?!"

Stanley and Charlie quickly joined their sister beneath the camera and started to signal with their hands and arms also, shouting at the device a mixture of demands and requests, their voices intermingled and desperate:

"Help us!"

"What do you want with us?!"

"Let us out!"

"You can't keep us here! I know our rights!"

After a long, slow two minutes without a response, Meredith sat down on the end of a bed, her brothers continuing to scream for attention. "It's no use," she said miserably. "They're not listening to us."

"Help!" Charlie cried one last time, before sitting at his sister's side.

"What are we going to do?" asked Stanley anxiously, stepping in front of the older girl. "Why are we here? What do they want?"

Meredith shrugged and shook her head. "I don't know," she replied, sounding small. She guessed it had something to do with what had happened to their mother and father, and most likely involved the girl she had once believed lived in her mirror.

Devoid of natural light, clocks, watches and television, the three children had little – or no – concept of time, except for the growing hunger that snarled within their bellies. More than three hours had passed since they'd given up trying to gain attention, and with nothing to do for entertainment, except for one game of eye-spy (*eye-spy with*

my little eye, something beginning with the letter 'b'; err, is it bed?),
they lay on their beds, whiling away the time by conjuring pleasant
thoughts.

The metallic sound of a lock being disengaged at the door
brought the children swiftly to their feet. The silver knob was turned
and the door gently opened inwards to allow a woman wheeling a
trolley laden with food to enter.

Meredith recognised her as the waitress serving dinner the night
before at her grandfather's house. She was still wearing the black and
white maid's outfit. "You!" she accused. "Where are we?! What have
you done with my family?!" Meredith made herself look big and
readied to charge at the newcomer.

The woman closed the door behind her and withdrew a handgun
from beneath her apron. "Uh-uh," she shook her head, waving the
small black weapon from side to side, pointing it towards the ten-
year-old. Meredith had no doubt from the way she looked that the
woman wouldn't hesitate to use it. "Now, sit! Enough belly-aching!"
One handed, the woman pushed the trolley deeper into the room, her
other hand still clutched around the handgrip of the gun.

Meredith sat back down, intuitively raising her hands in surrender.

"To answer your question, you're in 'sunny Scotland'; albeit on an
uninhabited island far from civilisation," the woman replied. "Don't
worry; no one will be able to find you here."

Meredith and Stanley shared a worried look. Hearts were sinking.

"I've brought you some breakfast and lunch..." She lifted a metal
plate cover to assess the meagre offerings. She replaced the cover and
said: "I hope you like Scottish food. We've got plenty of haggis for
later."

Although haggis made Charlie wrinkle his nose, the offer of food
emboldened the older of the two boys. If their captors meant to feed
them, it was hardly likely they were in any imminent danger. "Why

have you done this? Why are we here?" demanded Stanley, bitterness creeping into his voice. "What have you done with grandpa and the others?!"

The woman lowered the gun slightly, but it was still aimed perilously towards the children. "I should be more concerned about what's going to become of you," she retorted menacingly. "But, to answer one question. Your grandpa is okay... and most of the others." Although she said nothing about shooting Ryan, the tone she used implied an ill-fate had met someone.

"What do you want with us?!" demanded Meredith. "We're just kids."

"Are we going to die?" piped up Charlie.

The woman smiled warily. It looked more like a sneer. "Leverage," she said to Meredith, then tilting her head to one side to address Charlie, "and no... you're not going to die... IF our plans are carried out. Now, get your food whilst it's not too cold." She walked away from the trolley back to the door, tucking the gun away under the apron. As she exited the room, she muttered: "Enjoy."

CHAPTER THIRTY-TWO
POTUS

"**H**APPY NEW YEAR MR President..." Deputy Director Milo Calland made for the vacant seat opposite Avery Harrison ahead of the Resolute Desk within the Oval Office. His good mood was quickly quashed.

Already in attendance were the President's Chief of Staff, the Director of CIA Thawn Montgomery, General Bill Eastman and the Director of FBI, Elizabeth Reeves, amongst others less notable. The President was a little peeved at the Deputy's frequent tardiness.

"Sit," President Harrison ordered, not in the mood for small talk.

The morning had been full of drama, the very least being news of the multiple-organised heists occurring in Scotland late the night before, where some $60 million worth of American assets had been stolen.

The President stood up from his leather chair, making himself look even more imposing as Milo sat down, feeling small and inadequate. "I've just been talking with the British Prime Minister, David Humphries," he started, a smile threatening to appear on his lips. "It turns out the British Home Office knew of *her* whereabouts all along." He was implying Sophie Jennings, the elusive young woman who he personally blamed for the atrocities carried out at Area 51 in October, although his suspicions were under heavy scrutiny and now proving to be false. A short time before making the call, an event involving Agent Brayden Scott and Special Agent Christina Mullins had been reported, motivating the President into contacting his British counterpart to demand some answers.

"That's outrageous!" bellowed the General. "That's a violation of the *Peace Treaty*?" Bill Eastman was referring to a treaty signed by the United States of America and Great Britain at the end of the American Revolutionary War in 1783. He often spouted legal doctrine to highlight a point. The President gestured for the General to simmer.

"Let's keep a cool head," suggested the Chief of Staff.

"I hear you Bill," President Harrison acknowledged the General. "Not only that, Humphries tells me they have her listed as a SIS agent, and that she has been granted *absolute immunity*." He said it haughtily. "Apparently she has special clearance within the agency."

"Then, the British were complicit with her actions," stated Director Montgomery. "A deliberate act of aggression of such magnitude is surely an act of war?"

"Sir, we should respond decisively. Militarily, we have forces on mainland Britain who could strike within minutes." General Eastman, military advisor to the President was leaning forward, an excited expression filling his face. He was a Republican and firmly believed armed conflict solved every argument.

President Harrison sat down in his seat. "Calm down General, just listen; let's not be too hasty." He sighed in resignation. "Humphries denies vehemently and unequivocally that Great Britain had anything to do with the attack on our airbase, and... I now believe him. Agent Brayden corroborates his position. He's learned that Dominic Schilling appears to have masterminded the entire event, albeit with help from a rogue MI6 agent named Sir Marty Heywood – the man it would seem who put Mitch Youngs up to killing George Jennings.

"The Prime Minister said he'd already willingly given us access to all that British Intelligence had on the incident, and our agents are still on site completing their enquiries. Although they are a little aggrieved as you can expect."

"What about the reports of the 'invisible force' fighting against our soldiers within the underground laboratory? There's only one person with that capability." Milo Calland had received reports from a number of witnesses of the incident, and more than half a dozen had indicated a phantom adversary. "It can't be a coincidence surely?"

President Harrison shrugged. "Mass hysteria? Over-imagination? Who knows? I know one thing: there's no such thing as coincidence. The fact is, we have no *proof* the Jennings girl was involved. Sure, there were some strange occurrences at the base, but we have nothing concrete, no hard facts or compelling evidence that we can trust. Just speculations, conjecture and hearsay. None of which would be admissible in a court of law."

"But then, if she's invisible, there wouldn't be, would there?" asserted the General, a hint of sarcasm and dissent in his tone.

"So... we've been barking up the wrong tree, sir?" asked Elizabeth Reeves, feeling a little left out of the conversation.

"I didn't say that." The President shut her down. "For now, we have to go along with it. Bide our time. The Prime Minister has totally ruled out extraditing Sophie Jennings, and even if he so wished, he cited that the 'absolute immunity' granted her prohibits them from doing so. However," he smiled slyly, "Were an opportunity to arise whereby she comes into our custody *willingly*, that 'absolute immunity' order would become irrelevant."

The President's senior advisors sat around the table taking turns to look at each other as what the American leader was alluding to sunk in.

There was willingly, and there was *willingly*. The CIA had different understandings on how to interpret the word.

CHAPTER THIRTY-THREE
EMILY

T HE **CIA** AGENT HAD stormed out of the office, a hand still nursing the side of his head where Sophie had fired Mullins' gun, and a few curses being shouted as he went. A bitter exchange of words had passed between him and Emily before he threw up his hands in anger and made the decision to leave.

Special Agent Mullins was still in Ryan's SIS control room, the signed affidavit resting loosely in her hands. She had read and reread it countless times since being handed the document two minutes earlier.

"This is only valid in the UK," Mullins said, applying her own understanding of the law to the situation, which was exceptional but often bent to her own aspirations.

"And where do you think you are, Special Agent?" asked Emily self-righteously, "back home in America? This isn't Arkansas!"

"I'm from Connecticut," Mullins corrected, screwing her face up into a sneer. "Sophie will be made to account for her part in the crimes undertaken in America last year," she said, knowingly. "That's a promise."

Emily made no attempt at replying, her obstinate expression and folded arms conveying her riposte clearly enough.

Mullins thrust the legal document back into Emily's hands and left the office in a huff.

"Wow!" Standing up from hiding behind his desk in the

background, Mac, made his presence known. "You could cut the atmos with a knife!" he sounded exhilarated. "Did I just see that? Is *she* still here?"

"I'm here." Sophie reappeared beside the analyst, startling him.

"Jeez! You should wear a bell or somethin'," he complained, a hand involuntarily clutching his chest as though experiencing a mild heart attack. "I heard about what you could do... but, seeing... wow! Puts a whole different perspec' on it."

Ignoring Mac, Sophie sat down on the edge of a desk. "You okay?"

The colour had drained from Emily's face and she was physically shaking. She removed her spectacles and gave them a wipe with the lower part of her white blouse, exhaling deeply. "That could've gone better," she said, implying their encounter with the two American agents. "They had me worried for a sec. I hate conflict."

"Forget them," Sophie said, a hand reaching over to her friend, offering comfort. "We have more pressing matters." She allowed the woman to calm a little, before adding: "So, what now?"

Fully composing herself, Emily brightened. "We get off our backsides and set to work," she said. "It's more than a coincidence that your brothers and sister are taken, Ryan gets shot, and the massive theft-fest with what appears to be 'invisible' perpetrators all happening on the same night."

"Okay. That's the obvious bit. But where do we start?"

Emily inclined her neck and turned her head away from Sophie to face the garishly-dressed agent standing a short way over. "Mac, if you have no intention of going home to get changed, you can at least make yourself useful," she started. "I want to know everything about those robberies occurring in Scotland last night; find out what was stolen, where most of the thefts took place. See if there are any patterns, anything that might strike you as odd. It's New Year's Day... see if there is a convergence of heavy traffic in any one area that stands out... roads should be quiet north of the border the day after Hogmanay."

"Okay..." Mac nodded as he listened. A notepad and a pen had materialised within his hands and he had been scribbling obediently.

Emily continued. "We're looking for a base of operations, somewhere significant. Mark off on a map all the recorded incidents; see where there are concentrations of activity. Look out for absolutely anything that might come across as peculiar. I expect there'll be quite a few burglaries still to be reported what with it being a public holiday, but there's plenty to start off with. You may need to call in Jez and Belle to lend a hand." Jeremy 'Jez' Staff and Isa-'belle' Horris were junior analysts brought in by Ryan to act as assistants. He often just referred to them in the singular as *Jezebel.*

"Right you are, though I doubt they'll be happy with it being New Year an' all," replied Mac returning to his workstation.

"I'm not happy!" shouted Emily. Quickly she calmed herself. "Use CCTV footage, monitor traffic cams. Any surveillance footage that may give us a lead."

"I'm on it." Mac disappeared behind his desk partition.

"What about my brothers and sister?" asked Sophie solemnly, before adding a little belligerently: "You're not going to bypass my needs in favour of the 'greater good' again are you?" She was referring to the decision Ryan had forced upon them in October. They had bumped the search for George Jennings in favour of destroying his work. It was a decision which Emily had regretted ever since, and which Sophie constantly reminded her.

Shaking her head, Emily replied. "No. The hunt to find Meredith, Stanley and Charlie stays with us. Nothing's being left to chance. Not this time."

Sophie's face softened. "Thank you," she whispered.

The starting point was back at the scene of the crime. Grandpa Theo's house where Meredith, Stanley and Charlie had been kidnapped, where they'd all been drugged and where Ryan had been shot.

"What do we know about the caterers?" asked Emily. The two women were sitting around Emily's desk, a computer flat screen was flashing up images ahead of them. The workstation around them was cluttered with computer printouts, loose sheets of paper, and sundry personal items belonging to Emily, including a bunch of keys, her mobile phone and a large coffee mug emblazoned with the legend *I LOVE SPREADSHEETS* glazed around its side in large black letters.

"Not much," replied Sophie. "Theo booked them before I arrived for Christmas." She was still living in the apartment in Chelsea and was visiting her family for the festive season. "He told me that he'd found them advertised in the *Yellow Pages*." Moments earlier Sophie had called her grandfather to see how Camilla and himself were doing (that had been the pretext, and they assured her that they were 'fine'), following up with some questions regarding the New Year's Eve dinner, focusing in particular on the two individuals hired to prepare and serve it. "A company called *Velvet Grape Catering Services*, based in Norwich," she added. "I took the initiative and called them. They checked their bookings diary and it turns out they had nothing scheduled for last night."

"Oh?"

"That's what I said. I went on to explain to them a bit about my reason for calling, but they couldn't shed any light. Though they did mention that one of their vans had been stolen a week before; they reported it to the police at the time who recorded it on their national computer. I wrote down the details and asked Mac to run it through his surveillance tracker."

Hearing his name, Mac piped up defensively and a little flustered. "I'm on it!" This translated, until then, as completely the opposite.

"Delegating now, are we?" Emily mused aloud, half a smile playing on her lips. "You'd make a good leader."

Before Sophie could consider the idea further, Mac made a loud clap with his hands and a whoop of joy. "Girl... am I good or AM I GOOD!"

Emily twisted around in her swivel chair. "What've you got Mac?"

He stood up to look excitedly over his desk partition towards Emily and Sophie. "A van matching the one reported stolen was captured on a Highway Agency CCTV late last night heading northwest along the A47 towards King's Lynn.

"Using image-enhancing software I was able to zoom in on the registration plate, but a quick check on the number gave me a mismatch. The DVLA had the number plate registered against a *C4 Picasso*, not a grey *Ford Tourneo*. The *Picasso* had also been reported stolen at the same time."

"So the plates had been swapped... probably an attempt to throw us off the trail." Emily stood up from her seat and walked around to the other side of the partitioning to stand beside Mac. Sophie followed her.

"Yea," agreed Mac. "But it didn't work. Using the highway cameras' surveillance database, I was able to follow the van for miles. From the A47 they joined the A17, then the A1 where they drove continuously until stopping at a service station near Wetherby. There, a perfectly placed camera was able to capture a fantastic picture of both the van's driver and his passenger." Mac, still standing, stabbed his index fingers at a couple of keys on his computer keyboard. Two faces flashed up onto the large screen.

"That's them," said Sophie and Emily at the same time. They both turned to each other.

"I ran their images through facial recognition and, surprise surprise, we got a hit."

"You didn't expect to find something?" asked Emily incredulously.

"Actually, I was being sarcastic." Not adding anything further, Mac carried on: "Hector Degiorgio and Natasha Vincent. I'm surprised you didn't recognise them."

"Oh?" Emily looked puzzled.

"They're both listed as current employees of Kaplan Ratcliff. Isn't that your old haunt?" Mac knew the answer so continued. "Both are former military with stints in the French Foreign Legion and private sector work; currently on assignment as field agents within KR's Security and Intelligence division. It may not be a coincidence, but they were also part of Ryan's task force sent into Nevada to destroy Project *GYGES* in October. They were under Dominic's charge then..."

"And likely under his charge now," finished Emily. "Damn it! I do remember them. I should have recognised them at the dinner party."

"It's not your fault," Sophie reassured softly, her face hardening. "It's DOMINIC!" she hissed, a rage building within her. She fisted her hands at her sides, the feelings of anger once again rekindled.

Shooting Sophie a sideward glance, Emily noticed the young woman appear to 'shimmer', like she was fading in and out like a pulsating light bulb receiving a fluctuating electric current. Emily laid a hand on her arm in an attempt to mollify her. The action seemed to have a soothing effect, but only barely.

Oblivious to Sophie's distress, Mac continued:

"After the service station, they took the A66 at the Scotch Corner, where I was able to follow their route up into the north-west side of Scotland."

"Do you know where the van finally stopped?" asked Sophie hopefully, now calmer.

"Unfortunately, no. The last sighting of the *Tourneo* was on the M74 just past Paisley. I can guess that they travelled up A82, but I can't prove it, and beyond that is anyone's guess. None of the cameras along that stretch of road were functioning last night... for some reason. And not knowing how far they went, or in which direction they took thereafter, it's damn impossible to know for sure where their journey terminated."

Emily clapped a hand on Mac's shoulder. "No worries Mac, this is all good."

"Thanks. I'll keep on looking.... might get lucky."

From over the desk partitioning, Emily's mobile phone began to ring. She slipped past Sophie and sauntered across to her desk. Scooping up her phone, she didn't recognise the number displayed. She accepted the call and pressed the phone up to her ear.

"Hello?"

"Ah, hello. Is that Emily Porter?"

"Speaking."

"Hi Emily. This is Dr Morgan at Norwich and Norfolk University Hospital. It's about your father, Ryan Barber. Is it okay to talk?"

"Sure."

"I'm sorry to do this in a phone call, but I have some very bad news."

CHAPTER THIRTY-FOUR
DOMINIC

A T FIRST DOMINIC HAD thought Jennifer laughing at the other end of the phone was because she was pleased to hear that Ryan was dead.

"*You wish he was dead,*" she said in a cross between mirth and scorn, the amusement in her voice coming to an abrupt end. "*Especially now... now that your motives are becoming clearer.*"

"What d'you mean?" asked Dominic, slightly rattled. "The old fool avoided being drugged, got into a tussle and got shot for his endeavours. Twice!"

"*Shot twice, yes... but not dead. You seem to underestimate how resilient he is. He's still alive in a mid-Norfolk hospital.*"

"Okay," Dominic knew better than to argue with the woman. "I guess it's of no consequence, we got what we wanted."

"*And, where are the children?*" Jennifer asked curiously.

"They're with Hector and Tasha still." Dominic turned towards the *Ford Tourneo* where one of the three guards who had taken up positions around the vehicle stepped forward and helped Hector carry Stanley Jennings out of the back of the van. Natasha Vincent was standing in close proximity, watching. She still wore the waitress's outfit from the previous night, looking very cold and trying to warm herself up by smoking a roll-up cigarette. "I've assigned them babysitting duties. They're taking them to the island in one of our choppers shortly."

"Good. And what about you, are you ready to foster the next stage of the plan?"

Dominic turned and started to walk away from the sight of Hector, Natasha and the three guards, hurrying towards a black *Bell 206* helicopter. "Almost," replied Dominic assuredly. "After a long night, I thought I'd take the rest of the day off. Maybe tomorrow too."

"What about Sophie? She'll be beside herself with worry about her family. We don't want her to be a loose end for too long, you know how dangerous she is. "

"Don't worry your pretty little self. It's being dealt with."

"You sure?"

"YES, Jennifer. Get me the address of Ryan's hospital; I think his incapacity is going to serve a purpose. Now, leave me alone. I have a late champagne breakfast to attend." Dominic disconnected the phone and returned it to his pocket. A glance at his watch confirmed that he was more than late for breakfast.

If anything he was also late for lunch too.

Elspeth was waiting in the bar area of *Cuan Mor*, a restaurant, bar and brewery that offered a stunning view of Oban's bay. Nursing a glass of chardonnay, the ginger-haired woman looked bored and aggrieved when Dominic finally stepped into the establishment. She was tapping a foot agitatedly on the floor beneath her chair.

Looking around the bar, Dominic could only see one other patron. Everyone else was probably in bed still nursing New Year's hangovers he guessed.

The setting was ideal for an argument.

"Fadalach... Yous late," she admonished, raising her glass to her lips. The way she emptied its contents Dominic knew her mood was caustic and that he needed to tread carefully.

"There were a few stragglers," he said by way of explanation, slightly airily. "Here... I got you something." Dominic slipped a hand within his jacket. "Close your eyes and hold out your hands."

"I'm in nay mood for wee games." She placed her glass down hard.

"Just close your eyes woman!"

"Oka-yee!" Elspeth closed her eyes and held her hands palm outwards ahead of her.

"No peeking." Dominic removed his hand from within his jacket, retrieving an item inside his fist. "Here." He gently placed it onto the centre of her right hand. "This is the first of my two gifts. Now you can look."

"Oh... *Dominic*." The indignation in her voice along with her bad mood melted. "It's pure barry," she said lifting the *Suzanne* 18ct white gold diamond pendant up to give it a closer inspection. The 1.07ct diamond was fixed within a six claw setting and looked big and expensive. The necklace had been appropriated by one of the cadets during the night, stolen from a high-end jeweller and Dominic had fallen in love with it on sight.

"Of course, it's not as nice as the *Whisper of Persia*," said Dominic dismissively, "but it will look beautiful dangling from your pretty little neck nonetheless."

Elspeth blushed. "Thank you," she said. "Shame it's stolen."

After a lunch consisting of slow roast pork belly for Dominic and a hot smoked Cajun salmon salad for Elspeth, followed by a dessert of homemade apple and bramble sponge (served with creamy custard), Dominic settled the bill and handed Elspeth her second gift.

An A5 manila envelope.

"What's this?" Elspeth raised an eyebrow.

"Open it and see."

Elspeth tore open the envelope and poked a couple of fingers in.

"And there I was a thinkin' that yous only gettin' me a Burt Bacharach CD this Chris'mas." Pulling free her fingers, she retrieved a couple of tickets.

"Don't be so ungrateful," said Dominic playfully.

"Ah, Dom, yous special wee man." In Elspeth's hand were two tickets for the opera at Edinburgh's Playhouse. "*Die Fledermaus!*"

"You've been banging on about the opera for weeks. I thought we could take a break."

"To-deey!" she exclaimed upon seeing the date and time of the show. "Eight!" She pronounced it as 'eat'. Elspeth looked at her watch seeing that it was nearly 3:00 p.m. A look of concern flashed across her face. "Will we makes it?"

"Of course we will. If we get going now!" he smiled, standing up.

Hastening out of the quiet restaurant, they walked across to where Dominic's car was parked, a solitary vehicle in a large parking area. Even had it been packed, the flashy car would have stood out. A *Mercedes SL Coupe Torino*, metallic grey or what the salesman had defined as *palladium silver*.

It was a gift from Jennifer Ratcliff, and a replacement for the *Mercedes SLS AMG* which he'd wrapped around a tree last July. He had loved that *Mercedes*, but his affection was fast growing for the new one.

A couple of minutes short of three hours later (or 122 miles across country) Dominic was driving through Edinburgh's busy city centre, following a steady stream of traffic that took him up Queen Street, then onto York Place. At the roundabout he turned right and drove down Leith Street.

"Yous do knows where ye are a goin'?" Elspeth queried, a little apprehensively.

"Of course. Ah, there... see. We're here." Dominic steered the *Mercedes* across Princes Street and pulled up outside the stately

Victorian building that was The Balmoral hotel. "Come, let's check in."

The hotel's doorman was dressed in traditional Scottish attire that included a kilt and sporran. Before the car had stopped, he had approached the new arrivals. Climbing out, Dominic had a quick conversation with the man where he arranged for the car to be parked within the hotel's secure off-site parking garage.

"Spared nah expense!" Elspeth grinned walking ahead in through the hotel's grand entrance where a large, bright room decorated in creams and light browns met her. A couple of other doormen stood in various spots to either end, and a concierge stood behind a long reception check-in desk to their immediate right.

"We can afford it," said Dominic matter-of-factly, stepping up behind her.

Following a night at the opera and a lavish breakfast within the hotel's restaurant, Dominic led Elspeth on a tour of the city. They visited a whisky distillery (where they drank a few too many samples), before heading to the castle at one end of The Royal Mile, staying for the firing of the one o'clock gun, which deafened them for a good ten minutes after. Before the afternoon was over, Dominic took Elspeth on a leisurely stroll to Holyrood Palace, linking his arm together with hers.

"I might've knewn that you had more than one reason for whisking me 'ere," said Elspeth impishly.

"Huh?"

"Don' yous try the playin' dumb wit' me Dom'nic Schilling," she said, giving him a hard elbow to the side.

"Honestly, I don't know what you mean," Dominic protested with a twinkle in the eye. Elspeth knew the truth of it though. For two months the man had talked nothing but getting his hands on the *Whisper of Persia*. It was almost an obsession with him for some reason. And now they were heading towards the place where she knew it was currently on loan and on display. When quizzed about his infatuation for the diamond, all he would ever say was: *it's complicated.*

Holyrood Palace is the official residence of the British monarchy in Scotland, and like Buckingham Palace in London, has royal guards patrolling the premises at every turn, protecting its many treasures and on hand for when royalty or VIPs visited. When the Queen was in residence – like in London – guards would stand sentry outside the entrance, and the Royal Standard would be raised in place of the Union Jack; this only happened around once a year, usually at the beginning of summer when Her Majesty carried out a range of official duties and ceremonies.

Stepping into the palace via the central and only public entrance, Dominic was immediately taken aback by the sheer size of the building. Built in a quadrangle, he contemplated all the history that had taken place within those walls, most notably it being the home of Mary, Queen of Scots for a while.

Walking into the main corridor, Dominic first looked to his left and then turned to his right. Ahead of him he could see through the windows the large green square of the inner court surrounded by the four sides of the palace building; at its centre a concrete memorial in the form of a column atop three raised hexagonal platforms. Upon the Doric column two lanterns, once gas powered but now electric, were placed.

A second glance to his left indicated that the palace was closed to visitors in that direction; a rope boundary blocked the path. These led to the Queen's private chambers. The only way for visitors was via the corridor to his right, at the end of which was a door.

"Shall we," suggested Dominic, taking Elspeth by the hand and leading her like an over-eager parent and their less-keen child.

Although *The Daily Mail* newspaper had noted month's earlier that the diamond was going to be on display at Holyrood Palace, the actual diamond wasn't to be found in any of the rooms open to the public within the Royal dwelling. Instead, it was on display within the Queen's Gallery in a building adjacent to the entrance to the palace grounds, in a small room on the first floor, dedicated to its exhibition.

At the pay counter, Dominic helped himself to some leaflets and a colour guide and asked the cashier, a small dark-haired man wearing glasses and a *Bluetooth* headset: "Where will I find the big diamond?"

"It's in a small room at the back of the main gallery," he said. "You cannae miss it owing to the signs and the big security men hovering by the door."

Dominic thanked the man as he paid his and Elspeth's admission fee and then led Elspeth through to a large room where paintings were on display on the walls all around, and which he assumed was the main gallery. Paying little notice to the art, the former Director of Kaplan Ratcliff's Security and Intelligence Division, albeit only for a very short period, strode through the hall directly for the small room in which he knew the precious stone would be found.

The *Whisper of Persia*, a large vivid yellow diamond, described within the guide brochure as 'cushion shaped' owing to its square cut and rounded corners, took pride of place upon a black velvet cushion (the same one that had been used the summer before when it had been stolen from the *Masterpiece London Arts and Antiques Fair*) within a large toughened glass case in the centre of the room. It was the only item on display.

Two brawny security men who likely moonlighted as nightclub doormen or *Mr Universe* competitors, floated around the room in close proximity, their eyes scrutinising everybody who stepped in to have a look or walked up to the exhibit, their poise alert for any trouble or suspicious behaviour that endangered the exhibit.

Another guard stood just outside the room's door in the main gallery, equally big and just as ready to react were anything untoward to occur.

Dominic's eyes surveyed the immediate surroundings. He shot a glance towards the doorway he'd just stepped through, noted the recess within the frame and the edge of a metal security door retracted above it. A look at the display case easily identified it as being constructed from toughened materials by the prism and magnification of the glass.

They're not taking any chances this time, he thought.

"Wow! Is that the wee lass you've been makin' me ears bleed over?" Elspeth said loudly. Her eyes grew wide in her head. "Makes the wee trin-ket you fest-ooned on meh look cheap..."

"It is cheap... by comparison," replied Dominic. Although stolen, its intrinsic value was £7,500 – trifling against the diamond's current insured value of nine million pounds. He moved steadily forward and was soon standing up close to the glass and peering in.

Alongside the stone pinned into the cushion was an information card which glowed under the bright halogen bulb built into the glass case. Dominic had read it before:

> Very little is known about the origin of the *Whisper of Persia*; however it is thought to have once belonged to Cyrus the Great, founder of the Achaemenid Empire around 550BC. When he died in battle in 530BC, many of his treasures went missing, including a diamond matching the *Whisper's* description. For a while, it was suggested

the *Whisper* was the fabled Stone of Giramphiel owing to its unearthly appearance. In Arthurian legend, the stone was believed to be magical, granting the person who possessed it not only strength and bravery, but charm also. What *is* known about the *Whisper of Persia* is at 101.29-carats, it is one of the largest diamonds ever cut. It came into the possession of its current owner, the Viscount William Von Rothstainer, in 1988, who paid US $3,000,000 for it in a private sale from an anonymous proprietor.

Elspeth quickly scanned the information card, absorbing some of the facts detailed therein. "Hmpf," she grunted, tearing her eyes away from the display and turning to Dominic standing next to her, still transfixed by the diamond on exhibition. "Yous not just interested cos it's an expensive di'mond, is it? Yous b'lieve it somethin' else..."

Dominic sighed. "If you knew what I believed, you'd think that I was stupid... or mad... and the *look* you're giving me," he playfully elbowed her, "almost confirms it," he said.

One of the security guards glowered at them, a look of annoyance flashing across his face. Silently, he warned them to behave and walked casually around the display case to stand within a couple of feet of the two visitors.

Elspeth laced her arm around Dominic's and pulled him reassuringly close. "I dinnae say that," she said quietly. "Crazy, fo' sure. Stupid... nah." She turned back to the *Whisper of Persia* and drank in its beauty. "But," she shrugged, "I can see why yous like it s'much." The small ginger-haired woman looked back up to her companion. "Dom'nic," she said seriously.

His eyes met hers.

"Yous DO know... nuttin good will come'ff havin' t'is diamond."

A guilty look flashed across Dominic's face, like he was ashamed of how he felt, or that he had ever shared this secret with her. He was now starting to have regrets. He tore his eyes away from hers, his look falling upon the yellow diamond once again. "You're probably right," he conceded. "But in my heart... I feel it's pull... it's hard to explain. It's like a... *longing*. Like it's *destiny*."

It is jus' a stone, Dom'nic. The words were queued ready to speak, but by his expression, she thought better than to verbalise them. Instead, taking a long moment to form an alternative, all she could think of to say was:

"Maybe."

Dominic did not notice the doubt in her voice.

CHAPTER THIRTY-FIVE
RYAN

IN A PRIVATE OFFICE a fair walk down a series of corridors within the Norwich and Norfolk University hospital, Sophie and Emily sat ahead of a cluttered desk piled high with patient files and paperwork, the doctor who had called earlier on the phone was considering what to say next.

Staring past him, Sophie watched through the window as a flock of birds flew in a V in the distance. She wished she could be as free as them. Emily clutched her hand nervously.

The doctor cleared his throat. Unlike before when he was dressed in surgical scrubs, he was wearing a suit, shirt and tie combo; a pair of spectacles, slightly rectangular-framed, sat atop his nose. "Like I said on the phone," he started, "we did all we could for your father. The operation to repair his heart went well, quite straightforward really, but there have been 'other' complications."

"Is he going to die?" asked Sophie impassively.

The doctor smirked. "We all die," he replied. Seeing his humour was inappropriate, he made himself look serious. "But, to answer the question you intended: no. He might," he added, "wish that wasn't the case. When I told you this morning we had removed the two bullets, we had failed to notice the small amount of damage sustained to Mr Barber's spinal cord. Though slight, I'm afraid to say, it's large enough to have caused irreparable damage to his central nervous system."

"Yes, yes, you told me this on the phone. But WHAT are you saying?" Emily was growing frustrated with the man's long-winded, softly-softly approach.

"Miss Porter, Ryan is now affected with something we call 'quadriplegia', which simply means he's paralysed from the neck down."

"Is it permanent?" asked Sophie.

The doctor tried to look sympathetic but floundered with his response. "That's what irreparable damage means," he said, slightly sarcastic.

Ryan was propped up in the hospital bed with a countless number of pillows placed behind him. He was awake and looked almost happy lying there as Sophie and Emily stepped into the room. An ECG monitor bleeped above the bed and various drips and leads were still pinned in or poked out from numerous points about his body, hidden beneath a crisp, white sheet that had been drawn up to just beneath the man's neck.

"I bought you some grapes. And some kiwis," said Emily distractedly, shocked at seeing the broken man lounged out in front of her. Bought from a convenience store en route, the offering sounded pitiful, cliché-like, and felt like a stupid joke in the grand scheme of things.

The lack of any movement by Ryan could easily have been translated as ingratitude to the unwise. The man *was* paralysed from the neck down.

"Sit down, please. Both of you." Ryan barely moved his lips despite the quadriplegia not affecting his face muscles.

Emily looked for somewhere to place the fruit. To the left side of the bed was a large drugs' cabinet (which was locked) atop which a vase had been placed with a bouquet of flowers; a large white envelope was secured beneath with Ryan's name printed across it. Emily placed the fruit alongside it.

Together with Sophie, Emily did as demanded. They pulled up blue plastic chairs, the type that stacked easily and were often found in high schools and sat in silence.

"Forget about me for the time being. This..." he sighed, "... this doesn't matter." It sounded like a lie, his voice betraying his feelings. The fact that his life would never be the same DID matter, but for the moment the head of Emily's SIS team didn't want to dwell on it. There were more important things at stake. "Be so good as to bring me up to speed. Tell me everything that's happened since..."

Since I was shot last night...

Sophie and Emily turned to each other, clarifying who was going to speak or seeking permission to take the lead. As always, Sophie gave Emily the stand. She was more a *doer* than a *talker*.

"I think you were supposed to have been drugged at the dinner last night, but you got in the way. Theo, his wife. Sophie, myself. The kids... we were all unconscious. Something had been put in our desserts to knock us out, something fast acting. When Sophie and I awoke, we found that you had been shot. Twice – though, from the looks of things, it appears you'd put up a struggle."

"Yea, I remember," confirmed Ryan. "I'd heard a noise whilst in the living room. When I came back, I found you – everybody actually – out cold. Instinctively, I knew what had happened."

"Meredith, Stanley and Charlie are missing," stated Sophie desperately, unrestrained.

"It looks like the whole thing was staged to kidnap Sophie's siblings," Emily finished for Sophie. "We searched the house after, but there was no sign of them, and no clues as to why they've been taken."

Ryan sighed, disheartened.

"However, we've learnt that the kidnappers are Hector Degiorgio and Natasha Vincent, both are listed as current employees within Kaplan Ratcliff's Intelligence Division, and both former military," continued Emily.

"I know of the names," said Ryan. "Field operatives. They took part in our mission in Nevada last year."

"They were masquerading as caterers employed by Theo for his New Year's Eve dinner, having stolen a catering van. They somehow intercepted Theo's New Year's Eve party order."

"Kaplan Ratcliff... all along. Now it makes sense," he said, cryptically.

Emily ignored Ryan and carried on. "Why Meredith and her brothers have been taken is anyone's guess. So far, there have been no ransom demands or word from their captors. Our resources at MI6 – mainly *Mac* – have tracked the kidnapper's van travelling north into Scotland, but the scent elaborately grew cold. We lost it on the M74, just past Paisley. So far, we've been unable to re-find it."

Ryan sighed, though it sounded more like a wheeze. "I might've known she would pull a stunt like this."

Sophie looked puzzled. If Emily was surprised she didn't highlight it.

"What d'you mean?" asked Sophie.

"I'm guessing Emily never did tell you." Ryan closed his eyes, as though pained by the information he now had to disclose. He considered for a moment how best to proceed.

How could he come clean without admitting that he was to blame?

In the end he decided to fess up and to hell with the consequences. "It started in Alamo, after you and Dominic liberated those ninety children... after you both decided to go against my orders to eliminate them. We needed to hide the kids somewhere, and it was clear from the offset that MI6 couldn't be seen to have been involved." A tickle in the back of his throat caused Ryan to start coughing. "Emily…" cough-cough, "can I trouble you," cough, "for some water?"

"Sure." Emily stood and reached over to a jug, pouring water into a plastic tumbler. She lifted it up to Ryan's lips and gently tilted. He took some deep swallows, dribbling a little. Emily used a wad of tissues to mop the man's chin dry.

"Thank you, dear," he said. "Where was I? Oh yes. Sharing my concerns with Dominic," he muttered to himself before going on: "The man quickly put forward an idea, it was quite simple really, and fantastic! Of course, I should've realised that he couldn't be trusted, but at the time I had little option but to listen to him… and agree to his terms."

"Go on," urged Sophie wearily.

"We decided that Dominic would take the boys, and shoulder the blame for the attack on Area 51. It was imperative that MI6 NOT be linked to the incident as the repercussions would be catastrophic – not just for us – but for Great Britain; it would be a political nightmare. Dominic led me to believe that he would look after the children, oversee some of their training, but ultimately return them to MI6 when things had settled down and we were no longer under the spotlight. Imagine what we could achieve with ninety invisible soldiers!" Ryan trailed off as he fantasised over it. He blinked the thoughts away.

"But when Dominic forced Alby to fly him into Scotland without first clearing it with me, all but disappearing off the face of the earth, he crossed a line and I soon began to realise that things weren't as he'd promised. Of course, he had help, I suspected as much: Jennifer Ratcliff. And I confronted her with it, which she happily admitted.

I've spoken with her a few times since... but our last commune didn't go so well, and she made some threats."

"Threats? What threats?" Sophie demanded.

"Against Emily. Against you. Rhetoric, nothing too innocuous... so I thought."

Sophie turned to Emily. "You knew about this, didn't you?" she accused.

"Some of it," Emily admitted, awkwardly. "But I couldn't say anything. You mistrusted Ryan as it was, blaming him for your father's death. I didn't want to make things worse between you... he is your grandfather, after all."

"Only biologically," Sophie pointed out.

"Besides," Emily ignored the comment, "until now, Ryan still believed nothing untoward would come of their arrangement. It was irrelevant."

"Hmph! Some arrangement... Look where it's got us." Sophie turned and faced Ryan. Speaking softer, almost in pity, she said: "Look where it's got you."

Ryan looked solemnly at the young woman. "I'm not going to make any excuses, Sophie. I made a judgement call which you and Dominic forced upon me; I'm not proud of myself, but I had sound reasoning. Sure, it was a risk, which I thought was worth taking. And now it's backfired. Sometimes, things just don't work out the way they should. Life isn't scripted. It's just a coin toss."

"Okay, so what now? Where does that leave Meredith, Stanley and Charlie?"

Seeming not to hear Sophie's question, Ryan appeared to change the subject. "On top of this cupboard next to me, beneath the pretty flowers, there's an envelope. Go get it."

Sophie looked towards Emily for approval.

Emily inched her head up, peering across to the vase of flowers and gave the slightest shrug. Emily had no idea where Ryan was leading with this though recalled seeing the envelope there when setting down the bag containing her gift of fruit.

Sophie stood and walked around the bed and crossed to the cabinet. Unsure of herself, she reached for the white envelope and dragged it out from beneath the vase, one hand holding the ceramic container by its base, the other pincer-gripping the envelope.

"Evidently, you aren't the only visitors I've had today," Ryan said. Seeing the envelope in Sophie's hand, he smiled. "Okay, now bring the envelope over here and open it."

Inside the envelope was a black and white photograph.

Sophie gasped but didn't let go of the print. She handed it over to Emily.

"The nurse who opened the envelope thought there was going to be a 'get well' card inside. Instead, she found that photograph."

The photograph was of three children in various poses. One was lying on a bed, another was just sitting on the edge of a second bed and the third, the eldest, was standing looking directly at the camera, fear within her eyes. The image had been taken from overhead and Emily assumed it was a still from CCTV footage. Printed in the bottom left-hand corner were a sequence of numbers which Emily easily deciphered as the time and date the picture had been taken.

"It's from the kidnapper," said Ryan, stating the obvious. "On the other side there's a message. It's addressed to Sophie."

Emily turned the photograph over.

Sophie... if you want to see them again, call me.

A mobile number had been scribbled out beneath it.

"Why didn't you tell us about this sooner?" demanded Sophie, snatching back the photograph from Emily and waving it towards Ryan accusingly.

"Yea, Ryan…" Emily jumped in. "Can't you see we're beside ourselves with worry?"

"This could be life or death!" continued Sophie. "They're my family, haven't you betrayed me enough already, or does someone else I care about need to die first?!"

"Relax, both of you… they're fine."

"How do you know?!" demanded Sophie angrily, then again, more insistent: "How do you know?!"

"Isn't it obvious? You've yet to call that number. They'll be perfectly safe until you know what they want. My advice: don't call them. Not until, that is, you're ready to deal with the consequences of their demands."

CHAPTER THIRTY-SIX
BRAYDEN

Special Agent Mullins found Brayden back in his room at the London Marriott Hotel County Hall. Lying on his bed, he had a wet towel draped across his face providing scant relief, like the paracetamol tablets he'd downed together with a swig of *Russian Standard* vodka a short time earlier. Sophie firing Mullins' gun next to his head had given him a splitting migraine that pained him almost as intensely as the ringing that continued to scream within his left eardrum.

"So, what now?" Mullins sat, and then stretched out on the bed next to Brayden, resting her head on the pillow. Through the window she could see the Houses of Parliament with Big Ben foremost across the Thames, a few boats bobbing about on its dull-grey surface.

Through the towel Brayden made a noise that sounded like, "I don't know," but she might have imagined it.

"She'll still be made to account for her crimes." Mullins was still dwelling on Sophie Jennings, and the affidavit which precluded her from prosecution for any past transgressions.

Brayden dragged the towel free from his head and tossed it to the floor where it landed with a heavy thud. "What crimes?" He winced from the sound of his own voice which seemed to boom within his head. Speaking a little quieter, he said: "She was acting under orders. She's a fellow intelligence agent. Let's admit it; we would've done the same thing..."

"But Brayden, innocent people were killed... American people!"

"People die within our line of work all the time... you know that. Fact. It's the nature of the beast. No, we're to let it go... for now. The President wants us to focus on Dominic instead. If, as Emily suggested, he has some of the *GYGES* super soldiers, we need to locate them and take them back home. That's our latest priority."

"What about Sophie?" Mullins wasn't willing to give up quite as easily as Brayden, but then, she hadn't had a gun fired close to the side of her head.

"Maybe she'll give herself up to us... when this is all over," he said optimistically. "*Willingly*, of course..."

"Okay, so back to my original question. What now?"

Brayden closed his eyes for a moment; his pounding head was making it difficult to think. In the end he didn't bother. "I'm going to try and sleep this headache off. Why don't you do what you suggested at breakfast. Take some down time and do some of the sights. Maybe get in a show? It's New Year's Day... we shouldn't be working... not today."

"Seriously?" Mullins' mood seemed to brighten. "It would be good to take a break. Are you sure?"

"Knock yourself out. Take the rest of the day off. We'll get back together in the morning; hopefully I'll feel better. If anything urgent comes up, I'll call."

━━━━◆━◆━━━━

Stepping back into the SIS building the following morning feeling refreshed and completely recovered from his headache and deafness, Brayden found himself accompanying both Sophie and Emily along the many corridors towards their shared office. Walking in silence, the atmosphere was thorny and restrained. At the door, Brayden gestured the MI6 agents to go forward. "After you."

Emily smiled. Swiping her cardkey, the door glided open. Sophie rolled her eyes and followed the older woman in.

Agent Mullins was already there within the room. So too were Mac, dressed more suitably for an analyst in a shirt and tie combo, and a full contingent of analysts and agents milling around, including Jez and Belle, and a mix of MI6, FBI and CIA.

"Sophie... about yesterday," Brayden started, halting the woman's progress with a hand grab. He looked uncomfortable and awkward.

Sophie stopped just inside the doorway, Emily walking away ahead. She turned her head, an uneasy look upon her face. "Yes?"

"We got off to a crappy start. Can we put it in the past? Start fresh?"

Sophie's face drained of seriousness. She replied with a warm smile, exposing the full whites of her teeth. "Sure."

"Oh, and... just so you know there's no hard feelings... here. I've brought you something." Brayden had carried a black bag with him – like a rubbish sack – through the building. Both Sophie and Emily had noticed it but hadn't wished to impose by asking what was in it. Now Sophie was going to find out. He gently dropped it at her feet.

"It's not your dirty laundry, is it?" accepting the bag from Brayden. She tested its weight, noting that it didn't feel very heavy which added conviction to her guess.

"No, I have room service taking care of that," replied Brayden soberly.

Sophie pulled the bag open and reached in. "Is it...?" Her eyes lit up.

"Yep. It was recovered from the *United Airlines* plane you escaped from back in Fresno..."

Sophie pulled free her backpack and unzipped it smoothly. Inside were a few items of clothing and something familiar which immediately grabbed her attention.

"Flopsy!" she exclaimed, pulling the stuffed toy kangaroo free, acting like a kid – which, in reality, she was. After all, she was only celebrating her fourth birth year come April sixteenth.

"I thought you might like having them returned."

"You betcha! I thought I'd lost them forever!" Sophie raised the fluffy kangaroo to her face and rubbed it against her cheek. Feeling it, so soft, brought back memories of her father. He had gifted it to her after a day trip when he'd taken his wife and other children to London Zoo, a small consolation for being uninvited, but cherished nonetheless. "My father bought it for me," she said. "You don't know how much this means. It has sentimental value. Thank you."

"You're welcome," replied Brayden, grinning. All was forgiven it seemed. In that moment, it was hard to imagine Sophie being anything more than just an innocent, beautiful, young lady. Then a dark thought surfaced and he recalled how she had fought her way out of the terminal building, laying out seasoned field agents and evading capture from the best of them. He left Sophie holding her backpack and the toy, shaking his head, slightly bemused and joined up with Special Agent Mullins.

"Where've you been?" asked his partner. She'd looked for him at breakfast, and even knocked at his door shortly after, but found the CIA agent had risen early and had left the hotel building.

"Oh, went for a run, and then had to fetch something, is all." Peering over his shoulder, he saw Sophie pretend-walking the toy kangaroo on Emily's desk towards the bespectacled woman, like it were a Christmas gift. Both women were laughing, hardly a care in the world it seemed.

<hr>

"This is a photograph of Sophie's sister and two brothers: Meredith, Stanley and Charlie."

It was an hour later and Emily was standing at the head of the table in the conference room holding up the large black and white photograph. Around her were half a dozen senior analysts, as well as Brayden, Christina Mullins and Sophie, all sitting around on either side of the table giving her their full attention.

"They were kidnapped from their grandfather's home on New Year's Eve, and haven't been seen since. It was around the same time Ryan was shot. Yesterday, this photograph was delivered to Ryan's ward at the hospital. On the back..." Emily turned it over, "... this is written."

Sophie... if you want to see them again, call me.

Brayden raised his hand.

"Yes."

"Might be stating the obvious, but shouldn't Sophie just call the number?" Brayden looked about the table for endorsement. One or two nodded, which was good enough to motivate him further. "I mean, shouldn't we find out what they want?"

Emily half-nodded. "Sure. Maybe. Ryan was of the opinion that, by withholding contact, we'll have more time to prepare for dealing with whatever the demands are. It's not like they've given us an ultimatum or a specific timeframe."

"Yet," stated Agent Mullins weightily.

"Yet," Emily agreed. "So, whilst we decide when to call the number, we need to group our minds together and find out what we can about the burglaries in Scotland, where the perps' base of operations is, what's happened to the stolen property, and how this latest development," Emily flapped the photograph in front of her, "fits in. It would be great if we can find out what they plan next and pre-empt their next strike, catch them in the act."

Brayden's hand shot up again.

"Yes?" uttered Emily, a little abruptly.

"I don't get it. Sure, I understand the need to find out the answers to all those questions, but delaying contact with the kidnappers... that's high-risk strategy. I mean, you're putting lives at stake. Don't you think they will think something is off by not contacting them? They've got three hostages... at the moment. Plenty of flesh to bargain with."

Emily gave Brayden a withering look.

Brayden held up the flat of a hand in an apologetic manner. "It's what I would do, is all. Plus, it's something from the 'Idiot's Guide to Kidnapping' manual," he said, jokingly.

Some titters, sniggers and laughter erupted around the table.

Sophie glanced at Brayden and then across to Emily, reading their body language, their expressions and demeanour. Emily's was tense, her face challenging, almost stubborn. Brayden's was relaxed, confident. The twinkle in his eye indicated to her that he enjoyed sparring verbally, almost as much as he enjoyed physical conflict. Sophie returned her eyes to Brayden who caught and held them with his own.

"All I am saying..." Brayden said, seeming to speak directly to Sophie, "... is, hasn't Sophie lost enough family members... and friends, already?"

Emily, still standing, folded her arms across her chest, her cheeks slightly flushed and her form indicative of a woman scorned. "Agent Scott... I'd like to remind you that you are a guest, and that, whilst Ryan Barber is... *on leave*, I AM in charge."

A couple of the agents fidgeted uncomfortably in their seats.

Brayden raised his hands up in mock-surrender. "Apologies, Ma'am. No disrespect intended. But..." he turned again to Sophie, sitting opposite him, allowing his argument to go on unspoken.

"He's got a point," Sophie intervened, hoping to diffuse the situation. Immediately, Emily shot her a look of disapproval. "Who's to know what's being done to my brothers and sister whilst we sit here and argue what we do next. They are children. They are scared. I don't think we can afford to sit back and gamble with their lives on a theory that Ryan put forward from his hospital bed. I don't want to sound callous, but the man isn't in the best shape at the moment... plus, he's made some questionable decisions in the past," *like going after the sons of GYGES instead of my father*, she considered saying, but thought better of it. "I think this should be my decision."

Emily's demeanour softened. "Okay," she encouraged.

"I've decided that I will do what the note says. I want... no, *need*... to know what they want."

Brayden looked smugly towards Emily who sat down, dispirited, in surrender.

"Well... if there's nothing else," said Brayden, making movements to stand. "I think we should all crack on and get with it."

CHAPTER THIRTY-SEVEN
SOPHIE

"You don't have to** do this... not right now. Ryan's idea–"

"Ryan has had a lot of ideas these past few months... not all of them have ended well. Not for me at least. This time, we do this my way." Sophie interrupted Emily abruptly and icily. She was holding the black and white photo of her siblings in one hand and a phone handset in the other.

The two of them had stayed behind in the conference room, Brayden reluctantly leaving when it was clear his attendance wasn't wanted.

Emily looked downcast, slightly hurt by the venom in the young woman's voice. "Okay. Go ahead; I won't stand in your way. But you do it with our help. You're not going rogue." She gently placed a hand over Sophie's and guided her into replacing the telephone receiver back into its cradle. "Make the call outside." Emily indicated the operation room beyond the tough, soundproofed glass wall that separated it from the private meeting area. "The phone in here is secure. We would do better to use an open line and employ *StingRay* to help try and trace the mobile number." *StingRay* was an IMSI (International Mobile Subscriber Identity) catcher, or more simply, an eavesdropping device that helped locate the whereabouts of a mobile phone whilst in use, and, sometimes, when not. Widely used by American law-enforcement to track and trace criminals, it was less common owing to budgetary constraints within the UK. However, MI6 used it regularly for covert intelligence gathering, and London's Metropolitan Police were rumoured to use such technology, although nothing official had ever been proven and, when questioned, the Police Commissioner refused to comment.

"Whatever. Let's go do this."

A section at the back of the operation area was cleared leaving a large round table, upon which only a telephone with a multitude of wires attached to it was placed.

Around the table sat Sophie, Emily, Brayden, Mullins and Mac, giving the appearance of an ill-fitting group at a séance – the only thing missing was their holding hands and a dimly lit setting. Sophie was clutching the black and white photograph, like she was a spiritualist about to attempt communication with the dead and using it as a conduit to the afterlife, focusing and mentally trying to compose herself. She looked about nervously, and had emptied a cup of water with barely a gasp a moment earlier. Despite this, she felt like she had cotton-mouth and her throat was bone-dry. She coughed to try and clear it.

"Okay, we're all set. We're ready when you are," prompted Mac, contorted awkwardly over the back of his seat to a desk behind him where he stretched to reach a keyboard. A large flat LCD computer screen faced him upon which the *StingRay* compatible software glared out. He quickly keyed in some orders before twisting himself back to face his colleagues gathered in front of him.

Sophie stood a little to extend her reach for the telephone, set at the centre of the table. She pulled the wired object closer to herself until within range and plucked up the handset attached with a black coiled wire as she sat back down. Quickly, she punched in the mobile number that was scribbled on the reverse of the photograph, just south of its author's written demand.

Sophie lifted the phone receiver to her ear, hearing the ringing tone almost immediately. It trilled for a long time before being replaced by a woman's voice:

"We was a wonderin' whether yous was gonna call?" She spoke in a calm, casual manner. Sophie identified the woman as having a thick, Scottish accent, the lilt and pitch smooth and attractive, unlike some of the harsh, regional dialects heard north of the border.

"Who are you?"

The woman laughed teasingly at the other end. *"I'm jus' a wee smout... jus' goin' between."* She used the word smout, meaning 'unimportant' person.

"You have my brothers and sister... in the photo. You left a message for me to call. What do you want?"

The woman ignored the question. *"I s'ppose yous are try'n to track me wher'aboots... dinnae bother. I'll save yous the fasht..."* trouble.

Mac, who was carefully watching the LCD screen over his shoulder, shot up an arm, drawing attention to himself. "Found them!" he exclaimed with a fist pump. The location of the person at the end of the phone flashed up in front of him.

"Aye, we're here in Edinburgh... Waverley Station, to be preceese, gilravaging a bargain bucket of southern fried choukie."

"Waverley Mall Shopping Centre, next to the rail station," relayed Mac from the computer monitor. "Appears to be from within the food hall."

"What about the children? I need to know that they are safe," Sophie demanded.

"Aye, yous do. They willnae be hairmed, as'long as yous stay out of our bus'ness, that's a promise. And then there's the small matter of a di'mond yous owe."

"Diamond?

"*The Whisper of Persia… yous not forgotten it already?*"

Sophie fidgeted uncomfortably in her seat. She had her suspicions, and now the Scottish voice confirmed it. It was Dominic Schilling all along; him, seemingly, with his diamond obsession.

"*He wants to meet yous to discuss. Says he'll throw in a sweet'ner. He'll let you have one of the wee things back, but only if yous come.*"

"Okay. When?" Sophie relished the chance of seeing the man again. She had promised herself that when she did, she would kill him. Now she was going to be meeting with him, resisting the urge to strangle him was going to be very difficult. "Where?" she added solemnly.

"*He'll meet yous here, the-morn – that's tomorrow. Come alone. He'll be waitin' all efternuin. If yous not here, we'll still returns one of the wee things… only they's won't be breathing…*"

"I'll be there," seethed Sophie, her hand threatening to crush the phone's receiver in her grip, the skin over her knuckles were taut and bright white. Before she could add anything further, like the standard threat: *if you do anything to them, I'll kill you*, the line was disconnected.

"We've found them," repeated Mac for Sophie's benefit, "Waverley Mall Shopping Centre, Edinburgh, the food hall."

Sophie sighed loudly as she placed the phone's receiver back into its cradle. "*KFC* to be exact," she replied. "They knew we would be tracing the call, so made no attempt at hiding."

"We could have police at the scene within minutes, and agents within the hour," projected Emily, standing up, all abuzz. "Mac, access CCTV, see if we can find them on the grid, let's locate and follow them."

"Already on it," he replied.

"Wait!" Sophie spoke firmly. "Just hold on. They have my family.

Don't you think Dominic will know what we're capable of doing? Don't you think he's already planned for this? He knows how we operate, what surveillance equipment we have and he's prepared for it."

"I hate to admit it, but she's got a point," said Brayden cautiously. It was hard to believe that less than twenty-four hours earlier he'd wanted to arrest the blonde girl. Then, she had fired a gun next to his head in response, nearly deafening him. Now he was defending her, an act which appeared to surprise Mullins sitting next to him. "He'll expect us, and there are other things at stake." Brayden looked up towards Sophie. "What do you want to do, Sophie? It's your call."

Without hesitation, she replied. "We do as the woman said. I go meet with Dominic – ALONE – and listen to what the man has to say."

"Okay," Brayden was nodding.

"Okay," concurred Emily. "I'll get clearance from the Chief and start making the arrangements."

⸺ ◆ ⸺

The *Westland Puma* helicopter, with its dark olive-green paintjob, was preparing to take off from a short landing strip outside the control tower at RAF Northolt, its four-blade rotor system kicking up dust and causing wind to gust and batter the short line of passengers who alighted from two mini buses parked at the edge of the airfield; they were heading for the military aircraft taking big strides and looking keen for action. Accompanying Sophie were Emily, Brayden, Christina Mullins, four FBI/CIA agents and four MI6 field agents.

It was a little less than twenty-two hours since Sophie's call with the Scottish woman had ended, and preparations for their Edinburgh bound journey were complete. A quick glance at her watch confirmed it was close to the scheduled departure time of 10:00 a.m. Climbing up the step and onto the *Puma*, Sophie couldn't help feeling nauseous at the thought of flying on a helicopter again. She clutched the doorframe, unable to move forward. Sounds, images and smells from Nevada, of the *Chinooks*, flooded her memory.

"It'll be all right," reassured Emily. When learning of the travel plans, Sophie had voiced her concerns. Emily hadn't realised that the young woman had developed a phobia. Phobias were something an 'emotion inhibitor' would have eliminated... which her father had genetically added to his next batch of test subjects.

"Sure," replied Sophie, prising her hands free from the doorframe and forcing her legs to take her in.

On board the helicopter were three others waiting expectantly; two helicopter crew (one the pilot, the other a weapons system officer), both dressed in their all-in-one *Nomex* olive flight suits and wearing big headsets that concealed their ears, and one other Sophie recognised from the *GYGES* mission.

"Ladies..." Speaking in his gruff voice, the big man was quick to acknowledge Sophie and Emily and was smiling, genuinely pleased to see them. "I've saved you a couple of seats back here." He hadn't done any such thing; except for him and the two crew, the helicopter was empty. That soon changed. With seating for sixteen passengers, once Sophie, Emily and their FBI, CIA and MI6 entourage were strapped in, there were three seats left vacant.

The crew of the helicopter disappeared into the cockpit.

Sophie tried not to draw attention to her discomfort, barely acknowledging him. She took a seat behind the overly-familiar man.

"Liam... what are you doing here?" asked Emily, noting that he was dressed almost identical to how she remembered him from before: khaki-green T-shirt (still too small) and dark-green combat trousers. On his feet were the black *Alt-Berg* combat boots, though they were now a little scuffed and muddied. "You said you were retiring." The last time Emily had seen the man first encountered on Barry's *Bombardier* at Dulles International Airport, was in London when they had returned from California on the same jet, battle-weary and exhausted. They had said their goodbyes, and Liam had made noises that he had had enough, and that he was going to settle down somewhere and live a quiet life.

It was hard to believe that had only been two months ago.

"Well," Liam's smile faded, "I heard what happened to Ryan... and, with Barry dead," he said sadly, "I thought you might need a friendly face to keep you company."

In a window seat, Sophie peered out to look at gloomy London. It always seemed to be raining and a regularly overcast January day met her gaze. The noise of the helicopter steadily increased before it rocked a little from side to side and juddered as it left the ground, taking off gently, and rising fast into the late morning sky. Sophie clutched the padding of her seat, unable to subdue the unease enveloping her.

With a maximum speed of 159 mph, the pilot of the RAF helicopter announced that they were due to arrive at Edinburgh Airport around 1:00 p.m.

"It wouldn't have taken much longer had we gone by train," griped Sophie, though no one heard her over the drone and roar of the *Puma's* twin engines, and the statement wasn't strictly true. To travel by train from Kings Cross to Edinburgh was four-and-three-quarter hours.

Ahead, in the seats in front, Emily and Liam chatted animatedly, occasionally laughing. All around the cabin relaxed conversations were taking place. Brayden and Mullins. FBI and CIA agents. MI6 colleagues. No one was bothered by their method of transport, or by the situation they were flying towards.

But none of them came close to being shot out of the sky, she reflected. Sophie tried to close everything out and wished herself not there, a process that was now extremely simple. Although vanishing to nothing solved many problems, this time it didn't. Physically she was still in place and the change did nothing to alleviate the unease she felt.

She closed her eyes and tried to sleep the time and her fears away.

CHAPTER THIRTY-EIGHT
DOMINIC

Edinburgh's Hogmanay festivities run for three days and are famous, not only in Scotland, but the world over. Hundreds of thousands of revellers turn up for the New Year's festival; drinking, eating and enjoying the entertainment that brims from every pub, theatre and street corner, a gargantuan party unlike anything witnessed around the globe.

Although Dominic's visit to Scotland's capital was strictly for business, Elspeth's wasn't. It was difficult for him not to be swept up in all the excitement that seemed to flourish across the city, the small woman sharing and delighting in as much exuberance as Edinburgh had to offer.

Now it was over and the mood of the city was vapid, like everyone was nursing the mother of all hangovers, which for the vast majority – indeed most of Scotland – was entirely true.

But not for Dominic, who woke early that third January morning fresh and clear-headed and bolstered by the events laid out for the day. The same couldn't be said for Elspeth, who had imbibed too much alcohol late into the night and had buried her head deep beneath a pile of pillows, trying to lessen the pounding that seemed to emanate from deep within her skull.

"I'm going for a run," Dominic informed her. "I'll be back in an hour."

From beneath the pillows, Elspeth grunted.

Inserting small in-the-ear earphones, Dominic pressed play on his *iPod* and left the hotel room, walking the corridor and taking the elevator to ground level. As he passed reception, the concierge greeted him with a "Good morning." Dominic returned it, splashing a smile.

Exiting The Balmoral Hotel, he immediately set off into a light jog along deserted roads, heading in the direction of the castle, the mound and Princes Street Gardens.

After ten minutes and barely breaking a sweat, he sat down on a bench opposite to the Ross Fountain centrally placed beneath the castle within Princes Street Gardens. Reaching into his pocket, he fumbled for his mobile, a cheap pay-as-you-go phone he'd bought for twenty quid from a supermarket. It was caught up amongst a packet of tissues and some loose change, but soon came free. Pressing redial on the *Nokia* handset, he lifted it to his left ear.

The call was answered immediately.

"Hector. Are you ready?"

"*Aye. Just about to leave.*"

"Good. You know where to go. Remember, if you don't hear from me or Elsp-."

"*Yes, I know,*" Hector blurted, "*I'm to kill the kid and deliver her body to her grandfather's house in pieces, it's not gonna be a problem.*" Dominic didn't like the man's attitude and made a mental note to deal with him later.

"Don't let me down."

"*I won't.*"

Dominic pressed the end button and held the black *Nokia* for a moment in quiet contemplation. Yesterday, Sophie had been speaking to Elspeth on it. Just a cheap phone with an unregistered SIM placed within. The fact MI6 had likely traced its location did not concern him; not because he was unafraid of capture, or the fact that he was using his bargaining chip to protect his freedom, but because what MI6 had likely tracked was not the phone – or *his* – location, but a place he'd anticipated would be that afternoon's meeting point with Sophie.

A small high-tech device supplied by Kaplan Ratcliff the size of an *iPod* shuffle, which Dominic coincidentally called a 'shuffler', had been stuck discretely to the underside of a table in the food hall within Waverley Mall Shopping Centre earlier the previous day. Acting as a receiver and transmitter, the device intercepted any calls made to his mobile phone, broadcasting its carefully manipulated location for anyone wishing to attempt tracing it, before transferring the digital telecommunication signals onwards to the actual handset undetected. Although there was a slight lag between speaking and hearing, it was barely noticeable, and had anyone tried to intercept him using the 'shuffler's' transmitted position, they'd have turned up empty handed and totally out of luck.

Feeling significantly colder now that he had nothing to distract his thoughts, he stood up and began to jog some more for warmth, and because he wanted to return to the hotel for a shower before a hearty buffet breakfast. A couple of other people had the same idea regarding the brisk morning and were out jogging, running either towards or past him as he made his way along a path parallel with Princes Street towards the gardens' exit.

Soon he was running past the Victorian gothic monument erected to celebrate the life of the Scottish author Sir Walter Scott, and quickly beyond it, the Waverley Mall Shopping Centre and the railway station were coming into sight.

Crossing Waverley Bridge, Dominic visualised the forthcoming encounter with Sophie as he skirted the entrance to the shopping centre and continued contemplating it as he progressed his jog into a run, taking loping strides along the road in the direction of his hotel, suddenly eager to get back to his room where he could better prepare, hoping Elspeth had recovered enough so that he could enjoy some intimate time and burn off some of his excited energy.

CHAPTER THIRTY-NINE
MEREDITH

MEREDITH WONDERED WHO HAD kidnapped her and her two brothers, and why?

Locked within the room with three beds for furniture and nothing by way of entertainment, it was another seriously low point in their short lives. With no windows or toilet facilities, the only relief from discomfort – both physical (the need to pee) and mental (the need for a change in scene) – came just three times in the day; an hour after breakfast, an hour after lunchtime and an hour after dinner.

If they wanted the toilet at any other point, they soon learned the harsh reality: *you can't always get what you want.*

A slosh bucket placed in the corner of the room was provided for their use, affording no privacy. Charlie, to Meredith's amusement, had refused to use it, soiling himself on more than one occasion since being held captive. This infuriated their captors no end, an outcome that appeared to motivate him to do it more.

Toilet walks – or 'twalks' as they soon became known – were begrudgingly carried out on an individual basis. In turn, each of them would be collected from the room and taken for a short walk down a dark, sterile corridor as devoid of light as an underground catacomb, to a bathroom that had been built for purpose rather than comfort.

'Twalks' were carried out by either Hector or Natasha, the names of their abductors, which was all they knew of the pair, though

Charlie continued to refer to them as 'Scary' and 'Scarier', the man the former and the woman the latter. It was clear which one of them wore the trousers, metaphorically, and it wasn't the man from what the children had seen.

Meredith had learned their names during an overheard exchange between the two; this had taken place shortly after first encountering the woman on day one. Meredith had pressed her left ear up against the door and had listened intently for the woman, or someone's, return, an act that soon formed into habit and a daily ritual.

With meal times and 'twalks' the only interruption to the tedium of being caged like dangerous animals or a circus freak of old, Meredith quickly adapted to use the infrequent visitations to map out the day in a crude, ancient timekeeping fashion. Identifying the meal by the type of ingredients served, Meredith was able to track the time of day, and the approximate duration of their confinement.

Meredith had counted five meals since arrival.

The first had been paraded as breakfast and lunch, commonly referred to as *brunch*, but applying the term here was ridiculous. When the woman – Natasha – had lifted the metal cover on one of the food trays she'd wheeled in on the waiter's trolley, she presented burnt toast and butter. There was also two plastic cereal dispensers, one containing *Corn Flakes*, the other *Rice Crispies* and a serving jug half-filled with a UHT milk derivative, which tasted disgusting. Fruit juice cordial and water was also supplied. To say 'no expense spared' was an understatement.

Owing to their circumstances, they hadn't eaten much of what was on offer, and the man – Hector – soon came to retrieve the trolley. It was a little later that the routine of 'twalks' began.

The next food delivery, half a dozen hours later, was a cooked dinner comprising of potatoes, various vegetables, and a casserole containing a meat which none of the children could identify. When asked, Hector just shrugged and said that it was: "Meat." Now hungry, Meredith, Stanley and Charlie ate heartily, devouring every morsel.

Breakfast came next (the same as before, but with the added bonus of fruit, bread, and a mixture of preserves), followed by lunch (ham and cheese sandwiches); dinner again (steak pie and chips) and, most recently, breakfast.

Like the previous day, breakfast consisted of much the same offerings and Meredith, Stanley and Charlie filled their stomachs, relishing the relief from boredom that mealtimes provided. On collection of the serving trolley, Hector accompanied Natasha for the now routine 'twalk'.

"You." Hector, dressed in dark blue combat trousers, white T-shirt and a black leather flying jacket, pointed towards Charlie.

Charlie stood up from his bed and cautiously approached the man. As he passed him by, Hector placed a hand across his back. Charlie looked over his shoulder nervously towards Meredith who nodded slightly and half-smiled, willing him to be brave. Once outside the room, the door was locked behind them and Hector marched him away.

"I don't like this anymore," whispered Stanley miserably. "They took mum... now mum's –" *dead.*

"Please stop!" Meredith shouted unintentionally, borne out of frustration and the fact she didn't really want to dwell on it. "I wish they'd just tell us what they wanted," she added exasperatedly, standing up from her bed's edge and pacing the room again, clasping and unclasping her hands in agitation. Pacing was all she ever did; that and listening up against the door. "If we knew what it was, maybe we could help."

Stanley started to cry. "I want to go home," he said wretchedly.

"I know," she said, soothingly. She sat down next to the boy and draped an arm across his shoulders.

Charlie was washed and wearing a change of clothing when he returned maybe half an hour later. Meredith was guessing the time. He was wearing nothing fancy, just a plain grey sweatshirt and a pair of tracksuit bottoms secured at the waist with a drawstring. He sat down on his bed and watched Hector repeat the process with Stanley.

Another half an hour or so went by and Stanley returned, similarly fresh and attired as Charlie. Natasha was escorting him this time, relieving Hector from the task to go and answer a phone call.

"Meredith. Now your turn..." said the woman Charlie had nicknamed 'Scarier.'

Meredith had still been pacing when the sound of the door being unlocked filled the room once again. She was on the far side of the room, a step away from the slosh bucket when the woman had reappeared. Although relieved – or would be when she had been to the toilet – for a change of scene, something about the way the woman stared at her made her nervous.

"Come on, I ain't got all day!" Natasha did not hide her impatience and tapped her foot in agitation.

"I am!" Meredith back-answered. She grabbed Stanley's hand as she passed and gently squeezed it. He squeezed back for reassurance.

"That's right, sweetie. Say goodbye to your sister," The woman mocked menacingly.

In the corridor, Natasha halted Meredith with a tug at her arm whilst she locked the door behind her. The ten-year-old looked over her shoulder, peering beyond the woman down the length of the corridor, which appeared brighter than usual. Before she realised the source of the light, her escort shoved her in the back, forcing her forward. "Well, move then!" Natasha ordered.

At first Meredith couldn't move, her gaze transfixed on the natural light that entered through the opening at the end of the corridor.

Focusing on it she could see what looked like grey sky beyond the doorway, with a frothy-white and grey skirt undulating beneath it.

The woman raised her hand threateningly. "I said move!" she snarled.

Meredith turned away and pushed forward reluctantly. A second nudge from behind made the young girl look back angrily. "I'm going!" she hissed.

She needed little encouragement, knowing the direction of the 'twalk' from memory. It was now possible, she thought, to negotiate the way in the dark from memory alone; the excursion took them past five doors on one side of the corridor and six others on the opposite before branching left at the end. The bathroom facilities were just a little way further ahead.

At the door, she glanced to her left, her eyes following the passage which continued a similar length to the one she'd just trudged.

"Wash and shower. There are clothes on the chair." The door to the bathroom opened out into the corridor. Natasha twisted the silver knob and pulled it open; it swung gently away from her, the hinges to her left. "I'll be back in twenty minutes to collect you."

"Pity," muttered Meredith, stepping into the drably-painted room. She glanced around the familiar four walls, observed the lack of fixtures and fittings adorning the plain white tiled surfaces, unchanged from previous visits. Behind her, the woman closed and locked the door.

Above the sink was a mirror screwed into the wall. She quietly studied her reflection, noting how tired and haggard she looked and how lacklustre and lifeless her dark-blonde hair appeared. Forsaking herself for a moment, her eyes surveyed the area of the mirror surrounding her, searching for something, for –

– *someone...*

"Sophie," she whispered. "Where are you?" Meredith half-expected/half-hoped to see her sister appear in the mirror, like the girl had all of those magical times in the antique mirror, placed above her dresser in the old house when she'd first discovered her, when she believed the girl to be just a ghost.

This had been before they'd moved to Willoughby Rising; Sophie had appeared much younger then.

Now, Sophie was a woman having aged rapidly during the relatively short time she'd known her. Meredith didn't really understand it all, only that her father had done something to make it happen.

Unsurprisingly, Sophie's image did not appear alongside her own, and thoughts of her father surfaced, forcing sombre memories upon her.

"No Sophie," she said, feeling dismal. "No dad. No mum. You're all gone." The realisation stung like a slap and she flinched from its force and started to sob.

Meredith undressed quickly, turned on the shower and stepped into a glassed-off cubical, its swing-door gently closed behind her. The gush of hot spray felt refreshing and almost pleasant against her cool skin. Closing her eyes, it was easy to almost forget where she was. Soon the misery that had engulfed her moments before, and her tears blending in with the jet of water from the shower, dissipated.

Bottles of shampoo and shower gel were affixed to the wall within push-button dispensers and Meredith helped herself to each in good measure, washing herself from head to toe thoroughly, lathering herself up and scrubbing, raking her fingernails across her skin. Feeling relaxed as she washed the soap away from her body, she pulled the shower head down from its bracket and held it in one hand. Now serene, she asked herself one simple question:

What would Sophie do?

Of course, Meredith knew she wasn't Sophie, and without any

of her wondrous abilities she never would be, but a strange, exciting thought entered the ten-year-old's head.

"I can do it," she said softly, steel in her voice, accepting the idea as though it had been planted divinely. Were she to have studied her reflection in the mirror above the washbasin at that precise moment, she would have seen determination simmering within her eyes, staring back at her.

"I WILL do it!"

The shower disguised her voice, but even had it not, no one was nearby to hear it. Unbeknownst to her, the facility within which she was being held was almost deserted, and the hundred-plus inhabitants away. They were following orders that she was earmarked to play a small, but integral part in.

She stepped out of the shower, reached for a plain white towel, and dabbed herself dry, prolonging the moment.

As Natasha had mentioned on arrival, there was clothing on the chair. Like Charlie and Stanley before, matching sweatshirt and tracksuit trouser combos had been selected for her; someone unimaginative had gone shopping, most likely a man (Hector), and probably at *Primark*. He'd spared the expense. Unlike Charlie and Stanley, footwear had been left out for her (white unbranded trainers), as well as a red padded winter coat, one with a fur-lined hood.

Instead of questioning the choice laid out before her, she embraced it, dressing hurriedly. She was sure that her twenty minutes were over and willed the woman to hurry up and return.

As Meredith zipped up her coat, the telltale hint that the woman was back sounded from outside the door.

Jangling keys.

As Natasha swiftly inserted the key into the door's lock and placed a hand on the metal knob, Meredith quickly moved into position. When the door opened slightly, without thinking and on cue, Meredith launched herself.

The run-up provided the momentum needed to propel the door fully open, knocking Natasha completely over with a jumping kick, using her shock to gain the advantage. Bursting from the bathroom, she hurtled down the corridor in a sprint, turning onto the main stretch where she quickly counted down the doors as she passed.

Five on one side, six on the other.

They all looked the same; plain, solid, unmarked and unidentifiable. After the fifth door, she knew the next door led into the room within which her brothers were still being detained.

Looking at the lock, Meredith's heart sank. The keyhole was there, but the key was not. With false hope, she tried the handle.

The door didn't budge.

Behind her, the woman had regained her composure and was running after her.

"YOU! COME BACK HERE!!" she screamed pointlessly.

"I'm sorry," Meredith said to her brothers, leaving the door and charging off towards the exit at the end of the corridor, beyond which was the great outdoors and (she perceived) freedom. *I'll send help*, she told herself, making the decision to abandon Stanley and Charlie more bearable, giving it necessity.

Arriving at the end of the corridor, Meredith crashed into the door, throwing her full weight against the metal in tandem with her flailing hand that slammed down on the handle. She was sure it was going to be locked; expected it.

Satisfyingly, it wasn't, and the cold, murky, outside welcomed her with promises of salvation and hope.

Meredith didn't know what to expect as she jogged further out, stopping briefly to consider her options. It was drizzling, but the weather hardly mattered and didn't hamper her.

Ahead, she could see the sea between a number of ramshackle cottages in various states of repair, and over the top of a sandy hillock in the short distance beyond the cottages; a dirty dishwater grey, waves undulating and crashing against a narrow jetty that stretched out like an admonishing finger. A small fishing boat was moored to it, offering a glimmer of hope.

Behind her, the door crashed open loudly, Natasha spilling out, off-balanced. She sprawled to the ground, screaming: "Meredith! COME HERE!!" sounding like a witch in a Grimms' fairy tale.

Throwing a look back over her shoulder, Meredith saw the anger in the woman's eyes, and something else.

Fear.

Whilst considering her pursuer, she briefly noticed the building from which she had escaped. A large, windowless construction that looked almost alien and positively out of place within the setting, positioned as it was in the gardens of the row of old cottages that sprawled along an ancient cobbled road. She thought it looked a bit like a warehouse, the type often seen placed around the quayside of busy container ports.

It was black, matching her thoughts, and oppressive, like the designs of her captors.

Galvanised, Meredith ran towards the cottages, heading for a sizeable gap that fell between two where once another cottage had stood; crumbling brick and stones were all that remained, crunching under foot amidst nettles and sandy loam. The roar of the sea was loud, and she was soon clear of the buildings, bounding for the mound that had been originally designed and placed to provide a defence against flooding and a bit of a buffer from the harsh winds that battered the island, although she was not aware she was on an island – not just then – and had no thoughts as to which direction she should go; all she knew was she had to keep moving. She had to get away and get help – for her AND for her brothers' sakes.

"HECTOR!" The woman yelled for her companion who, unknown to Meredith, was around the side of the black building. On hearing his name spoken in such a pained tone, he came running fast and appeared within the clearing between the warehouse and the cottages to Natasha's right within seconds. "SHE'S GETTING AWAY!"

Hector watched Natasha give chase and started to laugh. The situation wasn't funny, but the way Natasha was running (like a school girl, arms flapping limply at her sides, her gait more shuffle than sprint), he couldn't help but be amused.

"No, sugar; she's not." He thought to use the gun that was stuffed beneath the waist of his jeans just above his left butt-cheek, but dismissed it.

Dominic wouldn't accept her being dead. It wasn't part of the plan... especially as, Hector thought, he'd just received instructions from the man informing him to deliver the girl to a place in Edinburgh.

"DON'T JUST STAND THERE!!" screamed Natasha desperately, charging away. Meredith was now on the other side of the hillock, no longer in her pursuer's, or Hector's line of sight. A shingle beach was all that now separated her and the sea, and both beach and sea stretched for as far as she could see, left and right of her.

"DON'T PANIC! I'VE GOT THIS!" Meredith heard Hector holler back. She decided to aim for the fishing boat bobbing up and down on the water tied to a post on the jetty, and started running hard towards it. As she closed in on the rickety wooden jetty, twenty metres (or just a little over) of beach between her and the first steps, the young man Charlie had nicknamed 'Scary' appeared impossibly at the top of the sandy bank AHEAD of her.

Not stopping, she ran harder, thinking she could outrun him, her chest heaving and breath laboured. She could see the steps leading up to the small pier clearly, but every stride caused her lungs to burn, and every exhalation came with a pained sound; a wheezing, braying.

Nearly there! Meredith encouraged her legs to keep on moving and willed her lungs to continue pumping oxygen into her bloodstream.

Yes... Nearly... The jetty was now five metres ahead, so close she could almost reach out and touch the wooden railing.

Like a marathon runner she found an extra ounce of strength in her limbs and urged herself forward, one final effort, just a little more... just a little more...

A whistling/flapping sound grew into prominence from behind, like a rope lasso being helicopter-rotored above one's head.

Thwapp!!

... she felt the ground rush up to meet her as both her legs became entangled and were swept out abruptly from underneath.

Falling forward hard, her body slammed with a THUD against the shingle. A groan escaped her lips from the force as she skidded, and stopped, a fingertip from the first step leading up to the jetty.

Not sure of what had just happened, Meredith lifted her head up, craned difficultly to peer down towards her legs and feet. Dismayed, she could see that they were entwined with cord, bound together tight by some weird throwing contraption.

"Nicely done. Thank God! What in hell *is* that?" panted Natasha trotting to within a foot of where Meredith lay. She was out of breath but did nothing to disguise the relief in her voice.

"A bolas," replied Hector. "It's a throwing weapon. I saw some of the initiates practicing with them yesterday, using dummies. Looked impressive, but I didn't think they'd be very effective... but, now trying it out for myself," he smiled, sounding compassioned, "proves their usefulness." Hector dropped down to Meredith, and straddled her back like she was a gelding. "I told you I had it."

"Get off me!" Meredith hissed, struggling beneath the man's weight.

"Yea, you'd like that." Hector slammed her face down hard into the sand, subduing her momentarily; there would be a bruise later. He pulled her arms up (Meredith yelped) and twisted a white heavy duty cable tie around her wrists, restraining her, before turning his attention to the girl's legs. The bolas, once used by *gauchos* (Argentinean cowboys), comprised of two interconnected lengths of cord with weighted balls attached to their ends. Hector unravelled it from around Meredith's shins before tying her ankles steadfast with a further cable tie. "You try anything like that again, and your running days will be over."

Twisting to face Hector, Meredith spat in his face. "You won't get away with this!"

"Let's kill her," said Natasha. A flick knife flashed open in her hand, pulled from a back pocket.

"Put it away," urged Hector. "The boss needs her. In fact, he wants her right away." He returned his attention to Meredith, using the sleeve of his leather jacket to wipe the girl's slaver from his face.

"Oh?" exclaimed Natasha quizzically.

Hector ignored her, his focus still on Meredith. "You've got some spunk," he said to her passively. "I quite like that. Sadly, you're not going to be mine for much longer."

CHAPTER FORTY
SOPHIE

THE **W**ESTLAND **P**UMA LANDED smoothly on the asphalt at 1:15 p.m. in an area clear from the main runways and a sizeable distance from Edinburgh Airport's terminal building. Special clearance had been granted for the military aircraft to land, and a welcoming committee provided by Police Scotland were waiting to collect and see them safely through security.

There were five vehicles, and they were parked in a row along the airstrip's edge. In the background an *Airbus A340* was approaching from the sky preparing to land.

Detective Inspector Hamish Bremner stepped out from his *Audi S3 Sedan*, its dark grey paintwork matching the sombre sky that looked no different to London, ready to dump a week's worth of rain on them at any given moment, a normal occurrence in Scotland.

The rotors above the helicopter began to slow as the aircraft began to power down and the nearside door glided gently open. First to disembark were the eight FBI, CIA and MI6 field agents who, from their clothing, were indistinguishable, wearing uniform MI6 combat clothing and *Kevlar* vests. About their waists they wore holstered weapons and radio receivers clipped to their belts. Behind them stepped out Brayden and Mullins, then Emily, quickly followed by Liam and Sophie who was no longer invisible.

"Welcome, I hope you had a pleasant flight. I see you've brought the English weather with you." DI Bremner spoke with a very slight Scottish accent and opened his hand, palm horizontal, feeling for rain. Swiftly, he turned and lowered it, offering it to Brayden to shake. The CIA agent took it and felt the Detective Inspector squeeze it hard.

"Appears so," grumbled Brayden, retrieving his hand. He opened and closed it a couple of times, flexing out the discomfort the man's grip had imparted.

"You must be Miss Porter who I spoke with earlier..." The DI continued, directing his pleasantries towards the auburn haired woman in glasses.

"Yes... and these are my colleagues, Sophie Jennings, Liam Cavanagh and Special Agent Christina Mullins," introduced Emily. DI Bremner shook each of their hands in turn, though the ladies gentler than he'd been with Brayden.

"All the arrangements have been made as requested... but, I do wish you'd impart some details as to what brings you to Edinburgh. It's discomforting having such a joint American and British task force in our presence, armed and dangerous-looking and not knowing the reasons."

"I wish it were possible, but our operation is sensitive, and sadly, classified."

"Aye... that's what the Chief Super tells me. Still, does make us a little agitated. Is my city under attack? Is it terrorists? Is there any immediate danger to me or my people?"

Emily laid a hand gently on the policeman's arm and smiled. "You've nothing to be worried about. Not today. We're here purely on a reconnaissance mission."

The Detective Inspector looked deeply into Emily's eyes. "I somewhat doubt that," he said.

DI Bremner pulled into a gap between a couple of buses towards the east end of Princes Street. It was on the opposite side of the road to Waverley Mall Shopping Centre, and within what Ryan would have said 'spitting distance' of their target; they could see the entrance to the building, its wave-shaped overhang a beacon to the steps that led down into the retail complex.

Brayden, Special Agent Mullins and Liam travelled with the field agents to a location a few roads away, where they sat conspicuously waiting in the backs of their vehicles for their next orders.

Glancing out of the window to her left, Sophie watched a stream of pedestrians walk along the pavement, some heading towards bus stops lining the road, or venturing to the shops running parallel with them, of which there were plenty to choose from.

"We'll be monitoring CCTV surveillance and listening in," said Emily sitting in the back of the car alongside Sophie. The passenger seat next to the senior police officer driving was vacant. "Any sign of trouble, or if you request it, I'll order our units in. We won't be far."

"Okay," replied Sophie, attaching the tiny microphone discretely to the collar of her utility-blue *French Connection Drummer* hood coat. "I'd feel better if I had a gun," she added.

DI Bremner raised an eyebrow, wondering if she was being serious. The look in her eyes seen from the rear-view mirror informed him that she was which made him shudder. The young woman was no older than his daughter Alice; she was still at university and barely knew how to operate an electric kettle.

"You and I both know that you don't need it," Emily assured her, taking her hand with one and patting it with the other.

Without another word, Sophie reached for the door release and exited the *Audi*, stepping onto the raised paving. Before leaving, she turned back and peered into the car. "Make sure you ARE watching my back. Meredith and the boys are depending on me," she said, slamming the car door a little too hard.

Sophie stepped around the rear of the vehicle and jogged across four lanes of traffic despite there being a pedestrian crossing a little way up the road. She joined a throng of tourists brandishing maps coming from the Scott Memorial, seen behind her, and integrated amongst them as they crossed Waverley Bridge.

Behind Sophie, the *Audi S3 Sedan* indicated, and then pulled out from between the two buses, merging into the stream of traffic. Emily watched the blonde haired woman bound down the steps into the shopping centre and disappear just as DI Bremner drove past.

⸺⸺◆⸺⸺

Dominic was sitting in a corner of the very busy food hall, set in the lower level of Waverley Mall Shopping Centre nearest to *KFC*, but not far from *McDonalds*, *Spudulike* or the escalator. At first, Sophie was not sure it was him. The last time she had seen the man he had a wider girth, long black hair and jowls.

Now, he was back to how she remembered him from their first encounter; she had seen him from a distance meeting with her father, sitting on a park bench in Chelsea Embankment Gardens reading a newspaper, trying to be obscure. Lean, short-haired and dressed smartly in a dark-grey suit and an open-collar shirt, he could easily pass as a bank manager out on his lunch break.

"I was starting to wonder if you were coming." Dominic stood up from his chair enthusiastically. "Please, take a seat. Thanks for coming..."

"Hardly gave me a choice," she replied frostily.

Dominic ignored the comment. "Can I get you something? Tea? Coffee? *Coca Cola*? Maybe something to eat? A *Zinger* burger, p'rhaps?" he offered pleasantly, like they were best buddies.

Sophie's stomach informed her that she was hungry but she didn't want to gratify the man. She chose to ignore it. "I'm good, thanks," Sophie replied, taking a seat opposite Dominic. She crossed her arms purposefully.

"You won't mind if I get a refill." Dominic indicated his large paper/wax *Pepsi* cup, a red and white striped straw poking out of its lid.

"Knock yourself out."

Casually, Dominic stepped away from the table and drifted through a crowd of young people towards the *KFC* serving counter, joining a small queue that didn't move very quickly.

Sophie sighed and groaned inwardly.

Five minutes later Dominic returned with his refill and a BBQ wrap. "Excuse me... I have this really fast metabolism, which means I need to eat something nearly every hour. Otherwise I get a bit cranky."

"I assume you've not kidnapped my brothers and sister to bring me to Edinburgh on a cheap, no-thrills date?"

"Don't you like my choice of restaurant?" Dominic feigned disappointment before breaking out into a big grin. "You're very perceptive," he replied, biting a large mouthful of his chicken snack, filling his cheeks.

"So, what now do you want from me? Isn't it enough you killed my mother already?"

Dominic finished his mouthful, licking his lips clean before answering. "Feels a bit like déjà vu, doesn't this?" he didn't wait for a response. "I'll come straight to the point. I'm calling in your debt."

"Debt?" Sophie looked baffled.

"Come come, dear girl. Don't tell me you have forgotten already, though you could be forgiven, knowing what you've gone through?" Dominic held the wrap in one hand and was waving it about as he gesticulated without thinking.

Sophie made no attempt at trying to decipher what the man was talking about. He looked slightly mad. Instead she sat resolutely opposite him, hoping her looking stupid would rattle him, her arms remained crossed in front of her.

"The diamond... duh!"

Sophie rolled her eyes and sighed. "Haven't we done this caper before, or am I missing something?"

"Not exactly, no. You see the way I figure, the first time you failed; I didn't get my diamond. Maybe the incentive wasn't adequate... or big enough."

"You killed my mother!" Sophie blasted, anger bubbling where the hunger had minutes earlier. A lot of people were looking at her from around the food hall.

"AND... I'll kill your brothers and sister too if you don't pipe down." Dominic took a sip of *Pepsi*, giving Sophie a moment to calm herself. "Listen to what it is I want you to do."

Sophie glared at Dominic for too long a moment, fidgeting on her seat. Uncrossing her arms, she opened up. She knew she had no choice. "Okay. Talk."

Dominic picked up his cup of *Pepsi* again and sucked deeply on the straw, concluding the action with an exaggerated gasp. He looked like he was enjoying the encounter. "The *Whisper of Persia*," he started. "It's on loan to the *Queen's Gallery* at Holyrood Palace. I want you to recover it for me."

"Always that diamond. What is it with that stone?"

"Call it... sentimentality," Dominic said quietly. He ate another chunk from his chicken wrap and chewed with his mouth open.

Sophie turned away so not to watch the man masticating his food. "Why don't you use the boys that you stole from us? I see you've trained them to use their abilities... the spate of robberies taking place up here in Scotland the other day..."

"Stole? They were hardly yours in the first place. Anyway, I could," Dominic replied, still chewing, all but admitting that he was responsible for the £200 million worth of treasures stolen on New Year's Eve, "but this is personal," he continued. He swallowed. "It needs someone *experienced*. Plus, the two – you AND the diamond – are somewhat intertwined. You had the diamond in your grasp, and then chose to return it. It's only fitting that you retrieve it for me."

"What if I refuse?"

"Does having all those abilities affect your memory, Sophie? I have your brothers and sister. Do you think I wouldn't hurt them?"

Sophie tensed up. Through gritted teeth she said, petulantly: "Okay!"

"Good. Glad we have an understanding."

"What about the 'sweetener' your friend mentioned on the phone? She said you'll let me have one of the children back... if I came. Well, I'm here... when do you live up to your piece of the bargain?"

Dominic smiled. "Here." He put the half-eaten chicken snack down and reached into his jacket pocket, removing his phone. With a couple of swipes and a stab or two of a finger, an image appeared on the screen. "So you know what you are working for."

The photograph was of Meredith, bound up, gagged, and lying in the back of what appeared to be a van. The girl had a large purplish bruise to the right side of her face, like she had recently been hit, and hit hard.

"You bastard!" Sophie flared. The urge to launch herself at him only just kept in check. She balled her fists at her side, rage threatening to overcome her levelheadedness. Diners in the hall once again directed curious looks her way.

"I know... and believe me, I've been called worse," Dominic grinned for a long moment before allowing it to subside. "Do what

I want and you get her back." He reached for his *Pepsi* and sipped it through the straw again. "That is, of course, after I get my diamond."

"And what about my brothers?"

"I was told never to place all my apples in the same cart. Simply, they're my insurance against any waggishness you, or MI6, contemplate. Once the diamond and I are safe, they'll be returned... unharmed... eventually."

"You'll return them immediately!"

Dominic smiled confidently. He had all the cards. "Don't worry, princess. You'll get them back... you have my word."

"How can I believe you? After what you've done?"

Dominic shrugged. "What choice do you have? Here," Dominic placed the guide book to the *Queen's Gallery* on the table in front of Sophie, "all you need to know about the diamond." The thin publication had been hidden on the chair next to him. "I'll give you..." he raised his watch-arm theatrically, gazing studiously at the timepiece, "... four hours. P'rhaps a little more. Call me using the number from the photo once you've done. I'll tell you when and where we'll meet up for the exchange. The diamond... for the girl; and NO funny business... I'll be watching." He swept up the remainder of his chicken wrap, peeled down a bit of the outer wrapper and took another bite. "Are you in?"

Without a word, Sophie snatched up the visitor's guide and sprung up irritably from the chair.

"A pleasure doing business with you," called out Dominic towards Sophie's back.

Disregarding the comment, Sophie stamped off like a sulky kid being forced into tidying her room. At the edge of the food hall she stopped, looked back over her shoulder and studied the man. He was eating the remnants of his BBQ wrap and looked pleased with himself. Bitterness burned inside her chest, followed by pure hatred.

Forcing herself to turn away before she was compelled to react, she stepped out of the busy dining room and followed a stream of visitors as they exited up the flight of steps.

CHAPTER FORTY-ONE
BRAYDEN

WHILST THE FIELD TEAM – comprising of four FBI/CIA agents and four MI6 operatives – sat in unmarked police cars a couple of streets away from Waverley Mall Shopping Centre, action-ready and waiting their next commands, Brayden, Mullins and Emily stood around a bank of video screens in a small room deep within the police station on Gayfield Square, a ten minute walk away. Street cameras had been manipulated to watch Sophie's every move, first from outside the shopping centre, then from within, internal surveillance cameras capturing the young woman's purposeful movements. With full control of the entire city's CCTV network, the three intelligence agents couldn't help but watch nervously.

On entering the food hall, Brayden teased the closest camera to zoom in on Sophie; the young woman's face momentarily filling the screen. Stating the obvious the CIA man said: "I see her."

"She's walking with purpose... I think Sophie has an eye on Dominic." Emily was pointing at the screen towards the direction Sophie was heading. She drew a line on the screen of her likely course. "Can we get a look... over there?"

"One moment." Brayden tapped a few buttons on the keyboard in front of him and the image from the video feed promptly changed. "There!"

"Got him."

Dominic Schilling was sitting at a table on his own. Observing

Sophie's arrival, he seemed to stiffen, then visibly relax, his shoulders dropping. He spoke a few words and Sophie appeared to respond. She then sat down opposite him.

"Is the hidden mic not working?" asked Christina Mullins, leaning over Brayden's shoulder.

"Oh damn, hold on." Emily tinkered with a handheld communications device, flicking one of the switches and fiddling with a dial. Ten seconds later and Sophie's voice filled the room: *"I'm good, thanks."*

"You won't mind if I get a refill," Dominic said cheerily.

"Knock yourself out," Sophie replied.

He stood up from the table and crossed the food hall to join a queue at a *KFC* serving counter.

Five minutes of watching Sophie twiddling her fingers and making 'tutting' sounds over the airwaves drew heavy sighing and sounds of exasperation from both Brayden and Mullins. When Dominic returned with his 'refill' and something that looked like a long, thin sandwich, the two agents and Emily were almost caught napping.

"Excuse me... I have this really fast metabolism, which means I need to eat something nearly every hour. Otherwise I get a bit cranky." Dominic's voice made them jump.

"I assume you've not kidnapped my brothers and sister to bring me to Edinburgh on a cheap, no-thrills date?" said Sophie.

"Don't you like my choice of restaurant?" Dominic started to laugh. He wiped his mouth with the back of his hand. *"You're very perceptive."*

"So, what now do you want from me? Isn't it enough you killed my mother already?" asked Sophie.

"Feels a bit like déjà vu, doesn't it? I'll come straight to the point. I'm calling in your debt."

Brayden's mobile phone started to chime and vibrate on the table in front of him. He quickly snatched it up and checked the caller ID. "It's Mac," he breathed, trying not to interrupt or talk over the wire-tapped exchanges. "I'd better take this." He stood up and left Mullins and Emily to continue listening in on Sophie and Dominic's engagement.

⎯⎯⎯•⫸⫷•⎯⎯⎯

Closing the door gently behind him, Brayden answered the phone abruptly: "Yea."

"*Hi Brayden, how's it going?*"

"Do you Brits feel the need to start *every* conversation with light-hearted chit-chat?"

"*I dunno… I guess,*" muttered Mac, hastily moving on. "*Listen, we've been alerted to something, could be relevant; might be bogus. Traffic police spotted a van matching the description of the one used by the kidnappers on New Year's Eve; a grey Ford Tourneo. They ran the plates and the same phony registration details came up.*"

"Where's it now?"

"*The police unit is following from a safe distance on the A84 and are waiting for advisement on how to proceed.*"

"Do we have access to overhead satellite imagery?" asked Brayden, unaware that he was casually walking along the corridor of the police station towards the building's emergency exit.

"*I checked, but no satellites are due over the area for at least a couple of hours. As a result, I took the liberty of commandeering an MQ-9 Reaper to track and observe.*" An *MQ-9 Reaper* was an unmanned aerial vehicle, more commonly known as a 'drone', and was one of a dozen the RAF used for covert operations. As well as providing high-altitude surveillance, the remote-piloted aircraft had military capabilities, often armed with air-to-ground missiles.

"Are you getting pictures yet?"

"Soon – the UAV is not yet in range, but should be... in about ten minutes. The traffic cops wanted to know whether they should intercept. I said no and told them to remain in pursuit without making themselves known; we don't want them rattled."

"Yea, we don't want traffic cops flubbing it," agreed Brayden. "When the *Reaper* begins broadcasting images, have them sent over to us. I want to know where that van is heading, and Mac?"

"Yea?"

"Good work."

"Thanks... before you go, that wasn't the only reason for my call. We're getting reports of some strange goings-on back here, in and around London."

"Go on," implored Brayden, slightly agitated; he wanted to return to the surveillance room and listen to more of Sophie and Dominic's chat.

"Daylight robberies," replied Mac eagerly. *"Of the New Year's Eve Scotland type and not the supermarket over-pricing variety."*

"Are you sure?"

"Well, only as much as I can relay. The Metropolitan Police are currently responding to a number of burglaries, robberies, thefts, muggings and heists... and they all have one thing in common..."

"Let me guess. The thieves appear to be ghosts?" Now at the exit door, Brayden turned and started slowly walking back.

"Bingo! Uncanny, right?"

"When did they occur? What time frame?"

"Occur? They haven't stopped!"

Brayden returned to the surveillance room just as Sophie's meeting with Dominic neared its end.

"*Are you in?*" Dominic sounded exuberant. He was holding all the cards, and everyone knew it.

Emily and Mullins watched Sophie snatch a thin book up from the table, looking very disgruntled and like she wanted to scrunch it up and punch it into his face.

"*A pleasure doing business with you,*" Dominic's voice followed, losing resonance as Sophie walked away.

"What did I miss?" Brayden stood alongside his fellow American. She had taken his seat when he'd left to make the phone call.

"Oh, just about everything," replied Mullins, slightly miffed. "I hope that call was important."

"I think so," retorted Brayden, nonplussed. "Mac... with something interesting. Fill me in and I'll update you."

"Oh, it's like that... I show you mine and you'll show me yours..."

Before Brayden had a chance to respond with something witty, the radio emitted Sophie's voice again:

"*Assuming you heard all of that... what now?*"

"I've got this," said Emily, her phone pressed against her ear. She was ringing Sophie.

Brayden perched himself on the edge of a table.

On one of the screens, a camera had picked out the young woman stepping out from Waverley Mall Shopping Centre back into the street. Her free hand (the other holding a brochure) making a mobile phone appear.

"Sophie, we heard everything. We'll send someone to collect you and we'll discuss the situation when you return."

"*Okay.*" Sophie's voice echoed through the speaker of the handheld communication device, slightly out of synch with the mobile. She didn't sound happy, which was understandable. The corresponding image on the screen corroborated her mood.

"Cross the road back to where we dropped you off, and then

make your way down Princes Street in the direction of the Scott Memorial..."

"*That ugly statue that looks like it belongs in a horror movie?*"

"Yes, that's the one; it's meant to be gothic. The next road you come to is Hanover Street; take it and cross over. Liam and the field agents are stationed a little way up. He'll be looking out for you. We'll talk more when you arrive."

Emily disconnected the call and returned the mobile phone to her jacket pocket. She took in a deep breath and let out an explosive sigh.

"So... what did that whack-job want with Sophie?" Brayden was intrigued to know.

Emily laughed humourlessly. "A diamond." It sounded lame coming from her lips. She shook her head in disbelief. "This is all over a bloody trinket."

Brayden turned towards Mullins. "Seriously?"

"Yep," confirmed the FBI Agent. "Dominic wants her to steal the *Whisper of Persia*... a diamond apparently on exhibition here in Edinburgh at the *Queen's Gallery*."

"Doesn't seem to make sense..."

"He's offering Meredith – Sophie's sister – in a trade. The diamond... for the girl," said Mullins. "He's keeping her brothers as collateral, to ensure his onward escape. He's not stupid."

"It can't be just about stealing a diamond," Brayden thought aloud. "He could have used his boys to do it; they're more than capable... except..." Something occurred to him. His face started to glow with enthusiasm. "... his boys are busy doing something else."

"Brayden, you're babbling," admonished Mullins blithely.

"No, no I'm not. Maybe this isn't just about stealing a diamond," suggested Brayden. Absently he raked a hand through his hair.

"No?" quizzed Emily.

"Maybe it's a diversion, a means just to get Sophie out of the way."

"Why?" Emily wasn't convinced. "Out of the way of what?"

Brayden took a deep breath. "Mac called to give me some updates, one of which related to those boys you've called the sons of *GYGES*. They're in play again, this time in–"

"London..." finished Emily, "...in our own backyard. Sophie is likely the only person capable of matching those kids for their abilities. According to the data we recovered, their DNA is almost identical to Sophie's."

"Stands to reason why he'd want her gone."

"What shall we do?" asked Mullins, joining the discussion.

"I wish Ryan was here. He'd have some suggestions," said Emily blankly.

"We don't need 'daddy', so let's not lose focus," stated Brayden seriously. "I don't see that we have much choice but to play out Dominic's plan. Sophie isn't going to want to do anything that will jeopardise the safety of her sister... OR her brothers. We need to think about getting that diamond."

"*And* we have less than four hours to do it," stated Mullins.

Brayden raised an eyebrow.

"Yep," Mullins continued, "we're on the clock. The whack job wants to do the exchange around 6:00 p.m."

"I guess we need to fathom how best to steal the diamond without causing too much upheaval," stated Brayden, adding: "Or upsetting the Queen."

"I'll speak with the Chief... see what he suggests. He's probably speaking with the Prime Minister, who's keeping Her Majesty up to speed on events." Emily hoped the head of MI6 could offer her some enlightenment.

"You do that," said Brayden with a hint of disapproval.

CHAPTER FORTY-TWO
GARRET

THE STAKES WERE NO higher than they had been set on New Year's Eve and the target, no less formidable. Tasked with overseeing the plan in Dominic's absence, Garret watched the initiates as they set off to carry out the man's request. He was dressed for warmth, trussed up in a thick brown winter coat, the hood crumpled down behind his neck, and a black beanie hat protecting his bald head from the elements. Despite wearing gloves, his hands were frozen, so he stuffed them deep within the coat's pockets.

Like before, all ninety of the boys had been left to plan their own jobs, the only caveat being: their jobs were to begin at exactly 1:00 p.m., and they had a three hour window to complete them.

Some of the initiates had made an alliance with others, plotting grander schemes that allowed much greater opportunities of plunder and wealth, but with sizeable risk. Most kept to themselves and aimed for smaller, higher value pickings.

A convoy of trucks and vans – mostly on hire – rolled out of the large warehouse under the steady gaze of Garret and Melvyn, two of the three Kaplan Ratcliff field agents that had survived the helicopter attack in Nevada back in October. They stood by the up-and-over warehouse door, as Dominic had done early New Year's Day. Melvyn was holding a clipboard and a pen. On a sheet of paper, he ticked off each initiate, identified only by their allocated number. None had been given a name, and as they were all identical, their number was the only way to separate them. As well as wearing an identification number pinned to their jackets, the corresponding number was also tattooed to their upper arm.

As the last truck rolled by, Garret gave the driver and the two initiates seated alongside him (which Melvyn ticked off as Seventy-One and Thirteen) a little wave. When the convoy disappeared around a turning and the smell of diesel had subsided a little, the man with the spiderweb tattoo on one cheek pressed a large green push-button on a cable that dangled from the wall. Instantly the up-and-over door began to clink and clank as it trundled without hurry down, the small motor powering it whirring as it rumbled with life.

"How much do you think they'll get this time?" asked Melvyn, making conversation. He stepped under the lowering door before the gap closed up and left him out in the cold.

"I dunno, a bit more I guess. London's richer."

"Shall we have a bet?"

Garret shrugged. "I guess it might make it a bit more interesting." It was going to be a long afternoon and they needed something to while away the time.

"Fifty quid that it's double."

"Fifty quid? Hardly seems worth it. Make it five hundred if you're so certain." A moment later, Garret laughed to see the younger man squirm as he weighed up the pros and cons.

"That's a day's wages," complained Melvyn, dejected. "I've got a kid on the way."

"Don't sweat it homeboy. Tell you what. How about I give you five hundred if you win... but if I win, you get a tattoo like this." Garret pointed to the web on his left cheek. "I got the stamp when I lost a bet ten years ago..."

"You got that from a bet? That figures. I did wonder why you'd had it done; thought it made you look a bit of a dick." Melvyn started to grin.

"Well... if you lose the bet, I'll be in good company."

Slightly over three hours later, Garret and Melvyn were behind the wall of LCD screens in the back of the mobile command centre. The *Mitsubishi Fuso* truck was equipped with high-tech surveillance devices and tracking software, and just like three days before, the two men watched in anticipation at what was about to happen.

"Okay cadets... are you in your starting positions?" Garret spoke into the adjustable microphone that poked out to the side of his headset. No longer wearing his beanie hat, his bald head shone beneath the overhead lighting that glowed brightly in the ceiling of the vehicle.

"*Copy.*" A chorus of affirmatives filled his ear as ninety kids confirmed that they were all in locations that were measured approximately fifteen minutes away from their targets. Like before, the initiates wore a tracker device on a dog tag pendant hanging from their necks.

"Okay... just leaves me to wish you all good luck! Be ready on my command," said Garret.

"T-minus two minutes." Melvyn tapped a few keys on the QWERTY keyboard in front of him. A digital timer appeared in the corner of the half a dozen VDUs placed around the walls of the command centre, the numerals counting down the minutes, seconds and milliseconds on every one.

"D'you want a coffee before we get started?" asked Melvyn affably, removing his headset for a moment.

"No, thanks," Garret replied. "The stuff goes straight through me... I'll need to go for a pee within a few minutes. I don't know about you, but I don't want to miss this."

"Suit yourself." Melvyn stood and scampered out of the truck. A little walk around the side of the vehicle, a dozen metres across the warehouse, he then came to the small office. Pulling open the door and stepping in, he trotted to the fully stocked drinks' machine and punched in a sequence of numbers that would produce a hot beverage in the style and preference of his choice. A paper cup was dispensed, followed by thirty seconds of squelching, sloshing, spitting noises that was soon replaced by a farting sound as Melvyn's coffee dribbled out.

As he stepped back into the truck, Garret threw him a reproachful look. "Cutting it fine... just thirty seconds..."

"What's your problem...? I didn't miss a thing." Melvyn sat down and pushed the headset back on.

Garret pressed the on button of his mic. "Okay cadets, on my word."

The digital timer flashed through the numbers and the two minutes were now nearly over.

Melvyn pressed a button on a flexible stem microphone that he'd dragged over from the back of the desk and which extended from a round weighted base. He spoke into its black foam covered head: "Okay, we have ten... nine... eight... seven... six... five... four... three... two... one..." As before, he made a gun with his right hand and followed it with a shooting sound, like a starting pistol.

Taking the place of Dominic, Garret addressed his audience of ninety teenage boys. "Okay cadets... this is it. Go! Remember... three hours..." a momentary pause, "... acknowledge."

Unlike New Year's Eve, the ninety boys were deployed during the day. Without the distraction or divertissement of a host of end of year and Hogmanay celebrations, some would say that the enterprise was foolish and reckless. If they had not been invisible, many of them would have agreed.

Fully 'immersed' the initiates entered shops, banks, museums, stately homes, car showrooms and jewellers and started taking things unchallenged, filling backpacks, holdalls, shopping trolleys and suitcases with as much as they could carry; like Sophie, every inanimate item they touched, disappeared. It wasn't until an hour later that the most daring heist took place.

It was a little after quarter-past two.

By now, law enforcement and the British government were aware that the nation's capital was under attack, and countermeasures were being deployed.

Garret watched the imposing building on Threadneedle Street appear on the sixty-inch flat screen from eight different viewpoints, cameras attached to the side of the ocular headgear that helped the initiates to see each other – like everyone else, they were invisible to each other.

"Isn't that?"

"You betcha," replied Garret, cavalier.

Since 1694, *The Bank of England* had presided over the country's finances, issuing the nation's currency in circulation, and was the fifteenth largest custodian of gold reserves in the world. Stored within eight vaults over two floors beneath the bank, there were more than 4,600 tonnes of gold stacked high within metal warehouse shelves valued at around £1,200 billion.

"Is it even possible?" asked Melvyn, awestruck. "It's supposed to be like Fort Knox."

The eight initiates entered the building by the only entrance. There were no other doors on ground level and no windows, giving it the dramatic appearance of almost impregnable security.

"We'll soon see," replied Garret, his eyes glued to the large screen. Running into the bank unchallenged, they entered the front hall where staff, security personnel and a few suited visitors stood around, some talking, others on mobiles. To the edges were a number of columns that gave the appearance of an old Greek temple, holding up the ceiling; in front of them were some large bronze uplighters, engraved with lions and eagles, symbolic to the past relationship between the British Pound and the American Dollar. Ahead, archways led deeper into the hall, security barriers barring access without clearance.

"*It's this way to the vaults,*" one of the boys said. Garret identified him as number Thirty-Seven. The boy wandered away from his companions towards a security guard. With ease, he seized the man's key card; the pass still attached to its elasticised belt buckle fob disappeared within his hands. He returned to the other seven boys. "*Come on, what are you waiting for?*"

"*You lead... we'll follow.*"

Each of the boys hurdled over the security barriers, ran a little deeper in and stopped just short of a scale model of the bank's building enclosed within a glass case atop a solid square table.

"*You sure you know where it is?*" asked another boy.

"*We take a lift.*"

"*More in point, do you actually know what you're doing?*" One of the boys sounded unsure.

To the left of the initiates, through another archway, they could see a cantilever staircase that led up and downwards. If they'd ventured towards it, they would have seen at its bottom was an old Roman mosaic, colourful and complete.

The lifts were to their right, along a short wide corridor.

"*Trust me.*" Number Thirty-Seven with the security guard's key card, spoke confidently. "*It's this way.*"

Garrett and Melvyn were watching mesmerised as the lift appeared, its doors gliding open accompanied by a long, loud, ear-piercing:

beeeeeeeeeeeeeeeeeeeeeeeeeeeeeeeeeeeeeeeeeeeeep!!

emitted from one of the surveillance speakers built within the wall of the truck.

"What the–" Melvyn jumped back in alarm, his attention no longer fixated on number Thirty-Seven's video feed or any of his seven buddies.

"It's a distress signal." Garret turned exigently in his swivel chair to check a computer screen behind him. The initiates appeared on a live, ever-altering list, which included their coordinates, their heartbeat, blood pressure and other vital signs. The numbers were all green, except one.

Number Twenty-Six.

His entire data line was flashing red. "Let's get a visual on number Twenty-Six," Garret requested of Melvyn, deactivating the discordant bleep sound, restoring tranquillity to the truck.

Melvyn tapped a couple of keys and the corresponding video feed flashed up, replacing the eight others that continued to broadcast the *Bank of England* robbery, no longer of current interest.

Garret activated the mic button and spoke into his headset. "Twenty-Six, what's your status?"

"*I'm hit!*" he screamed back over the airwaves. The image on the flat screen was nothing but a whitewashed wall with some red marks. A bloody handprint glistened upon it, and a long smear of crimson trailed for a short way. Garret knew that the blood belonged to the boy.

"What happened?"

Twenty-Six made some guttural noises followed by a gurgling sound over the truck's speakers. "*They were waiting for me. They knew I was invisible... they were prepared. They shot me, Garret... I'm dying.*"

"You'll be okay Twenty-Six, stay with me. I'll get you help." Garret turned off his microphone and turned to Melvyn. "Who do we have in the area?"

"I'll check." Melvyn turned to the monitor behind them and typed in a command. "Thirteen is close by, as is Eighty-Four."

"Send them both."

Before Melvyn had chance to acknowledge or turn away from the screen, the alarm sounded again, signifying another initiate in distress. He returned to the list and scrolled down. The entry for number 'Forty' was this time flashing red. He turned off the alarm and told Garret.

When the alarm sounded for a third time, a panicked look struck Garret hard across the face. "What the hell's going on?!"

"It's Fifty-Eight this time," informed Melvyn.

Garret thumped the keyboard in front of him with a fist and threw himself back in exasperation. "I don't like where this is heading. I wish Dominic was here."

Melvyn turned off the alarm again and quickly returned to the surveillance station next to Garret. Dragging the desk microphone over, he spoke into its head. "Numbers Thirteen and Eighty-Four; you're to divert to Hatton Garden where Twenty-Six needs urgent assistance, do you copy?"

"*Copy*," chorused through the in-built speakers.

Garret switched the video feed from Twenty-Six over to number Forty. "Forty, what's your status?"

Silence came over the airways.

"Number Forty, do you hear me?"

Melvyn swivelled around again to face the computer screen with the list of initiates. He scrolled down the names, stopping at a flashing red one. Number Forty. Alongside the identifier, his coordinates were highlighted. A little further along, the boy's blood pressure should have been detailed, in addition to his heartbeat. Neither of these was being recorded. Instead a '–' appeared.

"Forty, please acknowledge," said Garret desperately.

"I think he's dead," said Melvyn gloomily, peering around to his Kaplan Ratcliff colleague.

Ignoring him, Garret selected the video feed for number Fifty-Eight. The image immediately appearing on the screen was grey and out of focus. "Fifty-Eight, I'm getting your distress signal. What's your status?"

Silence.

"Fifty-Eight?"

Melvyn, still hunched over the computer screen behind Garret, sighed and shook his head. "He's dead too, Garret. His coordinates are the same as number Forty's."

"Jesus," Garret exclaimed. "Dominic's going to be pissed off when he hears this. What's their location?"

Melvyn selected the coordinates and keyed in a command. Before the computer had acquired the location, the alarm sounded once again.

"Oh bloody hell," uttered Melvyn at what appeared on the screen in front of him. It could equally have been at hearing the distress signal. "You won't want me saying this. Fifty-Eight and Forty... they were both with Thirty-Seven."

"Thirty-Seven?" Garret was confused. "Weren't we watching his feed a moment ago?"

"Yes, at *The Bank of England*. There were eight of them working together." Melvyn deactivated the distress signal again and hurriedly identified its source. Anxiously, he looked up. "What's worse," he groaned, "that distress alarm... it came from him. Initiate number Thirty-Seven."

CHAPTER FORTY-THREE
EMILY

THE CHIEF WAS IN no mood for any more bad news, so upon receiving Emily's brief regarding Dominic Schilling's demands with regards to Sophie, and the man's offer of a hostage exchange for the *Whisper of Persia* diamond (to be stolen once again *for* him), the head of MI6 was utterly incensed.

"We're in a state of emergency here in London, Emily. I'm not sure the Prime Minister is going to be too interested in what you're doing north of the border, and neither will Her Majesty. I've just had word that the Crown Jewels have been seized from the Tower of London; the Queen is most distressed."

"Oh."

"Somehow 'oh' doesn't quite convey the mood in the capital at the moment, Emily; the government are voting on whether to declare martial law, bolstering the insufficient police presence with the might of the military.

"But there are some positives. The flying squad foiled a gold bullion heist at The Bank of England; quite adventurous and impressive, honestly. The blighters were caught exiting the building and almost got away with it, but were intercepted by armed officers responding to a silent alarm triggered down in the vaults. After reports were being received of thefts taking place and items of value just 'disappearing' we quickly guessed that London was under attack by those responsible for Scotland the other

night, so rapid response teams were assembled and deployed. About eighty million quid's worth of gold was recovered, and three of the thieves were killed fleeing. There were others involved I'm sure, but how many we can only guess what with them being invisible an' all. Huh!" The Chief grunted, *"George Jennings has a lot to answer for!"*

"Well, I'm sure he'd condemn this misuse of his research and what his super soldiers are being reduced to, but as he's dead..."

"Yes... yes, I know. But... this can't go on, Emily. With those abilities, we have us a massive disadvantage. We need a way to match ourselves so that we can counter and put a stop to them, once and for all." The head of MI6 went quiet for a moment, wrestling his conscience with something. Just as Emily was about to ask if he was all right, the man spoke. *"I know you're not going to like what I'm going to suggest, and I wish to God we had another choice. I think we need to bring Sophie in and have some tests run on her; see if there are any ways to reverse-engineer her abilities."*

"Sir? That's abhorrent! She's one of us! I won't allow it!"

"I don't like it, but what else can we do?"

"There is something else," replied Emily after a lengthy pause, optimism in her voice.

"What do you have in mind...? Spill!"

"Give me twenty-four hours, sir; I may already have the answers to your prayers," adding cryptically, "I just need to see someone first..."

Ending the call, Emily speed-dialled another number. A ringing tone followed for a short while succeeded by a click as it was answered. Not waiting for a greeting, Emily spoke hurriedly: "Hi, it's Emily... that thing I sent you towards the end of October... did you make it?"

⬦

Brayden looked up expectantly as Emily walked back into the

surveillance room, as though the MI6 woman was blessed with the solution to their latest obstacle. Mullins sat nursing a cup of weak tea, too milky and way too much sugar added for anyone else within the room to like.

Heeding off questions, Emily spoke first. "We're on our own with regards to Sophie, the diamond and getting Meredith and her brothers back."

"What?" Brayden couldn't believe it. He swore. Mullins didn't say anything, just shook her head and wrinkled her nose.

"London has problems of its own," explained Emily.

"The thefts?" Whilst Emily was on her mobile speaking with the head of MI6, Brayden had tapped into a news feed on one of the office computers. So far, he was aware of at least thirty robberies, with reports that many more were ongoing. "Is it genuinely that bad?"

Emily nodded. "It's turning desperate." She detailed the theft of the Crown Jewels. "What's worse, I've been given new orders. I'm to return to London... immediately."

"What about Sophie? She's not going to like that," said the FBI Agent, stating the obvious. She took a sip from her tea.

"She'll understand. You should know Mullins, that whilst you and Brayden were chasing Sophie across America, I was helping and advising her on escaping you from the end of a telephone; we don't need to be joined at the hip."

— ⋈ —

The cars transporting the field agents – Liam with one group, Sophie travelling separately with another – arrived at the police station just as Emily was climbing into the back of DI Bremner's *Audi S3*. Electronically winding the window down with a push of a button, Emily leaned out to catch Sophie's attention.

Not waiting for her vehicle to stop, Sophie opened the door and spilled out half-running. "Emily! What's going on? Where're you going?"

"London. Something important has come up."

"London? Important?" said Sophie agitated, sounding whiney. She knew nothing about the spate of robberies taking place in the capital; despite the radio in the car reporting the incidents, her focus was engaged elsewhere. "What about me and Meredith? Plus we've only just got here," which was true; they'd only been in Edinburgh a little more than an hour.

"We didn't come here to sightsee," replied Emily harshly.

Sophie ignored the comment. "I can't do this alone..." she pleaded.

"You're not alone," Emily assured her. "You have Liam and the MI6 field team; plus Brayden, Mullins and their agents. I'll tell you later why, but trust me; I wouldn't go if it wasn't necessary. I'll come back... as soon as I can. Good luck."

Sophie was about to argue some more when Emily turned and gave DI Bremner the nod to drive. The *Audi* moved gently forward then sped off, joining traffic at the roundabout onto Antigua Street, then travelling in the direction of Queen Street.

Thirty-five minutes later and the telltale signs of an airport appeared on the horizon; aeroplanes descended from the sky, one after the other, with little time separating their arrival.

The *Westland Puma* was powering up when they drove into Edinburgh Airport, security personnel waving them through after expeditiously checking their credentials. The car pulled up a short walk from the aircraft.

"It was a pleasure meeting you," DI Bremner walked Emily towards the helicopter. "Shame you have to leave so suddenly... but I can understand."

"Goodbye Detective Inspector." Emily shook his hand before

turning and jogging the short distance to the helicopter. Once inside, the co-pilot closed the door and the aircraft juddered into the air, hovering at ten-feet for a moment before turning gracefully to change direction and gliding steadily up and away.

The co-pilot stepped past Emily as she secured the four straps of her seatbelt into the buckle she pulled up from between her legs. "London, miss?" he asked loudly over the noise of the military aircraft. The crew of the *Westland Puma* had received instructions from MI6 headquarters with regards to the woman's return and her onward travel requirements.

"Not yet," Emily demurred. "Tell me, do we have enough fuel to get to Devon?"

"Devon?" the co-pilot looked quizzically at her. "You fancy a holiday instead?"

"No... There's someone I urgently need to see."

The co-pilot's jokey demeanour slowly drained from his face. "Hold on. I'll check with Barnaby." Barnaby was in the cockpit, piloting the helicopter, now flying around 10,000 ft. Looking down through the window, sprawling hills and long winding roads could be seen below, with one or two matchbox cars travelling indistinctly in either direction. A minute later he returned, looking pleased with himself. "It's about 360 miles to Devon," he said excitedly. "Coincidentally, that's the mileage we can get from a full tank on this bird. We just filled up before we left."

Emily smiled. "That's good, it's settled then. Set the new course and wake me when we get there." She jiggled in her seat, making herself comfortable before closing her eyes. The co-pilot turned and disappeared back into the cockpit, pushing to the door behind him.

CHAPTER FORTY-FOUR
SOPHIE

When DI Bremner drove off with Emily in the rear of the *Audi*, Sophie felt lost and abandoned, and a wave of panic overwhelmed her. Almost hyperventilating, salvation came in the unlikely form of Brayden Scott, who had watched Emily drive off from the outskirts of the police building on Gayfield Square and who came to Sophie's aid after seeing her distress.

"Sophie... it'll be all right," Brayden soothed, stepping up close beside her. "You don't need her. Hell, you don't need any of us!" he mused. "Emily's an analyst... and she's got an important job to do back in London; she'll be back when she's done. Let's go inside and work out our next play."

Sophie calmed sufficiently enough to be led into the building where Liam had already disappeared. The field team of MI6, FBI and CIA agents moved aimlessly around outside the police station, looking menacing in their black clothing, body armour and matching bulletproof vests. Some carried weapons over their shoulders, but most kept guns concealed in holsters strapped around their waists. Their presence gained worried looks from the few pedestrians passing by.

FBI Agent Mullins was still in the surveillance room watching over video footage from the street cameras. Liam was sitting next to her, and both looked up as Brayden entered the room with Sophie close behind.

Liam plucked the ring-pull on a can of *Sprite*, fizzy bubbles frothing up over the rim. "It's not too late to make a grab for Dominic, ya know," said Liam, lifting the can of drink to his lips. "He's still in the food hall where Sophie met him."

"He knows that we wouldn't attempt it, not whilst he has my sister," explained Sophie. She peered over Liam's shoulder, looking at the man she had been sitting with barely twenty minutes earlier.

"Look at him... smug son of a bitch." sniped Brayden, joining the three to look at the screen. "Is that an *Oreo Krushems* he's eating?" Brayden was studying the man's choice of dessert, nostalgic for something American. Before anyone could answer him, his mobile phone started to ring. He glanced at the caller ID. "It's Mac," he announced, swiping the screen to accept the call as he turned away. He walked to the other side of the room.

"And he seriously wants you to steal him a diamond?" Liam spoke with a disbelieving expression on his face.

"Not just any diamond. This one..." Sophie dropped the visitor's guide Dominic had given to her in front of Liam and Mullins.

"The *Whisper of Persia*," read the FBI agent. "Sounds exotic..." she paused, before adding, "isn't that the diamond he got you to steal last summer?"

"The one and only."

"Bet you wished you'd kept it... would've saved us the headache," surmised Liam, taking a long pull from his *Sprite*.

At the back of the small room, snatches of one-way conversation between Brayden and Mac were overheard, but nothing that made any sense. The call was short and ended with Brayden hurrying back over as Sophie countered Liam's observation:

"I wish I'd shot Dominic in the back of the head when I'd had the chance... that would've been a better solution."

"Listen up," Brayden rejoined the group. Liam and Mullins

turned obediently like children in their chairs. Sophie, still standing, was facing him as he returned. "That was Mac. I'm not sure how this fits in, but the van used by the abductors of Sophie's brothers and sister has been spotted by traffic cops. They've been following at a discrete distance whilst a surveillance drone has been watching from overhead. Mac reports that the drone is now broadcasting live footage of the van and tracking its progress; it seems to be heading this way, towards Edinburgh."

"Shouldn't we intercept it?" suggested Mullins. "Bring whoever it is driving in for interrogation."

"We could... but we'd lose the element of surprise. I'm thinking it might be better to sit, watch and wait. Maybe that van will lead us to Dominic's base of operations, or at least to where he is keeping Meredith prisoner."

"Maybe it won't," disagreed Sophie.

Brayden ignored the comment. "Mac's sending us a link to the video feed... Liam, maybe you can take the lead on that and follow the van's progress?"

"Right, I'm on it."

"You see anything interesting, let me know." He turned to his partner. "Mullins?"

"Brayden," answered the FBI agent flippantly.

"You're with me."

An alarmed look flashed up on Sophie's face. "What d'you want me to do, Brayden?" she interrupted. "We're here because of that man..." she pointed to the screen which still continued to display Dominic Schilling eating his ice cream. He appeared happy and without a care in the world. "... and we have less than four hours to get what he wants."

Brayden swiped up the guide book to the *Queen's Gallery* and held it out to Sophie. "You're on your own," he said seriously. "But don't worry; we'll be on hand to help from the sidelines."

<hr>

"Honestly... I didn't think stealing a diamond would be something you guys would condone." Sophie stepped out from the back of the black *Ford Mondeo*. Christina Mullins was sat next to her and the CIA agent was seated in front alongside a field agent moonlighting as a designated driver.

"Don't think of it as 'stealing'. Think of it as 'borrowing'..." suggested Brayden through the crack of his open window. "Besides... the CIA does this sort of thing all the time."

Although close to 4:00 p.m., the car park abutting Holyrood Park was nearly full and made even busier with the arrival of Sophie, Brayden and Mullins in their car. The team of Anglo-American field agents were in the three others behind them.

"I still don't know why we couldn't just ask the gallery if we could actually 'borrow' it. I mean, we'd give it back after..."

"Sure," replied Brayden, adding sarcastically: "That would work."

"Just saying..." said Sophie petulantly.

Mullins climbed out from the other side of the *Mondeo* and walked around to stand alongside the blonde woman. "Okay... we'll wait for you here. Wear this two-way radio." The agent handed over a small discrete earpiece and a pin-on microphone, which Sophie inserted and attached to her body. A wireless transmitter pack she clipped to the waistband of her trousers behind her. "If you encounter any problems, give us a yell."

"Okay." Sophie stepped a foot away, and then stopped, turning back. "Last time, I had a knife!" she blurted.

"You won't need a weapon," replied Brayden. "The guards are

unarmed... they'll be no match for you. We went through the logistics of the theft; it'll be how you Brits say, a 'doddle'."

"I didn't use it to fight with... I used it to break the glass."

"Improvise," said Brayden disinterested. "I've seen you do that before."

Mullins smiled reassuringly towards the woman before climbing back into the car.

Alone, Sophie straightened herself up and walked away towards the pedestrian entrance that led into and exited the car park. As she stepped onto the footpath that ran the length of the road signposted as Horse Wynd, she willed herself invisible.

The change was sudden.

One moment there... the next – gone!

It was a transformation that she had done countless times and which she now took for granted. Her altered appearance had no significant impact on her faculties, but peculiarly did turn everything she wore or carried, invisible, a trick which did have its disadvantages.

Wrought iron fencing bordered the path, behind which trees lined the way all along to her right, and ahead, just before a bend, she could see a large gated entrance that led into the grounds of the Holyrood Palace.

Following the road round with the bend, Sophie continued on towards the building of interest. The *Queen's Gallery*. On the opposite side of the road, the imposing modernistic construction that is the Scottish Parliament building, a convention of windows, angles, concrete and abstract art thrown together with the easier-on-the-eye pond stretching out in front of it; it almost looked out of place in the shadows of the seventeenth century palace building that stood regally behind the gallery, a Victorian structure originally built as a church and used as a store room until 2002.

Without realising, Sophie was standing outside the gallery's entrance. Above the arched doorway 'The Queen's Gallery' had been sculptured and inserted within the brickwork, topped by a red heraldic lion holding a golden sword and sceptre.

"Oh crap," she said to herself using only her breath.

"*Is everything all right?*" asked Brayden within her ear, his sudden voice causing her to gasp.

"Warn me when you're about to do that!" Sophie berated with a hiss. "I'm going in." *Let's do this!* she roused herself, taking a step in through the arched recess.

Internal glass doors stood immediately in her way, and opening them with invisible hands surprisingly caused no shock or confusion to the two visitors dawdling just inside, or to the two cashiers seated behind cash registers ahead.

Sophie slipped past the admissions desk and continued forward, through to a large hall rich with oil canvasses adorning its walls and sculptures and pieces of antique furniture taking up prominence at various points around the gallery. Along with her, there were two others visiting the Queen's art collection, currently loitering in front of an oil portrait of a prominent figure from Scottish history.

Just as Dominic had two days earlier, Sophie gave none of the works a second glance, hastening ahead to the back of the room where a stencilled sign pointing left directed visitors to the gallery's latest exhibit: The *Whisper of Persia*. Two members of staff guarded the door. Muscular and looking like ex-military, they wore no-nonsense expressions on their faces. Dressed in green and blue tartan trousers (striped with lines of black, red and yellow), a black waist coat buttoned up over a white shirt and dark blue tie, the look was completed by plain tartan Glengarry caps perched on their heads.

"I'm near. Just ten feet from the room," Sophie commentated in a quiet voice. A bare moment later and she bypassed the two staff members and entered the small room inside which displayed the vivid yellow diamond. Although unseen, a peculiar feeling overcame the two guards as she moved past; they shared a puzzled look.

"Someone just walked over my grave," said one, shuddering with goosebumps.

Sophie paid them no mind; instead, she considered the staff member in the immediate propinquity. Like the two standing just outside the room's entrance, this one was similarly attired. Unlike them, he was smaller, and was moving about the room, though quietly. His hands were clasped together behind his back. From his appearance; five-foot-nine in height, narrow shoulders, slender frame, and a face that seemed hollow and gaunt/tired looking, he clearly wasn't ex-military. Nothing in this man – she weighed up – offered any threat or would trouble her abilities; but his presence wasn't meant to engage with any would-be robbers. He was there just to mind the diamond and be on the lookout for any signs of trouble.

As the guard drifted past, Sophie noticed the small gadget in one of his clasped hands; a remote device with a red panic button, a small LED light pulsed lime green upon it.

She correctly guessed that the simplest of movements would be all that was needed to sound the alarm, alerting and galvanising the big brawny guards outside the room into action.

A quick assessment of the area also indicated that there was surveillance cameras placed in the corners of the room. In addition, there were extra security mechanisms in place, far superior to what she had encountered in London back last July, when all she had needed to do was...

Smash and grab.

Her father's voice spoke the words in her head, reminding her how easy it had been then, seemingly a lifetime ago.

A glance at the doorway behind her revealed a recess built within the sides of the frame – like a track – and, where she expected to see the lintel at the top, the flat edge of a steel door could be seen.

In the ceiling were a number of small glass-bulb-shaped sprinkler heads… too many required for such a small area in the event of a fire. She could imagine what their true purpose was, and doubted it was water that would be pumped from them. *Probably chemical or gas*, she thought. A poison to incapacitate any would-be intruder.

Stealing the diamond this time around wasn't going to be quite as straightforward.

Sophie walked deeper into the room, careful not to step in the way of the guard still pacing vigilantly around the empty space.

How do I do this? She pondered, slowly approaching the glass case. Bright halogen light from the spotlight set in the ceiling above the cabinet made the yellow diamond glow majestically on the black velvet cushion at the centre of the display. It looked spectacular, and slightly magnified through the toughened glass.

Deferring any kind of action for a little longer, Sophie half-read the information card placed within the display, learning a bit about the diamond's fabled history, its link to Arthurian legend and the belief that it once belonged to Cyrus the Great. The claim that it had magical properties was all nonsense, she quickly dismissed as her thoughts moved onto the objective laid out for her.

There are three guards. One in the room; two out… If I take the one out in the room, the two outside will hear and be alerted to my presence, likely resulting in activation of the security measures… I'll end up trapped in here and likely 'laid out' by whatever comes out of those sprinklers in the ceiling.

If I make any attempt to break the glass, my presence will also become known and the guard in the room will likely press the button on his remote, activating the security measures. I won't have a chance, so likely outcome: see earlier conclusion…

Hmm.

Sophie wished she could liaise with Brayden and Mullins. Or Ryan and Emily, but to speak outside of her head would definitely rouse suspicion and alert the guards to her existence.

It wasn't ideal, but she was definitely on her own this time.

She looked around the room for inspiration. There were no windows, just bare whitewashed walls.

"*What's taking you so long?*" Brayden's voice blurted in Sophie's ear. Nervously, she whirled around to see if his voice (loud in her ear) had been heard by the guard. She was relieved to see that he was still ignorant to her presence.

"*Are you there?*"

Silently, Sophie backed out of the exhibit room and glided past the two big guards standing sentry outside in the main gallery. She hurried to a corner where a large portrait was hung staring down at her accusingly.

"I'm here." Despite speaking quietly, her voice carried a little in the large open room. Fortunately, the pair of visitors in the gallery were talking animatedly between themselves, gaining scornful looks from the guards, providing ample background noise to mask her talking. "It's no use, I can't do it," she bemoaned.

"*Is this the same girl I'm hearing who took on my best agents in California? Who thwarted my attempt at apprehending her in Washington with a decoy and who disarmed an FBI agent and fired her gun next to my head, all with the merest of thoughts?*"

"That was different," replied Sophie. "The security is too tight, there are three guards."

"*Three? They should be* easy," Brayden said cynically. "*What about a distraction? What if we tried to draw them out?*"

"It won't work. You coming in guns blazing would likely alarm them. Any sniff of a threat, they'll activate security measures." She explained what she had seen: the remote; the steel door; the ceiling sprinkler system. And that's without the toughened glass case which wouldn't be easy to crack.

"*I think you are over-thinking this. What do you normally do when faced with adversity? When I had you surrounded, there was no escape... but you still got away. How? How did you do that?*"

"I don't know... I didn't think. I just did it," she said, tonally.

"*Well, there's your answer. Just do what you do best... I have faith.*"

"Okay... but I hope you have my back if this all goes to hell." Sophie plucked out the in-the-ear com-piece before Brayden could reply and crossed the gallery to walk behind the two other visitors who were still talking, and who had advanced closer to where the pair of guards continued to watch over the gallery at the back.

A man and a woman, both in their early-thirties, and both looking like they were from privileged upbringing, had stopped in front of an early eighteenth century landscape and were commenting on the brush strokes used and the hidden detail within the painting. Over one shoulder, the woman carried a dark-brown handbag.

Barely registering what she was doing, Sophie barged the man and woman, and pulled off the woman's handbag where it vanished on contact. The man fell onto his knees and just grunted. The woman whirled around and cried out: "Hey!" Not registering the fact that there was nobody else in the room, she exclaimed: "Someone just stole my bag!" As the man regained his feet, she jabbed him in the side and criticised him unabashedly. "You're no help!"

One of the guards reluctantly stepped forward. "What's going on? There's no one else here!"

Sophie retraced her steps back to the corner of the room and dropped the bag on the floor where it reappeared, as if by magic.

"Look! What's that over there?" The guard pointed towards the far corner of the room, moving towards it. "You've just left it, is all!"

"Someone snatched it!" the woman disputed, though a look of relief filled her face upon seeing her bag.

With the handbag absorbing their full attention, Sophie ghosted past the guard, and then the two visitors, heading for where the other custodian continued to stand patrol ahead of the exhibition door.

"Well, it's found now," the gallery employee said, picking up the brown handbag and presenting it to the woman.

Tapping the man still guarding the diamond exhibition door on his right shoulder, he jerked his head around to see who sought his attention. Before registering that there was nobody there, Sophie wrapped an arm tight about his neck and carefully applied pressure, feeling him suddenly grow heavy. Unconscious from the compression, the man slipped from her grasp and fell silently into a heap at her feet.

From the other end of the gallery, the guard who had attended the woman with her handbag looked up to see his partner collapsing to the floor. "Pete?" He ran back towards his post and felt his legs become knocked out from beneath him.

Sophie lunged from one side, executing a side tackle like a seasoned footballer, bringing the guard down hard onto his chest with a grunt. Slickly mounting his back, legs straddling him, the young woman grabbed the guard by a fistful of hair and propelled his head down hard against the lacquered wooden floor, then again a second time followed by a third, hearing a sickening, wet, meaty thud as the man's nose broke under the final impact. Turning him slightly, she could see she'd knocked him out. His face was bloodied and showing rapid signs of bruising. A quick finger check to the man's jugular reassured her that she hadn't gone too far, that the man was still alive. She sighed and let him down gently.

Standing astonished, or maybe bemused a little way behind her, the man and woman had witnessed everything...

This wasn't exactly accurate. When asked later what had happened, their account would be rather muddled and deemed unreliable by the authorities attending. They'd claim they saw the man trip over his own feet, and had watched him headbutt the floor until he had knocked himself out; coupled with what had happened to the other guard, and what then progressed within the exhibit room, they would be detained for questioning and accused of being accomplices.

Completely invisible and therefore unseen by the two gallery visitors, Sophie left them to wonder at what had just happened.

No longer guarded, Sophie was amazed to find that the man patrolling the diamond exhibit had not heard or seen anything untoward from within the gallery. Instead, he continued to toddle around the cabinet in his own world, mapping out plans for the weekend or deciding upon what to eat for dinner. Whatever it was he contemplated, he did not hear Sophie creep up on him, and didn't know what had hit him when Sophie struck his neck with the flat underside of both hands, an action that quickly laid the man out cold and was fast becoming her signature move. Catching him in mid-fall, Sophie dragged the guard to one side, and laid him down. She prised the remote unit from his hand and discarded it somewhere safe and out of reach.

All alone, she advanced on the display case in the centre of the room, and placed her palms against the glass. Once again she saw the diamond on the velvet cushion, tantalisingly close. She closed her eyes and remembered how the precious stone felt in her hands and wished that to get to it all she needed to do was think it.

Opening her eyes wide, she concentrated, lifted her right hand and balled it into a fist, pulling her arm back. In full focus, she aimed a punch at the toughened glass.

Her fist cracked against the cabinet and bounced harmlessly to one side.

"Ahhh," Sophie winced, immediately clasping her hand with

the other, pressing it against her stomach. She cursed. The pain was immediate and lanced up her arm, making stars burst behind her eyes. It took a long moment to recover.

At the side of the room were four retractable barrier posts. When in use, a red pull-out strap would be linked to each post to create a safety border to manage visitors attending the exhibition; it would direct a queue around the display case one way, and lead it out from the other. Now, one of the posts was being hefted by Sophie. Too heavy to lift single handed, Sophie held the top with one hand, and the midsection with the other. The post's weighted end, she hoisted up to shoulder height.

Returning to the display case, Sophie's eyes flashed back towards the room's entrance; she raised the post a little higher, before swinging the weighted base in a forceful arc down towards the glass barricade facing her.

Beneath her full weight, the toughened glass gave no resistance. A large hole first appeared within the wall of the cabinet, before imploding in a scene of cascading crystals and falling pieces of jagged glass. Sophie jerked the post around the edges of the case to make the opening more accessible. Leaving the barrier pole jutting from the display case, the young woman reached in and snatched the diamond from the velvet pillow.

Immediately, a burglar alarm penetrated through the building activated upon removal of the diamond from the case. Synchronously, the metal security door positioned above the threshold to the room began to whirr into operation automatically, its intent very clear.

"Oh crap!"

Leaping forward with the diamond clenched within a fist, she made for the room's only exit. The steel door glided down smoothly, building momentum; it was almost halfway. Desperately, she threw herself forward, emulating a momentous, sliding tackle motion, throwing herself down as low as she could, and stretching her legs fast-forward to skid on the lacquered flooring, narrowly escaping beneath the closing jaws of capture with the thinnest of margins. All she needed was a hat to lunge back for, and it could easily have been a scene from an *Indiana Jones* movie.

Coming to a halt on her bum outside the room, the door banged closed behind her. She sighed with relief and bounced up to her feet.

With the alarm clamouring, a number of gallery staff had come running into the large hall to investigate the cause of the fracas. Sophie hurriedly ran past them.

One – a cashier from the ticket desk – saw a blur of a person (a girl?) reflected against the glass of one of the large paintings adorning the wall to her right; then it was gone and she quickly dismissed it once she caught sight of one of her colleagues lying unconscious across the floor.

⸻ ⬤ ⸻

Both Brayden and Mullins jumped up in alarm as the passenger door of their *Ford Mondeo* burst open, seemingly of its own volition. The driver had seen Sophie coming in the rear view mirror. Before the door closed, Sophie willed herself physically present, the seemingly vacant space on the back seat suddenly filled up with her existence. She looked out of breath and out of humour.

"Did you get it?" asked Brayden, knowing the answer just by the look on the young woman's serious face and by the sound of the burglar alarm blaring desperately in the near distance.

Sophie lifted her hand and unclasped her fingers.

The yellow, multi-faceted diamond sparkled under the slightest glimmer of light. It was steadily darkening outside and the clock on the dashboard confirmed the time at just after four-thirty.

Christina Mullins gasped upon seeing it.

Brayden whistled in admiration. "See. What did I say? I had total faith in you."

Disregarding the compliment, Sophie pulled the diamond back and concealed it in one of her coat pockets.

"I thought you'd be pleased," venerated Brayden.

Sophie looked down wistfully, then turned and peered out through a side window. "Getting it wasn't easy," she said. "I had to hurt three people..."

"Unavoidable, I'd stress."

Sophie didn't agree. "Let's just go, shall we," she suggested instead.

The driver turned the key in the ignition and set the *Mondeo* back into motion. The black vehicle moved out of the car park, closely followed by the three other cars carrying the unrequired field agents.

"Liam called a minute ago," said Brayden conversationally. "The spy drone followed the van all the way to a house here in Edinburgh. We know where Dominic's keeping your sister."

"Is she okay?"

"Liam didn't say," Brayden lied. The truth was Liam had told the CIA agent that Meredith was tied up, bruised and looking terrified. "I've prepared the team. They are just waiting my orders."

Sophie located her mobile phone and dialled the number she remembered from the back of the photograph that had been delivered to her via Ryan. "Do nothing until I say so," she instructed. "Whilst I have the diamond, I have the advantage."

The ringing tone sounded for what was a long time, and carried around the car's interior, played through loudspeaker. Whilst it rang, Sophie glumly watched the world outside as the driver took them past *The Queen's Gallery*, where police cars were parked haphazardly in front and behind two ambulances, blue emergency bubbles flashing atop their roofs.

Just when she thought the man was not going to answer his

phone, the ringing tone was replaced by his familiar voice. Hearing it made all her rage bubble to the surface once again.

"*Congratulations...*" Dominic said gleefully. "*We have a winner!*"

CHAPTER FORTY-FIVE
EMILY

Two HOURS AFTER CLOSING her eyes, the *Westland Puma* descended from its cruising altitude and made ready for landing. Royal Marines Base Chivenor, formally RAF Chivenor, was home to the Royal Marines, Commando Logistics Regiment and the 24 Commando Regiment Royal Engineers, and was situated on the northern shore of the Taw estuary on the north coast of Devon. It was the closest base to Emily's contact, who she had arranged to meet in a town not so far away. The pilot communicated into the cabin over the internal radio that they were cleared to land.

Emily, half-dozing, sat herself upright and watched out through the window to her left as RMB Chivenor came into sight and the helicopter suddenly lurched to one side as the pilot guided it towards an area of airfield indicated by the base air controller.

Landing smoothly, Barnaby the pilot powered the *Puma* down and the co-pilot reappeared in the doorway of the cockpit. "We're here," he said, pulling free his aviation helmet. Emily appraised his facial features for a moment, concealed behind a carefully trimmed beard and moustache, both ginger. They made him look older than he was. "What's the plan?" he asked. "Do you need us to wait for you, or are you taking some time out down here?"

Emily smirked. "I don't have the luxury of having some 'time out'," she complained. "No, wait for me here… I won't be long. Be prepared to fly to London on my immediate return."

"Very well." The co-pilot crossed to the door and turned the release handle. Once fully engaged he pressed against it and the door hydraulically opened out and glided sideways, revealing the military base beyond. "Go. We'll be ready for when you return."

***

Barnstaple was a ten minute drive from the Royal Marine's Base, and just fifty-four minutes from the cottage in Bude that Ryan had directed Sophie to drive to last July – the day her mother had died and her father had disappeared to America. Bude had been a place of refuge for Sophie and her siblings in the days following those traumatic events. It was now home to someone else, someone Emily had come to meet with.

Emily had never travelled to Devon before, but had spoken often to the man she was now meeting with in Rock Park overlooking the River Taw. Taking a taxi into the town, Emily quietly observed the meandering roads and the usual mix of town dwellings and business buildings that they passed as they travelled through Barnstaple, claimed by many to be the oldest borough in the United Kingdom.

Turning off Taw Vale onto New Road, a park came into view on the right. The taxi driver drove a bit further, taking the next turning onto Park Terrace, a quiet road that ran parallel with the recreational area and which merged with another road a bit further up called Ladies Mile. He pulled up steadily and stopped the car.

Emily paid the driver with a twenty pound note and told him to keep the change as she climbed out. The driver cheerfully accepted the tip.

Crossing the road, she entered the park through an opening big enough to allow vehicles, though made inaccessible for anything wider than a baby's stroller with the use of removable stainless steel bollards; a flagpole, naked without its pennant, reached up to the sky a little ahead on Emily's right as she followed a footpath that branched in several directions, though the one she decided upon led directly ahead towards what she could see was the river. She passed a large children's play area to her left where some youngsters were still playing, climbing large unwieldy apparatus or swinging back and forth on chairs suspended from chains. Despite the steadily darkening sky as evening encroached, and the colder-than-average January day, there were a good number of other visitors to the park wandering past or walking ahead of her; some walked dogs, others were out jogging.

Just after half-four, Emily was walking along the edge of the River Taw. Ahead, a man on a park bench that overlooked the river peered over his shoulder and acknowledged her with a wave of a newspaper. Emily's heart quickened with her final steps and she greeted the man with a simple smile. "Hello Thomas," she said. "Finally, we get to meet. Ryan's told me a lot about you."

"All true, no doubt, Emily," Thomas Mundahl replied, his Norwegian accent thick and easily discerned. He articulated each word succinctly.

"Well, you look how he described," said Emily casually, casting her eyes over the man. He had blond hair and designer spectacles and a striking, unmistakeable Scandinavian look about him.

"Likewise," Thomas replied. "I heard about Ryan's injury. Terrible. I was stunned. What happened?"

Emily explained the New Year's Eve attack, sketching out the kidnapping of Sophie's brothers and sister, and bringing the Norwegian up to the reason for calling him earlier that afternoon.

"I always believed George was a crazy man... but very smart, yes. What he managed to do... well... he was a genius. In genetics, I don't think there was anything he wasn't capable of achieving, you name it.

Sophie... his American super soldiers... they were just the beginning. And now he is dead," Thomas sighed with regret. "The silly thing is, it wouldn't surprise me to one day learn that he somehow managed to escape death," he said optimistically. "If anyone could, he could, no doubt."

"No one escapes death," said Emily unnecessarily.

Thomas considered his response for a moment. "Perhaps," he said simply. "But he still managed to contact us from beyond the grave," he referred to the video message George had left for Sophie, and with it the formula which had been passed onto him. "Here." He grabbed the black chunky holdall bag that was placed to the other side of him. He unzipped it a little and reached in. "I followed the formula exactly to George's specifications... Because of the number of hosts that need to be... *modified*... I troubled over the best way to administer the antidote. This is what I decided." Thomas handed Emily a dart-like object three inches in length.

"A tranquiliser dart?" Emily queried, turning the small, slender missile over in her hand. Inside it was a translucent fluid.

"Be careful," Thomas cautioned. "The needle is sharp!"

Emily tested the dart's point with the pad of one finger. A dot of blood appeared on the tip of her index finger, verifying the man's warning.

Thomas tutted and took the dart back to prevent the woman from pricking herself further. "It's a ballistic syringe loaded with George's counteracting agent. The needle is collared and has a barb-like circumferential ring that ensures, among a couple of things, the full dose is administered. All you need to do is load it into a dart gun, aim and shoot. The antidote is fast acting, so any host receiving the shot will feel the immediate effects."

"Nice work."

He slipped the dart back into the bag and re-zipped it up. "There's a couple of hundred rounds in the bag, though only one is sufficient per target. They'll fit within a standard tranquiliser gun. Don't worry if you stick a host with more though... you can't overdose on the stuff. And it's harmless to normal people... it will only work on those afflicted with the DNA enhancements prescribed by George... so keep it away from our girl, Sophie." The Norwegian stood up slowly, picking up the black bag and holding it out towards the woman still sitting on the bench. "Here you go: all yours."

Emily accepted the black holdall as she stood, and threw it over her shoulder. "Thank you Thomas," she said.

CHAPTER FORTY-SIX
LIAM

"**R**IGHT, I'M ON IT," Liam said, accepting Brayden's charge without complaint.

"See anything interesting, let me know." Moments later and Brayden led Christina and Sophie out of the room.

You betcha, Liam thought acerbically, taking up the seat in front of the wall of VDUs still broadcasting live surveillance footage from within and from outside Waverley Mall Shopping Centre, a closed-circuit camera still zoomed in and focused on a man in his forties who he easily recognised as Dominic Schilling. He was sitting at the same table where he'd met Sophie, talking animatedly into a mobile phone in one hand whilst holding a large *Pepsi* cup in the other.

Liam picked up a phone and dialled up Mac back in London.

After a couple of rings the analyst picked up. "*Big Mac*," the man replied at the other end.

"It's Liam... Brayden says you have a live video stream from an overhead drone... can you send me the link?"

"*Way ahead of ya, bro. Access the SIS database remotely. I've set up a feed within Ryan Barber's folder. I've called it 'DRONE'.*"

"That's original."

Mac ignored the comment. "*To access it you'll need to enter the pass code five-five-three-six-one, followed by the password, 'my mumma's a whore', all lower case.*"

"Seriously?"

"*Well, she's not... but she skipped out on us when I was five years' old, so—*"

"I mean, you picked *that* for a password?"

"*What's wrong with it?*"

Liam didn't bother offering a reply. "That'll be all Mac, thanks." Without waiting for a goodbye, he hung up and turned his attention to the computer keyboard in front of him. Quickly summoning a web browser, he typed in the address for the SIS database and hit enter. A few seconds passed and the screen directly in front flashed up an official-looking warning box advising access was for '*authorised users only*', along with a 'Log In' pop-up that prompted Liam to sign in.

Liam signed in his credentials and waited. An hourglass cursor started rotating in the centre of the screen, going round and round for longer than his patience tolerated. Sighing, the field agent leaned back in his chair and stretched out his arms. Glancing about the room, his gaze fell upon a couple of handheld communications receivers set aside on a table which Brayden or Emily had either used earlier, or brought along for spares. He stood up and reached over to one, feeling how solid and heavy it felt within his hand, a bit like an old mobile phone from the late 1980s.

Pressing the red standby button, the radio device crackled into operation and voices immediately rattled forth from the built-in speaker. Nothing interesting as yet, just Brayden making conversation with Mullins as they drove towards their destination. Liam half-listened, returning his attention back to the computer.

The screen had changed to display a menu page with a number of links and folders indexed.

Liam typed in a command within the search function and waited for Ryan Barber's folder to appear, which it did, surprisingly quickly.

A new list of files appeared, the bottom one of which was highlighted as: 'DRONE'.

Liam double-clicked on the file which instantly presented a security window with the access requirements:

PASSCODE:_______________

PASSWORD:_______________

Liam typed in 'five-five-three-six-one' next to PASSCODE, followed by 'my mumma's a whore' in lower case alongside PASSWORD.

Instantly the security window was replaced with a webpage on which Liam quickly found the link to the drone's live video connection. He guided the cursor over to it and double pressed.

Aerial footage, a few hundred feet above a dual carriageway, appeared in front of him, along with the moving image of a grey van – difficult to identify – and the unmistakeable sight of a marked police car trailing eight or nine car lengths behind it, a lorry and two cars separating them.

Using a map and satellite tracking function that looked like a glorified version of *Google* maps, Liam was able to follow the van within a separate pop-up window on the LCD screen, noting the vehicle was travelling between seventy and eighty mph and heading on a course that led unmistakeably towards Edinburgh.

Behind him, electronic conversations continued to play out on the communications receiver, just background noise.

Mac had informed Brayden that the *Tourneo* had been sighted on the A84. The drone tracked the vehicle as it turned at a roundabout onto the M9, and Liam followed it for the next thirty miles before – unsurprisingly – it took a junction signposted as A8 (Glasgow Road).

"*What's taking you so long?*" Brayden's voice blurted from the communications receiver. Liam assumed the CIA agent was talking to Sophie. He followed up by asking thin air: *"Are you there?"*

A long moment of silence ensued which Liam hardly noticed, his attention on the drone's live feed in front of him. *"I'm here,"* said Sophie quietly. *"It's no use, I can't do it."*

Liam turned away from the computer screen, transferring his attention for a moment to the radio.

"Is this the same girl I'm hearing who took on my best agents in California? Who thwarted my attempt at apprehending her in Washington with a decoy and who disarmed an FBI agent and fired her gun next to me head, all with the merest of thoughts?" Liam heard goading in Brayden's voice and knew the tactic. Brayden was trying to tap into the young woman's well of confidence.

"That was different," replied Sophie. *"The security is too tight, there –"*

Before Liam heard anything more the telephone on the desk began to ring. He snatched up the receiver. "Hello?"

"Liam," it was Mac. *"Police Scotland wants to know how to proceed with regards to the Ford Tourneo. If they're to intercept, they want to act now before entering the city. Shall I give them the nod?"*

Liam sighed. Brayden had said to just follow the van, see where the driver was leading to. He was hoping that by doing this, Dominic's base of operations might become revealed. "That's a negative Mac. Tell them to fall back; we've got this."

The live video continued to play the van's progress as it moved ever closer to Edinburgh's city, and the conversation between Brayden and Sophie continued to its conclusion behind him:

Brayden: *"I think you are over-thinking this. What do you normally do when faced with adversity? When I had you surrounded, there was no escape... but you still got away. How? How did you do that?"*

Sophie: *"I don't know... I didn't think. I just did it."*

Brayden: "*Well, there's your answer. Just do what you do best... I have faith.*"

Sophie: "*Okay... but I hope you have my back if this all goes to hell.*"

Five minutes later two things happened simultaneously that forced Liam to his feet.

The drone continued to broadcast overhead images of the van as it turned off the A8 onto Magdalene Crescent, then Douglas Crescent and Rothesay Place before leaving the main route into the city by way of turning onto Lyndoch Place and carrying on further through a number of side streets that were either lined with large tenement buildings or grey three-storey brick houses on each side; further on, the vehicle led to an area not far from a stretch of water that Liam identified as the Water of Leith.

The *Tourneo* came to a halt at the end of a narrow cobbled road bordered by trees along one side opposite a row of old houses, their doors a dusty-grey and windows framed in peeling white gloss paint. It was then that Liam got his first glimpse of the driver as he exited the van, slamming the door behind him and hurrying to the vehicle's rear.

Liam entered a command into the computer and ordered the drone to zoom in on the man as he opened the boot door up. The high definition picture panned in closer and a full facial shot of Hector Degiorgio filled his screen just before he leaned into the *Tourneo*, his upper body disappearing for a long moment. As he stood back up, he dragged something heavily out.

Not something.

Someone.

Behind him, the communication receiver flared into life with a long, ringing sound from an unidentifiable source, but one which he quickly took a guess at.

"*Oh crap!*" Sophie exclaimed distantly, surprisingly clear above the din of braying bells.

"This ain't good!" proclaimed Liam, standing, his attention tug-of-warring between the images on the VDU and the drama playing out on the radio. "THIS AIN'T GOOD AT ALL!!"

She was gagged and her hands and feet were bound, but it was undoubtedly the girl whom Sophie had been coerced into stealing the diamond over. With matching blonde hair that hung loose and untidily to her shoulders, Meredith bore a little resemblance to Sophie. A deep purple bruise to the side of her head looked ugly and sore and her wide eyes conveyed nothing but unparalleled fear.

"Okay little girl... I've got you. I've got you. You'll be safe soon." Liam knew Meredith couldn't hear him. He spoke more to pacify himself. Agitated, he watched Hector manhandle the girl up and over one shoulder, awkwardly slam the van's boot door closed and then carry her around to one of the dusty-grey doors. One handed, he unlocked it, used a foot to kick it open forcefully and stooped in, closing the door, and the spying Liam, behind him.

Liam reached his mobile phone and fast-dialled a number. Brayden answered on the second ring and Liam didn't wait to be acknowledged.

"I have identified the driver of the *Ford Tourneo*," he started. "It's Hector Degiorgio. He drove the vehicle to a house north of the city." Liam paused for breath. "He has the girl – Meredith – with him. She's bound and a bit beat-up, but other than that, she's alive."

"*Sounds great,*" Brayden sounded distracted. He confirmed almost as much: "*I'm a little busy at the moment Liam, but send me the location.*" Brayden hadn't received any word from Sophie since the alarms had begun jangling and concern accompanied his voice. "*Take the lead on this and get on over there. Be discreet and do not engage. I'll be in contact with you as soon as I can.*"

"Okay bossman," said Liam, the merest hint of mockery in his voice was lost as Brayden had already disconnected. Returning his phone to a pocket, the MI6 field agent sat back down at the surveillance desk and picked up the phone. He dialled, punching in numbers starting with the prefix '020', the code for London.

"*Big Mac*," the analyst replied.

"Mac, listen up. I'm heading out into the field... can you take up monitoring the drone footage?"

"*Sure.*"

"Let me know if you see anything I might need to know. If that van moves, have that drone follow it."

CHAPTER FORTY-SEVEN
SOPHIE

"**C**ONGRATULATIONS..." DOMINIC SAID GLEEFULLY. "*We have a winner!*"

"Okay... I've got what you want," Sophie replied. "Where do you want to do the exchange?"

"*Meet me at St Andrews Square Gardens at 6:00 p.m. I'll be waiting by the Melville Monument. Come alone.*" Not waiting for refusal, clarification or additional questioning, Dominic disconnected and the car fell eerily silent.

"You don't have to do this," said Brayden. "We know where your sister is being held. Just give me a wink and I'll have the field teams go in..."

It was tempting but Sophie shook her head. "No, there's too much at stake. I have my brothers also to think about." In the rear-view mirror, Sophie could see Brayden's contemplative look. "What's to happen to them if we go about this all wrong?"

Brayden sighed. He knew she had a valid point. "Okay, we'll do it your way." He glanced at the clock glowing on the car's dashboard. "What shall we do now? We've nearly an hour to kill?"

"Food," replied Sophie. The hunger hadn't abated any from earlier when she'd met with Dominic at *KFC*; since then she had gone on to lay out three security guards and steal a diamond. "I'm starving. Plus, I need somewhere to go for a pee..."

"How charming," muttered Brayden.

Six o'clock arrived without any fanfare or the toll of a church bell (St. Stephen's Church stopped ringing in the hour sometime during 2014 after the council received a handful of noise complaints).

Dominic was standing in front of the imposing Melville Monument that dominated the centre of St. Andrews Square, its fluted column commemorating the life of Henry Dundas, the first Viscount Melville. Despite checking his watch every couple of minutes, he felt relaxed and appeared to be waiting patiently when Sophie arrived. She melted into view having been invisible, sizing up the area and checking out the man undiscerned from close range for more than a couple of minutes.

"Good evening," he greeted upon seeing Sophie approach from the corner of one eye. He turned slowly and grinned warmly, as though he were regarding an old friend.

"For you, maybe," Sophie replied, bitingly. She walked to within a couple of feet of Dominic and stopped at arm's length, but easily within striking distance.

"Did you bring my diamond?"

"Did you bring MY sister?" Sophie volleyed back.

Dominic smiled sardonically. "I can do this tango all night..." he replied. "First, rid yourself of the hidden mic I know you have and remove the earpiece."

Reluctantly, Sophie plucked out the small in-the-ear device and tossed it to the ground. It bounced off the path, disappearing within wet grass. She then unpinned a small metal badge that was attached to the collar of her coat. Reluctantly, she flicked it away.

"Satisfied?" she spat.

"Almost... arms up." Dominic stepped closer to Sophie and started to frisk her down, his hands feeling for any signs of weapons or other strange protuberances, lingering a little too long at various places about her body. Absently, he felt the hard shape of the diamond buried deep inside Sophie's coat. For a moment, he thought about reaching inside her coat and taking it; swiftly, he dismissed the idea as foolhardy, and stepped away once the inspection was over. He'd seen first-hand what she was capable of, even if he did have Meredith to bargain with.

"I bet you enjoyed that."

Dominic ignored the comment but the twinkle in his eyes confirmed that he did. "Okay, Sophie... this way!"

A look of concern flashed up on Sophie's face.

"Don't be alarmed. I'm going to take you somewhere... safe; somewhere we can exchange *gifts* and part... as friends."

Sophie harrumphed at the suggestion.

Dominic once again ignored her. "I just need to make sure that you are alone first and that we are not being followed. If not, well... my colleagues have their orders. You might remember them from your grandfather's New Year's Eve dinner party. They are taking great care of the children. Meredith AND the boys. They have their instructions; if they fail to hear from me at a certain time... well, let's just say... you'll have a shorter Christmas shopping list next time round."

The metallic grey *Mercedes SL Coupe Torino* almost looked black where it was parked towards the western end of George Street, the entrance to Edinburgh's *Hard Rock Cafe* just a car-length in front of it. Through the large plate windows either side of the door, Sophie could see diners seated all around the bar restaurant franchise. *Guns and Roses* provided the soundtrack to the moment and could be heard pumping from wall-mounted speakers within: *Sweet Child O' Mine* played, Axel Rose giving the chorus his all.

Dominic unlocked the car with a button press on the key he held. "Get in."

Sophie raised an eyebrow sparingly at the man's choice of car. "I guess crime DOES pay," she said quietly to herself, hooking open the passenger side door and climbing in. The fragrance of car showroom newness assailed her nose, which wasn't unpleasant. The company on the other hand… "How far? I don't think I can last for too long. I'd hate to be sick in your nice flashy car."

"I don't recall you suffering travel sickness during our travels between California and Nevada and back…"

"Yea, well, for most of those journeys I didn't have to carpool with YOU, did I?" She buckled up her seatbelt.

"Touché."

Dominic reversed out of the parking space and drove down George Street and away from the city centre; they proceeded in silence. Taking a detour up along dimly lit roads and around short, narrow streets that were devoid of any traffic, the man soon determined that there were no obvious signs of cars following and set his sights on the course that would lead them to the location where the exchange was to take place.

Eight minutes later the *Mercedes* entered an even narrower road than any travelled before, which turned out to be a cul-de-sac. Dominic slowly manoeuvred towards the end, parking up behind a *Ford Tourneo* van. Bringing the vehicle to a halt, he turned the engine off.

"Home sweet home," said Dominic, releasing his seatbelt and opening the car door.

Stepping out, Sophie quickly assessed the area and the building which Dominic was heading towards. The row of terraced houses looked Victorian and in dire need of modernisation. Even with little light she could see the windows and doors were old, with paintwork reminiscent to something she imagined originated in the 1960s.

Dominic stopped at the front door of the second house along the row, a smudge of dull brightness glowing through a crack of curtain at its window. "What are you waiting for? Don't you want to see sister dear?"

Sophie quickened around the metallic-grey car, stopping at Dominic's back as he unlocked the front door and stepped in.

Hesitantly, Sophie followed him into the house, closing the door behind her.

"Go through to the living room... it isn't much. Take a seat." Dominic directed Sophie with an outstretched hand. He pointed into the first room along the short hallway and the young woman did as she was bidden, Dominic standing aside to allow her entrance.

It was like leaping back in time. A retro floor lamp with a brown woven wool shade stood in the corner splashing nicotine-stained light around the room. There wasn't any carpet, just bare floorboards with a dirty old rug sprawled out across the centre of the room. A tan-brown vinyl three-seat sofa and two matching armchairs were placed around an old black-and-white wooden-boxed glass tube television. Upon the top was a photo frame with an old wedding picture once belonging to the home's original occupant. A bookcase set within an alcove alongside a chimneybreast was filled from top to bottom with dusty old books deprived of their jackets, all hardbacks printed in the early 1900s. Except for a couple of Charles Dickens, Sophie didn't recognise any of the authors or book titles.

"Would you like something to drink? Tea?"

A feeling of déjà vu settled on Sophie before she recalled Dominic had said the exact same thing to her earlier that day at *KFC*. "No... Thanks. Let's just get this over with."

"Suit yourself. First... let's see the diamond."

Sophie unzipped her blue coat as though getting comfortable before casually reaching inside. The diamond was secured within an internal breast pocket. Filling her fist, she pulled the yellow stone free and produced it palm-outwards. Even in the dim light, the diamond sparkled majestically. "There... you've seen it," she said. "Now go get my sister."

Dominic's fixated eyes seemed to swell inside his head, giving him a *Beanie Boo* look but without the cuddly cuteness. Blinking, he forced himself to move. Saying nothing, he turned and left Sophie to continue holding the *Whisper of Persia* and was heard stomping up a flight of stairs that were concealed behind another door a little further down the short hallway.

He hurriedly ascended two stairs at a time.

Muffled talking quickly followed. Sophie identified Dominic, but not the other person. The sound of movement and creaking boards directly above her head, followed swiftly by heavy footfalls as someone descended noisily down the stairs.

Unseen, Meredith's abductor – Hector Degiorgio, who Sophie would have recognised as the waiter at Grandpa Theo's New Year's Eve dinner party – slipped past the living room door and exited the terraced house.

More thumping about upstairs ensued, before Dominic lumbered noisily down the stairs, pushing someone lighter down ahead of him.

At first, Sophie didn't recognise her sister. Meredith's wrists were tied together and grey duct tape had been fastened across her mouth, but the thing which seemed to alter her most was the large purple bruise marring one side of her face.

Dominic shoved Meredith heavily into the living room, but halted her from progressing further by holding her tightly by the plastic carpet tie restraining her hands.

"What have you done to her!" demanded Sophie angrily. She stood up and looked about to advance on the man.

"Uh-uh." Dominic shook his head and raised his right hand to reveal a lethal-looking combat knife. He snaked his arm around the girl's neck and pressed the knife's blade close to her throat. "I wouldn't," he warned.

Still standing, Sophie calmed herself. "Okay... don't do anything stupid. She's just a kid..."

Meredith was crying. Stifled mewing sounds emanated from beneath the tape.

"Now... the *Whisper of Persia*."

"Let her go first," demanded Sophie.

"Toss me the diamond or I will slit her throat!" The look he followed his threat with was cold and menacing.

"Okay... we do this together... on three?"

Dominic smiled. "On three." He withdrew the knife, the blade disappearing behind Meredith.

"One," started Sophie.

"Two," followed Dominic.

"Three!" said in unison. With an underarm throw, Sophie pitched the diamond carefully towards the man who released his grip on Meredith's restraints, freeing her to run over to Sophie.

Simultaneously, Dominic effortlessly snatched the diamond from thin air with his left hand and launched the combat knife with his right, using an overarm, no-spin throwing technique.

Perfectly balanced, the steel knife arced through the air silently and thumped Meredith hard in the centre of her back before Sophie had chance to comprehend what was happening.

"I'm sorry," said Dominic. "I just don't trust you." He backed out of the room, turned and ran out of the house.

"Nooooooooooo!!!" cried Sophie, Meredith falling headfirst into her open embrace. Lowering her carefully to the floor, Sophie quickly ripped the duct tape free. Immediately, a line of blood trickled from the corner of her sister's mouth.

"Sophie!" Meredith wailed. "It hurts... it hurts!"

Looking over Meredith's shoulders, Sophie could see the knife jutting out; its blade buried deep, the hilt within gripping distance. A small circle of dark red was increasing in size around the entry point, staining the grey sweatshirt and steadily growing.

"Hold still," Sophie calmed. She looked around the room for something to stem the blood flow, eyes scanning all over, seeking anything that might work. Finding nothing, she stood up.

"Don't leave me!" Meredith cried.

"I need something to help... I'll just be a minute." Running out of the living room, Sophie made her way down the hallway and entered a room at the end.

The kitchen.

Next to the sink there was a dirty tea towel. Not ideal, but in the absence of anything else, Sophie swept it up and sprinted back to Meredith's side.

"S-s-soph-ie..." Meredith with shivering. "I-I-I... f-feel... s-s-so c-c-c-cold!"

Sophie placed the tea towel around the protruding blade and applied pressure. "Hold on Meredith... it'll be okay."

"I... d-d-don't w-want t-t-t-to... die..." Meredith sounded weaker, speaking a little softer.

The front door to the house banged open forcefully and a big man lumbered into the hallway.

"SOPHIE!!"

She recognised his gruff voice and felt a small amount of relief. "LIAM! IN HERE!" she hollered desperately.

"Ah, Jeez!" Liam exclaimed immediately on arrival, falling down alongside Sophie and Meredith. He dug out his mobile phone and was dialling '999' before it was even out of his pocket.

"I'll... s-s-say 'hi' t-to m-mum..." Meredith spoke with just barely a whisper now.

"Please don't..." Sophie sobbed, applying more pressure against the dirty cloth and the wound, careful not to move or disturb the knife.

"I need an ambulance right away," Liam spoke urgently into the handset. "Knife wound..." he barked. "The victim is ten-years-old... she's lost a lot of blood... the knife is still in place... *hurry*." The operator at the other end asked for name and address details which Liam suitably replied.

"B-B-Bye... S-S-Soph..." Meredith closed her eyes serenely, accepting her fate, almost welcoming death.

"No! Not yet!" Sophie screamed into the girl's face. "I'm not losing you too!"

Meredith's eyes flickered open and appeared to shine brightly for a moment.

"It h-hurts," she winced pitifully.

"I know," soothed Sophie. "An ambulance is on its way. Just be brave... and fight." Unable to halt the tears, she cried freely and miserably. "Please Mer... fight for me. Don't give up... don't give up. Please! Please!" she sobbed. "Please don't... please don't you die."

CHAPTER FORTY-EIGHT
EMILY

ROUND THE SAME TIME Brayden was driving Sophie away from *The Queen's Gallery* in Edinburgh, Emily was travelling back to RAF Chivenor where the *Westland Puma* awaited on its designated landing pad, refuelled and ready for take-off.

After handing her the bagful of antidote darts, Thomas Mundahl had offered the auburn-haired woman a lift, which she accepted gratefully. Now, Thomas steered his pepper-white *Mini One* off the A361 at the roundabout, taking the first left. Ten seconds later as they approached another roundabout, Emily could just make out the green signage welcoming visitors to 'Royal Marines Barracks Chivenor' on a road branching away from the junction furthest on the right.

"Over there," pointed Emily.

"I see it," replied Thomas automatically. He indicated right and followed the circuit round; taking the unnamed final exit road that was only identifiable by its military welcome sign. A hundred metres down further progress was obstructed by security barriers remotely operated from within a small building set to the right of the road. Tall fencing bordered the perimeter for as far as could be seen – which wasn't far owing to the lack of daylight.

Thomas brought the *Mini* to a halt.

A soldier manning the gate came out from the small building and approached their car. Thomas, closest to the approaching guard, wound down the window fully, allowing crisp air to enter. Involuntarily, Emily shivered.

"State your business, sir." The guard was wearing the standard khaki uniform and a green beret upon his head. In his hand he held a weatherproof tactical torch, five-and-a-half-inches in length, its bright white beam pointed towards Thomas's face.

Thomas raised a hand to shield his eyes and squinted through the brilliance. "I'm here transporting Emily Porter..." he said. "You should be expecting her return."

"Identification, please."

Emily produced her MI6 warrant card. Thomas reached into a trouser pocket to retrieve his wallet and carefully picked out a Norwegian driving licence. Thomas handed both to the marine.

The soldier stepped back for a moment, scrutinising the IDs under torchlight before consulting a ten-inch tablet computer which he had also been holding. Momentarily, the torch disappeared, freeing up a hand to tap and select commands on his *iPad*.

Emily glanced at her watch: 5:41 p.m.

After what seemed like a considerable time, the marine returned at Thomas's window. "Here," he said, handing the two IDs to the man. "Miss Porter is cleared to enter... but not you Mr Mundahl."

Thomas accepted his driving licence and Emily's warrant card and thanked the guard. He turned to Emily. "I guess this is where we say goodbye," he said.

⸻◆⸻

At 6:00 p.m. Emily was back in her seat within the *Westland Puma* and Barnaby had announced through her headset that they were cleared for take-off. On her return she had instructed the pilot to set a course for London and had called the Chief of SIS to inform him of her actions, and about Thomas Mundahl and the serum which he had produced based on the formula George Jennings had posthumously given them. After, the Chief provided her with an update from his end; she learned that the thefts, burglaries and robberies had carried on until around 3:00 p.m.

There had been some deaths on both sides; it was inevitable.

One police officer had been killed when he had launched himself onto the bonnet of a fleeing car – like how you often see in the movies; unlike the movies, however, his hands had nothing to purchase and instead gripped flimsy windscreen wipers hopelessly. The result was foregone; the wipers snapped free leaving him clutching them uselessly as he shimmied speedily off the car, the driver turning sharply around a corner with shaking him free his intent. The officer tragically fell into the path of an approaching dustbin lorry.

Emily was aware of three *GYGES* soldiers dying during a failed attempt at stealing gold from the Bank of England; the Chief had told her that earlier; there had also been one other. There were no gory details, just affirmation that another of their opposing number had died, somewhere near Hatton Garden.

A moment of quiet reflection happened between the two before Emily spoke again: "What about Sophie and the team in Edinburgh?" she asked anxiously.

"No news," he replied.

Emily wrapped up the call, saying that she would meet with him when she arrived back at Vauxhall Cross later that day. Immediately after, she speed-dialled Brayden. It was now 6:15 p.m.

"Brayden… it's Emily."

"*Miss Porter… It's a terrible line. Where are you?*" The connection was bad, made worse for the FBI agent to hear from the noise of the helicopter's engine and rotors.

"I'm on my way back from Devon. How's Sophie? Did she get the diamond okay?"

"Yes... in a manner."

"Is she all right? Where is she?"

"Simmer down, boss. She's fine. She's currently meeting with Dominic... they should be about to make the exchange."

"They should? Don't you know?"

"Unfortunately we lost communication with her at St. Andrews Square. Dominic made her remove the mic and earpiece. We weren't able to follow her either... not without giving ourselves away."

Emily cursed.

"Chill, don't panic. We've got this. Dominic drove for ten minutes around the city before reaching his destination."

"How do you know?" Emily asked, curious.

"Because we knew exactly where he was going."

"You did? How?"

"You bailed on us before I was able to bring you up to speed. Traffic cops spotted a grey van matching that used by the kidnappers heading towards Edinburgh. Mac ordered a spy drone to follow it. Long story short, with our eyes in the sky, we followed it to a location north of the city, a stone-toss from the Water of Leith."

"Okay... are Dominic and Sophie there yet?"

"No – ah, correction! Yes... they've just arrived." Brayden sounded excited.

"Okay... get the field team over there on standby."

"Already on it. Liam is also situated close by."

"Good. Don't engage unless you have to. Have the drone follow Dominic... we need to find those super soldiers before they are fully developed. One will likely lead to the other."

"Sure. What about you? Are you on your way back?"

"No... not yet. I've got a meeting with the Chief and some things to do first. I'll explain later. Let me know when the exchange is done and you have Sophie and Meredith back safe."

CHAPTER FORTY-NINE
BRAYDEN

THE **MI6** **AGENT HUNG** up on him at the other end leaving Brayden to nurse his mobile handset, quietly contemplative. Mullins was seated next to him on the left, and both of them were back in the surveillance room loaned them by Police Scotland.

"Things all right?" asked Mullins.

Brayden slipped the mobile away. "Sure. Why wouldn't they be?"

In front of them on the LCD screen, a night-vision aerial video feed played out; broadcast live from the *MQ-9 Reaper*, hovering quietly thousands of feet high above the house to the north of Edinburgh. Too dark to transmit regular video images, the drone was switched to night time mode; the image was now black and white with an emerald-green hue. With a button press and the slide of the mouse, the image could grow or shrink on command.

"Sophie's gone in. Hopefully the trade will take place without a hitch," Mullins was speaking for the sake of it.

Brayden grunted acknowledgement but said nothing. Taking over controls of the camera, he zoomed in on the front of the property. Light could be seen shining through the curtains of what he guessed was the living area, but nothing much else could be extracted. Reaching out for a communications radio placed to the left of him on the desk, he pressed a button and spoke into it.

"Liam... Sophie's gone in."

"*Yea, I know,*" he replied.

"Be on standby. Field agents are close by."

"*Roger that.*" The communication device fell silent.

"I wish we still had a microphone on her... I'd love to hear what's going on in there. I feel so helpless." Back at St. Andrews Square, Dominic had ordered Sophie to remove her earpiece and the wireless microphone pinned to her coat. Helplessly, Brayden had listened as the small device clattered away with a whine and a whistle and transmitted little else.

"You of all people *know* that she'll be all right," asserted Mullins.

Brayden sighed, recalling in a flashback the two or three encounters he'd had with Sophie on the opposing side. "Yea, don't I know it?"

The first sign of activity came a little over ten minutes later. The driver of the grey *Ford Tourneo* slunk out of the house and crossed over to the *Mercedes* parked in front of the van that he'd been driving earlier that day. Climbing in behind the wheel, he manoeuvred the vehicle in a number of point turns so that it no longer faced the dead end but was headed in the direction back out of the cul-de-sac. Now straight, the driver waited patiently with the engine running.

"I think they're about to make a move," guessed Mullins.

Brayden snatched up the communication receiver and spoke into it again. "Liam... they're making ready to leave. Get ready to go in..."

Liam made no response. Brayden guessed that he was too close to the Mercedes driver to risk speaking.

"Do we even know *where* he is?" asked Brayden conversationally.

"In the trees, around here..." Mullins was touching a finger lightly against the flat VDU screen, "... I believe." On close scrutiny and a small amount of zoom-tinkering, the barest amount of movement could be made out behind an evergreen, just ahead of some prickly-looking bushes.

"I guess he can see for himself," resolved Brayden.

Two minutes later and the door to the house opened and the shadowy figure of Dominic Schilling hurried out, dashing the short distance from doorstep to the car in three quick steps. Before Dominic had closed the passenger door, the *Mercedes* started forward at speed.

Without summons, Liam sprung up from his hiding place within the trees, sprinted across the narrow cobbled road and burst into the house via the door.

"ALL TEAMS.... GO IN!!!" ordered Brayden into the communications receiver as he stood up. He turned to Mullins seated next to him. "Follow that *Mercedes*... don't lose them." Seemingly of its own accord, the video image was moving away from the house within which Liam had just disappeared and was making a slow course after the fleeing vehicle (currently not in view).

Christina Mullins made the video feed pan out to reveal a greater area of landscape, and making Dominic's getaway car appear once again. Unknowingly, Mac in London was ordering the drone's pilot to follow the *Mercedes*; and, so not to lose the vehicle, a small red dot was superficially added to the car's roof, making it easier to track.

The communications receiver crackled just before Liam's voice poured out. "*Ah, Christ... he's knifed her, Brayden. Stuck it deep in her back. She's in a bad way...*"

"What? Who? Sophie?"

"*Meredith*," Liam informed. "*It's bad... real bad.*"

For a moment Brayden looked lost. He raked a hand through his hair. "Liam... she can't die. Do whatever you must, but keep her alive." He ended the conversation.

"Where are you going?" Mullins asked Brayden as he dragged his coat free from the back of an unused chair. He was still holding the communications radio and wore a determined look upon his face.

"I need to speak to Meredith... *now*... before paramedics get to her..." *Or before she dies*, he thought to himself. "She knows too much, why else would Dominic want to bury a knife in her back?"

DI Hamish Bremner was in the corridor of the police station drinking a mug of coffee when Brayden hurried past.

Almost an afterthought, the DI sought to gain Brayden's attention. He quickly gulped back a mouthful of coffee. "Agent Scott... wait up!"

Brayden threw a look back over his shoulder. "I'm in a hurry. What do you want?" He was still holding the communications receiver and subtly turned down the volume level.

Bremner followed the CIA agent through a set of double-doors. "The theft at *The Queen's Gallery* this afternoon... what do you know about it?"

Brayden shrugged. "Only what I heard on the radio. Something about a diamond..."

The policeman didn't hide the fact he wasn't buying the man's response. "Amazing coincidence... don't you think? You being here when all this kicks off."

"Coincidence? Irrelevance, more like..."

"I have witnesses claim to have seen you and members of your team driving past the gallery just after the theft occurred."

Brayden stopped walking, turned and stepped up to the Detective Inspector. At six-foot-two-inches, Brayden towered over the policeman. "Listen... I don't care much for where this is going. I have a material witness in an ongoing investigation badly injured – possibly dying – who I NEED to see as a matter of urgency. You have a job to do, I get that... but you're a dog digging for a bone in the wrong garden..."

DI Bremner put up his hands in mock-surrender, half-smiling. "Okay, Chief. Tell me what happened... maybe I can help."

Brayden started walking again. "I doubt it... but you can drive; you know the city better than I do." He gave the suited man the address.

In silence, the CIA agent and the Detective Inspector walked out of the police station together on Gayfield Street, the policeman leading Brayden to his dark grey *Audi S3 Sedan* parked on the other side of the road.

Reaching into the car, DI Bremner pulled out a magnetic emergency strobe beacon and slapped it onto the roof. "We can be there in five minutes... three, if the traffic doesn't get in our way."

With siren wailing and the blue bubble flashing on the roof, the police detective was true to his word and steered the unmarked car around a circuit of streets and roads, coming to an end behind two other unmarked police vehicles and the grey *Tourneo* which Brayden recognised from stills pulled from surveillance footage. An ambulance in full emergency mode was screaming urgently close behind, but for now not in sight.

DI Bremner unclipped his seatbelt, making moves to get out.

"Wait here," said Brayden, climbing out, closing the door gently behind him. DI Bremner watched the CIA agent run across the road and disappear into a house through a busted-in doorway. Field agents were on the scene, two guarding the entrance nursing assault rifles, others in close proximity around the cul-de-sac and within the house.

"Where are you?!" Brayden shouted out as he crossed the threshold.

"Brayden, in here," replied Liam from within the first room off the hallway.

Brayden followed Liam's voice and stepped through to the dingily-lit room, quickly appraising the scene. Plastic-covered sofa and chairs; old television (*I haven't seen one of them since I was a kid,* he thought); bookcase with 'turn of the nineteenth century' books filling it; a disgusting, dirty-looking corner lamp that emitted the barest of light through an age-stained shade, and exposed floorboards with just an old rug for covering that seemed to benefit from having a young girl's blood spattered and soaking into it.

Meredith Jennings was lying on her front, her head twisted awkwardly to one side beneath Sophie's coat, being used as a pillow. A knife – the type Brayden recognised as military – protruded from the centre of the girl's back like an upright peg in a ringtoss game. Liam was applying pressure above a dirty tea towel around the knife wound.

Her eyes were closed and she barely moved.

She looked dead.

Adding credence to the conviction, Sophie was sitting on the sofa sobbing hysterically.

"Is she?"

Before Liam could answer, Meredith cried out in pain. Blood that had trickled in the thinnest of tendrils from a corner of her mouth now bubbled with spittle on her lips.

"Meredith? Meredith?"

The ten-year-old opened her eyes. They locked onto Brayden's, looking confused.

"I'm a friend of your sisters. Help is on its way," he reassured her. "You're going to be all right."

Meredith winced and shifted slightly. Her cheeks were damp and glistened from the involuntary tears that leaked from her eyes whenever she closed them.

"Don't move, Meredith," said Liam, feeling the girl tense beneath his weight. He turned to Brayden and shook his head, urging him not to carry on; his eyes were pleading.

Brayden took no notice. "Meredith... I need you to answer some questions... just a couple... what do you say? Would that be okay?" He spoke slowly and soothingly.

Meredith gently nodded her head, closing her eyes. Fat teardrops surfaced and fell to the jacket propped beneath her head.

"Your brothers... are they okay?"

"Yes..." replied Meredith, hoarsely.

"Do you know where they are being kept? Where did they take you? What can you tell us?"

Meredith shook her head. The movement hurt and she grimaced a little, a small moan escaping her. "I never saw the place before," she half-whispered, half-croaked. "It was across the sea... I... I... think," she went quiet for a moment. "I escaped... I left my brothers... to get help..." her voice seemed to gain strength. "... there was a beach on the other side of a hill... not far... before that... little houses in a row... most were ruins... but some looked used; lived in." With every few words a small amount of blood dribbled free from her lips, indicating an internal injury.

Outside, an ambulance turned up. The siren had been deactivated a couple of roads back but blue light danced brightly on the emergency light-bar attached to its roof. It threw flashes of blue into the room through a gap in the curtains.

Oblivious, Meredith continued: "Behind it... a big black warehouse... no windows. They locked us in a room... there were no windows at all... just..." she fought hard against a wave of pain that tore through her. For a moment Brayden thought that was going to be it, but then Meredith continued, "...three beds... they let us out a couple of times a day... we called them *twalks*... toilet walks... I escaped… but… they must've caught me… I woke up… found myself here…"

"Do you have any idea where they might've taken you?" Brayden pressed, seeing the light in Meredith's eyes begin to fade.

"…an island… …dunno… …feel so tired…" she replied.

"Meredith… STAY with me!"

"… need… to… slee…" She closed her eyes.

"No Meredith!" Brayden tried rousing her by slapping lightly against her face.

Behind them, Sophie continued to cry uselessly on the plastic sofa. For most of the few minutes Brayden had been in attendance, she had rocked back and forth muttering: "My fault…" over and over.

A paramedic in dark green uniform and wearing a high-vis yellow coat bustled into the room carrying an emergency bag. "Step out of the way, sir," the paramedic said. "I'll take it from here." Following him in, a colleague stepped in and walked to the other side of Meredith. He was carrying a yellow stretcher like it was a surfboard. He propped it up against the wall.

The two emergency first aiders busied themselves around the dying girl, one attaching a portable vital sign patient monitor via leads to her chest and arm, the other slipping an oxygen mask over her nose and mouth. A couple of bleeps and warbles were emitted just after being turned on and coloured lines and numbers flashed up on the monochrome screen.

"There's blood escaping her mouth with each exhalation; could be a punctured lung." He thought it likely from the placement of the knife protruding the girl's back.

"Pulse is weak," announced the second paramedic calmly. He had felt for a heartbeat finding none, but the monitor contradicted his first reaction. "Blood pressure is dropping."

"Oh God!" wailed Sophie, just a bit of background noise.

"We don't have much time," warned the first paramedic. "Quick… let's make her comfortable and get her to the hospital."

Brayden, feeling like a balloon seller at a funeral, walked to the furthest part of the living room, a finger space away from the old television in the corner.

Paramedic two stood up, crossed the short distance to the stretcher and laid it down flat. Together they carefully hoisted Meredith onto it, keeping her lying on her side.

"Is she going to be all right?" asked Brayden. He looked concerned. Sophie was now standing and closing in on her sister.

"Wait," said Liam, grabbing hold of the blonde woman, drawing her away, but not so much that she could not see what was happening. He was standing and the room seemed incredibly crowded all of a sudden.

"We'll do all we can for her," replied the first paramedic answering Brayden but directing his words to the worried woman being comforted close by. The portable vital-sign monitor started to jangle an alarm. "She's flat lining!" he exclaimed.

"This ain't good," muttered the other paramedic unprofessionally.

"There's no pulse… we're losing her. Quick! Find something to pack her back up. I need her lying supine without compromising the blade!"

"What about these seat cushions?" asked Sophie, between sobs.

"They might do."

Brayden and Liam pulled all the seat cushions up from the sofa and two arm chairs, and a paramedic manipulated them so that there was a gap for the knife's handle to be sandwiched between them whilst propping the girl suitably off the floor. The other paramedic used tape to bind them together.

The paramedics carefully turned Meredith and manoeuvred her into position. "Make sure the knife is secure," warned the first paramedic. "We don't want a shock to cause it to go deeper or move." They spent a little time to position and wedge the cushions, bandages and other packing into place.

"It's as good as it gets." The second paramedic retrieved a mobile defibrillator and attached self-adhesive pads to the girl's chest. "We're running out of time. Start CPR..."

The other paramedic pressed a hypodermic needle of adrenaline into Meredith's arm and tossed the spent syringe into a yellow sharps disposal bin.

The two paramedics hastily worked to prepare the girl for intervention, one applying compressions, the other charging the defibrillator machine, which hummed from low up to high in pitch. When it was ready, it made a double-ding.

"Not yet... we don't have a rhythm." The portable vital sign monitor displayed little except for four horizontal lines of inactivity. Half a dozen more compressions and the paramedic spoke again: "Now..."

"Clear!" said the paramedic with the defibrillator, pressing a button on the machine as the other paramedic ceased pumping down on Meredith's chest and jumped back.

Non-dramatically, the defibrillator forced 150 joules of electricity into the unconscious girl. She jerked violently, but didn't move off the pile of cushions beneath her.

The topmost line on the vital sign monitor began to oscillate and dance as a heart rate began to register. Other lines of activity sprung to life as measurements of blood pressure and respiratory rate were registered.

"Good job," self-congratulated the paramedic with the defibrillator. "Let's move her before her condition worsens..."

CHAPTER FIFTY
DOMINIC

"I'M SORRY," SAID DOMINIC. "I just don't trust you." He backed away from Sophie and her sister, the younger girl falling into the woman's outstretched arms like she were a long-lost lover, and edged out of the room. Turning into the hallway, he ran out of the house, slamming the door forcefully behind him.

"Was your visit successful?" Hector had turned the *Mercedes* around, the engine idling, and was waiting in the driver's seat. As soon as Dominic was in the passenger seat, Hector floored the accelerator. He closed the car door on the move.

"In more ways than one," replied Dominic, buckling his seatbelt. Concealed within his right fist, the *Whisper of Persia*... his prize for returning Meredith to Sophie, as promised. Of course, he doubted she'd feel very much gratitude, not for how he'd left things.

For a second, he regretted his actions, almost feeling pity. It hardly seemed right to plant a knife in the back of a child.

I've done worse, he thought, disturbingly.

Hector glanced Dominic's way as he drove above the thirty miles per hour speed limit through the streets of Edinburgh. "You all right?"

"D'you remember how it felt as a kid on the run up to Christmas; the excitement and expectation? The desires and hopes? Then you unwrap the one present you had wanted above all others... only to find... to *realise*, that having it isn't half as great as wanting it. Do you remember that?"

Hector shrugged. "S'ppose," he said.

"I feel the complete opposite to that. But... I do feel bad about leaving Elspeth here."

"We could go get her... if it'll make it better? She'd be glad to be with you, I'm sure."

Dominic sighed remorsefully. "Don't worry about me, Hector. Elspeth is best left here... for the time being. Just get us back to the rendezvous point. I'd like to be there to greet the initiates on their return from London."

"Yes boss," muttered Hector.

Dominic stowed the diamond in his coat pocket as he retrieved his mobile phone, sweeping it up to his ear at the same time as he tapped the redial button on the screen. It wasn't safe to be with him, but there was nothing to say that he couldn't still speak with her.

The ringing tone burred for two seconds before being replaced by Elspeth's familiar voice. "*Is it done?*" she asked excitedly.

"Yes," Dominic replied, "exactly as planned." He didn't elaborate on the bit about using Meredith's back for knife-throwing practice.

"*Good. Then yous hurry back belyve.*" Quickly. "*I'm lyin' here beneath t' sheets... nakit.*" Naked.

Dominic found himself smiling. Thoughts of the short redhead's body almost made him change his mind and tell Hector to turn back.

Almost.

"I wish I could Ellie," he started, feeling angry with himself. "You enjoy the hotel for a few more days, it's all paid for. You've got my credit card," it was in an alias, he mused, but it would function. "Use it to treat yourself to something nice and expensive; I've got some urgent business to attend. After that, I'll come back. We can pick up from where we left it."

"*Dom'nic... you s'id-.*"

"I know... I'm sorry." It hurt him to leave her behind like that and he meant the apology. "Listen, I'll make it up to you." Except, the feeling in his gut told him that he wouldn't.

"*You promise?*" There was doubt laced with pleading in her voice.

"I promise." Dominic ended the conversation with the slightest jab of an index finger and a pang of fear.

———

Nudging the speedometer above the limit for most of the journey, Hector steered Dominic's *Mercedes* into the fenced-in grounds of the warehouse.

Dominic checked his watch. 9:03 p.m.

Hector slowed the car down as he approached the up-and-over garage door, stopping a metre from it. From inside the warehouse, someone (it was Garret) pressed the button that operated the electronic door. Begrudgingly it seemed, the door groaned and clanked as a gap appeared wide enough to drive through.

Not waiting for the door to finish opening, Hector rolled the *Mercedes* forward and brought the metallic grey vehicle to a halt alongside the *Mitsubishi Fuso* truck.

Dominic lumbered out of the car, his legs stiff after three hours of non-stop sitting. Just inside the entranceway, Garret had depressed the button to retract the door. Dominic sauntered up behind the bald man as the door clattered to a stop, the bottom edge colliding with the concrete floor, ending its descent.

"How's London been?" Dominic asked.

Garret looked over his shoulder, a nervous tic taking up residence beneath his right eye, the movement made the spider web tattoo contract. "Um," he started.

The conversation went downhill from there as Garret floundered to find the best words to explain that four of the cadets had died; three during the heist at The Bank of England, and one at Hatton

Garden. "Aside from that… everything went great," the mercenary concluded solemnly.

"Which ones?" Dominic was referring to the cadets who had died.

Hector turned off the *Mercedes'* engine and climbed out, closing the door behind him. He walked to within a few feet of where Dominic was standing near to Garret.

"Twenty-Six, Thirty-Seven, Forty and Fifty-Eight…" answered Garret. He nodded towards Hector in acknowledgement.

"Thirty-Seven, you say?" All the cadets (or *initiates* as Dominic referred to them) were identical, like clones. Except, Thirty-Seven seemed to be a little more intelligent, a bit more advanced than all the others. He had exhibited leadership qualities unequalled by the rest and Dominic had singled him out for great things.

Now he was dead.

A rubbish bin placed a short walk from where the truck was parked bore the brunt of Dominic's anger and frustration. He kicked the half-empty bin an inch off the ground where it fell over to its side, a black bag spilling forth and splitting. He followed up with a tirade of swear words and curses that would benefit an '18' or 'R' rating in a movie theatre, mostly as a result of the pain that exploded in his right foot from the force of his toe punt.

Dominic was simmering down as he limped back to where Garret and Hector stood watching silently. "Where are they now?"

Garret shook his head. He didn't know exactly, but news footage had pictured one or two of them lying sprawled across the pavement, their bloodied and bullet-riddled bodies hidden beneath white sheets. "I guess police pathology will have them…"

Dominic closed his eyes and massaged his temple. A slight headache was forming. "Casualties were inevitable," he conceded. "What of the others?" he asked, dejectedly. There were eighty-six sons of *GYGES* still in the field.

"Their missions were a success. They should be arriving back…" Garret glanced at his watch, "… anytime now."

The first of the cadets returning from London arrived in a white *Ford Luton Taillift* truck shortly before midnight. Driven by a Kaplan Ratcliff mercenary, the super soldier, still invisible, was sitting in the passenger seat nursing a trophy from an earlier robbery.

In a repeat of the early hours of New Year's Day, Dominic greeted each of the initiates as they drove into the warehouse, directing them to points to park and giving instructions on where to unload.

At a quarter-to-one, the last of the returning sixteen-year-olds entered the warehouse in an ambulance. He was half an hour later than the rest who had been dribbling into the warehouse every couple of minutes.

"A bit unorthodox," commented Dominic as the emergency vehicle turned into the building. Garret closed the roll-up door.

As the invisible cadet stepped down from the passenger side of the ambulance, Dominic walked over to hand him a jet injector loaded with a vial of ochre liquid; it had become almost a routine. The boy accepted the gun-like object, making it disappear within his grasp.

A quick burst of high-pressure sounded, followed by the very rapid appearance of the boy. On his black Kaplan Ratcliff battle outfit, a number badge had been pinned to the front of his shirt: 63.

Dominic raised an eyebrow, aiming a look towards the yellow *Mercedes* ambulance; the blue light-bar at the front above the windscreen built within the panel of the roof was flashing. "Dare I ask?" he said in amusement.

Number Sixty-Three looked down gravely. "What I have isn't gold, but you'll agree, no less valuable."

"Huh?" It sounded a bit like a riddle to Dominic, and it was getting a bit late for brain teasers. Then it clicked, "Oh. You were with them… in the bank?"

"It wasn't easy recovering them… the bodies," said Sixty-Three. I know how… important it was… you know… to get them back. It wasn't easy, but I also managed to retrieve number Twenty-Six from Hatton Garden."

Dominic placed a hand on the young soldier's shoulder. "You did good," he said, gently patting him. He slowly removed his hand and indicated that the cadet join the others before walking to the back of the ambulance.

Twisting the handle of the double doors at the back of the vehicle, Dominic then pulled them open.

Placed in black body bags, the four dead cadets were laid out in the back of the emergency vehicle, squeezed in lengthways. A small moan escaped him with an exhale of air, taking him by surprise.

"Are you all right?" Garret appeared at Dominic's side from some place, he hadn't seen where.

Where a look of sadness had appeared on Dominic's face, stony resilience now replaced it. "We'll bury them at sea, on the way back to the island," he replied without emotion.

CHAPTER FIFTY-ONE
EMILY

ON HEARING THAT **E**MILY had returned to her office, the Chief of Britain's Secret Intelligence Service entered the small operations room and breezed over to her desk.

"I was about to pop up," Emily said seeing the older man approach. She was sitting at her desk, her handbag open in front of her and her computer in the early phase of booting up.

He waved off her protestations. "Can I have a word?"

"Sure." Emily stood from her workstation. "The conference room?" she suggested.

"By all means," replied the Chief. He followed Emily through the operation room towards the back.

Passing Mac, Jeremy and Isabelle on the second-from-last bank of desks (Mac watching a night-vision image of an aerial shot taken thousands of feet above ground), Emily led the Chief into the glass-partitioned office at the end of the room. He closed the door gently behind him.

"Things have escalated since we spoke on the phone," the Chief started. "I'm just back from a COBRA meeting with the Prime Minister, his cabinet and the Metropolitan Police Commissioner amongst others. A lot of very unhappy people, I can vouch!" He walked around to the other side of the large central desk, leaning over the top of a high-backed leather chair. "An estimated three-hundred million pounds was stolen from the capital today… that's a hundred more than New Year's Eve!"

"Amazing," said Emily, almost awestruck.

"Quite." The Chief didn't sound exactly impressed. "Amongst the items stolen were the Prime Minister's cherished *L.S Lowry* paintings taken from his private retreat, and the Queen's Crown Jewels right from under the Beefeaters' noses at The Tower of London." He tsked to himself. "The nation is in the grip of panic, aided by the media speculating as to where these… *transgressors* are likely to strike next." He barely paused for breath as he added: "There's rioting in the streets for heaven's sake! People are demanding answers and blaming the police, and the police are waggling their fingers at Whitehall for the budget cuts that are reducing their capability; the Prime Minister seems to think that the buck DOESN'T stop with him, but actually should lie at OUR doorstep."

"Oh."

"Yes, 'oh', exactly." The Chief fell quiet for a moment. "Ignore me Emily… I just needed someone to vent at. I wish Ryan was here… I'd be making his ears bleed instead."

"Me too, sir; wish that he was here, I mean."

"Yes… of course. How is he? Have you heard anything?"

Emily shook her head. "Not since yesterday; been too wrapped-up in this 'Dominic-ransoming-Meredith' business, to be honest."

"How is that progressing?"

Emily pulled out a chair and sat down. "Not too well." Before the *Westland Puma* had dropped her off on a piece of land within Vauxhall Pleasure Gardens just a couple of streets behind the SIS building, Brayden had called her with an update regarding Meredith. "Dominic stabbed Sophie's sister after the diamond exchange, thinking to use the distraction to safeguard his getaway. The ploy sure worked."

"Is the girl going to be okay?"

Emily didn't know. "She's in a critical condition. Brayden said he thought they'd lost her at one point, but paramedics managed to resuscitate her."

"And Sophie?"

"She's fine… upset… angry. Of course, she blames herself."

"What about Dominic?" asked the Chief, concerned. "I guess he's made off with this diamond he coerced Sophie into stealing?"

"He has… but we have him in our sights. At least that part of the plan has not been compromised." Emily told him about the surveillance drone currently tracking Dominic's movement as his car moved speedily away from Edinburgh. "Mac is out there watching him right now. Hopefully, he'll lead us to his base of operations."

"And ALL that loot I'd surmise?"

"Yes, with a bit of luck." She only sounded half-enthusiastic.

"That would promise a good end to a bad day," said the Chief optimistically.

"Or, if you were Dominic Schilling, a bad end to a good day, sir."

The time on her watch was 8:45 p.m. when Mac started making noises between mouthfuls of *Domino's* pizza and swigging *Dr Pepper* behind her. There was only the younger analyst and herself still in the office, 'Jezebel' having both left together an hour earlier.

"What's going on?" Emily asked, turning her head to the left, enough to peer across and above the partition separating her and Mac's VDU. She could just see the analyst's eyes.

"For the past three hours I've been following Dominic driving across Scotland. First along a stretch of the M9 which merged into the A84; after that at Lochearnhead he joined the A85, which he's driven the entire length of, heading into a place called 'Oban'." The spy in the sky continued to beam green-screen images to Mac's PC display.

He tapped a couple of commands on the keyboard and the overhead camera zoomed in on the *Mercedes*.

"Oban?"

"Yea. He's driving through the town centre and taking a number of turnings. It's possible he's checking to make sure no one is following; he seems to have gone in a circle a couple of times... either that...," he was now thinking aloud, his voice losing timbre, "... or he's lost."

"I somewhat doubt that." Emily stood up and walked around to her junior colleague, stooping down beside him to study the live video feed. "What's in Oban?" she asked, mildly curious for Dominic's choice.

"Not much... though it plays host to a lot of tourism, apparently; there are some castles and some ancient religious sites, and the scenery all around it looks stunning. There's a ferry port which services the Hebrides; according to the tourist info, the place appears to be thriving."

The surveillance drone continued to track the *Mercedes* as it left the clustered suburban streets of Oban and headed south-west of the town, passing a small railway station and joining a road mapped as Gallanach Road.

"Where... *IS*... he going?" Emily asked quietly. Mac didn't attempt to guess. Instead, he sat silent, watching the vehicle move into an industrial estate, wending and winding around a series of turnings that moments later appeared to lead to a dead-end.

"There!" exclaimed Mac, pointing a chubby finger at the screen.

"What is it?"

Using the directional buttons on the keyboard, Mac positioned the surveillance drone camera to pan in further on the *Mercedes* as it continued a course along a narrow lane that headed towards a warehouse. "Could that be?"

"The base of operations?" Emily didn't think so and was shaking her head. In the call with Brayden — after learning Dominic had buried a knife in Meredith's back — she had been briefed on all that he'd managed to extract from the ten-year-old before she had lost consciousness. "I know it's dark, but that place doesn't fit Meredith's description." Meredith had indicated she had escaped from a big black warehouse onto a beach after passing a row of small houses and over a steep hill. Although the bay of Oban, the nearest coastal body of water, was close, this warehouse and its surrounding area did not match Meredith's description.

"Where IS he going?"

The *Mercedes* slowed down to a crawl as it fell within the shadow of the industrial building coming to a brief stop, before surprising Emily and Mac by driving forward as though on a collision course with a boundary wall; except, instead of smashing into the warehouse, it disappeared within it.

"It could still be his place of operations... Where Meredith said she was being held captive, may just have been a hideout." Without thought, Mac picked up a slice of pizza and bit a large chunk from it.

It could have been, Emily supposed. "Whatever this place is, I guess it's the end of today's journey," said Emily. The time on her watch was now 9:03 p.m. She yawned. It had been a very long day and she felt the need for a rest. "Are you okay to continue monitoring the situation in case he leaves? I don't want to lose him."

"Sure," replied Mac, feeling tired himself. "Sleep deprivation has a lot of health benefits; plus, I need to maintain my high intake of caffeine so not to get withdrawal symptoms," he said sarcastically.

"Thanks," she replied sickly-sweet and unaffected. "Call me if he's on the move again... or anything else you think I might need to know. But Mac, only if it's important."

"No sweat."

Although there had been countless reasons to pick up the phone, it was three hours later when Mac was speed-dialling Emily from his desk. The sudden arrival of a white *Ford Luton Taillift* truck on the drone's surveillance feed hadn't gained much attention at first as it trundled along the narrow road leading into the grounds of the warehouse, disappearing within it in the same manner Dominic's *Mercedes* had. But the subsequent number of vans, lorries, cars and even an ambulance, that followed it in – Mac counted fifty-six in total – blatantly did.

CHAPTER FIFTY-TWO
BRAYDEN

MEREDITH HAD BEEN TAKEN by ambulance to the Royal Hospital for Sick Children in Sciennes Road, Edinburgh as soon as the paramedics had resuscitated her and the girl's vitals were stable. She had lost a lot of blood and her condition remained critical.

Following close behind the emergency vehicle, sirens blaring, DI Bremner drove the *Audi* through the otherwise quiet streets of Edinburgh. Brayden was in the passenger seat at the front and Sophie and Liam in the back. The mood was tense and nobody dared to speak.

At the hospital, Brayden jumped out of the car and opened the rear passenger door in a gentlemanly fashion.

Sophie slipped out while Liam climbed free the other side.

"I should really be coming back with you," said Sophie in dilemma. She wanted to be with her sister, to make sure she was okay, but at the same time the anger that frothed in the back of her throat urged her to go with Brayden to pursue the man responsible for all the woes that had befallen her and her family.

"Your place is here at your sister's side," Brayden said caringly. "There won't be much done tonight... not whilst we regroup and follow our leads regarding Dominic."

"I suppose."

"Besides," Brayden added, "I'm hoping to grab myself some shut-eye... I'm, how do you guys say it? *Naggard?*"

"Knackered," corrected Sophie.

Brayden smiled as he climbed back into the dark-grey car. The English accent made so many words sound eloquently dirty. "Liam can keep you company. We'll pick you both up in the morning."

"Keep me updated, won't you?"

Softly, Brayden nodded and smiled with reassurance. He replied: "Regarding your sister... ditto."

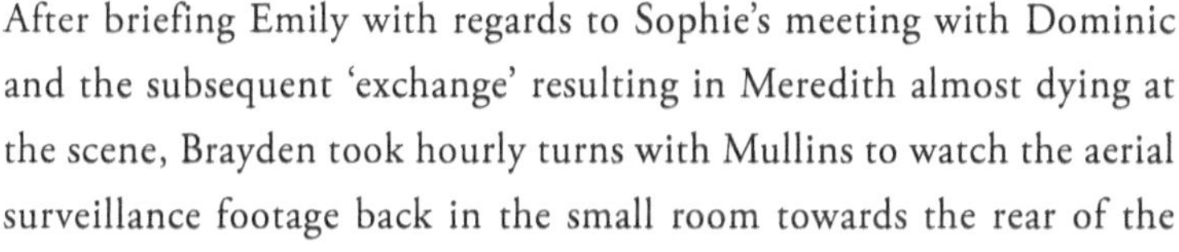

After briefing Emily with regards to Sophie's meeting with Dominic and the subsequent 'exchange' resulting in Meredith almost dying at the scene, Brayden took hourly turns with Mullins to watch the aerial surveillance footage back in the small room towards the rear of the police station. After dropping him off at the station's entrance, DI Bremner had left him for home for the day, driving the *Audi* off in another direction.

After two hours sharing stints staring at the green-tinged black and white video feed, the *Mercedes* that they were following entered the town of Oban via the A85. It was Brayden's watch and he felt a flutter of excitement burble in the pit of his stomach for some unknown reason. Takeout leftovers (Chinese) were in aluminium trays around the desk space in front of him. Without thought, he picked up a cold chicken ball, dipped it into a Styrofoam cup of sweet and sour sauce and took a bite. Behind him, Mullins was slouching in an office chair, her legs stretching over to another where her feet were propped up from the floor. She was asleep and snored subtly.

"Mullins," Brayden glanced behind him and spoke softly, as though being careful not to wake others even though they were in the room alone. "Mullins," he spoke a little louder.

Mullins didn't stir.

From a pile of directories and user manuals set to one side of the surveillance station, Brayden picked out a weighty-looking tome and slammed it down on the table behind him.

THWAPP!!

Mullins jumped up and rolled to the ground, a hand automatically reaching to the place where she ordinarily carried a gun. She had removed her holster and weapon and placed it on a table to the side before going to sleep.

Brayden laughed hard.

"That's not funny!" said the FBI agent, picking herself up. "Could've given me a heart attack..."

"It's a little funny," replied the agent, still sniggering. "Anyway... I thought you might like to see this."

The car they were following had weaved through the streets of Oban and had come out the other side, heading for an industrial estate towards the south of the town.

"Where're they going?" Mullins pulled up a chair alongside Brayden and sat down. She picked up an unopened bag of prawn crackers and started munching them like it were popcorn at the movies.

"I don't know... but I've got a feeling that they're nearly there," answered Brayden. It turned out to be prophetic.

Mullins and Brayden watched as the *Mercedes* followed a narrow road towards what appeared to be a large warehouse.

"Could that be...?" *the base of operations.* Mullins was half-thinking aloud, watching the vehicle stop outside the building for a moment before slowly moving forward and disappearing into it.

Back in London, Mac and Emily had been watching the very same images, sharing the same thoughts and conversation. Like Emily, he didn't think so. "No... it doesn't match Meredith's description." He had already repeated what the ten-year-old had said on arrival. "It's likely a meeting point..."

They continued to watch expectantly, but the picture on the LCD screen was frozen, like someone had pressed the pause button. After half an hour, Brayden's agitation manifested itself. He stood up and walked around the small room. Without announcement, he retrieved his mobile phone and selected a number on the contact list. A long ringing tone, followed by Mac's familiar voice filled his ear.

"Hi Mac, is Emily there?"

"*No mate… she's gone to get some rest. What's up?*"

"I'm guessing you've been watching the drone feed." Brayden had manoeuvred back to the surveillance desk and was leaning over the back of his vacant chair, staring at the video screen.

"*Sure.*"

"What do we know about that warehouse?" Brayden asked, staring at the large rectangular shape of the building.

"*I thought someone might ask that,*" replied Mac excitedly. Unlike Brayden and Mullins, he had spent the past thirty minutes online checking records and making enquiries. "*The warehouse – nay, the entire industrial park – belongs to a prominent UK based insurance company, but a little digging around… I've established the warehouse, along with another close by, have been leased to a shell company that indirectly belongs to a subsidiary of Kaplan Ratcliff.*"

"Kaplan Ratcliff?"

"*Yes siree. All arrows seem to be pointing her way. I think we need to have another chat with Jennifer Ratcliff.*"

Brayden didn't augment Mac's comment, instead he asked: "How long before we can assemble a team to mount an offensive?"

He didn't think it was possible, but at the other end of the line Brayden thought he could hear the man shrug. "*Oh, I dunno… logistically speaking, owing to your location and the time of day, about ten-to-twelve hours.*"

"Okay, that'll work. Begin the arrangements, but wait for further instructions. I'll need to speak with Emily first."

"Shall I get her for you?" Mac asked.

Brayden thought about it for a moment. He checked his watch before responding. It was 9:35 p.m. "No," he said cautiously. "Let her rest for a bit. There's no point disturbing her just yet… let's wait for something justifiable first."

He only had to wait two-and-a-half hours for that to happen when the first of a convoy of vehicles rolled along the narrow road leading into the warehouse, disappearing like the *Mercedes* had before them three hours earlier.

CHAPTER FIFTY-THREE
EMILY

BRAYDEN, MAC AND MULLINS had counted fifty-six vehicles entering the warehouse; the last – an ambulance – its blue light-bar flashing within the front edge of its roof, sped into the building moments before the roll down door was closed behind it. It was either responding to an emergency or an elaborate disguise to allow it safe passage through the roads leading through Scotland.

It was 12:45 a.m.

Emily had returned to the MI6 headquarters shortly after the first wave of vehicles had descended on the warehouse, actively commenting on what the surveillance drone transmitted onto Mac's screen, connecting with Brayden and Mullins and discussing its significance over speaker-phone. When little more happened after forty minutes of viewing what appeared to be a 'paused' image, the conference call was ended.

At 3:30 a.m. the roll down door of the warehouse was raised again and a stream of dark-garbed figures vacated the building, jogging in military-drill fashion in a column towards a coach that had appeared abandoned until then. There were eighty-six of them, which, on close inspection, easily identified them as the appropriated sons of *GYGES*. None of the figures appeared to be Dominic, and all bore a similar appearance to each other. Zooming out, the surveillance drone was able to track the coach as it drove out of the compound, taking a course that led towards Oban's small ferry terminal two miles away. A passenger ferry operated by *Caledonian Macbrayne* was berthed and received the contingent of super soldiers before immediately setting out to sea.

That was the first of two incidents of interest.

The second was the swift arrival of a *Bell 206* helicopter, landing a short walk outside the front of the warehouse precisely ten minutes later. Showing no signs of setting down passengers it soon became evident that its arrival was there to provide outward transport.

Sure enough, four individuals withdrew from the warehouse via a conventional hinged door, one of them lagging behind to lock up, securing a heavy-duty padlock and giving the door a reassuring tug before trotting towards the helicopter. Before climbing aboard, the spy drone camera had panned in on him.

"*That's our man*," asserted Brayden over the airwaves. The aerial spy camera fixated on the man's face and Mac pressed a key to pause the image.

"That's him all right," said Emily under her breath. "Who were his comrades?"

"*Beats me*," replied Brayden.

"One's Hector Degiorgio," interjected Mac, "The other two… probably armed goons going out for a ride."

"*That's helpful*," said Brayden sarcastically.

The helicopter took off with its four commuters, as the agents – separated by almost four hundred miles – watched from overhead; the *Bell 206* slowly rose up and glided across the sky towards the sea. From just below the clouds, the surveillance drone followed the helicopter as it flew past the ferry, and out further on a course west. The sea, far below, looked like a dark-grey broiling mass within the green image that played out on the live video stream.

"My guess is, that warehouse is where he's stashing the stolen loot from today's spree of robberies in London and those from New Year's Eve last week," presumed Emily. "Get local law enforcement to mount a raid… let's see if we can cheer up our Prime Minister and return the Queen her Crown Jewels."

"*I'm on it*," said Mullins, although sounding a little distant, as though from across the other side of the room.

Despite the *Bell 206* having a maximum speed of 138 mph, it cruised the night time sky at 120 mph, allowing the *MQ-9 Reaper* drone to easily follow its path as it flew across the Isle of Mull, before cutting a northern course on the other side of the island, heading further into the North Atlantic Ocean.

"Where's he going?" Emily pondered aloud. No one cared to respond.

One hour and twenty minutes later after two coffee breaks and countless trips to the toilet, the archipelago of St. Kilda appeared on their separate screens.

"*Jeez, I should have known it!*" exclaimed Brayden, still on speaker phone.

"What?" asked Emily within a stifled yawn. It was 5:10 a.m. and most of London outside the MI6 building overlooking the River Thames was still asleep.

"*St. Kilda*," replied Brayden, as though the name of the island explained everything. Not able to see the confusion on Emily's face via the phone, he sensed it by her silence. He decided to explain: "*After we extracted George Jennings from our black site last July, we had the warehouse 'cleaned'.*" Emily understood the term; it meant they were removing all evidence of their existence and signs that they had anything to do with the staged kidnapping that had ended terribly for Harriet Jennings.

"*Whilst 'cleaning',*" Brayden continued, "*Dominic was found unconscious within the room where Harriet was being held. Having served his purpose, we had no more use for him. I ordered that he be taken off site and dumped somewhere remote. I later learned that he was taken to the Outer Hebridean island of Hirta, one of four making up St. Kilda. I was led to understand that it was uninhabited... I guess that information wasn't correct. DAMN IT!"* Brayden banged something in the surveillance office in Edinburgh and Mullins could be heard trying to calm him. *"I should have done us all a favour and had him killed instead."*

On the computer screen in the MI6 operation room, Emily and Mac watched, simultaneously with Brayden and Mullins in their small back office surveillance room, Dominic Schilling's helicopter skirt the rugged landscape of the St. Kilda island of Dun, and begin its descent as it approached a stretch of coastline that belonged to Hirta. Without warning, a cluster of small buildings built in a single row appeared, and behind them, a very big square building.

"That's it!" said Brayden, like he had just discovered the final piece to a one thousand piece jigsaw puzzle. Although it was dark and the green screen image wasn't perfect, Brayden could see that it matched Meredith's earlier description by the shapes and outlines of the terrain. *"THAT's his base of operations,"* Brayden clapped his hands together. *"THAT's where he's been hiding those seized kids all this time... the ones you've been calling 'the sons of GYGES'."*

"It would also appear to be where he's still keeping Sophie's brothers," deemed Emily emphatically. "Mac, where are we with our strike force?"

Mac looked up from the aerial views still being displayed on the monitor ahead of him and glanced at his watch. It was now 5:25 a.m. and Dominic's helicopter was preparing to land on a patch of *Tarmac* clearly marked with an 'H' to indicate helipad, a short distance away from the warehouse.

"Personnel should be ready for deployment within a matter of hours."

"Good." She didn't ask him there and then to elaborate what 'personnel' he had procured for the mission but trusted the analyst's judgement. "Brayden?"

"*Emily*," he replied curtly through the phone's external speaker, confirming he was still in attendance.

"You and Mullins go get some rest. We'll pick you and the others up at Edinburgh Airport on the way."

<hr>

At 8:00 a.m., feeling much colder than she ought to have felt, Emily stepped out from a small terminal building at RAF Northolt and walked confidently towards the waiting *Westland Puma*. In one hand she carried the black chunky holdall Thomas Mundahl had given her the evening before, the other she shoved deep within her coat pocket. Once again, Barnaby was piloting the helicopter and the congenial co-pilot was on hand to greet her.

"Where this time, love?" the co-pilot asked pleasantly. Unlike Emily, he looked fresh faced and wide awake.

"Back to Edinburgh, but I'm waiting delivery of something first…"

"We're cleared to depart as soon as you give the order Miss Porter."

That delivery turned up sixteen minutes later. A plain white *Ford Transit* van pulled up alongside the helicopter and a female driver uniformed in khaki stepped down from behind the wheel and approached Emily. She wore a green beret on her head and the stripes on her sleeves indicated she was a lance corporal.

"Agent Porter?"

"Yes."

"One hundred *Lantec SFM6 Anti-Personnel* dart guns, especially adapted… as requested." The lance corporal led Emily to the rear of the vehicle and opened up the double-doors. Inside the van were ten large boxes, all sealed. The uniformed soldier dragged one close and used a utility knife plucked out from somewhere on her person, to cut through tape and bindings. "There's ten in each box," she said as she reached inside the box and pulled free a gun buried amongst polystyrene packing peanuts. She held out what looked like a normal assault rifle for inspection. The lance corporal felt the need to demonstrate its use by holding it ahead of her, one finger curled around the trigger, her other hand wrapped about the grip. She raised it up, levelling the sniper sight to one eye. "Specifically designed for use against humans, it's far more accurate than a conventional dart gun. With precision shots from two hundred feet, you'll hit the mark without any danger to yourself." She smiled wickedly, lowering down the weapon and handing it out to Emily for inspection. "It's a beautiful weapon. What's more, the built-in sound suppressor makes it virtually silent. Whoever you fire this at, won't hear you coming. It's great for sting operations."

"And it *can* carry more than one dart?" asked Emily, holding the weapon like a professional.

"It has a five-shot internal magazine. Here, allow me," the lance corporal accepted the rifle back and demonstrated how to release the magazine and load the gun. "And, before you ask, it's been modified to fit the specification of your darts, just as requested."

"Very good… I just need to see if I can find someone chivalrous… to help load these onto the chopper," said Emily, glancing towards the sudden appearance of the co-pilot, and throwing him a simpering smile.

CHAPTER FIFTY-FOUR
SOPHIE

THE DOCTOR STEPPING THROUGH the door looked solemn as he entered the room where Sophie and Liam were waiting. It was around two in the morning and Sophie was asleep in a corner chair, her head tucked down into her chest, her coat folded into a crude pillow behind her neck. Liam was sitting, leafing through a women's magazine, just for something to do.

The doctor made a coughing sound, both to clear his throat and to alert Sophie to his presence. It had the desired effect on each count. She roused herself up and forced herself to her feet. Liam tossed the magazine to the seat beside him.

"Doctor... how is she?" A panicked look flashed up on Sophie's face as she noticed the man lower his gaze, averting eye contact.

"Your sister lost a lot of blood and, as you know, required resuscitating on site by the paramedics. During surgery to remove the object from her back, your sister had a further myocardial infarction, requiring us to intervene for a second time. At first, she was unresponsive... but, we persevered and luckily she came back... she remains critical but stable. Her brain did suffer some oxygen deprivation, but we won't know the repercussions until we've run some tests. The next twenty-four hours are going to be crucial."

"Can we see her?" asked Sophie anxiously.

The doctor smiled. "Sure. She's in ICU," he said. "Follow me."

The doctor led Sophie and Liam along a short corridor, through a set of double-doors with the swipe of an electronic card, and a bit further, stopping short of entering a room where machines groaned, bleeped, hummed and wheezed. "We've placed her in a coma for the moment, to allow her body time to recover and heal itself, but you can take turns sitting with her if you like. Only one visitor at the bedside at any one time I'm afraid…"

Liam touched Sophie on the arm. "You go," he said. "She's your sister. I'll wait out here."

The doctor was holding the ICU ward door open. "Stay for as long as you like…" he said, "but there's really nothing you can do here, except wait for her to improve."

Sophie walked quietly into the room, following the doctor past a nurse's station towards a room with four bays separated by vinyl curtains hung from railings secured to the ceiling. Meredith was easy to spot as she was the only child in the ward.

A small whimper escaped Sophie's lips upon seeing the ten-year-old lying in the bed, a white tube protruding from her mouth connected to a ventilator which 'hissed' and 'plupped', simulating the girl's exhalation.

"It looks worse than it is," the doctor tried reassuring her, but his eyes betrayed him.

"Is it?" Sophie asked quietly. She curled a hand around Meredith's and gave it a squeeze. The girl felt warm to the touch.

***

A nurse shook Sophie awake. For a second she felt lost, unsure of where she was and certain that the events of the previous day weren't real. Stealing the *Whisper of Persia*; her sister being stabbed with a knife – nothing more than the invention of an over-active brain lacking good, solid rest and the nutrients of an honest-to-God healthy dinner.

The sounds of life-support machines quickly summoned her back to reality, banishing any hints of wishful-thinking to the ethers.

"The gentleman outside the room wanted me to get you," the nurse was crouching down to Sophie's level and spoke patiently.

"What time is it?"

The nurse glanced across to a wall clock at the other end of the ICU ward. "Just gone quarter-to-six," she said, half-turning before walking away.

Sophie stood up from the chair next to Meredith and stretched. Bones cracked with the effort. Before leaving, she kissed two fingers and placed them on her sister's forehead. "I'll be back shortly," she said softly, hoping her sister could hear.

Outside the ward, Liam was sitting on one of the cushioned chairs lined up along the wall. A stack of disposable coffee cups were at his feet with an empty sandwich carton. Wedged inside, together with a *Toffee Crisp* wrapper was a consumed bag of *McCoys* crisps, ready for disposal. He stood up in acknowledgement of the young woman's arrival. "I just got word from Emily," he said eagerly. "We know where Dominic is." He relayed the conversation he'd had with the MI6 agent a short time earlier, a verbatim account of the surveillance activities carried out through the night, and the discovery of Dominic's secret base of operations on the island of St. Kilda.

"What about the kids?" Sophie was referring to the sons of *GYGES*.

"They're en route," replied Liam. Upon discovering Dominic's location, Emily had used the surveillance software and the drone still broadcasting from above, to return to locating the *Caledonian Macbrayne* sailing across the sea, and cross-checking its details against the *Automatic Identification System*, verifying its registered use and scheduled destination. It had been chartered by the same shell company indirectly owned by Kaplan Ratcliff who had leased the warehouse in Oban. "They're on a ferry bound for the island," Liam asserted, "though they're not likely to arrive for another twelve hours… at least." Emily estimated that it would take approximately fourteen hours to travel there by boat; they had left some two hours earlier.

Liam continued: "We've received orders to link back up with Brayden, Mullins and the field agents now that our work here in Edinburgh is done. Emily's coming to pick us up on the way."

"On the way? To the island?" Sophie enthused, her heart quickening at the prospect of a swift reunion with Dominic and the chance of meting out some retribution.

"Indirectly, apparently," replied Liam. "We're meeting up with our strike force along the way, though she didn't say when or where."

"Oh?" Sophie sounded curious.

"All she would say was, she 'hoped' we didn't get seasick."

⸻ ◆ ⸻

DI Hamish Bremner escorted the contingent who included Sophie, Brayden, Liam and Mullins through Edinburgh Airport's security checkpoints and through the departure lounge to a section of the terminal off limits to most travellers. Owing to their matching black combat outfits, the MI6, FBI and CIA agents drew alarmed stares from civilians around the busy airport building, cutting a swath through the throng of travellers.

The joint force of field agents who, by and large, had sat on the subs bench for all of the previous day's action, were already at the airport and waiting in a transfer bus stationed at the bottom of a set of steps leading down from one of the departure gates.

DI Bremner led Sophie et al. out of the building and over to the waiting transport vehicle. A member of the airport's ground staff was waiting by the side of the bus wearing a high-vis yellow jacket and holding a *Motorola* walkie talkie.

"ATC indicate your helicopter has landed and is ready for boarding," said the man in the yellow jacket. "This way," he stepped on board the bus, turning out to be the driver.

"Thanks for the hospitality," said Brayden offering his hand to the Scottish policeman.

DI Bremner took it and gave it a firm shake. "Thank you for the heads up regarding the warehouse in Oban. Police Scotland will be celebrating that win for a very long time. Of course... the *Whisper of Persia* is still missing."

"That's a shame." Brayden took back his hand and moved towards the waiting bus; Sophie was already there.

"Good luck... with whatever it is you are doing."

Sophie, Brayden, Liam and Mullins climbed up the step onto the bus, walking down the aisle to sit on separate seats. The field agents were already seated, some animatedly talking; it was like they were going out on a day trip to *LEGOLAND*.

Once everyone was seated, the bus operator hydraulically closed the doors and set the vehicle moving, smoothly manoeuvring along the side of the terminal building a short way before taking the passengers towards an area of the airport adjacent to one of its two runways where a number of aeroplanes were either parked or preparing for take-off. Beyond was a stretch of asphalt that was almost empty except for a handful of cars and a *Westland Puma* helicopter.

Through the window, Sophie recognised the military aircraft as the one she had arrived in the day earlier. Standing by its open door, Emily was waiting expectantly.

The bus pulled up alongside the helicopter a safe distance away. Without prompting, the twelve travellers stood up and shuffled along the aisle towards the exit. One by one they disembarked in single file and marched across to where Emily stood. Sophie was in the middle of the procession and the auburn-haired woman placed a hand on her arm just as she was about to pass.

"Em," Sophie acknowledged. She sounded solemn.

"I'm sorry to hear about Meredith," Emily said soberly. "Is she going to be all right?"

Sophie slanted her head down. "Yea," she replied, lacking conviction. "I think she'll pull through." Emily squeezed her arm consolingly as Sophie added: "She has to."

Breaking their cheerless reunion, Brayden stepped between them. "The sooner we get moving, the sooner you can tell us where we're going."

"Okay," said Emily, rolling her eyes. "We'll have a proper chat later," she told Sophie as the blonde girl leapt up into the helicopter.

Brayden smiled down at Emily, satisfied that the line was moving again.

When almost all the members of the joint contingent were seated and strapped in, the co-pilot (who had greeted the travellers just inside the doorway) closed the door and disappeared into the cockpit of the helicopter, giving Barnaby the nod to leave.

Emily was unseated and stood at the front of the aircraft, her balance propped up by holding onto the backs of two aisle seats on opposite sides to her. Sophie believed the older woman was going to make some kind of speech.

The twin engines of the *Westland Puma* started to power up followed by the beating/whirring sound of the four bladed rotors beginning to rotate on the roof of the aircraft.

"Listen up," said Emily insistently, raising her voice to go above the increasing volume of the helicopter. "Some of you will already know that we have located our target – Dominic Schilling – and identified the place where he's been holed up. He's on an island called

'Hirta' two hundred and forty miles north-west of here." She lurched forward as the helicopter left the ground and started moving up and away. "Our plan is to link up with our strike team in a little over an hour's time and make our way to the island ready to engage Dominic and his force tonight, after dark."

"How're we going to do that?" asked one of the MI6 field agents who had been slightly miffed at spending the best part of a day waiting around, doing nothing. "I mean, these lads he has… aren't they going to be invisible and have other abilities?" he reasoned.

Emily was doing her best to stand fast between the two columns of seats as the helicopter gained speed and ascended higher into the sky. "I never said it would be simple," she replied. "But we have something that could make things a little easier." From a pocket she produced what appeared to be a tranquiliser dart. The rest were stored safely in the black bag Thomas Mundahl had given her the evening before, stowed in a cargo hold with the cases of rifles.

"We're going to trank them… great," scoffed Brayden, before dismissing the idea. "It won't work."

"This isn't a tranquiliser. It's an antidote, fast acting. Shoot one of these bad boys at an invisible soldier and 'poof" all their abilities… and our problems… all gone."

"Woah," exclaimed another of the field agents sitting close by, this one American.

"Each of you will be given a rifle which holds five of these," she held it between her thumb and index finger, "in a magazine. You'll only need to fire one. I've two hundred rounds… and there's eighty-six boys genetically modified, so you know we've got more than enough to go round… to treat them all. But make each dart count. Don't be trigger happy… we wouldn't want to let a handful of them escape… not the way they are. This is it, our only shot."

Emily returned the dart back to the pocket from whence it

came and started forward to take her seat. The turbulence from the helicopter was off-balancing and it had taken all her effort and the tensing of every muscle to maintain her footing. Before she sat, she had another thought but before voicing it she tumbled to the ground.

"Ahh!"

"You all right?" asked Liam, offering a hand.

"I'm fine," she gritted, picking herself up and straightening. She addressed the group once again: "Before I sit down, it goes without saying – *I hope* – but don't anyone go shooting Sophie by mistake. We don't want the bad guys having people who can make themselves invisible, but ours is for keeps. She's an asset. We like her just the way she is." Now Emily sat, taking a seat next to Sophie.

"Nice speech."

"Thanks," replied Emily, strapping herself into the seat. "Now for that talk."

CHAPTER FIFTY-FIVE
EMILY

HMS Ocean was an amphibious assault vessel, the fleet flagship of the British Royal Navy and fresh from a NATO exercise that was taking place within the Baltic Sea, recalled into action on the orders of Prime Minister Humphries. As Emily's *Westland Puma* touched down upon the landing platform, the ship was making progress not far from the north-western part of Scotland; the shores of Lewis and Harris, the largest island in Scotland, could be seen through binoculars, and was being observed by a crew member from the ship's bridge, overlooking the port side (the left, facing forward).

The *Ocean's* commanding officer, Captain Beresford, was out on deck, flanked by two Royal Marines and a Warrant Officer. They made up the greeting party and waited patiently as the co-pilot of the helicopter opened out the sliding door of the *Puma* and stepped down first, offering a hand for any passengers requiring support.

Emily, taking charge, was first to set foot on the warship. Not waiting for her colleagues, she strode out to the captain.

"Agent Porter I'm to assume," said the captain amiably. "We came as quick as we could."

"Thanks, Captain, I'm pleased to meet you. I know it was short notice."

"Well, we're trained for rapid response, on a cusp or a spur," replied the senior officer. "The arrangements have been made as requested. I have eight hundred Royal Marines stationed on board… and the best military might the British has at its disposal. Come, I'd like for you to tell me more about our mission. "

"What about the others," Emily indicated the stream of agents now making their way across the ship's deck behind her.

"They'll be taken care of by my Warrant Officer. They can enjoy some down time in our recreation rooms."

By 8:00 p.m. *HMS Ocean* was crashing through the choppy Atlantic waters to the west of mainland Britain, travelling at a speed of nineteen knots (which is approximately twenty-two mph), close to the vessel's maximum and making good time as they approached the Outer Hebridean islands of St. Kilda.

Emily glanced at her watch, noting the time. She was in the company of several senior seamen and military commanders in a room adjoining the ship's bridge. They were all standing despite there being enough seating for all placed around a table behind them. Sophie was there, as too was Brayden.

The captain had indicated that they would be arriving two miles east of Hirta at 9:00 p.m. Understanding the strength of the enemy, the ship's commander, together with others in charge of the military 'might' transported within the hull of *HMS Ocean*, agreed to the deployment of all its personnel and the use of its entire armament if necessary. Emily was humbled by the offer, but only asked for one hundred commandos.

Captain Beresford assigned a company from 3 Commando Brigade, under the charge of a Brigadier.

"When we anchor, we'll deploy the stern ramp. You'll set to shore on four *LCU MK10*s," the captain said. Landing Craft Utility (MK10s) were amphibious transport vehicles, each capable of carrying

120 commandos, a *Challenger* battle tank and other heavy duty utility vehicles. They would roll off the ship and power across the sea the rest of the way like boats, and then roll onto Hirta's shore. "We can also offer air support." He had a host of *Chinooks, Apaches* and *Wildcat* helicopters at his disposal, all armed with missiles and other heavy artillery.

"I don't think that will be necessary," Emily replied. "I'm hoping to take them by surprise and limit casualties. Most of them are only kids, but I think if we get to them fast, no one needs to get hurt."

Captain Beresford snorted. "You liberals with your crackpot idealism; you honestly think we can win a war without firing a single shot?" he scoffed before sighing. "All right, but, let me tell you, just from my own experience. Once you put a gun in the hands of a child, they STOP being a child. I saw it in Afghanistan, I saw it in Iraq… there's no distinction. If they fire a bullet at my men, they are trained to respond… and they are good at what they do. They will shoot, and they never miss their mark. If you don't like it…, well… I'm not forcing you to take the *Ocean's* commandos."

"You should listen to what she says," advised Brayden. "This isn't all that it may seem."

Unflinching, Emily looked the ship's commander straight in the eye. "I don't doubt your men are formidable against a normal opposition. When I say I want to 'limit casualties' I'm not talking about theirs; I'm talking about ours. These kids are nothing the like you've ever come up against, and I'm not just being cautious. Did you hear about what happened at Area 51 last October?"

The captain had heard a version of the events that had occurred in America's secret air base out in Nevada's desert, most of it fanciful or just plain nonsense. It had the properties of an urban legend. "There have been some rumours circulating about some secret tech being used, but nothing factual. An invisible soldier? Give me a break!"

"I know it sounds crazy, doesn't it?" muttered Brayden, smiling mirthlessly. One or two of the military commanders were smirking or laughing also.

Emily was deadly serious. "Say it was true, Captain, what then?" she didn't wait for an answer. "Now, imagine a scenario where you're facing not only one enhanced super soldier, but a whole host of them… eighty-six to be precise, what would you say to that?"

Captain Beresford joined the others, laughing contemptuously. "You're insane," he said. "I think I'm going to make some calls… this expedition is over."

"I wouldn't do that," warned Brayden. "You must've seen the news about all those robberies yesterday. What Agent Porter is saying is all true."

The captain was unconvinced.

"You're going to need a demonstration." Emily turned to Sophie standing a little out of the way, to the back of the group, half-perched upon a table. She had been so quiet it would have been easy to have forgotten she was there. "Show them."

All heads within the conclave turned to face her. Without blinking the blonde girl willed herself invisible. The transformation was instant.

"Good God!" uttered one of the commanders observing.

"Okay," said Captain Beresford, "you now have my attention."

CHAPTER FIFTY-SIX
SOPHIE

SHE HAD NEVER REALISED it could be so dark. Banks of thick cloud hung overhead, blacking out a quarter-moon and a billion stars. Internal lighting on the ship had been dimmed and all external lights, including the masthead light, the sidelight and the stern light, had been deactivated in an attempt to mask the *Ocean's* approach, all adding to the oppressive gloom. Peering through the *Yukon* night-vision binoculars, Sophie was able to make out the island's coastline just beyond the thick, oily surface of the Atlantic Ocean.

Beside her in the lead *LCU MK10*, one of the four amphibious landing crafts that had been launched for the operation from *HMS Ocean's* stern ramp, Emily was feeling anxious. "Do you see anything yet?"

In the background, the engines of the other three amphibious boats rumbled and whirred. They noisily competed with the crashing of the waves battering and jostling them from side to side.

Sophie shook her head. "No." She lowered the binoculars. "I'm not so sure doing this under the cover of darkness was such a good idea."

Emily disagreed. "We were not likely to see the boy soldiers during the day at any rate, not whilst they're disguised." She meant *invisible*. "At night... we have a better chance." Not least because the thermal night-vision glasses they all wore were more effective without the glare of daylight. Using them during the day ran the risk of getting dazzled or blinded by the sun.

According to the coordinates supplied by Mac, Dominic's base of operations was just thirty minutes away from where the warship had anchored. It was now 9:10 p.m., a little behind schedule.

Radio contact with the commanders on the vessel was maintained via operators in each platoon, of which there were five – with twenty commandos belonging to each. In addition to the commandos, agents Brayden Scott, Christina Mullins, Sophie, Liam and Emily, plus the eight field agents, all keen for some action after being kept on the sidelines for the entirety of the expedition north so far, were all preparing for the battle ahead.

As the shore rushed to greet them, the four amphibious boats fanned out, the pilot/drivers adjusting their velocity to allow them to arrive in a synchronised fashion, spaced ten metres apart. They glided onto the beach almost simultaneously. No sooner had the landing craft come to a halt, the exit ramps were released, clanging down against the shingle.

Now on the island, Sophie felt a tingly sensation as she recognised the setting from Meredith's description. Her palms felt sweaty; she rubbed them on the thighs of her black combat trousers. Although it was pitch black, the silhouette of the small jetty to the right of the beach was easily identifiable even without the binoculars; ahead, beyond a grassy mound, the large black building Meredith had described where she said her brothers were being held captive. It stood overshadowing everything else and looked almost alien within its surroundings.

"They're here. I can sense them."

Emily didn't respond. Instead, she spoke into a radio that was linked to the FBI, CIA and MI6 agents, as well as the commando platoon leaders. "This is command leader; you are green to go. Repeat. You are green to go."

A stream of commandos emerged from the four amphibious boats, garbed in dark camouflage battle uniform and combat helmets, and wearing thermal infrared ocular devices strapped across their eyes. Quickly they dispersed into an attack formation. All one hundred of them, standard assault rifles held at the ready, fingers curled around triggers.

There wasn't enough to go round, but those issued with *Lantec SFM6 Anti-Personnel* dart guns, kept them easily accessible, though hung over the back of their shoulders. The marines had laughed at them at first, deeming them a 'soft option' for military use. Emily had to explain that the enemy they were about to encounter wouldn't be what they were used to, and that the antidote would make them 'easier' pickings. As a compromise, the soldiers agreed to take the modified weapons, but showed no enthusiasm in likely using them.

Brayden and Mullins, who had crossed the sea in one of the other landing boats, walked up to where Sophie and Emily were still standing. Liam and the field agents had landed in the furthest boat from Sophie and were following the marines in the direction of the warehouse building; by the way they were running they appeared keen to get stuck in.

Then, as though triggered by motion or tripwire, what sounded like a single drumbeat echoed within the air as a number of high beam floodlights burst on from high posts planted within the hill every ten yards, illuminating the entire beach for as far as could be seen. Simultaneously, what sounded like an old air raid siren began to whine slowly and mournfully throughout the air.

"Now they know we're here, I hope they've put the kettle on," said Brayden dryly. Mullins smiled nervously beside him.

"You stay here. I'll see you inside." Sophie was holding her dart gun, the barrel pointed ahead of her. In various pockets in her combat clothing she carried spare darts. Strapped to her waist was a holster, within which she carried a deadlier weapon. A *Glock 19*, her weapon of choice, a more reassuring combat weapon in her hands. Back on *HMS Ocean*, she had picked up the handgun and felt its surge of power engulf her.

After Barry died, she had vowed never to use a gun again, except it was a promise she knew she wouldn't keep. Watching Dominic throw that knife at her sister, seeing her nearly die had made her change her mind.

"Sophie, remember what I said. We need Dominic alive," cautioned Brayden. He had stepped up close to the young woman, whose blonde hair was tied up and contained within a helmet that matched his, and all the other soldiers advancing on the black building, sent on the same mission. "The President was defiant with regards to that. The man needs to be held accountable for his actions Stateside; for the many American deaths. It's either him... or I have no choice but to take you."

"You could try. Besides, I have immunity," replied Sophie sullenly.

"Doesn't matter... Makes no difference to me. I need to take one of you back. Let's make it Dominic." His eyes were pleading.

Sophie glowered at the CIA agent for a moment. "I make no promises," she said, before vanishing to nothing.

"D'you think we can trust her?" Mullins asked Brayden quietly.

The CIA agent shook his head. "Not a chance. Come... come with me."

⸻ ◆ ⸻

The commandos were thirty metres ahead when the first shot was fired, ringing out within an echo, immediately followed by a yelp as one of the commandos was hit, accompanied by the dull thump as his body hit the ground. Urgent warnings and shouts of instruction were communicated between the marines as they took cover behind or within the ruins of the derelict cottages that lined the one road stretching adjacent to the shoreline, soon truncated by a sudden burst of automatic gunfire as they engaged with the enemy.

Through her night-vision eyewear, Sophie could see the line of soldiers preparing to advance, but bullets were flashing all around them, fired from Kaplan Ratcliff mercenaries who had taken up defensive positions around the perimeter of the building. Unobserved, she stood at the top of the hill that partitioned the beach, and scanned the scene ahead. Using her invisibility, she was able to get the lay of the land, see what they were up against. She counted eight opposition soldiers hunkering at various points around the building, some thirty metres beyond the row of houses. Hiding to the side of the building or behind hastily erected battlements constructed from wooden crates and oil drums just ahead of it, they used their defensive positions to their advantage.

Peering up towards the roof Sophie spied a sniper perched above. Using the toggle on the side of the ocular device strapped across her eyes she changed the setting from night to thermal and looked all around, searching for 'others'. She was relieved to see that there were none; the heat signatures corresponded with all the members of Dominic's welcoming force. There were nine of them in all… and none were invisible. They were just ordinary men.

Sophie reported what she had seen over the comms link built into the commando helmet she wore. "There's a sniper on the roof and eight combatants placed defensively around the perimeter; four at the front and two at either side." She toggled the goggles so that night-vision was restored. As the ocular devices were ineffective under bright light, it was fortunate that most of the floodlit area was aimed at the beach behind her.

Hearing Sophie's dispatch, one of the commandos ran out from cover, drawing fire away from his hundred or so colleagues. Gunfire rat-a-tat-tatted towards him; the distraction was intended to allow a marine to seek the sniper out on the roof. Less than five feet into his run, a single deafening shot rang out.

Sophie watched as a bullet punched a hole into the marine's face. He crumpled to the floor in a touchdown dive. Seconds later a barrage of bullets sprayed towards their hidey-hole, peppering another marine's chest and stomach.

"*Amberson's hit!*" cried a voice through their in-the-ear headphones.

"*So's Johnson!*" yelled another.

Like a call to arms, the commandos stood up and charged forward in frenzy, firing instinctively towards the positions Sophie had highlighted.

The sniper on the roof picked off soldiers as they advanced, felling five easily and injuring three others. Before a single enemy soldier was killed, thirty commandos were dead or mortally injured.

The sound of war filled the air. Gunfire was soon followed by grenades exploding and smoke bombs.

Sophie couldn't watch any further. "I'm going in!" Without thinking, she charged down the other side of the mound and ran into the roofless shell of the old cottage building she had seen the commando, Amberson, killed within and stooped by his body. By his side was his weapon, a *L96* bolt-action sniper rifle. She put aside her own weapon and picked up the dead man's weapon, trying it for size. Her *Lantec SFM6 Anti-Personnel* dart gun felt light and harmless compared to the weapon she now held.

Carefully stepping around the fallen soldier, Sophie pulled up the night-vision ocular device from her eyes, resting it upon her helmet. Stooping down, she picked up the sniper rifle and peered through its telescopic sight. Casually, she returned to standing. Although dark, the sight had a night-time setting and she was able to see the target easily through the lens with only the slightest adjustment. Perched atop of the roof the sniper was firing confidently, impervious to the danger. She carefully aimed the weapon, making a few adjustments to the focus and aligning the weapon so that her mark was placed at the centre of the crosshairs.

"I never knew you Amberson... but, this is for you," Sophie spoke tenderly. She pressed the trigger and fired a .308 bullet at her target. The gun kicked back against her chest (which was going to hurt later); it was immediately followed by the deafening roar of the gun, which sounded only after the man on the roof had tumbled over the edge and fallen quietly to the ground, only making a sound upon impact. He landed just ahead of one of the makeshift battlements.

Quickly adjusting her position, she aimed the rifle's sight on the field where bullets were flying from one side to another, viewing the carnage. It was clear to her that the marines were at an enormous disadvantage. Despite their skill, and mounting their attack from an open, unshielded area, it was akin to First World War tactics, where heavy losses were racked up in similar fashion during the Battle of the Somme.

Dominic Schilling's defences were a disciplined and very well-trained force and, from where Sophie was now standing, it appeared that they were clearly winning.

Bodies belonging to the Royal Marines were sprawled all over the place, some still moving or twitching, but most dead. Almost a third of the force was down... and barely two minutes had passed!

Sophie fixed the telescopic sight on a pair of mercenaries firing machine guns from behind one of the two makeshift, but effective, battlements. One of them was cowering down, reloading his weapon, and Sophie gently adjusted the position of Amberson's rifle so that he was dead centre of the sight's crosshairs.

"Let's make this a little fairer," Sophie said to herself, pressing the trigger on the sniper's rifle. The shot sounded loud again, but the kickback wasn't so fierce. She recovered immediately, quickly seeking out the second marine who had yet to realise that his fighting companion had keeled over behind him, preoccupied by the animus of defending Dominic Schilling's compound, and the eighty-six sons of *GYGES* hidden within. As soon as he fell within the centre of her crosshairs, she didn't hesitate. She fired for the third time, the rifle's spent bullet casing chinking to the cracked and broken concrete floor. Her mark flew backwards, still firing his machinegun into the air before coming to an abrupt end as he collapsed beside his friend.

The rifle's magazine carried ten bullets. She had spent three and assumed Amberson had kept it fully loaded. She quickly checked; there were seven shots left.

Sophie whipped the rifle to the right side of the building where two other soldiers were taking refuge. In quick succession she aimed, scoped each man, and fired. Like the two before, they collapsed inelegantly to the ground.

Surveying the other defensive positions, Sophie spied only one last soldier remaining, hunkering low behind the other pile of crates and oil drums. Commandos had killed the other three, leaving the lone gunman taking potshots at the advancing force, frustrating the attackers by doggedly avoiding them and getting lucky with his return fire. Sophie despatched him easily, showing zero remorse.

One of the platoon leaders spoke through her earpiece. *"All clear. We're ready to go in."*

The Royal Marines regrouped on the stretch of land between the row of cottages and the big black warehouse. Sophie counted fifty-three of them. They had taken heavy casualties, including half of Emily and Brayden's field team.

"*Can someone go open that door?*" another marine filled Sophie's ear.

"*On it,*" replied someone else.

From behind Sophie, an engine that had been rumbling low for the entire time, which the young woman had thought belonged to one of the amphibious crafts, began to resound louder, followed by squeaking and grinding as gears and pulleys moved and the diesel engine began powering the metal slab of a *Challenger* forward. It rolled onto the beach, soon climbing up and over the hill.

The hill had stood for nearly two centuries and could thwart the onset of a rising sea level and had shielded the once habited island from the harsh winds, but was powerless to stop – or even subdue – the advancement of this battle tank.

Once over the embankment, the *Challenger* came to a halt and the turret rotated in alignment with its 120mm, fifty-five calibre tank gun, rising up a couple of inches, taking up position to fire.

On the battle field, the commandos were hunkering down, taking cover and preparing themselves for something momentous to happen.

Sophie watched through the gap of the completely sideless building, fascinated by the tank's arrival. As it fired, the 'whoosh' of the armour-piercing 'discarding-sabot' round sounded, followed by an explosion as it hit the only front entrance into the warehouse, causing orange flames to billow for a moment before subsiding to reveal a rent torn into the metal wall the size of two double-decker buses.

"*Now!*" ordered a platoon leader and the fifty-three soldiers were up on their feet and running forward in an attacking formation. With no opposing soldiers to aim at, Sophie returned Amberson his rifle and retrieved her dart gun. Stepping out from the shelter of the old ruin, she started to jog after the advancing marines. It was when she was ten metres away from the rearguard that she realised that the advancement had stopped. When all the floodlights went out, returning the beach, the warehouse building and its grounds, and the entire surrounding backdrop, to complete darkness, Sophie knew something was wrong.

The first of many gunshots and the yelps and screams of soldiers from ahead of her confirmed it.

Unable to see, she pulled the night-vision eyewear back over her eyes as she walked, closing the gap between herself and the marines now seemingly within the thick of a skirmish.

"*What's happening?*" Emily had remained silent throughout the first phase of the operation, but with the lights going out, a tinge of concern had passed over her and laced her voice.

"*We seem to be encountering resistance,*" replied a platoon leader. "*But it's impossible. We can't see them!*"

"*Use your thermal settings!*" Emily instructed, flabbergasted.

"*WE ARE!!*"

Sophie flicked a switch on her ocular device, flicking from night-vision (where she could see the marines clearly) to thermal (where the scene changed to a multitude of colours on a dark background, concurrent heat signatures belonging to the soldiers).

"*They're amongst us!!*" screamed a marine.

Sophie switched views to night-vision as the soldier who screamed came into view. He had dropped his rifle and was jerking about in a bizarre dance, before his legs shot out completely from beneath him, as though swept out by invisible feet. He landed hard on his back and his body rocked and juddered on the ground, as though reacting to some sort of physical trauma over or above him.

Sophie changed back to thermal view.

Only one set of heat signatures appeared. No one else was close by. "I don't see them," said Sophie into her microphone. Yet, all around her, the marines were falling, as though succumbing to invisible assailants.

Screams were filling the air from ahead of her as other marines danced a similar tango.

"How's this possible?" Sophie asked herself. She frantically switched between thermal and night-vision and night-vision and thermal, hoping to see something, but what she viewed did not alter. There was nobody there… yet… the way the marines were acting was contradictory; it seemed to indicate they were in close hand-to-hand combat. Additionally, she sensed the presence of others; unseen, invisible others.

Maybe my father found a way to make the super soldiers truly invisible… Sophie pondered. George knew the only way to see *her* when she was invisible was through special glasses or thermal viewing devices. But that would mean genetically altering a subject's body temperature.

Through the ocular device, Sophie surveyed the field of battle. A number of marines were still standing but a good many were down, many dead or dying. Like the first soldier she had seen felled indistinctly, she saw another whose body was twitching beneath an unseen assailant. Still in her invisible form, she walked casually forward, the *Lantec SFM6 Anti-Personnel* dart gun pointing ahead of her, one hand wrapped around the pistol grip, the other holding the weapon steady via its magazine.

Screams and gunshots continued around her, and still no signs of the enemy. A bullet whistled past, too close for comfort, a puff of air brushing her ear. It was the same ear that had been clipped last October whilst escaping Washington's Dulles International Airport.

A couple of feet from the soldier, his chest still gyrating on the ground, Sophie fired her weapon towards a place, approximately knee height, above the fallen marine.

Instantly, like an illusion, the form of a soldier, clad in what looked to be silver-foil, appeared half-kneeling and half-straddling his victim. Unaware that he was no longer invisible, the sixteen-year-old carried on killing the marine beneath him. Using a combat knife – similar to the one Dominic had buried in Meredith's back – he rained down blow after blow, stabbing the marine mercilessly in a frenzy.

With just as little compassion, Sophie whipped out her *Glock*, aimed it at the back of the young killer's head and shot him. By now, the marine beneath his buckled body was dead.

"Emily, we're fighting blind at the moment. Dominic has found a way to block thermal imaging, some sort of reflective clothing. Sound the retreat. We'll need to think of something else."

CHAPTER FIFTY-SEVEN
BRAYDEN

"**N**OT A CHANCE. COME… come with me."

Brayden led Mullins away from where Emily was standing towards one of the now empty amphibious boats that was beached. When a big enough area had formed between them and Sophie was long out of hearing range, Brayden articulated his thoughts:

"Sophie means to kill him, which is understandable after what he's put her through," said Brayden knowingly, before adding: "So, it's imperative we get to him first."

"How, Brayden?" asked Mullins.

Brayden looked about the shore consciously, as though searching for the answer. Ahead, the floodlights illuminated much of the beach for a mile one way, and for as far as they could see the other. Some marines could be seen hunkering down low as they scaled the grassy hill and prepared for the fight on the other side.

"The marines have Dominic's defences tied up at the front. Maybe we could walk down there for a bit," Brayden pointed left, away from the warehouse, "walk inland a little; maybe then head on towards the building's rear; maybe there's a back entrance."

"I don't know Brayden, sounds like a lot of maybes."

"Do you have any better ideas?"

Mullins didn't. "Okay. Let's tell Emily and get some backup."

"There's no time and she's busy. Besides, our agents have gone in with the marines; they have their own battle to win. It'll be more evasive if we go in on our own… just in case this area is under scrutiny."

Mullins unclipped her gun holster and withdrew her weapon. Like Sophie, she had taken a *Glock 19*. She checked the magazine to ensure that it was fully loaded, and chambered a round. "Ready when you are," she said simply.

As they passed over the hill's summit, a glance to the right yielded a great view of the warehouse's foreground. They had travelled for a quarter of a mile, to a place they deemed a 'safe distance'.

Through the ocular piece that was secured over his eyes, Brayden was able to magnify his view. Crouching down low, hoping to avoid detection, he could see the defensive positions held by Dominic's mercenaries and ahead of them the force of Royal Marines taking cover within dilapidated old ruins, taking potshots at the enemy. As Sophie was invisible, he couldn't see her (not without changing to thermal setting), but he thought he could see some familiar faces. The big man Liam was standing clear of cover and was firing a *M60* machine gun. Next to him was an FBI field agent he recognised taking encouragement from the MI6 man. The 'rat-a-tat' of gunfire and what sounded like a loud 'putt!' every so often as a sniper rifle was discharged provided the soundtrack to Brayden and Mullins' advance.

"The way ahead looks clear," whispered Mullins, whose attention was focused on a patch of land that was dark where floodlighting was not directed; just before it there was an area that glowed as though under a spotlight.

"Let's go." Brayden tore his eyes away from the skirmish and set forth down the other side of the embankment. In a squat, they ran across the brightly lit area, seemingly taking an age to reach the canvas of darkness. Stopping for a moment to catch his breath, Brayden used hand signals to communicate their next movement. He directed towards the rear of the warehouse. To get to it, they would have to trudge through terrain that was overgrown with long grass and rugged with sand piles, hummocks and some very treacherous dips and inclines, a point proven when Mullins slipped and twisted her ankle after stepping down upon an animal's bolt hole, likely belonging to a rabbit.

"Ah, sh–" Mullins stopped mid-curse and hobbled for a bit.

"Are you all right?" asked Brayden in a hushed tone.

"Nothing an icepack and some *Demerol* can't fix," Mullins hissed back.

"Are you good to carry on? We're nearly there."

"I'll be fine," Mullins replied through gritted teeth.

Five minutes later Brayden led Mullins onto a path that seemed to follow a course towards the shadows of the hulking black warehouse. It was too dark to see, the metal-halide lamps not casting any light beyond the midpoint of the building. Both Brayden and Mullins had activated the night-vision setting on their eyepieces and were viewing the world through a greenish-grey tint.

"Look... over there," Brayden was pointing, "a rear door." Like the front of the warehouse, and both south and north side walls, there were no other signs of entry or any windows. "The way in," he said quietly.

From ahead, gunfire slackened and then stopped altogether.

That was over quick, thought Brayden. His opinion swiftly altered on hearing the dull 'thut' sound that seemed like a scratch in the air, followed by an explosion that made the ground quake beneath Brayden and Mullins' feet. The walls of the building appeared to shake and judder.

"What was that?" asked Mullins, already knowing the answer.

"My guess... a tank." They had been standing next to one of the *Challengers* on the boat coming in. "They've unlocked the door and are now about to go in."

"That'll keep Dominic's soldiers busy," said Mullins, blithely.

"That's also our cue; come, let's go..." replied Brayden. He started forward and didn't stop until he was at the rear door. Mullins, still limping, was slower but was soon at Brayden's side.

Comms links were issued to all as standard, and the earpiece in Brayden's ear crackled to life, followed by Emily's voice:

"*Agent Scott, where the hell are you?*"

Giving it no mind, Brayden removed the earpiece and dropped it into a pocket within his jacket.

"What was that?" asked Mullins, using the break to rub absently at her sore ankle.

"Oh, nothing," he replied. "I guess our absence has been noticed. I'll apologise to her later. Let's move in, hell waits for no one..." Brayden tried the door handle. As expected, it wasn't locked. They were on an uninhabited island, so why *would* it be? The door's only function was to secure the building from the encroaching elements. Before entering, he armed himself. Hanging behind him by the straps of a harnessed sling was the *Lantec SFM6 Anti-Personnel* dart gun, the barrel pointing downwards close to his rump. In readiness, he pulled it round to his front and hung it about his neck 'military patrol ready'. He curled a finger loosely on the trigger, whilst his right hand was hovering close to his deadlier weapon – like Mullins and Sophie, he had opted for a *Glock 19* also – holstered at his waist.

Brayden was about to move in, then stopped. He turned and faced Mullins before speaking softly. "Be alert. Remember back in Fresno when we were up against Sophie?"

"How can I forget?"

"That was kindergarten. There are eighty-six of them just like

Sophie inside here, so let's keep our focus. I don't care for any of these so-called sons of *GYGES*; it's Dominic we want." He pulled the metal door fully open and entered a large, empty room beyond. The lights were on, but nobody appeared to be home.

"I'm starting to wish I'd ignored you and told Emily where we were going now," muttered Mullins to herself, following Brayden in.

The room appeared to be a training or recreation hall, with a climbing wall at one side and obstacle equipment to the other. There were also some sports' facilities in close proximity: table tennis, five-a-side football goals, basketball hoop stands and judo crash mats.

The flooring glistened under the high overhead fluorescents and squeaked underfoot like that of an NBA basketball court. Brayden adjusted the viewing setting from night-vision to thermal, wishing he'd done that before stepping in. Just because the room appeared empty, didn't mean it was. Like Sophie, the *GYGES* kids could turn themselves invisible just by the merest thought.

Looking around the room through his altered lenses, he could see no one was in the room with them. Absolutely no thermal readings were registering, not even from behind the walls.

The air raid siren was still wailing from outside the building and distantly, the 'pop' and 'bang' of gunfire had started up again.

"I don't like this, Brayden," said Mullins quietly, "not at all." Something didn't feel right.

"Let's keep going." Approximately thirty metres from the building's rear exit were an internal set of double-doors. Without waiting, Brayden strode across the hall.

Behind him, Mullins started to follow then fell hard to the ground.

"Oomph!" Her *Glock* slipped from her hand and skidded across the lacquered floor. *What the hell!*

She had tripped on something and lay sprawled on her front.

Peering back over her shoulder a few feet, she expected to see the object causing her tumble.

Instead, there was nothing.

Brayden turned to see his partner slowly picking herself up from the floor. Mullins was reaching for her gun when the weapon shot away from her, skidding like a puck on an ice rink.

"What the –" Before she could finish, her head jerked back, as though she were struck hard in the face. Endorsing the theory, blood started to ooze from both nostrils, one trickle slightly faster than the other. She tried to focus on what had just happened, but before she could the world began to blur and fuzz over, followed by sheer darkness. She slumped forward unconsciously to the floor.

"Christina?" Brayden tugged free his gun and was hurrying back to the FBI agent's side. Where her gun now lay, he figured it was too far to have travelled on its own, not without third party intervention.

Which meant only one thing.

They weren't alone.

On realising, he was standing back on his feet, his *Glock* pointing ahead, his trigger finger a synapse away from ejecting a bullet.

Brayden pivoted his head from one side to another. The thermal setting on his goggles was still on, and his eyes searched painstakingly for signs of another within the room. He even looked skyward, towards the high ceiling.

No thermal images were being registered, not from any aspect of the room.

"How can this be?" he asked himself.

As if to answer him, an invisible rifle butt connected to the back of his head, and like Mullins a minute or slightly less before, he felt the moment and the world's entire problems swim away from him.

• • •

Nothing is more startling than a bucket of ice cold water being thrown into your face. Slushy water and ice chips cascaded down his body.

Brayden gasped, as though for his first (or last) breath, and felt his heart triple-somersault in his chest as a rush of adrenaline flooded his system, preparing him for fight or flight.

He could do neither.

It quickly became evident that he was tied to a chair in much the same way he had confined Harriet Jennings back in the Norfolk warehouse six months earlier. Cable ties bound his wrists and ankles, pulled tight to restrict movement. Unlike her, water was dripping from his face and had soaked through his clothing.

He shivered.

A bright operating theatre light on a cantilever arm attached to the wall was positioned a little above Brayden's head, the LED bulb blinding him to everything else in the room. He turned his head away, seeking a way to escape its glare.

"Agent Brayden Scott, what a pleasure it is to see you again." Dominic Schilling was buoyant and was standing alongside the restrained man. "Tell me, did you honestly think you had a chance against us?"

"How?"

"My initiates," he replied. "I knew you'd be able to see them… through your thermal imaging glasses, so we thought to counter that. It just so happened, Kaplan Ratcliff had been developing clothing that used *Mylar* foil, a material more commonly used in emergency blankets. It's good for containing body heat, so we had uniforms made out of the stuff. It's quite remarkable how effective they are; blocks infrared detection systems almost by one hundred percent. Cheap too! Though, gets a bit stuffy inside, I'm told. But what's a little discomfort?"

"We won't stand a chance."

"I know! That's the best part!"

The repercussions were enormous, cataclysmic even. He didn't want to think more on it. "Where's Mullins?" he asked instead, fear for the FBI agent suddenly overriding any other concerns.

"The woman? She your partner?" Dominic didn't wait for any reply. "I believe she's alive... a bit bruised and bloody, but still fairer to look at than you. I may let her live... when this is all over. But you... you're not going to be so lucky. You're going to be begging me to kill you... by the end."

Brayden tensed his arms and struggled against the white plastic strips strapping his wrists together, the motion caused his upright form to rock and buck on the wooden chair.

The cocking sound of a handgun caused Brayden to cease moving. "Okay Dominic. Let's not do anything too hasty... you can get out of this alive... I can help you..."

"You? Help me? Like you did last July, when you had me dumped here on this bloody island?" He was still bitter regarding the experience.

"That was a misunderstanding," Brayden said, sounding desperate. In truth, the man's dumping on Hirta wasn't his idea; he merely instructed that he be ditched somewhere... someplace remote.

"Doesn't matter; turned out to be a blessing, truth said. I never would've met the love of my life..." The thought of Elspeth, lying in bed at the hotel room in Edinburgh, flashed into mind.

"What do you want? Is it money? The President –"

Dominic interrupted the CIA agent. "– doesn't negotiate with terrorists," he finished. "We both know that. And your money? Naaahhh. Have you not heard the news? My men have amassed me more wealth than I could ever spend."

"What is it then?" Brayden pressed.

"What if I said 'world peace'?"

"I'd say you're the wrong sex; and you Brits don't do beauty pageants."

Dominic started to laugh. "I like *you Brayden*... really I do. You were always funny, like an everyday Jim Carrey."

"Maybe I should audition for an *Ace Ventura* remake."

Dominic ignored the agent's attempt at wit. He switched off the bright light and turned, gazing at a table at the side of the room. Upon it were Brayden's weapons. He gave them a cursory glance over before returning his attention to the American. "You see, the world needs fixing. There are too many wars and too much ill begotten wealth. Populations are over-expanding to breaking point and the exploitation of the earth's natural resources are at the expense of humanity itself. It can't go on forever. The world needs a new order. Things need to be done – *terrible things* – but all for the greater good."

"You sound insane, Dominic. You're delusional. Next you'll be saying you were visited by God in a dream."

He didn't deny it.

"Don't you see, Brayden? Something needs to be done. We need to save ourselves... from ourselves... before it's too late."

It was Brayden's turn to laugh. Long and mirthful, and so intense, his amusement brought tears to his eyes. It took every ounce of restraint for Dominic to stop from unholstering his handgun, and bringing the heel of it down against the American's head.

"I expected people to laugh," said Dominic dejectedly. "But they won't be laughing soon. None of you will... you'll see. Once we're finished with Britain, we'll take over Europe, then America, Asia, Africa... you name it. I'll even take the bits nobody wants."

"Even France?"

Dominic ignored the wisecrack. "We will be completely unstoppable," he continued. "We'll heal the world, and make it a better place."

"You've been listening to too much *Michael Jackson*."

"Keep making your stupid jokes, but I'll be having the last laugh."

"Honestly… Dominic, listen to what you're spouting. You lost four of your super soldiers in London yesterday… if you carry on like you are, the rest will follow."

"But that was before I had the diamond," said Dominic, as though it gave him a huge advantage.

"Well, that sounds crackpot."

Dominic made out that he didn't hear him. "The *Whisper of Persia* once belonged to Cyrus the Great. It was said that it was presented to him by God himself –"

"Here we go."

"– and with its innate power, Cyrus was able to conquer the Middle East, parts of Europe and the whole north of Africa. It was under his rule his people flourished in peace and prosperity. This is what we could ALL have. The legends are real, and with this stone…" Dominic presented the diamond using a parlour trick, making it appear from nowhere. It glowed under the ceiling lights majestically. "…I will take over the world."

CHAPTER FIFTY-EIGHT
SOPHIE

IT'S MADE FROM THE same stuff NASA use to line their space suits. It's radiation proof and helps regulate heat. AND it's also very good at blocking infrared, hence why you couldn't see the kids wearing it."

Emily was holding the suit and studying it under a spotlight built into the amphibious boat which she had travelled to the beach on. Beside her were Sophie (now fully visible), Liam and a number of marines. Upon discovering their inability to see their adversaries, Emily had sounded the retreat. Once clear of the battle zone, the tanks were ordered to fire a few rounds, to cover her soldiers' withdrawal. A few stragglers were now making their way over the hill, one half-dragging an injured colleague across his shoulder.

"Why didn't we think of that?" admonished Sophie. The idea was so simple, it almost beggared belief.

"Well, it's something for us to consider going forward," said Liam perfunctorily. "The question is: how do we get around it? They've got total advantage over us; if we can't see 'em, we can't kill 'em."

Emily appeared to be mulling over the problem when a marine platoon leader who had been pretending not to listen in stepped up. "What about radar?" he asked. His accent was pure Mancunian. Flecks of blood marked his face, none of which were his own. "We have some kit on board the *Ocean* which may help; new on the market. Handheld radar detection monitors, can scan up to fifty-feet; it'll detect animate and inanimate objects wherever you point it. We may not be able to see those kids, but if they're there, the radar will show them."

"Would that work?" Emily asked Liam.

Liam shrugged, "Only one way to find out."

A *Westland Lynx* helicopter delivered the order of handheld radar units within ten minutes of Emily's conversation with Captain Beresford. Five minutes later they had been unpacked and distributed amongst what was left of the strike force. Accepting one, Sophie and Liam led the way back towards the warehouse – forty-one marines following close behind them – over the grassy embankment and down the other side.

"*Keep a look out for agents Scott and Mullins,*" instructed Emily over the comms link. "*I want them found post haste.*" No one had noticed the Americans' absence, despite Emily's failed attempt at reaching them over the radio, until Sophie had returned with the *Mylar* combat suit, and that was only when Emily wanted to gauge the CIA agent's opinion on the matter.

Passing between the single line of cottages in their various states of repair, the marines steadied their handheld radar units, holding them like speed guns, directing them this way and that. The radar's LCD displays were rectangular, and adopted the C-Scope 'bullseye' view; the centre of the 'cross-line' symbolised the radar's host, or the originating point, and the four quadrants within the circular field represented an area fifty-feet in all directions; front right and front left (at the top of the screen) and back right and back left (at the bottom).

Abandoning their earlier bravado, the commandos were now carrying their *Lantec SFM6 Anti-Personnel* dart guns one-handedly, their more lethal weapons stowed over their backs or holstered by their sides.

Entering the open ground leading to the warehouse, the Royal Marines began to fan out. Ahead, parts of the black building were on fire and all around them lay dead marines.

Without warning, Sophie's radar screen pulsated red and started to bleep. A small 'blip' appeared at the top of the screen, followed by two more 'blips'. Beside her, Liam tensed up and prepared his weapon to fire.

Looking ahead, the way still appeared clear. Even with the night-vision goggles set to infrared, they could easily have been tricked into believing the foreground was still deserted.

"They're there," asserted Sophie fixedly.

"I see them," replied Liam, nodding towards the radar screen he shared with Sophie. A quick sideward glance to his left, then another to his right, signified that the marines accompanying them could see them also. "There's more too. Over there." Liam pointed towards the left side of the building. "And there." There was quite a force of others on the right side, lurking about, waiting as though in ambush.

Liam opened up the line on his comms link. "Let's coordinate our attack. At the moment, they think we are blind to them. Let's not spoil the surprise."

"*Copy that*," chorused over the airwaves.

"*Those rifles have a precision range of two hundred feet*," said Emily through their earpieces. "*Make them count.*"

At thirty feet, a shot rang out from ahead. One of the invisible super-solders had fired a pistol and, twenty-three soldiers along, one of their men collapsed to the floor, clutching his stomach and crying in agony.

"As Emily said, make it count. On three..."

Sophie counted: one, two, three, in her head, and fired the dart gun at the nearest target ahead of her. As the 'charge' required to fire the weapon was small and the weapon contained a built-in suppressor, the discharge was almost silent. Beside her, Liam fired at the same soldier. As the rifle carried five darts, Sophie took aim at a second target, fired, then a third and a fourth.

Within seconds, the seemingly 'empty space' ahead of them began to fill up with *Mylar*-foil garbed soldiers, initially oblivious to their altered state, but soon cowering for refuge as they realised they were no longer invisible, and their genetically heightened abilities were also radically reduced.

"Look… they're fleeing." Liam pointed to the left side of the building where the no longer 'super soldiers' were retreating; a stream of others were joining them from the right and centre. One or two stayed behind in assumed positions of leadership, and were waving their comrades on; a recently constructed barrier soon provided cover as they began firing machine guns at the advancing force of commandos.

Their aim was now erratic, desperate and ostensibly unskilled, though still very dangerous.

A 'crack' sounded as a sniper, using a rifle similar to the one Sophie had pulled from Amberson earlier, took a kill shot. The head of one of the sixteen-year-olds shielding his deserting companions exploded and his body rocketed backwards.

"They're going to be slaughtered," whispered Sophie, sadly.

Underscoring the point, a mortar round was fired from one of the *Challenger* tanks along the beach, the deadly charge exploding amidst the fleeing youths, killing some and injuring others.

Before the fulmination had a chance to subside, another 'crack' from a sniper rifle, this time felling the second youth providing his colleagues with cover fire, leaving the former super soldiers unprotected and exposed.

"*Platoon leaders, cascade the order to cease fire.*" Emily's voice filled Sophie and Liam's ears, though intended for the others in command on the field; almost immediately gunfire stopped.

"I guess that's our lead-in. Come; the way is clear."

Behind them, the *Westland Lynx* helicopter took off not far from where Emily was standing, and began to hover forward, billowing sand and sea spray into the wind for it to fall down in sheets upon the bordering mound and the row of abandoned cottages, a bright beam of light aimed towards the ground beneath it. Slowly, it floated over their heads and moved steadily towards the rugged expanse of land that bordered the large warehouse. Within the hills and dunes the sons of *GYGES* now spread themselves as they sought escape or refuge.

"THROW DOWN YOUR WEAPONS AND SURRENDER!" A marine wearing a green beret instead of a helmet was leaning out of the helicopter, amplifying his voice through an olive green, two-handled, megaphone. He was issuing his directive towards the fleeing figures below him. "SURRENDER NOW AND YOU WILL NOT BE HARMED! THIS IS YOUR ONLY WARNING!"

Guns clattered to the ground as many of Dominic's initiates, recently thinking they were invincible, stopped what they were doing and threw their arms fearfully in the air.

<hr>

The entrance into the warehouse was now a burning, gaping hole torn into the building's fabric by heavy artillery and mortar shells. Even without the flames from the blaze, and the soldiers defending it having retreated, the compound was just as dangerous to enter. Sparking, exposed cables hung like venomous snakes from the ceiling, bucking and dancing ahead and around them. Metal struts and mangled, misshapen pieces of framework strained under sections of collapsed ceiling, and piles of rubble were every which way they turned.

"Here... look... a gap." Liam picked out a path through the debris and found a less insidious route that required ducking beneath an electric wire that bucked and danced about their heads.

"The way appears to be clear." Sophie continued to hold the handheld radar pointed ahead of her as she closely followed Liam deeper into the warehouse. "Emily... we're entering the building," Sophie spoke into the comms link, activating the mic by lightly touching a small button on her earpiece.

After a long pause, Emily replied: *"Copy that. I'm sending a platoon in behind you."*

"Okay. Tell them not to shoot me by mistake!"

"I will. Over."

Sophie led the way deeper into the building, kicking away debris and ducking around a sparking cable.

"According to Meredith, she and her brothers were kept in a room on this corridor," said Liam elaborately.

"I hope we haven't killed them!" Seeing the destruction to either side of her, it was difficult not to feel sudden despair.

Thirty feet in, the mortar damaged parts of the building lessened and something resembling a corridor appeared, though littered with debris for quite a distance ahead. Overhead lighting flickered on and off and an electric current hummed somewhere close.

"They were apparently kept in a room on our left... six doors from the end of the corridor." Liam could see a T-junction ahead. To either side of him there were closed doors. Quickly he counted the number on each side up to the end.

There were nine doors to each side. There were likely more, but the mortar round fired from the tank had obliterated the rest.

"Point the radar over there," requested Liam, jabbing his right index finger towards doors five and six.

Two faint 'blips' appeared on the screen, beyond a solid thick line that Sophie identified as the corridor's wall.

"I see something," she said, each word coated with enthusiasm. She hurried over to the door and tried the handle. As expected, it was locked, exactly how Meredith had found it during her daring escape attempt a day earlier.

"Step back, I've got this." The big man waited a moment for Sophie to move aside then launched his body, shoulder first, against the metal door. Although the door was solid, the frame wasn't and it gave in easily with a metallic screech and clatter, forcing Liam to readjust himself before losing balance and falling into the room, onto his face.

What faced him hadn't been anticipated. Instead of just two children, there were two children AND two adults – a man and a woman. They were standing at the far side of the room, behind the third single bed.

Hector Degiorgio and Natasha Vincent.

Sophie's handheld radar scanner hadn't registered more than two people because both Hector and Natasha were pressed up close to Meredith's brothers, a knife held at both of their throats.

"We expected you to mount a rescue attempt. Dominic said that if you tried, we should kill them." Natasha was doing the talking, and to dramatize the threat she pressed the sharp blade against the neck of the youngest boy.

Before Sophie had followed Liam in, she heard the woman's voice and automatically willed herself invisible.

Charlie whimpered beneath his captor's knife, feeling its keen edge biting against the skin at his throat.

"Wo-ah, take it easy." Liam offered steadying hands, in one was his *Lantec* rifle, useless against these foes. He lowered it to the ground. "No one needs to get hurt."

Silently, Sophie walked unseen into the room, stepped around Liam and crept to the space between the wall and the ends of the beds. Before entering, she had swapped the radar device with her *Glock* and pointed it perilously forward.

"Now the piece at your hip," said Hector, indicating the gun holstered by his left side. "Remove the belt."

Dispirited, Liam unbuckled it and dropped it aside. "Seriously, I would recommend you giving yourselves up. Your army is in tatters. There's absolutely nowhere you can escape to, and if you mean to go on as you've started, you're both going to end up dead."

"Nice try, Sonny Jim. You speak as though it's you who's holding a blade to one of our throats."

"In a manner, I guess I am," said Liam, confidently.

Natasha turned towards Hector, who was already looking towards the woman. The pair of them started to laugh together, outwardly amused by the MI6 field agent's bravado.

"Last chance," Liam warned, seriously.

"Let's take him down a peg or two, Hector. Show him who's boss, right?"

"Right," replied Hector, flexing his wrist. The knife he held moved up and down an inch away from Stanley's throat menacingly, before he shifted position and prepared to slice down.

Stanley's bladder gave out; a dark stain appeared at the crotch of his trousers and urine pooled around his bare feet.

"No!" cried out Liam.

BANG!

The discharge from Sophie's *Glock* was deafening in such a small, enclosed room, causing the ears of both of Meredith's brothers to ring loud and painfully, and a dizzying, nauseating feeling to overwhelm their heads.

Aimed a centimetre from the side of Hector's head, level with the *pterion*, the softest part of the skull, a little above his ear and two inches to the right of his eye; the 9mm jacketed hollow point bullet penetrated through his head, tearing through brain matter and blood vessels before slicing asunder his middle *meningeal* artery, exiting the other side, its trajectory not entirely complete. The carefully placed bullet smacked into the front of Natasha's head, hitting her temple dead centre, and coming to a halt somewhere deep within a meaty section of her brain, close to the frontal lobe.

Sophie made herself present, appearing as if by magic, before gravity had done its business and helped Hector and Natasha to fall to the floor. Unlike the movies, there was very little blood, just a trickle from the entry wounds to the side and front of their respective heads.

"Sophie!" Stanley and Charlie bellowed together in delight; Stanley, the closest, wrapped his arms about her neck, oblivious to the gun still in her hand. Sophie swept him up carefully. Charlie was quickly at her side, muscling in for attention.

"Wo-ah, kids, there's plenty of me for the both of you."

The two boys reined in their obvious joy at being rescued and allowed Sophie to pull away and stand upright. By now, Liam was close at hand. He had kicked the knives across the room and was now crouching down, probing the bodies for signs of life. Satisfied there weren't, he stood up next to Sophie.

"They took Meredith!" whimpered Charlie. Now that Stanley was disentangled from the young woman, Charlie wrapped his arms about her waist.

Sophie returned the *Glock* to the holster at her side. "I know," she replied, placing a hand on the young boy's head before adding in a reassuring tone: "We found her. She's going to be okay."

"Can we go home now?" asked Stanley, relieved.

"Soon, I promise. I've just got something I need to take care of." Turning to Liam, Sophie then spoke to the MI6 man. "Can you see the boys safely to one of the boats?"

"Sure," Liam reacted, adding with a sliver of disappointment, "but what about Dominic?"

"Leave him to me," she replied. Sophie turned from Liam and the two boys and spoke once again into the comms link, her earpiece mostly silent throughout her encounter with the kidnappers, but occasionally crackling with updates from the conflict outside: "Emily… I've found my brothers. They're okay."

"*That's great news! What about Brayden and Mullins?*"

"No sign of them, but I'll keep looking. Maybe Dominic has them. He's close. I can feel it."

"*Don't go in just yet. Wait for the marines; they'll be with you shortly.*"

"I'm not giving them the glory," replied Sophie, ardently. "I'm going in now. Dominic Schilling's ass is no one else's but mine."

CHAPTER FIFTY-NINE
GARRET

" **I** WILL TAKE OVER THE world."

Brayden couldn't help but laugh. When it subsided enough to allow him to speak, all he said was: "Don't count on it."

A knock at the door put paid to any hope of having the last word or making a cutting riposte. Instead, Dominic turned away from the CIA agent just as the door opened.

Garret stepped in looking flustered. A glaze of sweat glistened on his bald head despite a cold draught blowing through the compound.

"Yes?" demanded Dominic at the newcomer's intrusion.

"Um, Dom…? A word?" He was slightly out of breath.

Dominic scowled at the mercenary, but allowed his annoyance to melt. "Go on," he said impatiently.

"It would be better in private," insisted Garret, treading backwards out of the room.

Dominic followed him out and pulled the door to, his hand remaining at its edge, keeping it open a knuckle's width. "Okay, what is it?"

"The initiates," Garret started, nervously. "They're fleeing."

"What!"

"The boys thought they were completely invisible as they approached them, thinking to take the attackers by surprise from amongst them. But that wasn't what happened. The enemy found a way to see through their *polyethylene terephthalate* clothing, and took us completely unawares. The cadets didn't have a chance." Garret rubbed at his eyes, as though clearing his vision from tears. "Before they knew what was happening, enemy marines were shooting them with some kind of dart gun."

"Tranks?"

"No. Something else, like the antidote." Garret was referring to the ochre countermeasure which the initiates injected to restore visibility. Kaplan Ratcliff had been able to provide a nonexhaustive supply. "Except... it's more potent. Unlike our stuff, the effects can't be undone by free will. The initiates tried to change back to invisible... but couldn't."

"What?!"

"I'm not sure whether it's permanent, but their abilities... they're gone."

"Sonofabitch!" Dominic turned to go back into the room, half-opening the door but stopping at the threshold. "Radio Melvyn and find the pilot of the chopper. We don't have much time."

Garret was speaking into a two-way radio as Dominic closed the door gently, almost contemplatively, behind him.

Brayden almost looked pleased with himself, sitting restrained in the wooden chair. It gave rise to Dominic's anger burning inside, and in one fell swoop, he landed a left hook against the side of the CIA agent's face, knocking him – with the chair – over. His hand sprung back and he clutched it with his right hand, recoiling from the burst of agony the impact caused. Brayden's face was like hitting concrete.

Far from showing signs of pain or injury, Brayden started to laugh. A small line of blood ran from his mouth where he had bit his tongue but he showed no other sign of injury. "It's over," he mumbled; it sounded distorted, his mouth numb and swelling. "If you give up now... I may be able to cut you a deal."

Dominic walked casually over to the table along one side of the room. Brayden's weapons, radio equipment, and sundry other items, were strewn across the surface. The former Kaplan Ratcliff Intelligence Director picked out a handgun, carefully appraised it, and then set it harmlessly back down before sweeping up the *Lantec SFM6 Anti-Personnel* dart gun.

"This is a curious thing," Dominic twisted his body, along with his attention, back to Brayden still lying on the floor. "Tell me, what concoction have you poisoned my super soldiers with?" He aimed the rifle towards the American's head.

Brayden started to laugh again. "Oh boy wouldn't you like to know? I can tell ya it's not the vaccine for bird 'flu," he replied, cryptically.

"Perhaps I should put it to the test, see for myself?"

The man just laughed some more. By Brayden's lackadaisical response, Dominic guessed that he was telling the truth. "It's not fatal... but permanent. In the end, George Jennings despised what he'd done... so gave his daughter one last gift... the cure to the *GYGES* project."

Dominic released the magazine containing the five darts, and plucked the topmost one out. Just three inches long from flight to tip, its potent chemical contained within a ballistic syringe. It was see-through, just like water. Dominic held it between thumb and forefinger, scrutinising the antidote, curious. His reaction was almost identical to how Emily had inspected one on taking delivery of them from Thomas Mundahl the evening before; like with Emily, the razor-sharp point caused a pinprick to his finger, making a small bead of blood appear.

Garret knocked at the door and entered. "Melvyn and the pilot are ready. They'll meet us up on the roof."

"Good. We don't have much time. It won't be long before she gets here." Thoughts of Sophie surfaced; an image of her face as he'd slung his knife at her sister's back. He didn't doubt that she would try to kill him if she were to reach them. Dominic returned the dart gun back to the table, pocketing the antidote dart almost as an afterthought. He then stuck his bleeding finger into his mouth and sucked it. "Come; help me get this sorry sack of faecal matter up. We're taking him with us."

⁜

Five feet was as far as they'd walked when the young woman appeared in the corridor behind them, screaming: "DOMINIC!!"

Brayden was walking ahead of Dominic and Garret, his hands still bound behind his back but his ankles were now free to allow swift movement. The barrel of a handgun was frequently thrust into his back. Now the gun was whirled away as Dominic levelled it towards his pursuer.

Seeing the danger, Sophie vanished just as Dominic pressed the trigger. A bullet ricocheted against a wall but missed his intended target.

Sophie reappeared, teasingly closer. She walked confidently nearer, a *Glock* in her hand.

"I've got this; I can have her," said Garret arrogantly, pushing down Dominic's gun arm, swaying his decision from shooting again. "You go ahead. I'll meet you up on the roof shortly."

Dominic nodded appreciatively but doubted the bald man's bravado would match the blonde girl's abilities. He turned and ordered Brayden to hurry forward: "Get going!" They headed towards a door at the end of the corridor, beyond which a metal staircase led up to the roof.

Garret stood in the centre of the corridor, making himself

look big and imposing. He carried an assault rifle, which he aimed aggressively towards the girl.

"I remember you from Nevada," said Sophie, closing in on the Kaplan Ratcliff soldier. "You were one of the three who kept the kids safe after the *Chinook* exploded."

"Finally get to put a face with the voice," Garret trilled. "What gave me away?"

Sophie shrugged. "Your bald head… your fragrance… but mostly, the spiderweb tattoo on your face. Not many out there could pull that look off. Tell me, did you actually want that inked or was it from losing a drunken bet?"

Garret smiled sheepishly. "Bingo," he said, before adding: "I'm going to enjoy killing you."

"I seriously doubt that." Sophie walked to within a few feet, and stopped. "Let's make this a little bit more of a challenge." She released the magazine from the *Glock*, watching it skid across the floor, and then unchambered a round; the bullet clattered to the tiled floor. She tossed aside the gun then unsheathed a pair of *SOG* fighting knives, the type favoured by Navy SEALs.

"Even better! All right. Let's do this *mano a mano*." Garret flung the assault rifle away and unholstered a handgun, which he unloaded in a blatant fashion before disposing it. Mirroring Sophie, he produced a pair of blades, each slightly longer than the 12.4 inch knives she was brandishing. "Don't think that because you're a woman, I'm going to go easy."

Sophie grinned devilishly. "You're one of those 'woman-beating-types' I figure. Don't worry, I was counting on–" Before she could finish her retort, Garret lunged for her. Side-stepping, and twisting her body backwards, she just managed to avoid the man's attack. She threw him an angry look.

"I'm sorry," he chuckled, "hadn't you finished talking? I thought we were here to fight, not fornicate." Garret swung his right blade towards the young woman's face in an arc, following it with his left, aiming towards the centre of her stomach, grunting from the exertion.

Sophie jumped back and just managed to tuck her stomach in as the double blades skimmed past her body. Not finished, he sliced the air some more, dangerously close to her chest and neck. Still she managed to dodge the man's frenetic attack.

Changing tact, Garret launched himself with a leap, double kicking Sophie – once in the stomach, then to the face – the contact propelled the woman backwards into losing her balance, knocking her to the floor.

"The way Dominic was going on about you, I thought you were something special. Turns out, you're nothing much, just a stupid little girl!"

"Is that the best you've got?" Sophie harried, executing a 'kip-up' move, drawing both her legs up to, and beyond, her chest, and with her hands placed against the floor, she propelled her legs skyward whilst simultaneously pushing off with her hands. Feet first, she rotated her body and righted herself mid-air before landing into a crouch, her fighting knives gripped tightly in her hands. With almost no pause, she made her move, slashing the blades ahead of her, this time forcing Garret to duck, dive and retreat in much the same way she had been moments earlier, before he regained composure, parrying and returning close combat manoeuvres.

"There you are," he hissed, blocking a stroke and landing a cut to Sophie's forearm.

Barely registering the wound, Sophie countered, her blades flashing ahead of her in jabs and curves, this time one connecting with a part of his ear, slicing a piece of flesh from his left lobe. Immediately, blood trickled down his face and neck, soaking into his jacket.

"You sure you wanna carry on?" Sophie asked, as though she cared.

"I've had worse, princess."

Taking Sophie by surprise, Garret dropped down low and performed a spinning sweep kick, taking her legs out from beneath her and dropping her to the floor.

Sophie was on her back, momentarily stunned.

Righting himself to standing above the girl, he raised his right hand parallel with his head, the combat weapon loosely gripped within his fingers, and propelled it in much the same way Dominic had released his knife into Meredith's back.

Alert to the danger, Sophie did two things instinctively and synchronically. She rolled to one side out of the blade's trajectory, whilst at the same time willing herself invisible.

Garret's knife clattered to the floor and skidded away, knocked further with the aid of a sly foot. It ended up quite a way down the corridor, out of reach and any risk of further use.

"Resorting to gimmicks now, are we?" said Garret, scornfully.

"It's been fun, but you are just an appetiser. My main course is waiting for me... getting cold."

Garret swapped the knife from his left hand into his dominant right, and aimed a stab at thin air towards where he heard Sophie's voice.

Sophie reappeared next to him as his knife met nothing. "Boo," she whispered, then vanished once again.

Garret whirled around, the knife slashing erratically ahead of him.

"Now I'm here," she said, flashing into existence again a few feet away, just behind him. As Garret turned, she disappeared and waded in on him, planting a knee heavily into the man's groin.

Crying out in pain, he went down on his knees, clutching himself hopelessly, slightly winded. In self-defence, there's no quicker way to momentarily incapacitate a man than to aim a blow to his nether regions.

It had the desired effect. Sophie almost felt sorry for him as her image came back into focus alongside him. "You had enough?"

Garret responded by lashing out angrily towards Sophie. She dodged back, but too slow. The knife sliced through the front of her shirt and gouged her skin an inch above her bellybutton. It was just a flesh wound and hadn't registered with her pain receptors yet, but the action reminded her that she wasn't invincible.

"Too bad." Sophie disappeared again and walked out of Garret's reach.

Garret, encouraged by his lucky strike, stood back up and limped forward a bit, the pain in his groin lessening, his ears straining for the slightest sound. The girl could have left him there, moved on to her 'main course', which he guessed was Dominic. But he sensed she was still there, lurking somewhere close by, waiting to pounce. He just needed to concentrate and listen.

When Sophie made her move, Garret was completely oblivious and looking the wrong way. Tapping his shoulder lightly, playfully, gained her the desired result.

He immediately turned to face her. As he did, she punched an intense blow with the solid base of the knife's handle, gripped tight within her right hand, against the front of his neck, deliberately crushing his throat, fracturing his larynx.

Garret dropped his knife, throwing up both his hands to his neck, pulling, clawing and massaging at it desperately. "Hclegh!" he uttered hoarsely, struggling to breathe. "Hclegh!" he repeated in panic, falling to his knees.

"Not a stupid little girl now am I?" Sophie crowed, materialising five feet away with her back to him. Re-sheathing her *SOG* knives, she headed towards the door at the end of the corridor which Dominic had taken only a couple of minutes earlier. Along the way, she spoke into her comms link: "Emily? I know where Dominic is," she said, reclaiming her *Glock* and the magazine from the dusty floor. She heeled the clip of bullets back into place and chambered a round.

"*Where are you?*" Emily asked anxiously.

"Heading to the roof; there's stairs leading up to it," Sophie replied, leaving Garret to die noisily on the floor behind her. "Emily, I've found Brayden. Dominic has him. I think he means to use him to help his escape. But don't worry; I'm not going to let that happen."

CHAPTER SIXTY
SOPHIE

THE ROOF OF THE warehouse was flat and, stepping out through the doorway of the bulkhead at the top of the metal stairs, Sophie thought she was too late. The noise from the *Bell 206* helicopter was loud, its rotors 'thwap-thwap-thwap-thwap-thwap-thwapping' repeatedly in the air, a beam of bright light illuminating a spot just a little way ahead of her. Following it with her gaze, she saw the dark outlines of Dominic and Brayden just a little further, roughly twenty metres, standing by an area with a large yellow 'H' painted within a circle, waiting to cadge a ride.

The helicopter was just arriving, not leaving.

Sophie sighed relief and started forward, allowing the door to swing with a metallic clatter behind her. A stinging sensation at her stomach caused her to recoil, and she placed her free hand cautiously to the gaping hole in her uniform shirt. It came away wet with warm, sticky moisture. Blood. As nothing was hanging out, she knew, despite the life fluid, the wound was superficial.

The light from the helicopter had now picked out Dominic and Brayden, and Sophie could see that the man who had killed her mother and thrown a knife at her sister's back, was holding all the cards; in this case, his handgun, a *Beretta*. Like Sophie, he had a favourite weapon, and it was pointed threateningly towards the CIA agent's head.

Sophie aimed her own gun towards Dominic's head, each stride cutting the distance between her and the two men by half a metre.

Dominic said something that Sophie couldn't hear; his voice was absorbed by the clamour of the helicopter as it came down steadily to land. Brayden moved away, closer to the edge of the roof, Dominic dangerously behind. Detecting Sophie's presence, he positioned himself so that Brayden was now between him and the blonde woman, his gun now pointing not only at Brayden, but in Sophie's general direction.

A passenger in the helicopter aimed a sharp shooter assault rifle out through a window, Sophie within his sights.

Observing the danger, Sophie willed herself invisible just as the rifleman fired. The gunshot was barely heard over the helicopter, and neither was the one discharged from Sophie's *Glock*.

The bullet hit Melvyn's head dead centre, the propulsion hurling him back into his seat.

The pilot, fearful of a similar fate, put the helicopter back into motion, using the cyclic control lever, and a combination of foot pedals to manipulate the aircraft desperately back into the sky.

"Wait!" yelled Dominic, turning his *Beretta* towards the pilot. The helicopter turned sharply in the air, blocking his line of fire, before beginning to ascend and drift away from the warehouse. The illuminance from the spotlight deserted them, returning the roof to almost pitch blackness. "Gutless…" his expletive went unfinished as Sophie reappeared in front of him.

"Give it up Dominic. It's over." Despite the growing gloom, it was still easy to identify the villain of her life's story.

Dominic moved in closer to Brayden, pressing the barrel of his gun against the back of the agent's head. "It's not over, Sophie. Not by a stretch."

"Don't do anything rash, Sophie," pleaded Brayden. "I need him alive, remember."

Dominic laughed as he brought the *Beretta*'s heel down on the back of the CIA agent's head. It was hard, but not hard enough to knock him unconscious or to cause him to lose balance. Brayden grunted and swore.

"One step closer and I'll do more than just boff him."

Sophie readjusted her grip on the *Glock*, her finger tightening around the trigger. "What makes you think that I give a damn?"

Dominic shrugged. "My confidence in your weakness. Unlike my initiates, you have a conscience."

"Your initiates are finished…"

"No thanks to you. Tell me, how did you see them? Their uniforms were infrared resistant; your night-vision goggles would have been useless." Far from being angry, Dominic was curious.

Sophie unclipped the small electronic device that was stowed on her belt. "Radar," she said, flicking a switch to activate it. The LCD lit up as it booted and took a moment to settle before displaying its familiar tracking screen. The unit began to pulsate and highlighted the two men ahead of her within its front right quadrant; red 'blips' and a corresponding, but subtle, bleep followed. As the radar device continued to probe the area, an additional 'blip' appeared on the screen; this one in the lower left quadrant – signifying a place behind her. Another 'blip' joined it, then another.

Sophie wore a puzzled expression. Peering over her shoulder, the entire roof behind continued to appear vacant.

"What, Sophie? You didn't think I'd commit ALL my soldiers to the front offensive?"

Four 'blips' had by now been picked up on the radar, invisible to the naked eye, but on the roof nonetheless. They approached stealthily.

"I can play this game," she whispered, invoking her predominant ability. She sprinted across the space, skirting the invisible soldiers who had entered the upmost level through the bulkhead, the roof's only access point. Unable to see things she held whilst invisible, she reappeared to quickly glance at the radar screen, pinpointing the newcomers' whereabouts; they were still moving in Dominic's direction.

Having circled around the four super soldiers, Sophie now thought to advance on them from their rear, first taking cover behind the bulkhead construction built atop of the roof. Turning the sound off the handheld radar, she stepped out from behind her cover and advanced on the dots appearing ahead.

Checking the radar's LCD again, she did a double take. "That's not right," she muttered.

The screen still displayed six 'blips'; Dominic and Brayden, the only people NOT invisible on the roof, were easily viewed from where she was standing despite the gloom. They were the furthest 'blips' appearing on the gadget. The other four were positioned between her and them, except – where they had been advancing on her previous position, they had now stopped. Instead, they had changed direction and were moving back, heading towards her.

"How's that possible?" *Can they see me?*

As if answering her question, a gun was fired and a bullet whistled past her head, clanging against the metal outbuilding, and sending a firework of sparks to rain down just behind her. A hot sliver of metal landed on her cheek, burning her.

"Ouch!" She cowered back. Checking the radar she watched the four red 'blips' representing the super soldiers begin to separate, moving steadily apart.

Sophie knew the tactic; encirclement – an offensive strategy.

Surround the target and come at it as one, guns all blazing. The odds of surviving weren't favourable, which was usually the whole point.

In the background, a helicopter could be heard flying nearby, its sound growing into prominence. Most likely Dominic's ride returning, she thought.

"There's only one thing to do." Sophie stood, raising the *Glock* to shoulder height, aiming towards a place she knew one of the super soldiers was lurking. Before she was able to fire a single shot, a volley of bullets dashed against the metalwork next to her as one of the initiates fired a burst from his assault rifle. A bullet tore into her shoulder, spinning her to the roof.

"Aghh!"

"I got her!" one of the boys hollered out in triumph.

Winded and in intense pain, Sophie dragged herself around to the back of the small bulkhead, taking shelter from further attack whilst she inspected the damage. "Well, this sucks," she said, placing the gun in her lap, and pressing a hand against the wound at the top of her left arm. It was bleeding profusely and she knew it needed medical attention. Burning agony flared from the compression causing a wave of dizziness and nausea, followed by a burst of stars that danced behind her eyes.

"*Sophie... are you there?*" Emily spoke into her ear.

"Yea... I'm here," she groaned, lifting up the radar screen. The four super soldiers had surrounded her and were beginning to slowly approach.

"*Are you okay?*"

"Yea... nothing a–" Sophie didn't finish the sentence. One of the four invisible soldiers was coming into view. She lifted her gun and fired.

Uncharacteristically, the bullet missed. The boy came even closer. She sensed that he was getting ready to shoot, and as if to confirm things, a tactical red laser sight light appeared from thin air and seemed to penetrate through her.

There was no time to fire her *Glock*, and to attempt it she knew the game would be up. Just to accentuate how futile it was to continue, another red laser beam entered her from a different angle, followed by two more. The four sons of *GYGES* had her in their sights, their guns trained on her.

"*Sophie?*" Emily sounded anxious in her ear.

"They have me surrounded," Sophie said, exasperated.

"Throw out your weapon!" one of the boys bellowed.

"*Hold on,*" urged Emily. "*Help is on its way.*"

The sound of Dominic's helicopter grew more prominent and approached the warehouse from the sea, behind Sophie who was cowering dejectedly, its bright spotlight once again providing illumination to proceedings.

Dominic, seeing the return of the chopper and receiving word via a two-way radio that Sophie was surrounded, brazenly walked forward. He shoved Brayden heavily ahead of him, jabbing the barrel of his gun into the small of his back for motivation.

Hovering fifty feet up in the sky, it was difficult to identify the pilot of the aircraft from roof level, and owing to the bright 1,600 watt *Xenon* lamp burning bright beneath it, the other, shadowy silhouette half-leaning out of the helicopter, was not seen either.

"I told you it wasn't over, Sophie!" Dominic amplified his voice to be heard over the helicopter. "You may as well show yourself."

Sophie tossed her *Glock* away and abruptly reappeared almost directly beneath the spotlight's effulgent glow. She was standing with one arm folded across her stomach, the other held up in surrender.

Even had the 'thump-thump, thump-thump' sound of the helicopter not been so prevalent, no one would have heard the shots being fired from the *Lantec SFM6 Anti-Personnel* dart gun.

Four in total, each shot made in quick succession; the ballistic syringes hitting their marks and taking instant effect. The super soldiers flinched from the stinging impact of the darts, feeling woozy from the genetic properties contained within the injected serum. All that was left of the sons of *GYGES* took on solid form, looks of surprise and fear concealed behind the night-vision head gear clipped to their helmets.

"THROW DOWN YOUR GUNS... THIS IS YOUR ONLY WARNING!"

Sophie recognised the pitch and tone. It was Liam, his gruff voice amplified through a megaphone. A break in the clouds above revealed a sliver of moon that lightly dusted the surroundings not lit up from the helicopter's spotlight with a soft, silvery glow. From the small amount of light, she could see that the helicopter wasn't Dominic's *Bell 206* after all, but the *Westland Lynx* that had flown the radar units in from *HMS Ocean*. The side door was pushed open and Liam was squatting in the back, the megaphone in one hand and a rifle in the other.

The four super soldiers were puzzled as to what had just happened. They could see that they were no longer invisible, but the true extent of their change wouldn't be learnt for a few hours yet. One of the initiates, number Sixty-Three, who had earlier transported the dead bodies back from London within a stolen ambulance, believed his longevity would not be compromised. Foolishly, he raised his weapon, aiming it towards the helicopter.

Liam fired a single bullet from his rifle, dropping the initiate with a head shot. He collapsed sideways to the roof's surface.

"ANY MORE?" Liam bellowed, threateningly.

"Hold your fire!" ordered Dominic. He was still standing behind Brayden menacingly, though now manoeuvring the CIA agent into a more defensive, shielding position.

The three sons of *GYGES* dropped down their rifles and raised their hands up in the air. No sooner had they disarmed, a stream of Royal Marines spilled out from the bulkhead doorway, assault rifles pointing forward.

"YOU TOO, DOMINIC!!" ordered Liam from above, the *Lynx* helicopter lurched a little to and fro, buffeted by a sudden gust of wind.

Ten Royal Marines spaced themselves out on the roof, surrounding the three former super soldiers. With the swing in fortune, Sophie lowered her arm. Unfazed, Dominic continued to hold Brayden captive, his *Beretta* pressing hard into the agent's back.

"I'm going to kill him if you don't do as I say!" countered Dominic. He took a step backwards, pulling Brayden with him. "Lower your guns!" he shouted towards the marine commandos. "I mean it! I'll kill him!" He pressed the gun even harder into the CIA agent's back.

"Lower your rifles," ordered Brayden, urgency in his tone.

The marines looked to each other for confirmation or reassurance, then to the soldier in charge. The platoon leader nodded, giving affirmation. "Do it," he said.

"There's nowhere to go, Dominic; there's no escape," said Brayden. "Give yourself up."

Dominic wore a mixed expression; one of panic, and the other, blind madness. "You don't get it… none of you do. This is going to be the beginning of a new age. You can't stop me. None of you can." He let go of Brayden for a moment, his gun still fixed at a point in the man's back. With his hand free, he reached into his jacket pocket and made a fist around the yellow diamond inside for encouragement. Touching it made him feel more powerful, more invincible. He never felt surer of anything in his life, and the diamond seemed to egg him on, pulsing like a heart within his grasp, willing him further. It felt hot, like a burning ember straight from a fire. "You can all join me! Even you Sophie; it's not too late! Together, we'd be unstoppable."

"I'd never join you Dominic." Sophie stepped forward from the place she had initially taken shelter, where she had begrudgingly surrendered to the super soldiers. Now they were crushed, and she was back in play. Her gun was on the ground, within easy reach, but she walked past it. She kept on walking until she was four feet away from Brayden. The CIA man's hands were still cable-tied behind his back, and Dominic's gun continued to press against his spine, a finger slip away from ending his life.

"Do you honestly think I'd want anything to do with you? After what you did to my mother? To Meredith?" Lightly, she touched the bullet wound at the top of her shoulder, wincing.

Sophie was surprised to see a hurt look appear on the man's face. "I didn't have a choice," he offered meekly, but not explaining his reasoning.

"Let Brayden go," advised Sophie. "This only needs to be between us."

Dominic removed his left hand from his pocket; it came out in a fist, like he was concealing something or about to throw a jab. The *Whisper of Persia* he left in his pocket, its weight feeling reassuring against his stomach. "Yes… you're quite right," he replied conciliatingly. "This could just be between you and me. But, you see, I know that as soon as I take my gun off the *yank*, either the lug in the helicopter, or any one of those *marines*," he spat the word out vehemently, "is going to try and shoot me. He is my guarantee…"

Seemingly taking offence, despite not being able to hear him, Liam – the *lug* in the helicopter – didn't wait for Dominic, or for the opportunity to present itself freely. He fired his rifle at Dominic, the bullet smashing into his gun hand, knocking the *Beretta* free from his grip and pulverising three of his fingers. Brayden, trained for quick reactions and taking his chance, leapt forward, and started running in Sophie's direction.

"Arruugghhhh," Dominic howled, holding up his mangled right hand for inspection. Just his thumb and little finger remained, making it appear like he was giving a gory 'call me' hand sign to someone. "My bloody hand!" he cried. The mutilated chunks of his fingers looked like minced up sausages strewn about his feet. "Have you no decency?!"

Sophie unsheathed one of the *SOG* combat knives. "Have you not heard the saying 'what comes around, goes around'?"

Without his hostage, Dominic no longer had any bargaining chips. This resulted in the immediate reinstatement of marine weapons being trained eagerly his way.

"Get these ties off me," grunted Brayden, irritably. He half-turned, presenting his restrained wrists towards Sophie.

With barely any thought, Sophie obliged, slipping the blade beneath the plastic cable tie and applying a small amount of pressure, the knife's keen edge slicing it through like it were butter.

Seeing the young woman's intent, Brayden repeated his earlier warning: "Don't, for your sake. I need him alive."

Sophie said nothing, turning away from the American and taking big strides towards Dominic, the knife hanging at her side. She ignored the gunshot wound to her shoulder for the time being.

For the benefit of the ten marines who looked like they were gearing themselves to take a shot, Brayden repeated his remark louder: "I NEED HIM ALIVE!"

Seeing the blonde woman coming towards him, Dominic looked around desperately. His eyes clocking the *Beretta*, but getting it was suicide. There was no way he could reach it, not without receiving a ten gun salute aimed at his head or chest. When he looked back to where Sophie had been approaching, she was gone.

Although many within the strike force were aware of her abilities, all of the marines standing around had never witnessed her actually metamorphose. Seeing her vanish before their eyes elicited a chorus of gasps and interjections; awe, fear and surprise. One even said: "Where did she go?" like he'd never even been given the brief.

Sophie zigzagged a course away from Dominic; her intention, to engage him from behind.

Dominic, no longer able to see the young woman and fearful of what she was about to do, threw up his hands. "I give up! I GIVE UP!" he screamed. "Just don't let that crazy bitch o–" *on me*. He finished his appeal in his head as the desire to continue speaking it aloud left him when he felt cold steel press up against his throat. No one could see the knife or the girl wielding it, but they were both there all the same, and the thin line of blood appearing on his neck was testament to it.

"I dare you to struggle with me, Dominic," almost a whisper. He remembered her saying those very words to him before, back in that rundown motel on the outskirts of Washington DC; this time he believed the threat. "It would make this so much easier."

"You don't have to do this... I'm unarmed."

"Just like my mother was, when you killed her?" lamented Sophie.

"I told you before; *that* was an accident," he said.

"And my sister? Was that an accident too?"

Dominic had no answer for that.

"Sophie!" Breathlessly, Emily ran out onto the roof through the opening of the bulkhead. "Don't!" She was wearing night-vision goggles; the infrared setting was switched on, and she was able to see Sophie standing behind Dominic, the knife at his throat. "Let us take him in. He'll get the death penalty."

"Listen to Emily, Sophie!" recommended Brayden, seriously. "You'll get your justice. The President has stated as much."

Sophie felt trapped for a moment. Torn between doing what she wanted – nay, *needed* – to do and what was right.

"Sophie… please!" Emily begged. "Don't do this."

Hesitantly, Sophie retracted the *SOG* combat weapon from pressing against the front of Dominic's neck, slowly withdrawing it so that it was hanging harmlessly at her side, pointed towards her feet.

Dominic exhaled deeply with relief.

Gritting through the pain in her shoulder, Sophie raised her left arm and rested a hand on Dominic's shoulder to remind him that she hadn't left. "Okay… move. Try anything funny and I'll carve my initials out in your innards."

Brayden indicated for the marines to move in, to take the man into custody. The embroilment was over.

Or so it seemed.

After taking only two steps forward, Dominic dropped to his knees and energetically carried out a low spinning hook kick. Although she was invisible, he guessed her position correctly and swept her out from under her feet, and pounced. The sound of her scream of surprise, and the metal shaft clanging away from her hand, was satisfying as he straddled the invisible hump on the roof, momentarily pinning her down.

The knife flashed into view on the roof a couple of feet away.

Dominic knew his advantage would be fleeting. He was no match against Sophie's strength or agility, even if she was injured; already he could feel her tensing beneath him, preparing to execute a move that would see her escape and likely bring about his downfall. Taking his chance, he raised his fisted left hand, and stabbed it down hard.

It connected with a thump.

"Ahhh!" A small bee-sting of a prick was felt beneath the blow.

The ballistic dart had been in his palm since he had sought comfort from the diamond, his hand chancing upon it completely by accident, though subconsciously he'd always known what he was likely to do with it. Finding the small missile had set his mind abuzz; it was just a matter of waiting and hoping for the right moment.

"If I can't have my super soldiers, then neither can they..." he spoke down to the woman beneath his weight.

The special design of the hypodermic dart released its contents on impact, the collared needle fixing to the skin to ensure complete fulfilment of its injected drug.

Dominic hadn't been able to see where the small arrow had connected, but it didn't matter. The translucent payload entered Sophie's bloodstream regardless and began to work immediately.

"What have you done?!" screamed Sophie. Dim and very slowly, she began to evanesce back into view; the transformation under the adverse circumstances lacked its former spectacle or excitement. She kicked Dominic off her and jumped to her feet. In less than five seconds she had completely materialised and was in full view.

The special dart was sticking out of her chest. In shock, Sophie reached up to it and pulled it free, the barbs of its tip leaving a small puncture hole beneath her clothing to the top of a breast. She flung it aside and screamed, raw and animalistic. Rage engulfed her and she started forward after Dominic Schilling, a murderous look on her face.

"Sophie, no!" yelled out Emily, running towards her.

Sophie punched Dominic in the face and aimed a kick to his solar plexus. Despite her injuries and the noticeable reduction in her strength, her fighting knowledge had not deserted her; with adrenaline fuelled by her anger pumping through her veins, she meted out more punishment, punching and kicking, forcing Dominic to backpedal hopelessly across the roof, towards its unhindered edge.

"Stop!" shouted Brayden.

"Please..." Dominic had had enough, "just finish it." He tripped over his feet, falling hard onto his rump. He was now three feet from the roof's precipice, lying on his back. "Put me out of my misery."

"No chance... I haven't finished yet." He made to get up; Sophie's foot connected against his chin, forcing him back with momentum. He collapsed to the roof and something sparkly fell free from his coat pocket. It rolled a short way.

"The diamond," murmured Sophie.

Dominic laughed humourlessly, shaking his head. How things could have been different had he not been so obsessed with it. "My... *precious!*" he was still laughing.

"Who d'you think you are? *Gollum?*" she snarled. "Pitiful." She stamped down on his good hand, hearing carpals break.

Dominic screamed. The pain in his left hand now competed with what remained of his right.

"That was for Meredith!" Before Sophie could land any more blows, Brayden grabbed Sophie from behind, wrapping his arms around her waist and pulling her away.

Despite the rage that burned inside the woman, the CIA agent was comfortably subduing her. Either his determination, or the sudden absence of Sophie's abilities and weakness from losing a lot of blood, Brayden was finding the intervention very easy. "Enough, Sophie!" Brayden dragged the woman, kicking and screaming, towards where Emily and a few marines were standing. "It's over!"

Behind them, Dominic had crawled to where the diamond had rolled to and had retrieved it, difficultly closing his hand around it, one or two of his fingers sticking out awkwardly. He stood up on unsteady feet and took a step back, teetering close to the roof's overhang.

"Dominic, NOOOOOOOO!!" Emily was the first to read the situation, and no matter what she would later think when retrospect provided time to reflect and analyse, nothing would have made a difference. His intention was finite. It was too late. Dominic had found a way out.

Without a single word, Dominic stepped sideways off the roof, disappearing into the darkness below, the sound of the *Lynx* helicopter and Emily's voice the last things he would ever hear.

Brayden let Sophie slip from his hold, allowing her to trot to the place Dominic had just dropped from. Above her, the *Lynx* moved slightly forward, beginning a slow descent towards the painted landing spot on the roof, taking with it the main light source.

Peering over the roof's sheer drop, Sophie expected to see Dominic lying somewhere below, but with the light dwindling behind her and the moon now submerged once again behind thick clouds, it wasn't possible; she only saw absolute darkness. A wave of vertigo pervaded her head and she heeded the flash of warning that came with it, dropping down to the roof heavily, almost collapsing. She found lying on her back comforting, so she stretched out and stared at the sky, wishing she were able to see the stars.

"Sophie!" Emily sprinted to where the younger woman was recumbent, her breathing shallow. Kneeling down by her side, she took Sophie's hand, resting on the tear at her stomach. It was wet and sticky with blood.

"I don't… feel so good," said Sophie, quietly. "When I close my eyes… I see white light… I think it's calling to me."

The helicopter had landed noisily behind them and Liam, still carrying his rifle, jumped down and ran to where he could see Emily stooping over Sophie.

"Ignore it, Sophie. It's just…" Emily said some more, but Sophie didn't hear it. Exhaustion overcame her and the light – powerful and bright – appeared to offer comfort and hope, and an answer to her problems. Following it with her mind, she thought she could see the silhouette of a man standing in the distance in the centre of the light, indiscernible but familiar. He was holding a stuffed toy; *Flopsy*. Closing in on him, he grew into prominence and offered her a hand for reassurance. He was friendly and filled her with calm.

Come, he said telepathically within her head. His voice was exactly how she remembered it.

"*Dad?*" she heard herself say, reaching out for his grasp.

George Jennings smiled. It was warm, but sad. He took hold of her hand and led her deeper into the light.

CHAPTER SIXTY-ONE
POTUS

THE PRESIDENT ACCEPTED THE video conference call sitting within his customary leather chair. He was at the head of the table in the White House Situation Room within the basement of the West Wing. Deputy Director of the CIA, Milo Calland was with him; for once arriving early, along with others closely tied to the fallout of project *GYGES*; his Chief of Staff, the Director of the CIA Thawn Montgomery, General Bill Eastman, the Director of the FBI, Elizabeth Reeves, and several others in positions of importance. All the seats around the long, rectangular table were full, and a few dignitaries had to stand at the back and around the sides of the room.

"*Mister President,*" started Brayden Scott taking up the centre of the large fifty-inch screen attached to the wall opposite to President Harrison. It was clear that he was connecting with them from a British location by the portrait of a young Queen Elizabeth II on the wall behind him. He looked tired, which was to be expected after having no sleep in almost two days, the decision to brief the President outweighing his personal needs.

"Agent Scott," President Harrison acknowledged. "So, the mission was a success," he said, leaning forward over his crossed arms. He had already received sketchy details as they had emerged regarding the operation from intelligence operatives within the CIA, but none of the fine detail, and certainly nothing from anyone who was live at the scene. The President was also fresh off a phone call with the British Prime Minister, David Humphries.

"Not without casualties," Brayden replied wistfully. "The *GYGES* soldiers have been neutralised… the hideout has been destroyed… and Dominic Schilling is dead." It all sounded so clinical and matter-of-fact.

"Good." The President wore a satisfied look. A predecessor had said the same thing when learning Osama Bin Laden had been killed.

"What about my agent, Christina Mullins?" asked Elizabeth Reeves, deeply concerned for the FBI employee.

"I'll spare you all the detail, but she's alive, ma'am. Currently in hospital for observation; there are some minor injuries, but she'll make a full recovery." Royal Marines had found the FBI agent bruised and bloody in a room a couple of doors away from where Brayden had been detained. She was unconscious when discovered but came around shortly after. Before interrogating Brayden, Dominic had worked his charm on the woman. When that failed, he used his fists. "She should be discharged in a couple of days. I'll stay in England until she is fit to travel. We'll return to the capital together."

"And our girl?" asked General Eastman optimistically. In a private meeting, the General had convinced the President that Sophie Jennings, regardless of her *absolute immunity* status, needed to be seized and taken into American custody. Her abilities made her a clear and present danger to the United States, and if – the General reasoned – she was held in trust, they might be able to convert her to their cause, or at the very least, harness her powers for other benefits through scientific research. There were people within the scientific community keen to take over from where George Jennings had left off.

Brayden looked down towards a spot not in camera-shot. He

hesitated, raising a hand to his forehead where he massaged a worry line and the beginnings of a headache.

"Well, Agent Scott?" pushed the President, adjusting himself impatiently within his leather seat.

"I'm afraid she was one of the casualties," Brayden said miserably. "She was dead before we could get her to a hospital. A GSW," *gunshot wound*, "she lost a lot of blood."

There were groans of dismay erupting around the table and General Eastman punched the table.

President Harrison felt the same disappointment. "I see," he said solemnly.

"Um, if it's all right with you Mister President, will that be all? It's been a helluva long and telling day. I'll send you my full report some time tomorrow."

The President nodded in agreement. "Very well agent Scott; we'll talk some more in the White House when you return to Washington."

"Thank you, Mister President." Brayden disconnected at the other end and his portrait was replaced by a screensaver of the presidential logo sitting in the centre of a completely blue background.

"Well, that's a big kick in the nuts," said Milo Calland, his only contribution to the meeting. It was at that precise moment that the President decided to replace the Deputy Director of the CIA.

CHAPTER SIXTY-TWO
RYAN

HER FATHER HAD STILL been alive the last time she had sat within the living room of the small house, hidden beyond a row of trees that did well to conceal it from the road despite it being winter and the branches of the oaks, elms and silver birch trees being free of leaves.

Ryan's safe house; the place Sophie had been directed to seven months earlier after her mother had been killed, and her father (seemingly) abducted. The car she had driven in was still parked out front, the blue *Peugeot 206* a shameless reminder of that day's terrible events, was dirty and uncared for, brown and white bird droppings caked the windscreen, bonnet and roof, and blood still stained the interior upholstery. Thomas Mundahl's pepper-white *Mini One* was alongside it, sparkling clean by comparison.

It was now the first week of February, and her wounds had practically healed. The damage to her shoulder had required surgery to remove the bullet, but aside from the dull ache, the numbness around the surface area and the round, jagged scar, no one would have known. The knife wound to her stomach, and the cut to her forearm, both inflicted by Garret, were completely gone. Surprisingly, her body was still able to regenerate the flesh and tissue around the knife wounds to near perfection, but was less successful with deeper, bullet damage.

"I can't stay here forever," said Sophie, accepting a steaming cup of tea from the Norwegian. He had collected her from the hospital only the night before.

Thomas offered her a plate with an assortment of biscuits that were left over from Christmas. She rejected them with an outward turned hand.

"It's nice here. You could grow to like it. It's very peaceful. The people in the local village keep themselves to themselves. No one asks questions. No one cares." Thomas spoke carefully, articulating each word in a concise way, his accent rich. He placed the plate of biscuits down, helping himself to a ginger nut. He dunked it in his tea. "It's safe here," he continued, "the perfect place to lie low and be dead to the world."

Sophie looked down at the tea. Both her hands were wrapped around it, as though drawing warmth from it. She wasn't cold; far from it. A gas fire burned brightly in the centre of one wall, heat billowing out. "I didn't ask Emily to fake my death. I'm sure I could have handled things."

"It was for the best," Thomas replied. "Even without your… abilities, the Americans would still pursue you. You know that. After Dominic threw himself from that roof, it stood to reason; they wanted you still in connection to the Nevada attack last year." He sighed. "This way, you can live relatively free."

When Sophie had collapsed on the roof of Dominic's warehouse, her pulse was weak and the truth of the matter was she almost died. With little time, Liam had transported her in the *Westland Lynx* back to *HMS Ocean*, where she received enough treatment to keep her alive. Shortly after, once her vitals were stable, she was secretly transferred by helicopter to a private hospital in London. Whilst travelling, the news of her 'unexpected' death was announced to Agents Brayden Scott and Christina Mullins (found bound and beaten within the warehouse a short time earlier).

Emily believed announcing Sophie's death was the tidiest outcome.

"Being in hiding isn't 'living free', is it?"

Thomas Mundahl understood her resentment. He'd felt much the same when Ryan had whisked and hidden him away, after George had destroyed the laboratory and killed his colleagues. But he soon adapted and learnt to live with it.

A dark-blue *Mazda* MPV pulled into the driveway outside the house, and parked up a little out of view. Following the sound of the engine turning off, a couple of car doors could be heard to bang shut, indicating more than one visitor.

"Ah, Ryan's here," muttered Thomas, standing up. He placed his cup of tea down.

"Ryan?" Sophie looked puzzled. "Shouldn't he still be in hospital?"

Thomas shrugged. "He insisted on visiting... as soon as you were discharged. You know what Ryan is like. He can be very... persuasive." He smiled. "I won't be a minute." He exited the room to welcome the newcomers.

Sophie knew exactly what he had meant.

The visitors took a long time to make their entrance, owing to Ryan's disability. Since visiting him at hospital on New Year's Day, his prognosis was unchanged; he was still paralysed from the neck down.

Someone was lowering an access ramp from the rear, passenger side, and then helping the wheelchair bound occupant onto the driveway. A few seconds later, pleasantries were exchanged between Thomas and Ryan, followed by greetings to Emily and another, unknown accomplice. Shortly after, Emily pushed Ryan into the living room.

"Ryan!" Sophie stood and crossed over to him, planting a kiss to his forehead. Two months earlier she had found it difficult to share a room with him. Now that he had lost the ability to walk or move a single muscle she'd found it in herself to forgive him… her pity had helped her find inner peace; finally, she believed Emily's assertions that the MI6 man had nothing to do with her father's death… even if he had been so vocal about *wanting* revenge on the man responsible for Clara's death.

"Sophie… glad to see you looking so well. How are you feeling?"

"I feel great," replied the blonde woman, sounding genuine. "Hi Emily," she acknowledged the auburn-haired woman, though her natural, blonde colour had begun to appear at the roots and streak within it.

"Hi," smiled the slightly older woman. She applied the brakes on the wheelchair then sat in a seat across from Sophie.

"Thomas will be with us shortly… he's just outside. I brought an assistant to help me in and out of the people carrier; borrowed him from SIS. Before entering the man happened to notice a plant that caught his interest. Thomas said he'd take him on a tour of the garden. I do believe it was the *monkshood* that got him excited. We've got loads growing about the garden. Quite pretty when in bloom, but highly poisonous; I grew it for precisely that reason. Anyway…" he changed the topic, "what about… your…" he struggled for the correct word. "… *enhancements*?" He could have been talking about breast enlargements had Sophie not known what he was referring to.

"Gone," Sophie said. She had tried to think herself invisible, whilst laying in the bed at hospital a couple of days after surgery. Concentrating, much the same way as she had all the times before, she focused on changing, on disappearing. But nothing happened. Her abilities had deserted her.

"Oh. That's too bad. Seems like we've both lost something precious to us," said Ryan, slightly subdued.

"It's probably for the best. My father was right: nothing good would ever come of being able to become invisible." Sophie then changed the subject. "How's Meredith?"

"Doing very well; your brothers too. She's back at home now, though a few weeks away from returning to school. They all miss you. Theo too. They all took your death badly."

This made Sophie feel terribly sad. She swallowed hard. "Well, I'd be there with them if it were up to me."

"Someday, maybe," replied Ryan agreeably, "when the dust has settled. You do understand... it's for all your sakes?"

Sophie turned her head away. Reluctantly she conceded. "Sure. Thomas said as much."

Ryan felt the need to elaborate further. "Alive, you're a wanted woman, with... or without... your strengths. Some would go to extreme lengths to find you. Let us do what we must to protect you... and your family."

It made sense but she hated hearing it. Dismissing it for the moment, she changed the subject. "What else have I missed?"

"Have you heard about Jennifer Ratcliff?"

"No."

"She's been taken into custody for her part in proceedings. She denies it, of course; however the evidence linking her and Kaplan Ratcliff to the entire enterprise is overwhelming; they funded everything and were involved in all of Dominic's schemes. Monarchists are calling for her to be tried for high treason just because of the theft of the Crown Jewels, but in all likelihood she'll be convicted under the *Anti-terrorism, Crime and Security Act*. Either way, she'll be spending the rest of her life behind bars."

"Good," was all Sophie could think to say, her mood downcast.

"I brought you some of your things," Emily interposed breezily in an attempt to cheer things up. She removed a bag from her shoulder and handed it to Sophie.

Sophie unzipped the backpack and pulled free *Flopsy*, her soft toy kangaroo. There were other items; clothing, her dad's *Nexus* tablet, some photographs, but the only other thing she removed was an A5 manila envelope with her name written across its centre. It was unsealed and reminded her of the one her father had left her within the aluminium attaché briefcase at Fresno Airport.

"I thought you might like that back… now that we've done with it," stated Emily.

Sophie upended the envelope and allowed gravity to assist its descent into her hand. A two-and-a-half-inch thumb drive. She felt a pang of regret overcome her. "Thanks. I'll keep it together with the photograph – the last things my dad gave me."

"Photograph?" Ryan threw Sophie and Emily puzzled looks.

"Now's not the time," advised Emily.

Sophie ignored her. "When my dad left me this thumb drive, he included a picture. It was of him… with your daughter, Clara." Sophie stood up and reached for a wallet she kept in the seat pocket of her jeans. She opened the plastic billfold and plucked out a folded photograph. She held the image up so Ryan could view it.

George Jennings was smiling, looking happy. He had his arm around the shoulders of Clara. Together they looked intimate. Ryan made a little whimpering sound, seeing his daughter again; and seeing her murderer embracing her.

"There's an address on the back. *Norská 561/10, 101 00 Praha, Czech Republic.* Does it mean anything to you?"

Ryan blinked back tears. After careful consideration he said: "No. Except *Praha* is Czech for Prague."

"I did some checks back in the office… but found out nothing; it's just a private residency," ventured Emily, adding nothing of value to the conversation.

Sophie studied the picture. The faces of her father and her

biological mother stared back at her. Carefully, she refolded it and slipped it back away. "Maybe I'll take a trip, check it out..." Sophie saw a flash of concern flit into Ryan's eyes, adding: "... one day... when the dust has settled, of course."

Out in the hallway, the front door banged open. Ryan's assistant followed Thomas into the house, closing the door behind him.

"Ah, that'll be my right hand man returned from his excursion around the garden," Ryan brightened. "You may know him."

Following Thomas into the room, Agent Barry 'Barrington' Abney stepped in with the dignity of a rugby scrum half. "Sophie!"

"Barry!" she squealed in delight, jumping up and charging at him like an excited kid. "I thought you were dead!" she exclaimed. "A heart attack, they said... at the hospital."

Barry accepted the young woman in an embrace. "You're not the only one's death they faked," he said.

A short time later, Barry was giving Sophie the same tour Thomas had given him on arrival. It was the first time they'd been able to relax together since the hotel room in Miami.

"Monkshood," he said, pointing out the plants bordering the garden.

"I know. I saw them in bloom last year. Quite poisonous, I believe."

Barry was amazed she knew that. Was there no end to her talents?

"I really thought you were dead," she said. Barry reached for her hand, and together they took a little stroll around the garden.

"I guessed you might. I don't know how they managed it; somehow they simulated a heart attack I guess. Probably the nurse, she injected me with something just before it happened. One minute I'm lying in a hospital bed when I start feeling a lot of pain in the chest… I quickly black out… and the next, I wake up here… in England, two days later. I've been in hiding ever since."

"Don't you ever leave me again! D'you hear?"

"I promise."

"Good. Then that settles it." Sophie stopped walking and pulled free her hand. She reached to the seat pocket of her jeans and tugged free the wallet.

"What you doing? You paying me?"

"No. I want you to see something. It was in the locker in Fresno, amongst other things." Sophie reached inside and withdrew the folded photograph. "It's my father… with Clara."

"They look cosy."

"Indeed." Sophie didn't sound impressed. "On the reverse is an address, somewhere in Prague." Sophie turned the photo over, giving him a look. "It's in my father's handwriting," she said.

"What are you thinking?" asked Barry contemplatively.

"Fancy taking a holiday? A stroll on the Charles Bridge over Vltava River this time of year is supposed to be very romantic. Maybe we can have that talk you promised me; back in that cheap hotel we stayed in in Miami." That awkward moment in bed entered both their minds.

Barry smiled, slightly embarrassed. "I don't know. What about Ryan?"

"Might be better that we don't tell him," Sophie said, evasively. "He wouldn't be pleased."

"About us eloping?"

"About me coming out of hiding," she said.

"I don't know." Barry sounded hesitant. He was mulling over the prospect of another journey with the young woman. "Nothing good is likely to come of it."

"Nothing good ever comes from the things I go after…" Sophie was full of sorrow.

Barry took Sophie's hand in his, and they walked on in silence for a bit. When they'd done a full circuit of the garden, Barry stopped. "I almost forgot. I have something for you." He reached into a pocket and removed something that fitted snug in his enclosed grip. "Close your eyes and hold out your hand."

Sophie did as bidden.

Barry placed the solid object into her hand and she flinched. It felt ice-cold to the touch.

"The *Whisper of Persia?*"

"We thought you might like to keep it… as a souvenir, after all the trouble you went to in getting it – twice! We prised it from Dominic's dead hand… he'd been determined to keep it, even after death."

"Maybe you should've let him keep it."

Barry shook his head. "I don't think he was going to need it where he was going. His body was cremated three days later."

"Even so… It doesn't belong to me," she replied, resolutely. "I guess it should be returned to *The Queen's Gallery*, to its rightful owner."

"It belonged to a Viscount who has expressed no desire for its return, claiming it to be cursed or bad luck. He's cashed in on the insurance already… twenty million quid and change; if it's recovered, he won't see it… it'll just go to the insurer."

Sophie gave it a moment's thought. "It's not right for me to keep it, and besides, what could I do with it? What would you do?"

Barry shrugged. "It's yours to decide what to do with. Keep it, or return it. You choose."

Sophie sighed, raising the diamond up close to her face so that she could see light through it. For a long moment she studied it.

The multi-faced stone glistened and almost shone as it appeared to draw in and capture the rays from the cool, midwinter sun. "No good would come from me keeping this stone," she finally said. "Or anyone else, for that matter."

EPILOGUE
SOPHIE

THE SMARTWINGS FLIGHT LANDED at Václav Havel Airport in Prague just a little over one hour and forty-five minutes after taking off from Gatwick. Unlike their last flying experience, Sophie and Barry disembarked the *Boeing 737* like every other passenger, using the exit door and walking merrily into the departure building, looking like an ordinary couple away on a romantic break to celebrate Valentine's Day. Passing through border checks was a formality, and despite feeling nervous, the passports they travelled with identifying them as Barry Jenkins and Sophie Matthews, gained only the slightest scrutiny. They were waved on casually, and within ten minutes were outside hailing for a cab.

It was dark, arriving in the Czech Republic's capital city a little after 8:00 p.m.

A yellow *Skoda* pulled up responding to Barry's upraised thumb, and the Czech driver leaned across from the left-hand side and spoke to them in his native tongue.

"Um… what did he say?" Sophie asked Barry, puzzled.

"Why are you asking me? Didn't you learn almost every language in the world?" Barry retorted, slightly stunned.

Sophie laughed, throwing him a wink. She stooped down and peered into the taxi. "Dobre rano. Mluvite anglicky?" *Good morning, do you speak English?*

The driver made a face that indicated uncertainty, wobbling his head a bit like a nodding dog, then made a sign with his thumb and index finger to imply 'a little'. "*Trochu*... small pieces... yes."

"Can you take us to Charles Bridge?" Barry took over.

"Ano," pronounced 'ah-no', replied the driver in a positive tone. "Charles Bridge."

"No?" Barry was disappointed.

"He said yes," reassured Sophie. "'Ano' means yes. 'Ne' means no. Come; let's get in before he thinks we're stupid tourists..."

———⟫•⟪———

Walking across the old Bohemian sandstone bridge was very romantic. Charles Bridge was built in the 14th century, construction beginning in 1357. There were a few other couples walking along it, but not nearly as busy as during the summer months. February was one of Prague's least touristy months despite its romantic setting.

It was cold, around minus one degree; a few flakes of snow were falling, but not enough to settle. Heavier snowfall was forecast for later that night.

Electric bulbs glowed within the lanterns set all along the balustrade between the alley of statues that stood like sentinels keeping watch. There were thirty in all overlooking the 620 metre length of the bridge, baroque in style and depicting saints and patron saints, the most notable, *St. Luthgard* the Holy Crucifix and Calvary. Three watch towers protected the river crossing, two of them at the Lesser Quarter end, and one, the more impressive, at the Old Town end. It was towards the Lesser Quarter towers that Sophie and Barry were heading, the steeples of St. Nicholas church could be made out in the background behind them.

"Are you sure you want to do this?" Barry asked, stopping the young woman almost at the centre of the bridge, the Vltava, Czech

Republic's longest river at 270 miles, flowing beneath them. He placed his gloved hands on her shoulders and studied her face.

"I've had a few weeks to change my mind; I haven't yet."

"Okay. Just saying… there's no going back once it's done." Stating the obvious was something Barry often did.

"You don't want me to do it, do you?" Sophie asked, slightly disconcerted. She pulled free from his clutches and stepped away, towards the low wall of the balustrade facing south of the city.

"I didn't say that. I just think… you could keep it, it's historically important. I did some research… it apparently belonged to Cyrus the Great –"

"Yada, yada, yada. I read the info blurb at the gallery." At the bridge's edge, the wall stopped just shy of reaching her waist. Without a thought, she pulled out the *Whisper of Persia* from her coat pocket, leaned slightly over and outstretched her arm. Her hand was clutching something. Barry guessed what it was.

"Don't!"

"Nothing good will ever come of it," Sophie warned, glancing back towards Barry. She opened her hand and felt the yellow diamond roll across her fingers before tumbling free, dropping weightily to the inky-black surface of the Vltava with a gurgly-'plunk'.

"I guess that settles it." Barry was a little disappointed.

Sophie stepped away from the low wall and rejoined the MI6 field agent. "I guess so." She linked her arm within his, and together they began to stroll back to the other side of the river.

⟡

They picked up a ride in a taxi at the intersection of Legerova and Rumunská outside a bar and restaurant called 'Legenda', a *Jameson Irish Whiskey* sign above the entrance door. Twenty minutes later, the Czech driver, who spoke better English than Barry, stopped the car and indicated that they had arrived. Barry paid using a crisp 200 Czech Crown note.

"Are you sure you want to do this?"

"I wish you'd quit asking me that question," grumbled Sophie, stepping out of the yellow cab.

"You don't even know who lives here." Barry climbed out of the car from the other side after accepting his change and walked around to the pavement. The taxi took no time to drive off. "Maybe it would be better to come back in the morning; we haven't even checked into our hotel yet."

"I'm doing it now, before I change my mind."

The building of *Norská 561/10, 101 00 Prague, Czech Republic,* was nestled within a long row of five storey properties. A chestnut-brown double-door stood between the pavement and the apartments within, an arched leaded window in the top half of each, allowing just a glimpse of the inside. Giving the door a tug, Sophie instantly determined that it was locked. To the right of the entrance was an intercom and door buzzer system screwed into the wall. Sophie stepped over to it, giving it half-measured consideration.

"Are you going to buzz?" Barry asked, walking up close behind her.

Sophie shook her head. "What would I say?" She had been so focused on getting to Prague that she hadn't given any thought to how she would approach the mystery behind who lived at the address written on the back of the photograph.

One of the double-doors opened out as an occupant, a man in his sixties wearing a flat cap and a thick coat, exited the building. He paid the young couple no notice and the door gently swung back towards closed. Barry lunged towards the door, stretching a foot out into the jam. "Quick," he said, "let's get in off the street. We look conspicuous outside." He took hold of the door's edge and pulled it open, allowing Sophie to enter before him.

The hallway was wide and dingy; grimy black and white ceramic floor tiles click-clacked under Sophie's feet as she walked deeper in. At the end of the hallway was a large staircase with an ornate handrail, a lion's head was carved at its end. Beside it was an old elevator which no one other than a fifth floor resident would give any trust, an electronic number panel above it flickering on and off.

A quick survey concluded that the apartment they sought was not on the ground level. They guessed the culmination to their journey would be found on the third floor.

Without speaking, Sophie led the way.

Two minutes later, Barry slightly out of breath, they stood outside the apartment numbered: 10.

Nervously, Sophie placed an ear against the solid wooden door and listened. From inside, the faint sound of a television could be heard. Canned laughter and a familiar tune followed belonging to a popular American comedy show.

"What are you waiting for?" pressed Barry.

Spurred into action, Sophie rapped her knuckles against the door. Slow and deliberate, she struck the wood three times.

Inside the apartment the scraping of chair legs against tile or wooden flooring, immediately followed by footsteps, the echo indicative of a sparsely furnished or recently decorated dwelling.

A metal chain inside rattled as it was put in place, then a series of bolts were dragged aside before a key was turned, unlocking the door.

The door of apartment ten opened a few inches, just wide enough for the inhabitant to be able to see who visited her at such an hour. Barry glanced at his watch and the time, still set to GMT, was 9:15 p.m. Czech Republic was an hour ahead and Barry had already done the simple math.

It was a bit late to be visiting someone uninvited.

A woman in a plain fleece dressing gown spoke nervously to them. "Dobry' den?" *Hello.* She was pretty, in her mid-to-late thirties, and had similar, delicate features and an almost identical eye colouring to Sophie. Unlike most Czech women, who had a light brown colour or brunette hair, she had golden blonde tresses tied behind her into a bun. A pair of spectacles rested on her small nose.

"Um." Sophie didn't know where to begin. "Jmenuji se Sophie Jennings." Pronounced 'menooyi se': *my name is Sophie Jennings.* In her hand she held her wallet. She tugged it open and pulled free the photograph her father had left her. "Můj otec mě sem poslal," pronounced 'mooya o etme asem pos lal': m*y father sent me.* Unfolding the picture, she offered it to the woman through the gap of the door.

Tentatively, she accepted it, precipitously closing the door after.

For what seemed like an age, Sophie and Barry stood patiently outside the apartment. When Barry was about to voice his belief that the occupant was not going to come back, the chain on the other side of the door clinked and jangled as it was withdrawn, the door quickly opening up fully.

The woman stepped out of her apartment and took Sophie in an embrace, the photograph she clutched tightly in one hand. She drew the younger woman close, her arms wrapping around her tight. She started to cry, tears freefalling down her cheeks. "Oh, Sophie," she whispered. "I never thought I'd see the day." She spoke perfect English, with no sign of an eastern European accent. "Your father said we'd be together one day... I just didn't believe it."

"Clara?" Sophie couldn't believe it either. She pulled back to get a clearer look. The young woman in the photograph bore a striking resemblance to the person standing in front of her, though time – coupled with fear and worry – had done a little work to harden her appearance.

"Yes," Clara said, still crying. She didn't think she could ever stop.

"You're my mum?"

Clara nodded over-enthusiastically, a grin stretching across her lips. "I am," she said softly, happily.

"Hello Sophie," George started cheerily. It was close to midnight when Clara convinced Sophie to dig out the thumb drive to play George's recorded message. It had been over four months since Sophie had last seen the video and Clara selected the file eagerly after inserting the SD card into the slot of her laptop.

It had been three years since Clara had last seen the man, back in the laboratory. *"I guess, if you're watching this, things have gone bad and are beyond my control,"* he continued uninterrupted for a bit, Clara watched the man through moist eyes, listening to his voice rapturously. She barely registered the words he was saying, they hardly mattered; seeing his face once again was enough.

Sitting beside Clara on the two-seater sofa, Sophie was equally mesmerised. George went quiet for a moment as he disappeared from the screen, going off to retrieve the vial of blue liquid which Sophie had already drunk back in the Chelsea apartment in October.

"I wish I could've tested it more thoroughly," George began saying, *"but I simply ran out of time. Don't worry, it's fine... and no animals died making it! You will, however, need to get used to the modification as you won't be requiring the injections any more. I'm sure that'll please you! Plus, the changes it will make to your DNA, they're irreversible, which means nothing can ever be done to change it... so, if you were ever hoping for a cure... I'm sorry... it's not going to happen..."* George continued speaking some more, but Sophie stopped listening, instead replaying that phrase over and over in her head:

If you were ever hoping for a cure... I'm sorry... it's not going to happen... If you were ever hoping for a cure... I'm sorry... it's not going to happen... it echoed within her mind.

"*Remember that,*" George's voice cut through her thoughts, so loud and clearly, he could have been in the room with her. When Sophie looked up at the screen, George was staring at her. For a moment, their eyes seemed to lock, and then the illusion passed.

"Are you okay Sophie?" asked Clara, "you look like you've seen a ghost."

Sophie didn't hear her; she was still playing her father's warning over and over in her head, like it were a sound byte set on a loop:

Remember that... Remember that... Remember that... Remember that... Remember that... Remember that...

"Sophie?" Barry sat up from resting his head on the back of a sofa, a bottle of *Gambrinus* Czech lager in one hand. He opened his eyes and a look of concern crossed his face. "Sophie?" he persisted, more urgently.

Sophie blinked away her thoughts, focus returning to the people in the room. "What?"

Clara paused the video playback. "Are you okay, dear? We seemed to have lost you there for a bit?"

"I'm fine," Sophie replied unconvincingly. "Just fatigue, I guess," she yawned. "May I use your bathroom?"

"Of course," replied Clara. "It's through there, at the end of the hall."

"Thanks. I'll be right back."

As Sophie wandered towards the bathroom, her father's voice began once again, following her along the hallway until she reached the bathroom door. It was open a little and she could see the ceramic washbasin and toilet just ahead; the wall behind them was mirrored and spotlessly clean.

Closing the door behind her, she crossed to the sink and turned on the tap, cupping some icy-cold water. She splashed her face a few times and felt refreshed, her tiredness immediately subsiding. She grabbed a towel from a nearby hook and dried her face and hands.

If you were ever hoping for a cure... I'm sorry... it's not going to happen... Remember that.

"But the antidote?" Sophie asked her father, as though he were there in the bathroom with her. Dominic had stabbed her with one of the special darts and immediately after she had lost her invisibility, becoming normal. So it seemed... or had she just assumed it?

Have you tried to use your abilities since? Her conscience conjured a response, mimicking George's voice.

"A couple of times... but nothing happened."

"Try again!" her father appeared to speak within the room and Sophie flinched, spinning around with a start.

Unsurprisingly, there was nobody else there.

Feeling suddenly unsteady, she turned back and took hold of the washbasin with both of her hands, staring at her reflection in the mirror. She felt nervous and nauseous and her heart pounded in her chest. She dismissed the feelings, forcing calm to flow over her by using meditation together with some deep breathing exercises. Now relaxed, she allowed her focus to blur and directed her concentration on a point deep within her mind, going to the place within to summon her external alteration, the place she could never describe but felt was at the core of her being.

She closed her eyes and willed herself to change.

Warmth began to flow through her veins, starting at the tips of her fingers and the points of her toes, slowly coalescing into her feet and hands. Gradually, the sensation permeated up her limbs and throughout her body, going deep and deeper, tingly and electric, affecting four different areas all at the same time, coming together at her centre just below the fall of her breasts.

Sophie opened her eyes. In the mirror, she looked no different.

Almost complete – but not quite – the perception consuming her body continued upwards to the only part bereft of the temperate conclusion; the heat coursing into her neck and on further, into her head – until it had nowhere else to go.

When that moment arrived, Sophie's entire body felt consumed by an inner fire; synapses in her brain fired and an ethereal awareness overcame her.

Sophie opened her eyes.

She was still leaning over the sink, the mirror reflecting her exactly to how she was a moment ago; not a hair out of place or a change in colour to her skin.

She sighed. "I knew it wouldn't work," she whispered, dejectedly. Standing up, she caught sight of her self –

or lack of it!

How could I forget?

A curious by-product to her father's genetic enhancement was her appearance could be reflected, even when completely invisible. It was how Meredith had first seen her, why her sister had called her 'the girl in the mirror'; naively, the nine-year-old had thought that she somehow lived inside it.

On face value, it didn't look like anything had happened, not staring back at her from the silvered glass. But taking a big step back from the washbasin, to allow her eyes to scan her body from her feet upwards, her metamorphosis became evidently clear.

Sophie Jennings had totally vanished.

A knock at the bathroom door startled her. It was Barry coming to check up. "Are you okay in there?" he sounded worried.

She took a deep breath and concentrated on being visible once again.

"Sophie?" Barry twisted the knob and opened the door just as Sophie, suddenly alarmed, transformed into full view.

"Can't a girl go to the toilet in peace?!" she grumbled, a flash of annoyance crossing her face. The fact that she was standing facing the mirror did not come into any question.

"Sorry," he muttered meekly. "You've been gone a quarter-of-an-hour, we thought you might've fainted or fallen down the hole or something."

"Hmmm, okay." Sophie softened and appeared to be glowing.

"Are you sure you're okay? You look… *different*." Barry couldn't put his finger on it, but there was a perceptible change in the young woman's demeanour.

Sophie smiled, ignoring the question. She took hold of Barry's hand. "Come… there's something I need to tell you… and Clara," she pulled him out of the bathroom, leading him back towards the living room. "Then," she continued in a mysterious manner, "I've got something to show you."

ACKNOWLEDGEMENTS

A GREAT DEAL OF WORK went into producing this book, and it would be remiss of me to mention those who played a part – big or small – in helping me see it through to the end.

As always, my wife Beth, who gave me the space to write when it was needed, even when her stomach rumbled for lunch! I'll always be indebted to you for your encouragement and for allowing me to follow my heart and my dream.

My dedication at the front says it all, but Laura Ling, thanks again for sparing your time (and red ink!) in helping with the editing of the book. When I've strayed, you've kept me in check.

Paul and Lynne Cotton, my lab-rats this time around. Thank you for reading the early draft of the book and for your constructive feedback.

Sometimes, all that is needed to nurture an idea is a couple of pints of beer. Those times are usually had in the company of Darren Staff, a good friend who often lends an ear to entertain my imagination and weird sense of humour.

And to those of you who have taken a chance and bought this book. I always had you in mind when I first sat down to begin writing this series. I hope you enjoyed it. Please feel free to tell me by dropping me a line or leaving feedback on *Goodreads*.com, or any online forum for that matter. It's always appreciated!

ABOUT THE AUTHOR

PHILIP J GOULD was born in Ipswich in 1974, and still lives in Suffolk with his wife Beth, and three children, Rebecca, Sophie and Matthew. At an early age he discovered a vivid imagination and an affection for the written word. Leaving school at sixteen, he went onto work in shipping and insurance, and is also a qualified personal fitness trainer. He quit the day job in 2012 to develop his career as an author and to spend more time with his family. His first book was *The Book of Alternative Records*, first published in 2004 by Metro Publishing Ltd.

Be the first to hear news and read exclusive content
on the official website: www.philipjgould.com

Join the official Facebook page:
www.facebook.com/philipjgouldbooks

Follow Philip on Twitter @philipjgould